G000060064

THE LUXURY ORPHANAGE

GRANT FINNEGAN

ALSO BY GRANT FINNEGAN

The Seventh List

Flight 19, Part 1

Flight 19, Part 2

For Sharon

THE LUXURY ORPHANAGE

Human beings.
We are the most intelligent creatures on earth.
Our kindness towards each other knows no boundaries.
Neither does our cruelty.

Grant Finnegan
2020

PROLOGUE

My body has been trapped down here—how long? I don't really know.

I can only count up to ten. So I think it's been much longer than ten years.

Finley was the one who taught me how to count using all my fingers.

He said unless I take my shoes off and use my toes, he didn't know how to teach me to count any higher.

He said there was a way, but it would take much longer to teach me. He said he would the next evening, after dinner.

But Finley left the next day.

They said he was sent back to an orphanage in Scotland, because Scotland was where he was from.

I liked Finley.

We all did.

He was one of only a few of the older orphans who tried to protect us.

See, I was too little to be able to defend myself.

I never knew what the world *adult* meant, but Finley tried to explain it to me one day. He said it's what they were. They were much bigger, to us.

Those who worked here, most were mean to us.

Really mean.

One day I was picked up and thrown against a wall. I still don't know what I did wrong to deserve it. It hurt so bad.

I wished Finley was there to protect me.

But he was gone.

But what these mean people never knew was what we knew, after being sent down here ourselves.

Finley was never sent to an orphanage in Scotland.

He didn't even leave this orphanage: the Ravenstone House for the Less Privileged.

Like I said, I liked Finley a lot.

But so did two of the workers at the orphanage.

They liked him in ways I never understood.

So when it came time for the adults to grow tired of Finley, and the things they did to him, and him trying to protect the younger orphans, they said he'd gone to an orphanage in Scotland.

But it was a lie.

And we all knew it.

Because he was sent down here.

With the rest of us.

But now, they are doing things to the orphanage above us.

And Finley has an idea.

CHAPTER ONE

Lacham, Borough of Wandsworth, London, circa 1984

RAVENSTONE HOUSE HAD STOOD IN DISREPAIR FOR close to twenty years. It had been condemned as uninhabitable somewhere in the early to mid-seventies and subsequently boarded up by the local authorities. Then it became a popular haunt of junkies, the homeless, street kids, anyone who needed a dilapidated roof over their heads. And *haunt* was an apt word to use. Most only stayed there for a handful of nights.

Why?

Because the place gave anyone who stayed there the creeps—even the kids who spent most of their days at Ravenstone as high as a kite on drugs, or blind as a bat on booze.

If it wasn't the leaking ceilings or the coldness that seemed to come from deep below, it was the sounds only heard in the darkness of the night.

Children. Whispering through the long and dilapidated corridors, heard in every room.

'Help us.'

'It's not our fault.'

'We did nothing wrong.'

The voices crept along the back of their necks, sending a shiver down their spines.

And more often than not, when the whispers ceased, the drops of water always began.

Weird.

Creepy.

Creepy and weird.

As most of the guests were off their faces, they passed all the strange occurrences as a by-product of their spaced-out minds.

Hallucinations.

A few, the more ballsy types, thought it was all joke.

They would invite their friends to come and stay the night, to experience the spook show with their own eyes.

But even those twits would soon realise.

You don't mess with the children of Ravenstone.

The last moments of their lives had been horrific, to put it mildly.

The monsters did not discriminate. Whether their victims were boys or girls, raped and sodomised they would be dragged through the dark corridors by their hair, and downstairs into the basement.

Down there, the darkness is so infinite, it's as if the blood running through your helpless little body has turned the colour of the night sky.

Only death brought relief from the immense pain.

But the darkness would remain forever.

It's not our fault.

We did nothing wrong.

So you'd agree, reader.

The spirits of these children, somehow trapped below the floorboards of Ravenstone House, would not take well to anyone who wanted take the piss.

So when the time was right, the voices of the children heard in the rooms and corridors of Ravenstone House would suddenly cease.

And when the squatters, hoping to spook their invited guests, thought the freak show was over, they would stomp their feet on the floor and throw empty bottles of whatever they were drinking down the dark corridor in disgust.

'What a fucking waste of time, you fucking git,' one such guest said to his friend who was bunking up at Ravenstone, this particular night.

If the three men standing there at one end of the corridor hadn't been drunk as skunks, they would have wondered why the bottles they'd thrown into the darkness hadn't smashed into pieces.

But it was a moot point now.

As the guy who'd spoken gave his mate a clip over the back of the head, it happened.

'What the fuck!' the third guest screamed.

He'd been hit fair and square in the head with the very beer bottle he'd thrown down the corridor only seconds ago.

As the others turned and began to laugh at him, another bottle came flying back at high velocity, and smashed into the corner of the corridor wall centimetres away.

'Who the bleedin' hell is throwing bottles back at us?' the squatter shouted.

As the words left his mouth, another six bottles came spinning out of nowhere, hitting all three men hard.

'What the fuck?' one shouted, before they all dropped to the ground bleeding, and wincing in pain.

'Let's get the fuck out of here,' one pleaded to the others.

His mate had other ideas.

'Fook off, ya pansy,' he stood and said, 'Let's run down there and find out who threw these bottles at us.'

He took a step forward.

Under his foot, he felt the floorboard creak.

He wiped the blood trickling from a cut in his forehead.

As he turned back to see where his friends were, one made a weird sound, apparently unable to speak.

The guy raised his left arm to beyond where his friend was standing, and pointed.

When the guy turned back, he pretty much pissed himself.

At the end of the long and dark corridor a light, weak as if it were a thousand miles away, had appeared, a pinprick in the curtain of the darkness.

It was enough for him to barely see, with his whole body now trembling, something in front of the tiny light.

Two children standing there, still as pieces of furniture.

One was short, a girl. Standing alongside her was what appeared to be a boy, much taller.

The taller one pointed at him, shaking his head from side to side.

CHAPTER TWO

Four years later

'WHAT DO YOU THINK?'

'How long did you spend at Westminster University studying architecture?'

'Excuse me?'

'I think you spent the whole time at the Undercroft, not studying like most of us did.'

The two architects smiled at each other.

There is an inherent issue when one of your work colleagues is also one of your oldest friends. The banter at work is as perpetually thick as a pint of Guinness.

Quentin leant forward and cleared his throat.

'When you are a born architect,' he ensured Tim was making eye contact with him, 'there is no need to attend class.'

Tim checked the office to ensure no one but 'Q' would hear his response.

'When you are a born plonker, with your hand on your willy instead of a pencil, you should be in class instead of the pub.'

The two men shook their heads at the same time as they struggled to suppress their laughter.

Quentin Brookes felt a wave of satisfaction. He knew his best friend Tim Bentleigh liked the latest plans laid out on the table. Tim loved to take the piss out of him at every opportunity. It was one of the things Q loved about him.

Quentin Brookes stood at precisely six feet tall—handy as an architect, since it made viewing plans on a flat table easy. A keen cyclist and amateur football player on the weekends, Q was fit and in good shape. His thick, mousy-blond hair, always kept short except in his late teens, sat atop a well-structured face. With striking blue eyes and perfectly straight teeth, finished off with a square, set jaw, the guy was unabashedly good-looking.

His last name was synonymous with one of the two most influential cities in the world, alongside New York.

You'd hear it on the streets, in Parliament, and in the British tabloids on a daily basis.

His father, Bernard Brookes, was the current lord mayor of London.

⊏══⊐

Tim walked around to the side of the table and put his arm around Quentin, not taking his eyes off the plans.

'Another dog's bollocks masterpiece in the making,' he said, grinning.

Tim Bentleigh made Q look average in height. He towered over his friend by at least half a foot. He'd been in the school basketball team from an early age, and at the ripe old age of nineteen, his height had topped out at a more than respectable six foot seven.

Lanky was an apt description for Tim, but after ten solid years of university and work, he was a tiny bit more filled out these days. But he enjoyed tennis more than anything of late, and still made it to his local gym most weeks. Like his best friend, he was also in good shape.

A mop of jet-black hair, these days shaped by a classic short back and sides cut, suited the beanpole of a man. Think Clark Kent stretched out, minus the big glasses, with friendly brown eyes, a slightly pointy nose, and a smile permanently set on his full lips.

Q nodded at Tim's 'dog's bollocks' comment before the most random feeling came over him.

He stared at the plans for one of the most ambitious renovations the firm had ever been tasked with designing, and wondered how his gorgeous fiancée would take to the idea.

They'd been in the market for a little while, looking for their first home to buy together. And this development was in their borough, which made it all the more attractive. He knew the price tag would be a little out of their range, but he'd worry about it later.

'Cat got your tongue, mate?' Tim asked quietly. He took his arm from around Q, but remained standing next to him.

Q was still staring at the plans, but a grin appeared on his face a moment later.

He turned to Tim and said, 'I think I've come up with a rolled-gold idea.'

Tim screwed his face up and set his eyes on Q.

When his friend said nothing, he added, 'Come on, Willy Wonka, out with it.'

Q stared down to the plans, in particular Flat Two.

'I fink me and the missus should buy this one righ' 'ere,' he said, affecting a cockney accent. Quentin reached over and rested his index finger on the center of the lounge room of Flat Two.

Tim thought about it for a moment before patting

Quentin on the back and saying, 'Mate, you are full of good ideas today. Sounds like a grand plan, but…'

Quentin waited for Tim to speak, but it didn't come.

Tim had done it for effect, so Quentin would eventually look him in the eye. When he did, a moment later, Tim leant in closer and said, 'You've heard the rumours about the place?'

Quentin rolled his eyes before scoffing at his best friend's comment. He obviously didn't believe in the hocus-pocus ghost stories virtually anyone involved in the project had heard about.

'Come on, mate,' Quentin said, shaking his head.

Tim shrugged and inverted his smile. 'All I'm saying, Q-man…' He glanced back down to the plans of Flat Two.

A second later, a drop of water landed right in the middle of the paper.

CHAPTER THREE

QUENTIN WATCHED MARY ACROSS THE DINING TABLE. She was eating the spaghetti bolognese as if she was trying to break the land-speed record for food consumption.

She caught Q looking at her and said, 'I could eat a horse. I was run off my feet today.'

Q smiled and as he shook his head, said, 'You are one of the hardest-working hotties I know, my dear.'

And he was right, for sure.

Mary Campbell was a charge nurse in a ward of one of England's biggest and most revered children's hospitals.

The Great Ormond Road Hospital, Camden.

At the ripe old age of twenty-nine, a strict exercise regime was not a priority, thanks to her being run off her feet most days of the week.

But she'd always been in good shape, and had easily attracted the attention of a university student studying architecture about five years earlier.

At five foot six, she was a little shorter than her 'Super-Q', as she often called him, but it had never bothered her, or him, in the slightest.

Long locks of blonde hair, most of the time in a thick ponytail, surrounded her small and pretty face. Big blue eyes sat between a small, almost elfish nose, and her smile was the one thing every single child which came through her ward fell head over heels for. Some of the more confident boys even suggested marrying a ten-year-old was surely legal somewhere in the world. When she wore one of her many summer dresses out for a weekend stroll, Quentin's head would wobble with overwhelming pride so often his neck would eventually ache, especially if he was holding her hand.

But to add to her impressive looks, Mary was perfectly suited to her profession. She loved children, and knew how to make kids feel at home in her ward. Compassion came almost instinctively to her. But she was also intelligent, and the type of 1990s late-twenties-something who was no shrinking violet when the need arose.

But Quentin was still nervous about what he was about to say to her over the dinner table.

He knew she was serious about their budget for the purchase of their first home. She was brilliant with their finances, and Q knew this was a great thing.

His proposal would see that budget stretched to its very limits. But he could not escape the pull of Ravenstone House. He knew he had to try.

'Darling, we've pretty much completed the plans for the renovations today,' he said, to get the ball rolling.

Mary glanced up from her dinner. He couldn't help but grin at the sight of her sauce-red lips.

'You've worked hard, Q. You'll have to show me what you've done,' she said.

This lifted his confidence, so he pushed forward.

'Funny you say that.' He nodded towards the bedroom. 'I've brought the plans home.'

In their small flat, the only spot big enough to roll out the plans was the double bed.

'Very good. You can show me after dinner.'

Quentin smiled as she continued to eat with vigour. Q decided to do the same. The quicker they ate, the sooner he'd be able to see what his fiancée thought of his idea.

CHAPTER FOUR

Quentin insisted on doing the dishes.

It was a ploy to get Mary relaxed and in a good frame of mind.

A glass of wine was also helping with this little plan.

Mary sat at the dinner table, sipping on her wine while Quentin did all the cleaning up. With hindsight, later she would realise why he'd been so chatty before, while doing all the chores. That's how he gave himself away, when he was nervous. Bless him, she thought.

'So, now all the dishes are done,' Quentin dried his hands on the dishcloth and took a deep breath, 'I can show you my masterpiece.'

Mary slipped from her chair, bringing the glass with her. Since he'd done all the cleaning up, it was only fair to devote herself to hearing him talk about his work.

The thing she loved most about Quentin was his passion for everything in his life, especially her. He took immense pride in his work, and to her, this made him all the more attractive.

'Lead the way, you sexy man,' Mary said as he walked

past her. She gave him a playful pat on his behind for good measure.

Q turned on the light in the bedroom before stepping over to the bed. Mary was by his side a moment later.

'May I present to my beautiful future wife,' he turned and met her eyes, 'the new and completely renovated Ravenstone House Flats.'

Quentin spent the next five minutes explaining many details of the plans. As Mary finished her glass of wine and started to get a little fidgety on her feet (having spent most of the last nine hours standing up), Q picked up the signal and knew it was time to roll the dice.

'So, what do you think, honey? Do you like what you see?' he asked, a little nervously.

She shrugged her shoulders before placing her empty glass on the nightstand.

'Darling, it looks fabulous. Now if you don't mind—'

Quentin cut in as diplomatically as he could.

'Mary, I'd like to know what you think of an idea I've come up with. It involves you, me…' He could feel his nerves getting the better of him.

'…and Flat Two.' He turned and put one finger directly on the plans, where the lounge room of the flat would be.

She pulled his hand up and held it in her own.

A faint smile appeared on her face, but only for a moment. She put her hand on his cheek and said, 'Quentin Brookes, I love you. But I imagine the flat would be way out of our price range.'

Quentin could feel his hopes evaporating. But he knew he had to try.

'I know the developer quite well. If I could get a firm price on the flat, would you consider doing the sums?' he said.

Mary let out an exasperated breath, but not at Super-Q's

proposal. It was more from exhaustion. She'd always liked the idea of living in a freshly renovated flat, especially one that mixed old and new, like this would.

Something deep inside her told her to be completely open-minded about the proposal.

'Okay.' Mary turned to make Quentin's night. 'Talk to the developer and find out the price. We'll look at the numbers. At some point, if it all seems possible, we should go and have a look at the place.'

Quentin could feel the excitement building in the pit of his stomach. 'If we were a bit short on the finance, I could ask Dad to consider helping out, if he were interested.' He ended on a questioning note.

Quentin wondered if he'd overstepped the mark.

Mary had told him a few times before that she'd always wanted to buy a place with him, but without his father's involvement whatsoever.

Suffice to say, Mary had never warmed to Quentin's father.

She ignored Quentin's comment as best she could, and gazed down at the plans once more. After a few moments of awkward silence, she decided to change the subject.

She studied the plans a little closer before turning back to Q.

Smiling, she said, 'If this all goes ahead—do me one favour, Super-Q.'

Quentin put his arm around her. 'Name it, my lady.'

'You make sure you get all the skeletons out of the closet. Old Ravenstone House has quite the reputation.'

Quentin nodded. 'I will.'

He needn't worry about the skeletons in the closet.

That's not where they were.

The morning after talking with Mary about Flat Two, Quentin called the developer.

Doug Lozel used Quentin's firm to do most of his design work, and the two men had known each other for years. Doug was on the fast train to retirement, and was hoping Ravenstone House would be one of his last jobs before he and the missus headed for the endless summer of Costa del Sol, in the Andalusia province of Spain.

And in the end, it would in fact be his very last project.

He'd already built his holiday home in Costa del Sol a few years ago, so as far as Doug was concerned, there was no time to dilly-dally.

This worked in Quentin's favour when it came time to sweet-talk Doug into giving him a special deal on Flat Two, on the ground floor of Ravenstone House.

Over a fresh brew of English Breakfast tea, and possibly the world's biggest pound cake, Quentin went to work on trying to talk Doug into giving him a reduced price. To his surprise, he found Doug in a generous mood after only five solid minutes of sweet talking the big guy.

'Quentin, you know, I've known you a long time,' Doug said between gulps of tea and a piece of cake so large it might have floated down the middle of the English Channel like an iceberg.

When his mouth was finally free, he went on: 'So plying me with tea and cake and telling me what a good developer I am,' he smiled, 'isn't necessary.'

Quentin wasn't sure how to take being caught out, so he sat and smiled awkwardly.

Doug burst into laughter, leaning over to slap Quentin hard on the right shoulder.

'Now before we talk figures,' Doug stopped laughing and leant forward conspiratorially, 'can I ask you one question?'

Quentin, still nursing his right shoulder and wondering

what in God's name was going to be thrown at him, said, 'Sure, Doug, fire away.'

'Does your father know you want to buy a flat at Ravenstone House?"

Quentin stared at Doug for a moment.

'Dad doesn't know about this, so, no.'

Doug sat back for a moment, and Quentin fleetingly saw something odd in the big guy's demeanour. But a second later it was gone.

Now it was Quentin's turn for questions.

'Can I ask why you asked me?' he said.

The oversized developer, a victim of his own love affair with long and boozy lunches, took another sip of his tea before looking back at Quentin.

'A little curious,' Doug said.

'Is this about the fact—'

Doug cut Quentin off rather abruptly and said, 'No, they're only rumours, my boy. I can't imagine your father believes in ghosts, any more than I believe in exercise.'

Quentin smiled, but a feeling of apprehension swept over him. He was old enough now to make his own decisions about his life. Still, his dad could be difficult sometimes.

Doug sat forward and patted Quentin on the knee. 'I want to make sure that Bernard won't get upset with me for selling the flat to you even though you and your lovely woman's finances are stretched,' Doug lied.

Quentin took a deep breath and knew it was time to push on and get to the point.

It only took another two minutes of discussion before Quentin believed he had achieved his goal.

As the men shook hands, they had considerably differing thoughts.

Quentin—was over the moon. He couldn't wait to get home to tell Mary. They'd secured the flat for only £75K more than what their slightly stretched budget allowed. They could get this over the line. No sweat.

Doug—was relieved he would be moving to Spain soon. When Bernard Brookes found out he'd sold Flat Two to Q, there might be hell to pay. He never understood why his old pal Bernie had a problem with this development. In the end, he didn't care. Now he only had one more of the ground floor flats to offload, and the development would be sold out.

He'd eventually get over the fact he'd sold it to someone he knew. The fact was as straight as a die: he was desperate.

Most of his workers had refused to work on the three ground-floor flats. In the end, he had to import labourers from Romania.

Even on a mild day, the ground floor and basement were so cold you could see your own breath. Most of the workers wore winter parkas all day. But the cold wasn't the only issue.

There were also the strange sounds.

And the constant drips of water.

The morning sky was a cobalt shade of blue, which the residents of Lacham welcomed with open arms.

Quentin and Mary stood in front of the busy worksite, ensuring they remained within the direct rays of the morning sun. Holding hands, they watched tradespeople coming and going, all hard at work for another day. The renovations were on track to be completed in about a month or so.

Doug told Quentin he would meet him out the front at the stroke of 9am. At a quarter past nine, Mary was growing anxious and annoyed. Although she had the morning off, she didn't want to spend it standing out the front of Ravenstone House waiting for someone tardy.

As she was about to politely ask her fiancé to call Doug, they heard a voice coming from down the street.

Both of them turned to see Doug walking in their direction. He looked out of breath.

'I see what he means by the stroke of nine,' Quentin said confidentially. 'Maybe he meant he will have a stroke at nine.' He smirked.

Mary couldn't help but smile back. It washed away the annoyance of standing there for the last fifteen minutes waiting for the man.

'I'm sorry,' Doug said, as Mary wondered whether a defibrillator within arm's reach wouldn't go astray.

'It's fine,' Quentin said.

'It's all good, Doug.' Mary leant forward and gave the man a peck on the cheek. It made him feel all the more embarrassed.

Doug caught his breath for a moment, wiping his brow before turning to face Ravenstone House. 'I got held up at home,' he panted. 'Sorry for being late. Now, let's go inside and take a look at the flat.'

As he stepped towards the bottom of the five steps to the main door, he could feel something stir in the pit of his stomach.

It certainly wasn't the gigantic cooked breakfast he'd devoured only thirty minutes earlier—the sole reason for him being late.

It was a sense of dread.

Ravenstone House gave the guy the creeps.

CHAPTER FIVE

DOUG IGNORED THE PAIN IN HIS CHEST AND PUSHED on. He handed Quentin and Mary a high-vis vest each, which they put on.

Mary scanned the foyer of Ravenstone House.

The place was still an organised mess. Plastic sheeting covered the floors, along with the ladders, tools, and piles of debris you'd normally see on a construction site. Two painters sat atop portable scaffolding, busily painting the ceiling.

Mary could envision the foyer after the renovations. It would be stunning.

'Follow me,' Doug said as he began weaving his way through all the mess and activity in the foyer.

Halfway down the main hallway, Doug came to the staircase leading up to the first floor, which sat ominously to the right of the foyer. Ahead and to the left, the ground-floor hallway continued to the three ground-floor flats, and ended with the entrance to the basement. Doug had only gone down the stairs once. That had been enough. Most of the rumours he'd heard about Ravenstone being haunted centred on that basement. He'd left his site supervisor in charge of any problems down there.

Doug walked another six feet before coming to an open door. He turned and smiled queasily to Quentin and Mary. 'Here we are.'

The couple returned the developer's smile and followed him through the entrance.

The last time Quentin had been at Ravenstone House, the place had been vastly different. He could now see the flat coming together. It was almost ready for its new owners to move in.

After taking the couple on a tour of the flat, Doug pulled up in the middle of the lounge room.

'So this is it. Tell me,' Doug raised his eyebrows and tried to muster up some enthusiasm, 'what do you think?'

Mary stared at Doug for a moment and gathered her thoughts.

A second later, a sudden gust of cold wind passed through the flat.

Mary turned around and met Quentin's eyes.

'Where did that come from? Is it because we're on the ground floor?'

Quentin turned to the developer. Big Doug had gone pale and was shrugging his shoulders.

'These old houses are well insulated with the two or three floors above. It's handy in summer, but not so much in winter,' he lied.

Quentin walked over to Mary and put his arm around her. She didn't look entirely convinced, but eventually went to the windows of the main living area and stared outside.

'I guess if the heating is up to scratch,' she spun around to her future husband, 'this won't be a problem, right?'

Quentin nodded. 'The central heating utilises the latest technology.' He turned to Doug for reassurance more than anything else. 'So we'll be fine. Right, Doug?'

Doug wished he'd eaten earlier. He felt nauseous.

'No expense was spared on the heating of the flats in his development, I can re—'

What made the moment so bizarre was that Doug was actually looking up towards the ceiling when it happened.

Doug had stopped his bullshit line mid-sentence, about no expense being spared on the heating for Ravenstone House.

He blinked heavily, wiping his face with a handkerchief he'd pulled from his pocket.

'What is it, Doug? Are you okay, mate?' Quentin said.

'It was nothing. Got something in my eye,' he said.

Doug Lozel had lost count of the amount of times the Romanian labourers had complained about the leaks. He didn't want to tell the couple for fear of the two backing out of the sale.

Even after they'd replastered and checked all the water pipes, the problem continued.

Doug had now experienced the problem first-hand and twofold.

The drops of water had somehow done the impossible.

They'd hit both of his eyes.

Doug Lozel would soon feel the heat of the Spanish sun.

But he would not be able to see it.

———

Fifty days later

Whoever said moving house was fun was completely stark raving mad. Moving house is, for most, a right-royal pain in the buttocks. It's hard work. It's stressful.

Quentin was over it. The small flat they'd rented in

Tooting Bec was only a stone's throw to Lacham. That at least was something.

The main move took place in the early hours of Sunday morning. Quentin was keen to get it done well before the permitted cut-off time of midday.

One of the reasons he loved Mary was she was a minimalist. She didn't own piles of things she never used, so the number of boxes they had to pack was pretty manageable. The painful part was getting all the furniture down the ridiculously tight staircase from the third floor. Lifts are meant to work all year round. But the lift at their flat in Tooting Bec had shit itself the day before the scheduled move. Nothing more than bad luck, but it meant everything would have to come down the stairs. Fantastic.

At least when they arrived at Ravenstone House, all they needed to navigate was the five stairs from the pavement to the front door.

As Quentin drove down Lacham High Road, he could see another moving van sitting out the front of Ravenstone House.

'We've got company,' Mary said as they pulled up.

'Maybe it's our neighbours over at Flat One?' Quentin said. Flat One was the closest to theirs on the ground floor.

⸺

As Quentin passed a box to Mary, who was standing on the pavement, his question was answered.

A couple walked down the steps and headed to the other van.

As they reached the back of their van, they spotted Quentin and Mary standing there holding a box.

The woman smiled and said, 'Are you guys moving in here today too?'

Quentin nodded. The woman's partner dropped his box and smiled.

He walked to Quentin and Mary and said, 'Hi there. I'm David, and this over here is my wife, Christine.'

Quentin dropped the box in his hands to the pavement for a handshake.

Wow, Super-Q thought, make a mental note never to upset my new neighbour. Though Quentin would have pegged his age at a youthful sixty, the guy was built like a fridge, and his hands were the size of baseball mitts.

'So, we are in Flat One,' the fridge's wife said, shaking Mary's hand before Quentin's. 'Which is yours?'

Quentin could feel his pulse in his right hand, but ignored it. 'We're in Flat Two,' he said.

David and Christine shared a genuine smile before they turned back to Quentin and Mary.

'Well, it looks like we're going to be neighbours,' David said.

Mary checked him over.

She'd have agreed with Quentin if she could read his mind. David was built like a major kitchen appliance. He wasn't tall, probably somewhere between five eight to five nine. He appeared to be in his late fifties. His hairline and weathered face said as much. But his demeanour was warm and friendly, with grey eyes and a genuine smile. He was dressed in activewear, which told Mary he was about to go to the gym, or did something like martial arts. As she got to know David Banks, she'd find out she was right on both accounts. He trained regularly at a gym, and was also a third-dan taekwondo instructor.

Christine stepped a couple of feet closer and said, 'Well, when we are settled in, we'll have you two over for some nibbles and drinks, if you like.'

Christine's blondish hair was in a ponytail, exposing a

decent set of earrings either side of a friendly, attractive face. Quentin met eyes with Mary, and he could tell she welcomed the idea.

'We'd love to,' Quentin said.

CHAPTER SIX

QUENTIN WAS EXHAUSTED. WITH THE LIFT OUT OF action in the old block at Tooting Bec, he felt as if he'd moved three times in one day.

His back ached somewhat, but he took consolation in knowing that at least they'd only had to get all the furniture *down* three flights of stairs, not up. His tired body yearned for a good night's sleep, and he expected that once his head hit the pillow, he'd be out like a light. He felt he could fall into a coma-like sleep and not be woken until the dawn crept its way through the curtains.

The one thing that had taken most of his energy to move was Mary's four-poster bed.

He was certain her enormous contraption of a bedframe had been designed and built during the Industrial Revolution. His suggestion, back when they'd moved into Tooting Bec together, to sell it in favour of his own bed (which was a much better fit, being considerably smaller), found Quentin almost thrown out of his very own flat by someone who'd not officially moved in yet.

So the wrought-iron four-poster bed was pulled apart

and shipped over to Ravenstone House. It was safe to say it weighed a tonne.

After a dinner of takeaway pizza, washed down with a couple of beers, Quentin found Mary in their bedroom making up the bed.

Mary tucked in her side of the bed and said, 'Our first night in our new home. This is very exciting indeed, my Q.'

'And how's all this space around your beautiful bed?' Quentin waved his arm around. It was quite the novelty to be in a bedroom at least three times bigger than the old one.

She patted the bed. 'You look beat. Why don't you get cleaned up and get yourself a well-deserved night's sleep?'

———

When Quentin hopped into bed, he relished taking the weight off his aching legs and arms. Mary got in a moment later and the two snuggled underneath the duvet. Both were dog-tired from the long day of moving house, and it would be a short race to be the first asleep.

Quentin's eyelids felt as if they had turned into slabs of concrete. As he lay there, knowing sleep was only a few moments away, Mary propped herself up and studied the man who would one day be her husband.

'I love you, Quentin Brookes,' she said.

Seconds before sleep came to him, he said, 'I love you too, honey.'

———

Quentin hit the accelerator harder, ripping at the gearstick and smacking the pedals with his left foot. Racing down the main stretch at Silverstone, he couldn't believe how fast he was going. As he saw the corner coming up quickly, he mashed the stick in perfect harmony with his feet.

As he cleared the bend and began to accelerate up the hill, the woman's screams in his headset made no sense at all.

He'd normally hear instructions from the technicians, along with the odd 'well done,' not the sound of a woman wailing.

But when he realised an arm was pulling at him, Quentin's mind quickly pulled him out of his favourite dream: Quentin Brookes, British Formula One champion.

As he opened his eyes, he felt the first stab of fear. He was stone cold, like someone had pulled the duvet off and thrown it to the floor.

What made his blood run cold was knowing who was screaming.

Mary, his fiancée.

She grabbed at him and shrieked. 'Quentin, Quentin! Are you awake? Please, please, wake up!'

The fog lifted from his mind as his eyes began to register shapes in the darkness.

Something was completely wrong with what he was seeing.

The main light source was a slit at the top of the closed curtains on their bedroom window. Usually, when they were lying in bed, that slit was well above them.

Mary's screams had stopped, and now she whimpered. She'd already latched onto him as if her life depended on it.

'Quentin! What's going on? I'm so scared,' Mary said.

Now fully awake, Quentin sat up and realised why he was so confused.

For good measure, he decided to confirm it by looking directly above.

No way.

'What the—'

This is not happening, he thought.

The slit at the top of the curtain was no longer higher than the bed.

It was below.

The tops of Mary's wrought-iron bedposts were touching the high ceiling.

Quentin shifted to look over the edge.

A wave of nausea, two beers, three quarters of a pizza, and sheer terror tumbled around his stomach.

'Quentin, we're off the ground!' Mary squirmed.

As Quentin grabbed Mary and wrapped his arms around her—it happened.

The bed dropped.

It hit so hard, and with such a bang, Quentin was certain the legs would pierce the hundred-year-old floorboards like a nail hitting a piece of balsa wood.

Mary's screams continued.

'It's okay, honey,' he lied.

Mary shuddered in his arms, but then whispered, 'Look.'

When Quentin turned to the bedroom door, he swore his heart had turned to lead.

Two children stood there, staring at him and Mary.

It's not our fault.

We did nothing wrong.

CHAPTER SEVEN

QUENTIN AND MARY MANAGED TO FALL ASLEEP, somehow.

It was a good effort considering they spent the rest of the night on their couch, which was not designed for two adults to sleep on.

Mary had insisted that Quentin pull the couch over to the island bench of their kitchen so he could wedge it underneath the overhang. While designing the flat, Q had envisioned this as the place where they enjoyed casual brunches. That's why he'd extended the kitchen bench out. This was not part of the vision.

But you don't have to be Einstein to figure out why Mary had made the request.

After seeing the children standing in the doorway, she'd been too frightened to sleep in their bedroom.

Mary had insisted they leave the flat immediately, but Quentin wondered where they would go. He was still exhausted from moving, and had come up with a second option—the couch. When Mary reluctantly agreed, she did so only on the proviso it be pushed underneath the overhang.

That, she hoped, would keep them from waking up again in mid-air before being dropped like a bag of spuds.

Quentin was able to slip off the couch without waking Mary, and quietly went about brewing some coffee and making toast.

When Mary woke, she sat up and got her bearings. As her head bobbed out from underneath the overhang of the island bench, Quentin smiled.

'Is that my Sleeping Beauty?' he said.

Mary rose to her feet, feeling groggy. Having the shit scared out of you must be similar to a big night out.

'How's my future wife holding up?'

Mary took a deep breath before glancing towards the doorway.

She turned back to Quentin and shook her head. 'Last night was one hell of a first night here.'

When the bread popped out of the toaster, Quentin smiled and said, 'Come, sit.' He patted the top of the island bench. 'Let me get you some coffee and toast.'

———

'What are we going to do?' Mary said after taking a bite of toast. She followed it up with a big gulp of coffee.

Quentin gathered his thoughts.

He'd fallen in love with this flat. That he'd also been the chief architect only made it worse. It was the first time he'd been able to buy something he'd designed.

But there was something else. He couldn't put his finger on it. It was as if something had drawn him here.

'We need to figure it out, babe,' Q said before taking a sip of coffee.

He studied Mary for a moment.

'Tell me what you're thinking, Mary Lee Campbell.'

She shook her head.

'We'd both heard the rumours. And now it looks like they're true,' she said.

She closed her eyes and continued to shake her head.

'I don't want to live in a haunted house,' she said.

When she opened her eyes, she found Quentin staring into the distance. When he eventually met her eyes, he nodded.

'You and me both, honey. I guess we need to monitor the situation. If it happens again—' Q cast his eyes to every corner of the room while reflecting on his words.

With fear in her voice, Mary said, 'If it happens again, we'll have to consider our options. Do we stay and see if we can fix it, or do we cut and run?'

Quentin met his fiancée's tired eyes. 'I know I want to make it work here. I'm hoping last night was a freak of nature, so to speak. A one-off.'

⊏⊐

Mary closed the front door of her flat. She was relieved to be on her way to work, to be honest. She heard footsteps in the hallway behind her a second later, loud enough to expect it was probably not a ghost or anything similar. So she hoped.

She spun her head around to make sure.

It was Christine from Flat One.

'Good morning, neighbour,' said Christine, bright and chirpy. 'How was your first night?' she asked.

Mary caught herself hesitating for a moment, wondering what to say to this woman who was still little more than a stranger.

'It was okay, I guess. You know, a new place always takes a bit to get used to.' Mary thought she'd done well at masking what she was actually feeling.

Christine was all smiles.

'I know, right? It always takes me a little while to get used to a brand-new home,' she said.

When they arrived at the front door to Ravenstone House, Mary opened it for Christine.

'You didn't by chance hear a loud bang last night?' Mary asked.

Christine smiled, though her eyes said something else. She was hiding something. She stared at Mary for a moment before shaking her head. 'No, I didn't hear anything other than the usual sounds of London at night.'

Mary couldn't believe it. To her, the sound of her impossibly heavy bed dropping six feet onto the floorboards had been like two cars colliding at 60 miles an hour.

Christine checked her watch. 'Which way you headed?'

Mary nodded towards the entrance to the Tube not far down the road, 'The Tube, you?'

Christine started to walk off. 'Come on, we can go together.'

By the time the two had reached the station, they'd learned a little more about each other. As they arrived underground, Christine tapped Mary on the arm and said, 'Well, I'm heading this way.' She pointed to one platform.

Mary was glad she'd bumped into Christine.

'Nice chatting to you,' Mary said.

As Christine was about to walk off, she stopped. 'We must get together for that drink and nibbles. Why don't we do it on the weekend?'

Mary thought it would be a great idea. Christine seemed very sociable. It wouldn't hurt for her and Quentin to get to know them.

'I'll check with Quentin, you check with David, and we can let each other know.'

Christine waved, as she could feel a rush of air. Her train was fast approaching, and she wanted to be on it.

'Will do!' she shouted over the noise.

As Christine ran for her train, she wondered why she'd lied to Mary about the noise last night.

She supposed she was more embarrassed than anything else, considering the bang had come from her own bedroom.

Or so she'd thought.

CHAPTER EIGHT

10 days later

Q<small>UENTIN AND</small> M<small>ARY SPENT ONE FURTHER NIGHT ON</small> the couch in the lounge room after the flying bed incident. Although Mary was reluctant, as you'd expect her to be, she then mustered the courage to return to their bed. This owed much to Quentin's improvisation: the architect had rigged two pieces of timber between the bed and the ceiling. It was the only way he'd been able to talk her around.

Nothing unusual had happened since. Tonight, drinks and nibbles were planned at David and Christine's flat.

'Come on, pretty boy,' Mary shouted from the kitchen as she placed plastic wrap over the dish of hors d'oeuvres she'd made. Quentin was in the bathroom brushing his hair.

When he came around the corner, Mary burst into laughter.

Quentin had fashioned his hair into a mohawk with gel. His hair in the middle stood on end. Mary didn't mind it—it made Q look like he was five years old.

'Ah-ha.' Mary walked over to him and planted a firm kiss

on his lips, 'I see you're out to impress the neighbours tonight,' she said.

'All in a day's work, my darling.' Quentin turned around and headed back to the bathroom.

A couple of minutes later, the couple stood in front of the door to Flat One.

Quentin tapped lightly with the doorknocker a couple of times.

It swung open with vigour a few moments later.

'Hello, hello,' David said, greeting the couple with a warm smile and a handshake Quentin thought may break a bone in his own hand. 'Lovely to see you both. Follow me.' David ushered Q and Mary into the kitchen.

The couple found Christine behind the kitchen counter preparing food.

Sitting across from her were a man and woman Quentin and Mary hadn't met before.

'You guys may not have met yet,' David said, nodding to the couple sitting there.

'Quentin Brookes, and this is my fiancée, Mary Campbell,' Q said.

'Pleasure to meet you. Andrew Parsons, and this is my wife, Yukiko.'

Quentin studied the couple. Andrew had an unmistakable American twang to his voice. The guy stood up from the stool and reached out for Q's hand. Around six feet tall, with an average build, the guy was dressed smartly in a crisp white shirt and black suit pants. Smiling brown eyes nestled behind a small set of rimmed glasses, matching a neat, short mound of brown hair.

His wife was petite, probably no more than five foot two. A mane of thick black hair done up in a ponytail stretched far past her shoulder line. She greeted Mary with sincerity in an accent still tinged with Japanese.

'Andrew and Yukiko are fellow neighbours. They moved into flat number three last week,' David announced as he held up a bottle of red wine to his guests. 'Who's for a red?'

Quentin and Andrew nodded, while the women all opted for white instead.

When everyone had a glass of wine in their hand, Christine held up hers and said, 'Here's to our new neighbours at Ravenstone House.'

'Hear, hear,' everyone said as they all leant in and touched each other's glass in a toast.

Andrew spoke of his career as a computer programmer. Quentin zoned out for most of the story. Yukiko's job was even less interesting: she worked in administration at a law firm.

The wine flowed for the next couple of hours, with second bottles of red and white soon opened and heading for empty.

'So you're the man who designed the flats?' Andrew asked Quentin at some point.

Quentin nodded proudly. 'Yes, I am. Are you guys happy with your place?' he said.

Yukiko put her glass down and nodded. 'You're obviously very good at what you do.'

Andrew took another sip of wine and rested his glass on the table.

'But we're going to have to maybe get a plumber in,' he said, turning to Quentin. 'It's not constant, but there seems to be the odd drip leaking from the ceiling, especially in the lounge room.'

David and Christine shared a glance that did not go unnoticed by Mary and Quentin. A moment of awkward silence ensued. For the first time that night, they were lost for conversation.

Christine leant forward and spoke quietly. 'It must be something about the house, because we've had the same thing in our flat.'

Andrew now met his wife's eyes, and they reflected on a conversation from only the night before.

The American hesitated, clearing his throat before saying, 'Someone told Yukiko yesterday. There are rumours about Ravenstone House.'

Mary swallowed air. Quentin took a deep breath. David and Christine knew what was coming.

'Apparently this place is haunted.' He took a drink of his wine, then added, 'by orphans who died here.'

Andrew scanned the eyes of everyone sitting around the table.

'I think it's all a load of bullshit,' he said.

Yukiko shifted uncomfortably in her chair. She wondered if her husband was getting drunk. But he wasn't done.

'Haunted houses are a figment of people's imagination,' he continued. 'I'm sure no orphan died in this house. It's all made-up spook stories from people who need to get a life.'

The dining table suddenly shuddered.

It then rose three inches into the air.

But as quickly as the table went up, a second later it came crashing down to the floor.

Everyone's glasses of wine and water crashed sideways along with the wine bottles.

As the women screamed and the men swore, the lights in the flat—went out.

The room plunged into darkness.

'Nice one, Andrew,' Yukiko said, 'what did you say that for?"

David spoke calmly to his wife. 'Darling, second drawer behind you. Candles. Pull one out.'

He took a deep breath and said stoically, 'Power outage for sure. These things happen.'

Quentin heard Mary shift her seat right next to his, and then her breathing, short and panicked.

Christine placed the candle in the middle of the table, everyone around her a grey smear on the backdrop of total darkness. She could feel the fear rising inside her.

First her bed floated in the air before crashing to the ground, and now this. She knew for sure it was what Mary had heard a couple of weeks ago.

As the flame from the candle brightened, David sighed with relief.

The feeling was short lived.

Christine screamed at the top of her lungs a second later.

Surrounding the entire table were dozens of children.

Ghosts, of children.

It's not our fault.

We did nothing wrong.

CHAPTER NINE

THEY HAD ALL SEEN THE CHILDREN.

They knew they had to be the ghosts of orphans who had once lived at Ravenstone House.

Andrew would be the only one of the six who didn't believe what had happened. Some people deal with events such as this in their own way, and his was to go into denial.

What struck the others was—how many there were.

The ghosts stood swaying from side to side, staring at the adults around the table as if it were the first time they'd ever seen another human being.

The children took in what the adults were doing, how they were dressed, what they were drinking and eating, and the way they talked like they hadn't a care in the world.

Their memories felt like a thousand years ago. The tastes and smells. Daylight. Blue skies. The sun, the wind, and the rain. The feeling of air passing in and out of their lungs. The warmth of hot food in their mouths, and in their tummies. The feeling someday things would get better.

They had hoped, one day, to move out of Ravenstone and into a house with a mum and a dad, who would hold them tight and say the words, 'I love you.' Brothers and sisters would play with them in the backyard.

It was the dream of most orphans, and for some it had come true: the lucky ones who got to leave Ravenstone House for the Less Privileged through the front door.

―――

Dinner with Quentin's father was, for Q and Mary, quite the chore lately. Five years after Quentin's mother had passed away, his old man kept becoming more difficult as each year rolled on.

They had seen his demeanour change. He was often abrupt and dismissive, and it had only grown worse in the last few years. The dinners, while Quentin's mother was alive, had taken place every two weeks like clockwork. Now, they were lucky to be every three to four months.

What grated Q and Mary was that when Bernie Brookes put his work hat on, you'd think the guy was made of steel. He ruled over London as if he were Batman and London was Gotham City. But at home he was anything but a superhero: he was a seething, grumpy old bastard with nothing positive to say.

After most of his dinners with Q and Mary, he would trudge up and down the Persian rug in his lounge with a whisky in his hand, whining to them about everything and anything which came to mind.

It was laborious, to say the least.

People made fun of it all the time, but none did it to his face. He was known for his moods, and telling the guy a squirrel had fallen asleep on his scone would be asking for trouble. Toupees were not meant to look that ordinary.

―――

'Why don't we call him and tell him we can't make it?' Mary said as they walked into Bernie Brookes' street.

Quentin shook his head. 'Babe, we're 250 feet from his front door.' He squeezed her hand. 'We can't pull out this close to the time. He'll flip.'

Mary let out a sigh and eventually nodded.

'This will be the first dinner at his house since we moved into Ravenstone,' she said.

Quentin knew exactly what she was saying. He'd spoken to his father briefly around the time he and Mary had signed for the flat, but they had not seen him since.

Bernie Brookes had told Quentin that buying the flat at Ravenstone House was a bad idea. He told him Doug Lozel had a reputation for doing shoddy work and couldn't be trusted, and that Ravenstone House was rotting and falling apart. Bernie had told Quentin the place should have been demolished decades ago. 'Forget about the fact the place is possibly haunted,' his old man had thrown in for good measure.

Well, Quentin and Mary were now fully aware that at least this part of Bernie's assessment held true.

And now they would have to endure a couple of hours of the Bernie Brookes show, live in person.

The roast lamb was good. It always was. Bernie's live-in housekeeper was a seriously good cook. Mary was a sucker for the roast potatoes, vegetables, and a gravy good enough to be sold in a wine bottle.

It was just a pity they weren't eating this amazing meal somewhere else.

Outside of a smattering of conversation, the awkward silence around the dinner table was palpable. Mary wondered if time itself had stopped.

Bernie eventually finished his meal, letting out a sound of satisfaction as he wiped his face with his napkin. He then took a big drink of his wine, avoiding making eye contact with his guests.

'So, you guys bought the flat in Ravenstone,' he said, and after a few seconds met their eyes.

Q and Mary shared a glance before Q turned to his father.

'Yes, we did, and of course you know I designed the flats myself.'

Bernie glared at his son for a second and Mary could see something brewing in his eyes.

'Out of all the flats in London. Out of all the flats you have probably designed, and probably more in the future, you had to buy one there of all places,' he said coldly.

Quentin stared at his old man for a moment. Without taking his eyes off Bernie, he took a drink of wine himself.

'The place is sound,' Quentin said with a slight edge to his words.

Q let his comment hang in the air. Mary was sure she could see steam rising from the ears of the lord mayor of London.

The two men stared at each other for a few moments.

'You'd never speak to me that way if your mother were still here,' Bernie said with a tone befitting a man of authority.

Mary went to put her hand on her fiancé's, but he pushed it away.

'And you'd never speak to me like that if your wife was still here,' Q said.

Mary now wished they had cancelled dinner when they had the chance.

Bernie leant forward and sneered at Quentin, 'Don't you dare speak of your mother,' he hissed.

Quentin felt his rage building.

Her sudden death had been the hardest thing Quentin

had ever had to deal with. He thought about her every day. He missed her, and wished she were sitting at this dinner table right now, so she could stick up for him. Like many mothers, she put her children at the front of the line.

After half a minute of the most uncomfortable silence, with the two men staring at each other, Quentin turned to Mary and spoke quietly.

'Get your things.' Q slowly turned and glared in his father's direction. 'This dinner is over.'

As they rose from the table, Bernie stared at his glass of wine, as if in a trance.

Mary leant forward and, as quietly as she could speak, said, 'Thank you for dinner.'

Bernard didn't even meet her eyes. He nodded, but his face remained stone cold.

CHAPTER TEN

Mary hopped into bed and lay next to Quentin. She could see that dinner with his father was still on his mind. Q stared up to the ceiling, lost in his thoughts.

'Do you want to talk about it?' Mary said softly.

Quentin took a while to answer.

He turned and reached out for her.

'Dad's getting worse as the years roll on. I don't know if he's ever going to be the same. I wish Mum was here. I miss her more than ever.'

Mary gave Quentin a firm kiss on his cheek.

'I know you miss her, honey, but you'll always have me by your side.'

Quentin nodded, but Mary could tell he was still upset.

'He got to you tonight, didn't he?' Mary said.

She knew pushing the matter wasn't a good idea. So she put her head on her own pillow and looked up to the ceiling.

'Mum was always careful. She'd brought me up drumming the same words into my head everyday,' Quentin said.

Mary slowly turned to him, not sure what he was referring to.

'Always. Stay. Behind. The. Yellow. Line.'

It came to her a moment later.

Quentin's mother had slipped off the platform and into the path of an oncoming train one morning.

Quentin reached over to his bedside light and turned it off.

He gave Mary a kiss before turning over.

Mary turned off her light a few moments later.

Eventually, sleep came to her.

⎯⎯

'Nurse Mary.'

The voice was so small it could only be a child.

It was barely a whisper.

'Nurse Mary, I want to talk to you.'

Mary could hear the words, but remained confused.

Dreaming of work was nothing unusual for her.

She spent a good chunk of her time there, so it had to have drifted into her subconscious, where some believe dreams originate from.

But this dream was different.

The voice sounded so close. As if it were in her ear.

Mary, in her dream state feeling as if the voice were a little fly buzzing around her ear, tried to shoo it away.

'Nurse Mary, can I please talk to you?'

As Mary went to roll over, a strange feeling overcame her. Even asleep, she could feel the hairs on both her arms stand on end. A tiny shiver washed over her from head to toe.

As she opened her eyes and faced her edge of the bed, the first thing she saw was her own breath coming out of her mouth.

The second thing, standing next to her side of the bed, was a little girl.

Mary's immediate instinct was to scream louder than she'd ever done before.

But suddenly, as Mary's hand shot up to her mouth and she thought she was about to pass out in sheer horror, the little girl reached over and placed her tiny hand on Mary's.

As soon as the girl's touched her, an immediate and powerful calm passed through Mary's hand and to every corner of her body.

Mary felt as if she was on an operating table seconds after the anaesthetist had injected her with the drugs that would send her off to la-la land.

The calm was incredible. Mary no longer felt the urge to scream.

The little girl leant forward and, to Mary's amazement, gave her a peck on the cheek. Mary couldn't believe she felt it so vividly, as she could still feel the little girl's hand on her own.

'I live here in Ravenstone House,' the little girl said.

Mary stared at her. Whatever effect the little girl had on her was powerful. She felt as if she couldn't speak if she wanted to, but no longer felt the urge to scream.

When Mary finally spoke, she could feel her lips moving but could barely hear her own words.

'Which flat do you live in?' she said.

The tiny girl slowly shook her head. Her pigtails bobbed from side to side.

Mary could not believe how pretty the child was. She hoped one day she might have a daughter that would grow to be this beautiful. She wore a dress that was old and frayed at the edges, but her face beamed with an almost angelic glow.

'We live below the flats,' she said.

Mary stared at her for a time before she said, 'What is your name, my darling?'

'Heather,' the girl eventually whispered.

'It's nice to meet you, Heather,' Mary said.

The little girl's face lit up with a bright smile.

'We feel the goodness in you, Nurse Mary,' Heather said. 'That's why we believed you would talk to me tonight.'

Mary felt as if she'd been talking to Heather for hours, even days, but knew it had only been a few seconds.

As Mary could feel a deep sense of calm and what felt like sleep coming towards her, Heather said, 'Nurse Mary, can I ask you a question?'

Mary responded immediately. 'Yes, of course.'

Heather leant close enough that Mary swore she could feel the warmth of her breath.

'If I brought one of my friends back to visit you one night, would it be okay with you, Nurse Mary?' the little voice said.

'Yes, I would happily talk to your friend. If they're your friend, they will be mine too,' Mary said.

The little girl smiled before leaning forward and once again kissing Mary so lightly on the cheek that she barely felt it.

'Sweet dreams, Nurse Mary. We're so glad you're here,' she said.

As Mary could feel her eyes closing and sleep about to wrap around her, she said, more to herself than the ghost of the beautiful little girl, 'When I wake up in the morning, how will I know this wasn't a dream?'

And she fell soundly asleep.

━━━

When Mary opened her eyes, Q was already up and buzzing around the kitchen. She could smell the aromatic waft of brewing coffee infused with toast. She could hear music and

Quentin's singing over the top of it. Her fiancé was no Freddy Mercury.

As she peered over to the window, studying the morning light seeping through the cracks, the previous night's events sprang into her mind.

Mary took a deep breath and wondered if she'd ever had a more realistic dream. It had been incredibly vivid. She remembered feeling the little girl's hand. Her little kisses. Mary thought she was the sweetest little girl she'd ever met.

She remembered the few words Heather had said. She wanted to bring a 'friend' to see her.

With a sense of trepidation, Mary wondered who this friend was.

Mary remembered the last words she said to the little girl.

'How will I know this wasn't a dream?'

But Heather hadn't answered.

The coffee and toast were calling out to her. Or maybe it was Quentin's version of 'Ice Ice Baby'.

As she climbed out of bed, something caught her eye.

Something on her bedside table—out of place.

Mary's breath caught in her throat.

There it was, sitting right in the corner, closest to where her head had been on her pillow last night.

It was so small she almost missed it.

She caught herself wanting to smile but cry at the same time.

It was the tiniest little ring she'd ever seen.

A little girl's ring.

CHAPTER ELEVEN

MARY WAS CAUGHT BETWEEN THE PROVERBIAL ROCK and a hard place. Should she tell Q about what had happened last night? Would this sound as if she'd taken leave of her mind? Would Quentin think she'd gotten caught up in the legend of Ravenstone House?

But he had seen the children around the table too.

And of course, there was the levitating bed episode. How would you ever explain that?

Quentin Brookes was a level, decent guy. His mother had brought him up well. One of his values was to always keep an open mind. But, and there was always a but, as there is with most people, this mindset could only be stretched so far.

As Mary nibbled on her toast, in between sips of her coffee, Quentin rattled off in quick succession all the things he had on that day. It went in one ear and out the other.

Her mind was elsewhere

On Heather.

'Go get 'em, tiger.' Mary knew Q loved her saying this as he ran out the door. She always did her best to ensure she was in striking distance to his well-proportioned derrière, so she could swing her hand and give it a cheeky whack as he headed for the door.

'Have an amazing day, you spunk.' Quentin grinned before disappearing through the front door.

Mary hoped that one day he would come up with a new term of endearment. She'd told him once before what a chunk of spunk loosely referred to in nursing circles. He'd clearly forgotten.

Mary was due on shift at midday.

She'd made the cautious decision to not tell Quentin about the meeting she had during the night with a ghost —not yet.

But now, she wondered what she'd do with herself, and how she would be able to fight the urge to tell at least *someone* about Heather.

—

After a hot shower, Mary dressed and stood in the kitchen for a few moments. The random thought came from nowhere.

Maybe I should go and check out the basement, she thought.

There were two main issues with this. One: Mary was petrified of the dark. And two: with the spook show now going on strong, she was shit-scared about what might happen down there.

But the cat curiosity killed was still well and alive in her. Sometimes it was her undoing. But she couldn't help it.

Mary found a torch and decided she would do the unthinkable—face her greatest fear.

You go, girl.

As she closed the front door of her flat, she took a deep breath.

This is it, Mary thought.

She took six steps before she got the fright she was expecting.

—

'Good morning, neighbour!' Christine bellowed out of nowhere.

Mary came close to fainting on the spot.

'What are you up to?' Christine said.

Mary had gone pale.

'Er, I was going to look for the, um,' Mary fumbled her words, 'the boiler.'

Christine stood there none the wiser.

'Well, once you've finished, feel like getting a coffee?'

Mary, now feeling the colour in her face return to normal, thought it sounded like a great idea.

She would suss out her new neighbour and contemplate telling Christine about what had happened last night.

The boiler would have to wait.

—

The closest coffee shop to Ravenstone House was an arduous three-minute walk away. Actually, Mary welcomed at least a few moments of fresh morning air.

As the coffees were delivered to their corner table along with a freshly baked apple-and-coconut muffin, Mary could feel herself growing nervous at the idea of talking to Christine about 'it.'

But after five minutes of healthy conversation, she felt as if Christine might be the sort of person who could be open to the existence in the world of 'unusual' things.

Mary decided to take a leap of faith.

When Christine took her last sip of her coffee, Mary sensed the time had come.

'Can I ask you a slightly awkward question, Christine?'

Christine to her credit remained calm and unperturbed.

'Shoot, young lady,' she said.

Mary stared out the window for a second. She'd come this far, she thought, there was no point in turning back.

'Obviously, we all saw what we saw the other night.' Mary spoke quietly to ensure the other patrons in the cafe did not hear her. 'But can I ask you—do you actually believe in the paranormal?'

A small but discernible smile crept across Christine's face.

'Can I tell you a story, Mary?' Christine said in a whisper.

'Yes,' Mary said.

'I once had an elderly neighbour, Mavis, bless her,' Christine said as a faint smile crept onto her face, 'who had recently lost her husband of seventy years. When I bumped into her out the front one day, she told me something which sent shivers down my spine.'

Mary held her breath in anticipation.

'Mavis told me, in the last few weeks, her husband had started to come and visit her late at night. She'd wake to find him sitting on the edge of the bed. They'd talk for a while. The look on her face told me Mavis really believed it was him. Before shuffling off that morning, Mavis said she was looking forward to passing away, so she could be with him again, where she belonged.'

Mary shook her head. 'My God, I can feel shivers running down my neck right now,' she said.

Christine smiled, and this time the smile stayed a bit longer.

'So if you're asking me if I believe in things which are not of this world, be it aliens or ghosts, you can safely say I do. I always have.'

Mary finished the last of her coffee, lukewarm at best but good all the same.

'Now you've asked me this,' Christine grinned, 'I can ask you why you asked, or,' she leant over and placed her hand over Mary's, 'you can cut to the chase and tell me what you want to tell me.'

Mary took a drink of water and decided there was no point mucking around anymore. She could tell her neighbour liked her as much as she liked her neighbour, and there was the potential of a good friendship in the offing.

'Alright.' Mary shuffled in her seat and sat forward and to attention. 'What I'm about to tell you is obviously to stay between us.'

Christine raised her eyebrows before pouting. 'Sure. You will come to learn I can be trusted. And David too.'

Mary nodded before resting her elbows on the table and locking her hands together.

'I had a visit last night.' The words fell out of her mouth quicker than she had expected.

Before Christine could say anything, Mary added, 'By one of the orphans of Ravenstone House.'

Christine sat back in her chair as if she'd been slapped in the face.

She leant forward so the two women were only inches away from each other.

'Go on,' Christine said, looking as if she had more to say but wanted to wait until Mary finished.

'She was the sweetest, most beautiful little girl I have ever seen.' Mary could feel her emotions rising. 'She even introduced herself to me. Her name was Heather.'

Mary watched Christine for a moment, not sure if she should continue. Christine seemed lost in thought.

After a couple of deep breaths, Christine nodded to Mary and once again leant forward closer to her.

'I don't believe this,' she said.

Mary for a moment thought she'd offended her.

She caught herself feeling awkward, and it must have shown in her body language. Christine smiled and placed her hand quickly on Mary's again.

'It's okay, Mary,' she said.

The two women stared at each other for a few moments.

Christine checked their surroundings in the cafe, to ensure no one was in earshot.

'When David woke this morning, he was in a bit of a fizz.' Christine shifted in her seat. 'He said he'd had one hell of a scary, and very realistic, dream.'

Mary could feel the pulse in her neck pressing against her skin.

'What happened?' she said.

Christine swallowed, then studied her empty coffee cup for a moment.

'David said he dreamed a little boy was standing next to his side of our bed,' she said.

An apprehension crept up from deep within Mary, of something dark and disturbing. She felt a flush of heat wash over her.

Mary took another drink of water. She longed to be outside and breathe the fresh morning air again.

'Did the little girl say anything to you, other than her name?' Christine asked.

Mary nodded. 'She asked if she could bring a friend to come and talk to me.'

Christine's face was turning ashen. 'Oh, boy.' She shook her head and under her breath said, 'What have we gotten ourselves into at Ravenstone?'

'Did the little boy say anything to your husband?' Mary said.

Christine stared at the table for an eternity, much to Mary's chagrin. But when she eventually spoke, Mary wished she hadn't.

'He asked David if he could come under the house and let the kids out.'

CHAPTER TWELVE

Quentin was not impressed.

The look on his face said it all.

But he softened after Mary had spent five minutes explaining why she had ended up talking to Christine about what had happened in the night, before telling him.

Dinner the night before with Q's father had been stressful. Quentin had hopped into bed and spoken of his mum.

Mary felt lumping him with another problem first thing in the morning was unfair. She'd planned to tell him that night.

And now she did. Mary told him about her encounter with Heather, as well as what Christine had told her earlier in the day.

When she produced the tiny ring from her pocket, Q was clearly taken aback.

Mary handed the ring over to him, placing it in the palm of his hand. She knew his heart could feel the pain and emotion she'd felt when she met Heather.

'Shit.' Quentin stepped around the from the island bench of the kitchen and hugged Mary. 'This is intense.'

When he pulled away from her, she said, 'I think it's time

we had a chat to Christine and David about this.'

Quentin checked his watch, which showed a stroke past 9pm. 'Don't you think it's a little late?'

Mary shook her head. 'Christine told me if we wanted to see her and David tonight, any time before 10pm was fine. I get the impression she was keen to talk to us about this with David.'

―――

'Coffee, tea,' David smiled, 'or something a little stronger?'

Quentin and Mary shared a glance before they both nodded. 'Tea may be the better option tonight, thanks,' Mary responded.

'Me too.' Quentin took a deep breath. 'Although I am very tempted to opt for the stronger option depending on where the conversation goes,' he said lightly.

The four residents of Ravenstone House sat as couples on the two couches in David and Christine's lounge room.

David was the first to speak.

'Obviously, we have an issue here at Ravenstone,' he said matter-of-factly.

Christine sat forward and instinctively found herself peering down towards the floor.

'The notion of moving again concerns me. We could lose money, or not be able to sell the flats at all. We are not wealthy. Walking away with nothing and having to buy another property is not an option for us,' Christine said.

David could see the concern on his wife's face. He placed his hand on her back and rubbed it gently.

'We're not keen to move either,' Quentin said. 'This place —there's something about it. I can't put my finger on it. It's as if we were meant to be here. I know this sounds silly, but this is what my gut is telling me.'

Mary reached for Quentin's hand and squeezed it gently.

She felt exactly the same.

'So what do we do?' Mary was the first to say what they were all thinking.

The discussion went on for about ten minutes.

Quentin had mentioned the word *seance*, but this was unanimously ruled out. A few moments later, David wondered if an exorcism was in order, but this too was quashed. It was Christine who then brought up the idea of a late-night visit to the basement. Even this was debated, but was clearly the better option.

Mary eventually made a suggestion they could live with.

Wait for Heather to come back to her, with her friend.

From there, if it were possible, Mary would ask Heather and her friend if they could come back another time, and this time talk to all of them together.

Mary felt as if she were in an episode of *The Twilight Zone*.

But as she and Quentin lay down in bed a little later, she knew it was the most sensible idea to start with. They would consider all other options if this one didn't go to plan.

'Alright?' Quentin came within kissing distance of the woman he was crazy about before planting one on her.

Mary stared into her future husband's eyes for a moment and hoped it was the best idea to start with.

'I'm ready and willing,' she lied.

Mary was shitting her pants.

⸺

Ten days had passed with no sign of Heather. Nothing paranormal had happened since the night she'd visited Mary, and the ghost of a little boy had visited David.

The two couples were starting to wonder if maybe

nothing more would come of it. But this was wishful thinking. Mary and Quentin knew in the pit of their stomachs there had to be more to come. For it to stop now seemed too good to be true. The place was rumoured to have been haunted well before they came along.

Mary had kept Heather's ring. She kept it in her bedside drawer in a pouch, on a couple of occasions taking it out and studying it. It was slightly rusted on one side, and as fragile as the smile on Heather's face the night she first laid eyes on Mary.

One particular night, Quentin came home late from fourteen hours' straight working on a new project with a ridiculous time frame for design and completion, which had put the firm he worked for under immense pressure. He went straight to bed, and as soon as his head at hit the pillow, he was out like a light. Mary read for a while in bed, but found it hard to concentrate on the book with her fiancé snoring steadfastly not two feet away.

She considered smacking him over the head with the novel, but quickly did away with the idea.

As she put the book down and went to turn off the light, the most random feeling came to her, compelling her to reach to her bedside table and pull out the pouch containing Heather's ring.

Mary took the ring out and held it in between her index and middle finger for a moment. She thought about the poor little thing. What had happened to her? What had her life been like? The more she thought about her, the sadder Mary became.

She put the ring to her lips and kissed it lightly before saying, in a whisper, 'I hope you are okay, my darling, wherever you are.'

Mary rested the ring on top of her bedside table.

It was, though she did not remember, the exact spot

where she first found it.

———

'Nurse Mary.'

The sound was distant, as if the winds of the night had brought it from somewhere far, far away.

'Nurse Mary.'

Mary was in a deep sleep. Her dream found her standing in the middle of thousands of revellers at the Glastonbury Festival. The Cure were front and centre, and the crowd was absorbing every note that came out of the giant speakers.

Mary, with a drink in one hand and her other balled in a fist, punching the air, found herself singing at the top of her lungs. The Cure were one of her favourite bands.

'Nurse Mary.'

As Mary continued to sing, she felt something press up against her leg.

When she glanced down to see what it was, she froze.

Heather.

The little girl's eyes spoke of curiosity. She'd never seen someone dance before.

Mary dropped her drink on the ground in shock. The music abruptly stopped. And when it did, all the people around her at the Glastonbury Festival disappeared, to be replaced by thousands of—

Children. All dressed like Heather.

They stood there staring straight at Mary, who was the only adult as far as the eye could see, and before she could say anything, she felt something on her hand.

Heather had placed her hand around Mary's index finger.

Mary could feel a rush of mixed emotions come from nowhere.

Suddenly, she felt her body jolt.

When she opened her eyes, she was in her bedroom, staring at the ceiling.

The shock of the dream started to dissipate as Mary drew long, deep breaths from the darkness.

Her left hand was hanging over the edge of the bed.

When she went to pull it away, Mary found she could not.

Something was holding it down.

———

'Nurse Mary.'

Mary spun her head to her left and realised why her sixth sense was firing on all cylinders.

Heather stood there, closer than last time.

She held onto Mary's index finger. Mary couldn't figure it out.

Ghosts were meant to be foglike things, she thought. Apparitions, right?

They weren't meant to be able to touch you.

'You kept my ring.' Heather spoke gently but excitedly. Mary was still in a state of shock, but could feel her heart rate slowly decreasing.

Mary could hear Quentin lightly snoring behind her. Part of her wanted to kick him and wake him up so he could see Heather with his own eyes.

'Nurse Mary.'

Mary smiled at Heather and nodded. 'You told me, when you visited last time, you wanted to bring a friend with you.'

Heather leant closer to Mary and spoke softly.

'His name is Finley.'

Mary could see nothing but the darkness of her bedroom beyond Heather. A sliver of light emanated from the middle of the curtains in the window.

'I don't see anyone but you, Heather,' Mary said slowly.

'He will come when I tell him it's safe to,' Heather said.

Mary took a deep breath, still settling from the fright of seeing Heather again.

'Maybe we could go into the lounge room, and I could meet him there? I don't want to wake up Quentin,' she said.

A pretty smile came across Heather's face as she nodded.

'Quentin had a long day today. He must be very tired. Finley said Quentin has much good in him. Like you.'

Mary was surprised by what Heather had said.

But for now, she wanted to do the unthinkable: meet another ghost.

—

Mary tiptoed into the lounge room and sat on the couch. The room was draped in the kind of darkness you could feel on your skin. Her heart beat against her chest like a drum. She hadn't felt this nervous in years.

Heather had disappeared from view when Mary's feet touched the bedroom floor.

Mary wished Quentin was there with her. She always felt safe in his presence, as if he wore an invisible suit of armour. The guy wasn't afraid to stick up for himself, nor to intervene on Mary's behalf if the situation called for it.

But for now—Mary was all alone.

She felt Heather's presence before she saw her. It was a tiny prick of nerves behind her ears, before the sensation of a breeze passing over the back of her neck.

'Nurse Mary.'

Heather came close enough that Mary could see her little figure standing almost directly in front of her.

'I'm here, Heather,' Mary said.

Mary's heart was now in her mouth. Her short breaths

came out cold and laced with nerves.

'Would you like to meet my friend?'

Mary nodded before she said, 'Yes, Heather.'

She could see another figure slowly walking towards her from the darkness.

He was much taller than the little girl, close to double her height. For a second, Mary wondered if it actually were Quentin coming to see what she was doing.

When the apparition came to a stop next to Heather, the little girl glanced up before reaching for his hand.

Mary could make out his youthful face. As he took Heather's little hand, a faint smile appeared on it.

Mary figured he couldn't be more than fourteen or maybe fifteen years old.

His clothes like Heather's, were old and a little ragged, but mostly clean.

The young lad had a decent crop of dark hair, neat and brushed to one side.

He was a good-looking boy. Mary could see his square, set jaw and big eyes. If he'd lived to be Quentin's age, Mary thought he'd have had to fight off the ladies with a big stick.

'This is the one who protects us.' Heather smiled to Mary.

Mary nodded.

'Hello, my name is Mary. Mary Campbell.'

He crouched down next to Heather, still holding her hand. He held out his other hand to Mary, and once again she wondered how it was possible for her to feel anything when her hand met his.

It didn't make sense, and probably never would.

'Hi, Mary. My name is Finley Sproule.'

Mary detected what sounded like a Scottish accent. Faint, but it was there.

'Well, it is a pleasure to meet you Finley,' Mary said.

For a long moment, Mary wondered if she should pinch herself. Could this be a dream?

'I know you are thinking you are dreaming this,' Finley said, as if he could hear her thoughts.

'I won't lie to you,' Mary said. 'The thought had crossed my mind.'

'Let me show you.' Finley turned his head towards the lounge room door before returning his gaze to Mary.

He flicked his hand and the door closed. It happened quickly, but silently.

If Mary thought this was mind-blowing, there was more to come.

Finley turned his attention to the kitchen, and two seconds later the range-hood light clicked on over the cooktop.

It was enough to give off a faint light that shone across the island bench and over to the lounge room.

Now she could see clearer.

Her mind was a jumble of thoughts. How was this possible?

Years ago at work, one of the children in her ward died in front of her.

And on that occasion, her senses, less than a minute before the little girl passed away, had felt something else in the room.

The last thing the dying girl said to Mary, as clear as a summer's day, she would never forget.

'My friends are here to take me.'

Mary knew she was the only person in the room apart from her patient.

The little girl smiled. 'Can you see my friends, nurse? They're right there.' And as she waved to no one Mary could see, she closed her eyes and put down her arm. Seconds later, she passed away.

Mary sat there and continued to fight the urge to call out for Quentin. Partly from a sense of fear, and partly because she wanted him to see what she was seeing.

'We aren't here to harm you, Mary,' Finley said.

Mary stared at Heather for a second before turning to him.

'Why have you come to see me?' she said.

Finley stared at her for a time.

She wondered if she'd offended him.

This was not the case. He'd waited a long time for this moment, and wanted to choose his words very carefully. A lot was riding on what he was about to say.

He glanced around the flat before resting his gaze back on Mary.

'We can feel the good in people, and the bad. You and Quentin, and the people across the hall,' he said, indicating David and Christine.

'But especially you, Mary Campbell,' he said.

Mary nodded before Finley continued. 'You are the closest thing to an angel we've ever felt.'

Mary had been called a lot of things, but never this.

She was one of the most popular head nurses in her hospital. A big part of it was as simple as it was straightforward: she loved what she did. They say enthusiasm reflects interest. It showed in Mary every day. She loved caring, especially for children.

Mary smiled. It was a compliment she would never forget.

'Finley,' Mary said, leaning forward, 'you seem to be a good boy. I can see why Heather thinks so much of you.'

Heather stood a little taller and beamed.

'I feel privileged to have met you two.' Mary meant every word. 'Is there something I can do to make things better for you?'

Finley put his hand to his mouth.

It had been close to forty years since he'd lost the ability to feel tears fall across his cheeks, but he remembered the feeling of overwhelming emotion.

This time around, it wasn't from sadness or pain; it was from joy.

'Nurse Mary,' Finley said, speaking more confidently now, 'we are trapped here in Ravenstone. We've never been able to leave. We believe we know why, but we can't do anything about it. I believe you may be able to help us.'

Mary peered over to the range hood in the kitchen. It was her only source of light. She felt more comfortable now; the fear in her bones had slipped away. Something deep within her heart came to life. Maybe it was the angel comment that did it.

Mary once again found herself staring at Heather.

Such a sweet little girl.

And for whatever reason, her spirit, along with Finley's and possibly many others, had never been able to leave Ravenstone House.

A thought came to Mary.

'Finley, I need to ask you a question,' Mary said softly.

Heather turned and met Finley's gaze, and they both smiled faintly.

'Can I bring Quentin and our neighbours the next time we talk?'

Finley didn't take his eyes off Mary. Eventually, he smiled and put his hand on Heather's head before patting it gently.

'Heather,' Finley said, 'we need to go now.'

Mary suddenly felt disappointed, but she need not have.

'If this is your wish, Nurse Mary,' Finley said, 'it will be done. Remember, you need to leave Heather's ring out so she knows it's safe. She'll come and get me.'

Then they both disappeared into the shadows.

73

CHAPTER THIRTEEN

'GOOD MORNING, YOU BEAUTIFUL THING.' QUENTIN kissed Mary on the cheek. 'I'd kiss you on the lips,' Q smirked, 'but my morning breath might knock you out.'

Mary smiled. 'You never know, mine may do the same to you.'

Quentin slipped out of bed and stood up. 'Did you sleep well?' he said as he searched for his slippers.

Mary stared at him for a second before she said, 'Heather came back last night, with her friend.'

Quentin's mouth went wide. He came around to Mary's side of the bed and sat down.

'You okay?' he asked, before reaching for her hand and holding it firmly.

Mary nodded, 'I'm fine. Why don't I tell you over breakfast? I'm quite hungry after last night.'

━━━

Mary recounted the previous night's encounter to David and Christine over afternoon tea.

Quentin found their response to Mary's story remarkable.

They seemed to take it all on-board and in their stride. He admired how open-minded they were.

When the couple asked questions, Quentin could tell they seemed to care more about the spirits of the children than the whole deal with living somewhere which was clearly haunted.

As the conversation appeared to be drawing to a close, David asked the other three an interesting question.

'Do you think we should bring anyone else who lives here in on this?' he said.

The four observed each other's faces carefully to try and gauge their thoughts.

Christine went first. 'Andrew and Yukiko?'

Mary shrugged her shoulders, 'Andrew seemed to be quite averse to the belief in ghosts or anything supernatural.'

They all agreed.

'But Yukiko,' Quentin finished the last of his tea, 'I'm not sure if she shared her partner's view. She seemed to take quite an offense to his attitude the night it happened.'

'Well, we may have to suss the couple out a little first,' David said.

They all agreed.

'What about anyone upstairs?' Mary instinctively peered up towards the ceiling.

'I've only seen one of the couples from upstairs, and from a distance. It's amazing we all live under this one roof but you never see any of the other tenants coming and going,' Christine said.

'We could always go knock on their doors and introduce ourselves,' she added.

David broke into laughter. 'And what, introduce ourselves as the British chapter of the Ghostbusters?'

Christine gave him a light-hearted slap on the arm before laughing herself. Quentin and Mary joined in too.

When the laughter died down, Quentin said, 'Maybe we keep it in-house for now.' His expression grew slightly serious for a moment.

'But depending on what transpires downstairs, we may need to potentially involve the people—upstairs.'

Mary had left Heather's ring out on her bedside table in the precise place she believed she left it the night before.

Once Mary had spoken to Heather, she would wake Quentin, who would go and lightly tap on Christine and David's front door. They would leave their own bedroom door open and listen for the signal.

Mary suggested their lounge room was the best place to come together. The hope was they would all get to meet Heather and Finley.

Christine implored David not to follow through on his promise to come to the meeting in his fluorescent leopard-skin G-string underpants. She said it might scare everyone off, living and deceased. He agreed gingerly.

'Nurse Mary.'

Heather.

Her voice was as faint as the autumn breeze blowing the leaves through St James's Park.

Mary had only been asleep for about an hour. She woke easily, and as it was the third time she was being woken by the ghost of the beautiful little girl, there was no feeling of fear or fright.

'Hello, my darling Heather, it's so nice—'

Heather cut off Mary's words by kissing her on the cheek.

Mary, it appears you have a fan.

'Heather, you are the sweetest girl.' Mary sat up and smiled at her. 'Has anyone ever told you this?'

Heather leant in so her face was now the closest it had ever been to Mary's.

After a few moments of silence, Heather shook her head from side to side. 'No, Nurse Mary. No one has ever said it to me.'

Mary smiled.

'Well, you are, my darling. I think you are. Don't you forget, okay?'

Heather stared at her. It was so sweet, Mary thought.

'I guess you want me to go and get Finley?' she said.

Mary nodded but whispered, 'Remember, I'm going to wake Quentin, and David and Christine too. They will come and talk to Finley too. Can you give me a minute?'

Heather stared at Mary for a long time before she said, 'Yes, Nurse Mary. Finley said you are an angel of the living.'

And with those words, Heather slipped into the darkness of the night.

CHAPTER FOURTEEN

Quentin had admitted to Mary he was awake when Heather had arrived at their bedside. He said he didn't want to sit up or say anything and jeopardise the moment. He said he could barely hear her speak, mainly because he decided to remain half-buried under the duvet to avoid detection.

Quentin had arrived back in their lounge room a few minutes later with David and Christine. Three wore nightgowns.

David, in true martial-arts style, wore pyjamas that looked like a kimono.

'Come, sit over there,' Mary said to her neighbours before ushering Quentin to sit next to her on the main couch.

Following Mary's directions, Quentin had already made sure the only light on was the one from the range hood in the kitchen.

'Let me do the introductions,' Mary said. Quentin was quietly impressed with her leadership. David and Christine silently nodded. 'Everyone take one last big breath,' she added, 'and no one freak out or make any sudden move-ments, right?'

———

Thirty minutes later, the foursome was becoming concerned. They wondered if something had happened. Were Heather and Finley coming back at all? Last night, Heather had brought Finley back within a couple of minutes, tops.

When Mary's antique clock chimed, they all knew precisely what time it was.

Midnight.

'Maybe we should call it a night?' Christine said five minutes later.

As the last word left her mouth, Mary let out a tiny gasp.

She'd spotted Heather and Finley behind her.

As the other three people in the room sat in complete awe, Heather shuffled right up to Mary.

She smiled before turning and waiting for Finley to arrive.

'Nurse Mary,' Finley said clearly, 'we're sorry for being late.'

His focus remained on only her, as if the other three people were not in the room.

'It's okay,' Mary said.

Finley stared at her for a few moments.

Mary was starting to believe this was how it went with Heather and Finley. Their responses were always slow, as if they needed longer than a living person to respond. She was right.

'There is one who is here,' Mary knew Finley meant here in the house, 'who is not with us below.'

Mary could feel the hairs on the back of her neck stand upright.

'What do you—'

Finley responded quicker this time, though Mary realised he hadn't finished what he was saying.

'She lives upstairs. On the stroke of midnight, she's always standing at the top of the stairs, staring down to the ground floor. She's a mean, scary old lady, Mary. She hates us. I don't know why. I decided to wait until after midnight so she didn't see us coming to visit you.'

Mary took a deep breath. Great, now we also have the ghost of an old lady who lives upstairs and hates children, she thought.

'Finley, Heather, I would like to introduce my fiancé to you, and also our neighbours and friends,' Mary said nervously.

Heather seemed to step back a little, as if she were intimidated by facing Q, Christine, and David all at once. She stepped closer to Finley and reached up for his hand.

The real reason was as disturbing as it was sad. It was because Quentin and David—were males.

That was why she'd taken such a shine to Mary.

Men scared her. Even now.

Finley held onto Heather's hand and studied the other three people sitting with Mary.

'My name is Finley Sproule.' He spoke quietly but clearly.

Christine and David shared a glance. Christine was breathing heavily but slowly. It was obvious to the others that her nerves were still settling. David put his hand on her back and patted her gently. The guy had nerves of steel, or so it seemed.

Quentin personally was freaking out on the inside, but on the outside he remained poised and calm.

It was as if Mary had been made for this. She was taking

it all in her stride. No wonder she's so revered at work, he thought.

Finley whispered something to Heather.

A moment later, she sat down on the floor.

Finley followed suit, sitting down next to her.

Mary, Q, Christine, and David sat there looking down at the two. Heather remained close to Finley as if he would protect her if need be.

Finley reached over and patted her on the head.

'Do you want to go back and wait for me?' he said to her.

Heather shook her head.

'I want to stay with you here,' she said.

Finley smiled at her.

'Alright, my bonny Heather,' he said, 'but I want you to sit behind me and close your eyes and ears. I need to speak to these people for a few moments.'

Heather stared at the four people sitting on the two couches. Without a further word, she shuffled behind Finley and disappeared from view, albeit with her little legs sticking out.

⸻

Finley studied the four sitting there watching him.

He'd waited forty-five years for this moment.

'I've waited a long time to have people back in Ravenstone. Flesh and blood but with kind souls. Not like who was here before. They did unspeakable things to us when we were all flesh and blood.'

The adults all shifted uncomfortably, one way or another, almost by instinct.

Mary found Quentin's hand where she latched hers onto his. A chill passed over her whole body.

David leant forward and spoke slowly. 'Finley. How

many children are,' He hesitated, though after a deep breath he composed himself enough to finish, 'with you?'

Finley stared at him for a time before he bowed his head as if in shame. Admitting the evil of Ravenstone House had always troubled the young man.

He said a number, so quietly the four could not hear him.

Once he'd repeated it, it would haunt the four for months to come.

'One hundred and fifty, including me,' Finley said, audibly now.

Instantly, Christine started to sob.

'Finley, can I ask you the most uncomfortable of questions?' This from Mary.

Finley found himself feeling something unusual emanating from upstairs.

He glanced up towards the ceiling, but the feeling passed.

He returned his eyes to Mary.

'Ask me anything,' he said.

She swallowed and took a deep breath.

'How did all of those children die?'

Finley stared at her such a long time she wondered if she shouldn't have asked.

'Fifteen,' he said, before once again finding something in him wanting to look up towards the second floor.

Mary shared a curious glance with Christine, who lightly shrugged her shoulders.

'Fifteen, Finley?' Mary said, not sure what this meant.

Finley studied Mary and wondered how she would react.

'Babies, and some a little older. Maybe two or three about Heather's age.'

Mary could feel a sense of dread rising within her. Later, she'd know it was because she felt what was coming before she even thought of it.

'Fifteen of the children with you, Finley—'

'Died. In their sleep. Not—'

David peered over to Quentin, and the two men locked eyes with each other. It was a dark stare they shared, but not for each other.

Finley said the word *killed*, but he needn't have.

They'd joined the dots.

A hundred and fifty children had died at Ravenstone House at one time or another.

And a hundred and thirty-five of them had been murdered within the walls of Ravenstone House.

'Oh no,' Finley whimpered a second later.

Heather had sprung to her feet and literally leapt onto Finley's lap, where she held onto him.

'I'm sorry Nurse Mary, please forgive—'

———

Finley and Heather evaporated into thin air.

Suddenly, the range-hood light blew out, plunging Quentin and Mary's flat into sudden darkness.

The air went cold in an instant.

Mary reached for Quentin in the darkness.

The last thing she heard was Christine's whimpers to her husband, something like, 'What's going on?'

Then every door in the flat blew open.

Every kitchen-cupboard door flew open at the same time and immediately started to bang open and shut.

Objects started to fall out of the cupboards, smashing onto the kitchen floor. Others flew across the room and broke when they hit the walls.

At this moment, the real terror began.

The couches started to move.

Mary gripped the couch with both hands.

'What the fuck?' she heard David shout over all the commotion.

Christine was screaming, and latched onto David with all her might.

When Quentin wondered if this was the mother of all nightmares, he pulled Mary under his right arm and said, 'Hold on, my darling. This will be over—'

His words were cut off by the very woman he was trying to protect.

He couldn't recall the last time he'd heard Mary scream.

All she managed to say to him was, 'Look.'

When Quentin turned his attention to the island bench of the kitchen, the apparition of an old lady stood on top of the bench.

She was dressed in clothing from a hundred years ago.

When Quentin saw her face, he froze.

She was gaunt, wrinkled, and downright ugly. Her teeth were jagged and hideous, as if she were devoid of lips at all. Her hair was thin, and moved as if floating in water.

She proceeded to point a long and bony hand in their direction.

'You,' she hissed, her voice clear above all the racket.

'Stay. Away. From. The. CHILDREN!'

Christ almighty.

The two couches rose swiftly into the air.

David and Christine's flew straight up, colliding with the light fixture before it came crashing down.

Quentin and Mary's flew across the room and hit the wall.

They heard crashing sounds upstairs, too.

Every piece of furniture, in all the upstairs flats, had been thrown into the air at exactly same moment.

CHAPTER FIFTEEN

CHRISTINE NURSED HER BROKEN ARM.

Two whole days after what was Armageddon for the residents of Ravenstone House, things were starting to return to normal, at least on the surface.

Other than Quentin nursing a sore neck, Christine's broken arm was the only injury inflicted during the ordeal.

Quentin and Mary had worked that Monday as normal. Well, as normal as they could make things look from the outside.

After work, they'd come straight over to David and Christine's to see how they were holding up after fright night.

'So the million-dollar question now is,' David smiled to the others as he dunked his shortbread biscuit in his tea, 'what in God's name do we do now, people?'

Quentin sat forward. 'Obviously, all the tenants upstairs are now aware Ravenstone House is legitimately haunted.'

He shared a concerned look with Mary before adding, 'But none know what we know. They don't know about Finley, Heather, and the other kids yet.'

Christine grunted as she shifted her arm before taking a

sip of tea. 'I think at some point we should probably all get together. All of us, who live here.'

She could see the sudden look of concern on Q and Mary.

'No, I'm not talking about telling the upstairs people about the kids. But we should find out what they all know. A fact-finding mission, so to speak.'

David finished his shortbread and said, 'Good idea, darling.'

Quentin reached for a shortbread before sitting back and nodding in agreement. 'Do you think we'll get another visit from Finley and Heather?' He turned and met Mary's eyes. 'Something tells me there was more he wanted to tell us.'

Mary nodded before turning to her neighbours. 'What do you two think?' Before they answered, she added, 'There has to be more than being scared of the witch.'

David sat up. A thought had just come to him. He took another sip of his coffee and ignored the urge for a third shortbread biscuit.

He turned his gaze towards Quentin.

'Maybe, my young friend,' he smiled before winking at him, 'it's time you and I went on a little expedition.'

Quentin was unsure where he was referring to. And when his question was answered, a cold sweat would form under the collar of his shirt.

'Where?' he asked.

David turned his gaze to the floor and raised his eyebrows.

'The basement.'

———

Quentin and David made the decision after further discussion over tea, coffee, and shortbread biscuits (yes, David succumbed to his third) that the expedition would take place the following night.

Quentin brought home all the plans he had at work for Ravenstone House. They went back to the turn of the century, and had been found in a wall in the house during the renovations. How and why they were there was anyone's guess.

David contributed too: he found his torch but decided it didn't have the juice this sort of event needed. He told Quentin he would pop out the next day between his taekwondo classes and pick up a couple of torches with more grunt.

———

Mary had the day off, and welcomed the idea of a spot of brunch.

After she and Christine had ordered, Mary was the first to spot her.

Yukiko.

She hadn't yet seen Mary and Christine sitting in the dead centre of the cafe.

Mary pointed her out to Christine before raising her hand in the air. 'Yukiko, fancy seeing you here!'

Yukiko spotted Christine and her worried look dissipated.

She waved back, but Mary was already motioning for her to come over.

'Hi, neighbour. How are you this fine day?' Mary said as Yukiko drew closer to their table.

'All things considered,' Christine and Mary knew exactly what she was referring to, 'I am okay.'

She spotted Christine's broken arm and felt guilty at her own self-pity.

'Christine, your arm, are you okay?' she said.

'I may not be playing tennis for a wee while. But other than that, I'm fine and dandy.' She smiled.

Christine met Mary's smile and without saying anything, they knew they were thinking the same thing.

'Care to join us?' Christine said. 'We've ordered coffee and food. You're welcome to have whatever tickles your fancy.'

Yukiko checked her watch and took a breath. She knew she had some time up her sleeve. And besides, a few minutes with her female neighbours would be nice.

'Thank you,' she said as Mary pulled one of the spare chairs at their table out for her.

Yukiko wasted no time unloading her woes on Mary and Christine. 'Andrew is a bit freaked out by what happened on Saturday night. He's being a real prick about it.' She put her hand to her mouth in an instant. 'I'm sorry, I didn't mean to be rude!'

Mary and Christine shared an amused glance.

Both women had heard far fruitier words in their time.

Mary patted Yukiko on the hand and smiled. 'Darling, if only that were the worst profanity I'd heard in my time as a nurse.'

'He blames me for all this,' Yukiko said before peering down to her cup of coffee.

Christine frowned before sipping her tea. 'I don't understand,' she said. 'How could what happen possibly be your fault? Did you pick up every piece of furniture in Ravenstone House and throw it around?'

Yukiko smiled faintly before shaking her head.

'I mean, I pushed him to buy the flat. I took a real shine to it. I can't explain it.' She glanced up at the two women. 'I was…' She seemed to blush from embarrassment. 'I felt as if I was drawn to the place.'

Christine and Mary once again met each other's eyes. They'd had this feeling too.

'So what does Andrew want to do?' Mary asked.

Their brunches arrived a moment later. Christine had opted for porridge, which came in a bowl the size of Wembley Stadium, while Mary went wide-eyed at a bacon and eggs ensemble that would tide her over until 8pm that evening. Yukiko had passed on food.

As the two women began to poke and prod their dishes, they realised Yukiko hadn't answered Mary's question.

Yukiko's eyes started well up before she finally spoke, wiping her nose at the same time.

'He told me we need to sell as soon as possible, and move out.'

'I'm sorry, Yukiko,' Christine said.

Yukiko took a long drink of her coffee, which seemed to help her composure.

'There's more he said,' Yukiko added.

'He told me if I am not "on the same page", he's going to pack his bags and leave. With or without me.'

'Bloody hell,' Mary mumbled in between bites of a piece of bacon as big as her forearm.

Once she finished chewing, she said, 'It's a bit rough, isn't it?' She turned to Christine for consolation.

'Yukiko, what are you going to do?'

As she put down her now empty cup and signalled to the waitress for another, it was as if she'd taken a mask off to reveal someone else altogether.

Her face stiffened, and as she wiped something from her left eye, she took a deep breath and all of a sudden was much more confident and resolute.

'I don't appreciate threats.' She narrowed her eyes as her gaze shifted from Mary to Christine. 'Something tells me I am at Ravenstone for a reason.'

Mary and Christine were taken aback by the change in Yukiko, and impressed. Although she was petite, she appeared to be one tough little cookie underneath her visible persona.

'If he wants to walk, so be it,' she said a second later.

When her second coffee arrived, Yukiko took another long sip.

She watched the two women eating their brunch, as if she were waiting for the right moment to say something.

'Remember when I told you both I work in administration for a law firm?' Yukiko said, leaning in closer.

'Yes, I remember,' Christine chimed in, followed by Mary's 'Me too.'

Yukiko smiled.

'Can you ladies keep a secret?' she said.

'Loose lips sink ships,' Christine said.

'My lips are as tight as a fish's bumhole.' Mary grinned, delighting in the humour of the moment.

Yukiko nodded, and this time came in closer still to the others.

'I'm a forensic investigator at one of London's top private investigation firms.'

Christine sat back and appeared surprised. Mary shovelled some egg into her mouth before nodding. Wow.

'I know what you're both thinking,' Yukiko smiled, stealing a glance at the waiter behind the counter. The guy was three ways killer cute. She turned back to Christine and Mary. 'Why did I tell you this?' she said.

They both nodded, and Yukiko wondered if her heart would handle a third coffee. She decided to pass.

'Because I am going to find out everything that was ever known about Ravenstone House.'

'What are the chances of keeping your two new neighbours in the loop as to what you find?' Christine said. 'We'll be sure to return the favour.'

Yukiko took one last look at the cute waiter. She wondered if he had a temper like her husband's. She was starting to wonder if she wanted her husband to be her husband anymore.

The guy caught her checking him out and returned her smile. It made her day.

But bumping into Christine and Mary was definitely a bonus too. She felt a kind of bond with her two neighbours.

'It's a deal.' Yukiko shifted her feet and took one step towards the door of the cafe, but stopped and stepped back momentarily. 'Please don't tell Andrew about any of this, right?'

'Deal,' Mary said, as Christine smiled and pulled an imaginary zip across her lips.

CHAPTER SIXTEEN

Quentin and David had spent a while skimming over the plans of Ravenstone House, and David was champing at the bit to put them away and get on with it so he could put the new, more powerful torches to the test.

Quentin, trying not to kill David's enthusiasm for recent purchases, carefully reminded him there were actual working lights down there.

When they worked, Quentin.

The Q-man was in no hurry to venture downstairs. He was worried he'd bump into the witch, in all her glory, missing lips and all. But a small part of him was also curious.

Mary and Christine opted to stay together in Q and Mary's kitchen.

David had donned what appeared to be army pants from the Korean War, or that vintage. They were faded and as tight as, well, the fish Mary had mentioned at the coffee shop earlier that day. He wore a black skivvy that hugged his rather impressive muscular and well-proportioned upper body. Actually, it made Quentin feel slightly better—he felt as if he almost had a bodyguard there to protect him during the excursion.

Quentin, obviously not aware of the dress code, wore blue jeans and a dark-green hoodie.

'This is it, ladies,' David quipped as he reached over and put his arm around Quentin. 'Call in the light horsemen if we're not back soon.'

'You be careful, my man,' Mary said as she watched her fiancé and neighbour venture towards the front door of their flat.

Quentin raised his arm and waved the big torch back in Mary's direction. He wondered if anyone would have noticed if he'd sneaked an incontinence pad in beneath his jeans.

Probably.

———

The lights in the ground-floor hallway were dim. The design brief had always been tilted towards subtlety. No open-heart surgery would be taking place in the hall, so there was no need to light it up like Piccadilly Circus after sunset.

That night, Quentin would have been happy to have signed off on the second option.

The floorboards creaked a bit as they ventured towards the closed door that was the entrance to the basement. Quentin wondered how this could be possible when all the boards were supposed to be brand new.

When David arrived at the door, he turned to Quentin and could see the younger man's face growing paler by the minute.

'You good, Q?' He smiled.

Quentin took a deep breath and mustered up some courage. 'I'm good to go,' he lied.

When David put his hand around the doorknob, he gasped.

It was ice-cold.

A shiver went up his arm and into his lungs. He caught a breath that felt as cold as the doorknob itself, and saw the vapour leaving his body.

Maybe he was at the base of Everest. So it seemed.

The handle shifted slowly before he opened the door.

Inside was the kind of darkness you normally find when you shut your eyes in the darkest moments of the night.

'There's a light switch somewhere, right?' David asked.

Quentin found the switch.

After six attempts at flipping it up and down, he laughed at the lunacy of the moment.

'You've got to be kidding me,' he said.

The light at the top of the stairs didn't work.

David took it in his stride. He reached for the switch on his torch and a second later, the top of the stairs was bathed in a stark, bright white.

Quentin's eyes adjusted, though the same couldn't be said for his heart rate. He took some long breaths through his nose, which calmed him a touch.

'Are there more switches downstairs? More lights?' David enquired.

Quentin expected there would be, but wasn't sure. He damned well hoped there was, but he wasn't across the electrical plans and layout of most of the buildings he designed. 'Not sure, to be honest,' he said, 'but at least we have these big torches.'

Even David, with balls of steel, was starting to feel uneasy.

This place was creepy.

The air was unusually cold.

David reached the top of the stairs and shone his light downwards. He had the strange impulse to turn back.

Quentin closed the door behind him and took a long

breath of cold air. He wondered if holding David's hand would seem weird to the third-dan taekwondo master.

———

The basement had undergone extensive changes over the years, from the original layout it had when the house was built well over a century ago.

Servants' quarters had become bedrooms for some of the orphans.

Most of these had very little light, or in the case of two of the rooms, none at all. How anyone could make children sleep down there was the sort of question any decent person would ask the people who once ran the orphanage.

A door to the basement out the front of the house had long been blocked off, and interestingly the chasm left behind, where stairs once led downwards, had been filled in and made into a pitiful-looking garden, though plants always died within days of being put in the soil.

Discussions between the developer and Quentin's firm about converting the basement into another flat had found both parties in agreement. It was unsuitable. The ceiling was significantly lower down here, and the general thought was it wouldn't work.

But there was more to it.

Anyone who spent long in the basement eventually lost their shit. And one construction worker literally did. Only the Eastern European labourers lasted longer, and this was because they were all were on speed or something you snort up your nose. The sounds, the bitingly cold temperature, and freaky happenings were tolerable when you were out of it. High standards of building construction were virtually non-existent down here for the obvious reason.

So half of the basement had been ripped out and became

one large area. Cages were put in to be used for storage for the flats upstairs.

Most of the tenants had not ventured down here.

The other half of the basement stayed as it had been when Ravenstone House was an orphanage. There, three small rooms ran along the far wall across from the cages.

One, to the far left, had no door. In this room were the boilers and other items associated with the flats upstairs. David could make out the low hum of a machine idling in there.

Of the two other rooms, both still had doors. Both were shut.

Although the Romanian labourers had been snorting half their wages up their noses simply to get through a workday down here, no amount of speed could get the men to work on those three rooms.

Doug Lozel gave up on trying to get the rooms renovated for other purposes.

All but one of the labourers quit a week before the work was scheduled to wrap up. As most of the eight Romanians weren't known to each other outside of work, the seven who quit were completely unaware that the one who stayed back lost his life on his way home to Romania the following weekend when the contract officially ended. Mystery surrounded his death by drowning after he walked up to the railing of the ferry and simply fell overboard.

Doug gave up at that point. The basement would stay as it was.

CHAPTER SEVENTEEN

QUENTIN WAS FIRST TO SPOT IT: ANOTHER LIGHT switch.

He scampered over and flicked it downwards.

Light.

David and Quentin shared a surprised look.

Only one light had come on, a solitary globe hanging from the ceiling. It bathed the immediate area in a weak, yellow hue. And the globe itself was swaying, in an arc wide enough to make every hair on the two men's necks stand upright.

'Great,' Quentin said, 'we have enough light here to have a romantic dinner. I'll have to bring Mary down.'

David ignored the half-decent jibe and panned his torch around the basement.

Even though he'd had direct contact with ghosts merely two nights ago, which you'd think would have given him a confidence boost in the basement, David still felt on edge good and proper.

He felt physically off, which was rare for someone as fit as he was, but there was also something much, much deeper in him.

It was a feeling he couldn't put his finger on.

He remembered visiting a Nazi concentration camp in Austria many years ago. Out the front of the entrance to one of the saddest places he'd ever set foot in, two big signs sat on either side of the pathway in.

These identical red signs had an image of a dog, with a big cross painted over the animal.

Dogs were not allowed to be taken into the concentration camp.

Why?

Because they would go crazy.

If that's not proof that there's a sixth sense, even if it's only in dogs, I'm not sure what is.

David was starting to feel like he was a dog being led straight into the concentration camp.

The longer he was down there, the stronger the sensation grew.

It was as if he wanted to scratch—his soul. It itched, and he found himself increasingly unable to stand still.

He'd later admit to Christine that this was the most uncomfortable place he'd ever set foot in. Worse than the concentration camp in Austria.

And to think, this was directly below where they lived.

━━━

'You okay?' Quentin asked.

David turned and met Q's eyes.

'This place is getting under my skin,' he said.

Quentin nodded. 'You and me both. What do you say we check out those two other rooms with the closed doors, before we call it a night?'

David, now clearly fidgeting, as if there were a bull ant crawling up the inside of his army pants, agreed.

The two men walked to the door of the middle room.

'Bloody hell,' Quentin said as he grabbed the handle, 'it's as cold as ice.'

The door creaked as if it hadn't been opened in forty years. As the door swung all the way open, both men felt a gust of wind.

The room was tiny, no more than the size of a second bedroom. The walls were white, but peeling everywhere, and the floors were old and in serious need of repair.

It surprised Q that there were no cobwebs. Not one. Even the spiders seemed to be scared of the basement.

The room was completely empty, save for a coat rack that ran the full length of one side of the room. The hooks appeared to be two hundred years old: big and robust, but now rusty and almost falling apart.

Quentin noticed something about the wall about halfway down from the coat hooks. There were strange scuff marks all the way along the wall, at intervals between each hook.

David walked up and stood next to Quentin. They now both stared down to the marks and began to wonder what they were.

'Oh, no bloody way,' David said a few moments later.

He crouched down a little and ran his hand over some of the marks.

When he stood back up and turned to Q, Quentin could see David had gone a little pale, but his eyes burned with rage.

'Those fucking bastards,' David said sharply.

'Who?' Quentin said.

David took a long, careful breath.

'You know what these marks are, right?' he said.

Quentin shook his head.

David gritted his teeth.

'They're scuff marks of kids' boots, shoes.'

As soon as he said it, the penny dropped for Quentin.

'You've got to be bloody kidding me.'

Children had been hung up on the coat hooks somehow.

The marks showed where they'd kicked in a futile attempt to escape.

'This place is—'

David didn't finish his sentence.

The door suddenly slammed shut.

Both his and Quentin's torches ceased working not one second later.

'Fuck!' Quentin shouted, as the panic burst through his body.

'We're out of here—now!' David shouted before making for the door.

David collided with the inside of the door less than three strides from where he'd been standing.

He felt so ill, he wondered if he was going to throw up.

He desperately wanted to be upstairs.

As he groped for the handle, he could feel Quentin behind him.

'I've got the door handle, but hold onto me if you want.'

Quentin grabbed the back of David's jumper and held on for dear life.

David realised, as he opened the door, that the torches were still out. He fumbled for the switch, but nothing happened.

To his horror, the one light in the basement had also gone out.

But a second later, it came back on, ten times brighter than before.

'Arrggh,' he shouted as his eyes adjusted to the sudden burst of light.

Shit.

There was something else.

The basement was full of children.

Shoulder to shoulder.

Standing there staring at David and Quentin.

Not a sound was heard.

They stood there like statues.

David was frozen with a fear he'd never felt before.

He was about to make a run for the stairs when he sensed movement to his left.

He heard a door open.

The door to the third room.

He turned to see how Quentin was going.

Quentin's breath was short and shallow, but he was at least standing. How long for was anyone's guess.

When he turned back and wondered what he was going to do, he saw someone come from the left.

Heather.

And directly behind her was another familiar face.

Finley.

'David, and Quentin.'

Finley turned and stared across the basement.

'These are our new friends. Please make the men feel welcome, everyone.'

In an instant, all the children grew big smiles and their demeanours changed. They raised their arms and started waving.

'Now, off you all go,' Finley said in a calm and friendly tone, 'let us have a few moments alone with our new friends of flesh and blood.'

As David watched Finley, he gasped.

All the children had disappeared in an instant.

Quentin walked out from behind David and tried to compose himself.

'We weren't sure if we would see you again,' Finley said.

David nodded, 'The old lady upstairs scared us.'

'She's always hated us,' Finley said.

Both men stood there, now longing to be upstairs.

Finley sensed how the men were feeling.

He smiled. 'I know you can feel it down here,' he said. 'You want to go back up.'

David nodded, but with kindness. 'You're right. I'm ready to call it a night. I don't feel so good.'

Finley whispered something to Heather.

'Yes,' she said.

'Before you go upstairs, would you allow me to show you something? Oh, and could you give permission for Heather to try and make you feel better?' Finley said.

David turned and met Quentin's eyes. They both wondered what this was about.

David turned back to Finley. 'Okay,' he said.

Finley patted Heather on the back before saying, 'David, do you mind crouching down?'

David nodded and dropped to a crouching position.

Heather took one more look up to Finley, who smiled down to her and said, 'Off you go.'

She walked to David, who was now feeling strange. Heather was literally inches away from him.

She lifted her hand and rested it on his shoulder. David would spend the rest of his life trying to figure out how he could feel her hand. But if you thought this was weird, wait.

'Thank you for thinking kindly of us, Mr Bank.' She leaned forward and gave him a kiss on his forehead.

As her lips touched his skin, he felt some sort of electricity pass through him. But it wasn't like a shock: it was a wave of the kindest consciousness he'd ever felt in his life.

106

Immediately, the feeling of being physically ill or freaked out disappeared.

When David opened his eyes, he smiled at Heather, who had stood back a foot or so. But the smile on her face and the happiness in her eyes were mesmerising. He felt a pang of sadness that such a beautiful little girl had been taken from this earth at such a young age, and had apparently now, in death, spent all this time below this awful place.

David turned to Quentin and said, 'If you're feeling a bit off, I suggest you let Heather do the same to you. She must have some sort of angelic power. I feel completely fine now.'

Quentin decided to let Heather do her work. When he described it to Mary later, she'd tell him she felt the same sensation when Heather first visited her.

Finley smiled, 'Well done, my bonny Heather. You are an angel,' he said.

David took a deep breath. 'Finley, what would you like to show us?'

The smile that always seemed to be on Finley's face slipped away.

He whispered to Heather, who a second later was gone.

David and Quentin shared a glance before turning back to Finley, who took a sideways step and pointed into the open doorway of the third room.

'Follow me,' he said.

CHAPTER EIGHTEEN

'THEY'VE BEEN A WHILE,' MARY SAID.

Christine shrugged one shoulder, keeping the other still thanks to her broken arm.

'They'll be back soon; they're big boys,' she said.

Mary nodded. 'Alright, I'll try to be patient. Another tea?'

Christine had already downed two. What would be the harm in a third?

'Yes please—'

The knock on the door made both women jump two feet in the air.

Knock, knock.

'Hold on, my man,' she said, loud enough for Quentin to hear through the closed door.

'I thought you were going to take—' Mary continued as she opened the door, but stopped mid-sentence.

But it was Yukiko, from Flat Three.

'Err, hello,' Mary said, 'long time no see.'

Yukiko checked to see if anyone was in the hallway.

'Can I come in for a moment or two?' she said.

Mary could tell immediately from her neighbour's body

language that she didn't want to be caught standing there talking to her, and she wondered what was going on. But in a flash she smiled and stood aside, waving her right arm. 'Sure, come on in.'

As she closed the door, Mary said, 'I just put the kettle on. Come.'

Christine stood up from her kitchen stool when Yukiko walked in with Mary close behind.

'Yukiko, what a surprise,' Christine said, ushering Mary's new guest to sit next to her at the bench.

When she sat down, Mary said, 'Tea? Coffee? Water?'

Yukiko met Christine's eyes before turning back to Mary.

She hesitated for a moment, maybe a little too long, before she said, 'Got something stronger?'

Mary nodded. 'Name your poison.' She met Christine's eyes and together they both wondered what was going on.

'Vodka, neat,' Yukiko said.

After Mary made a tea for Christine and herself, and poured Yukiko a small glass of vodka, she pulled a bar stool around to the other side of the island bench.

By the time she'd sat down, Yukiko had already downed the entire glass.

Christine shot Mary a concerned look.

Yukiko was already reaching over for the bottle when Christine said, 'Bad day at the office Yukiko?'

Yukiko poured herself another vodka.

'Depends on what you classify as bad,' Yukiko said, studying her glass before meeting Christine's eyes.

Mary took a sip of her tea. A little too hot, it singed the tip of her tongue.

She wondered if a shot of vodka would soothe it.

Yukiko sat in silence for a moment, deep in thought. She slipped her fingers around her glass, as if it comforted her, and took just a sip this time.

Without looking at either of the women, she said, 'Remember how I told you both that I'd do some digging on our wonderful new home, Ravenstone House?'

A chill ran down Yukiko's spine.

Mary said, 'Yes. You were going to find out all about the place.'

The private investigator shuddered, and she took another drink.

'Well, let's just say,' the look on her face was serious, 'I sort of wish I hadn't.'

Christine leant over and patted her on the arm. 'I get the feeling you want to tell us what you found out,' she said.

Yukiko nodded, 'I think you both better remain seated,' she said.

———

David and Quentin came to the open doorway.

The light bulb out the front of the rooms had returned to its normal intensity, and the faint yellow glow cast a long shadow across the open doorway.

David and Quentin peered into the room. They couldn't see much until David switched on his torch.

The room was almost identical to the one next door, but there was no coat rack on the side wall, just an empty and eerie space.

The floor was in a terrible state, and looked too dangerous to walk on.

Finley stood and watched the two men carefully as they studied the room. He wondered how they would react when he told them about it.

Better still, he believed that if he took the two in and they stood in the 'circle,' they might feel it.

He hoped that if they did, they would consider his audacious proposal.

Finley slipped past David and walked into the room.

When he reached the spot, he turned to the men and said, 'I want you both to come in. There's something you might want to see.'

David and Q met each other's eyes.

They could see into the room fine from where they stood. Something deep inside them said, 'Do not enter.'

But to David's credit, he knew he had to.

'We're all ears, Yukiko,' Mary said.

'Before I go any further, Andrew knows nothing of me looking into this place,' Yukiko said intently. 'He's working late tonight, which is the only reason I came. I know you'll want to talk to your men about this, but please,' she ensured she met both their eyes, 'I don't want him to know anything. I'll figure out what to do with him later, okay?'

Christine nodded, 'As we told you at the cafe at brunch, you can trust the both of us. And Q and David too.'

Mary agreed.

'Alright,' Yukiko said, and took another drink of her vodka before placing it on the bench and sitting back. She took a deep breath. 'I'll do my best not to bore you. I have a habit of going on a bit. It's a side-effect of my job. I give the full story. Please be patient.'

CHAPTER NINETEEN

'RAVENSTONE HOUSE WAS ONE OF THE LAST GEORGIAN-style country manors, constructed on Lacham Hill in the year 1831.

'Officially built with three floors, the attic, or unofficial fourth floor, was where you would find the servants' sparse living quarters.

'The basement was home to the manor's kitchen, food storage, and other utilitarian facilities not seen in the light of day.

'The original owner, Viscount Henry Lloyd III, would spend most of his weekends at Ravenstone House.

'Some weekends, his family would come with him. Other times they would remain at his main home in Peckham, Central London, but Viscount Lloyd would still go to his country home—only on those weekends, with his mistress.'

'The dirty old dog,' Christine said.

Yukiko didn't seem to find her quip funny, and pressed on.

'Upon his death in 1890, the home remained in the Lloyd family.

'But at some point, years earlier, maybe around 1870, his wife died in the house. Her name was Rose, and records mention an accident which saw her fall from the top of the stairs. She was found dead at the bottom of the main staircase.

'But here's the thing. Her own children said she never left Ravenstone House. What I think they meant was, her ghost remained there. And she was not a happy ghost, either.'

Mary and Christine shared a disturbed look.

'Christ,' Mary said, 'this information was recorded somewhere?'

Yukiko nodded. 'We have access to libraries and files going back hundreds of years. You would not believe the sort of information you will find there.'

She took a quick sip of her drink.

'The grandchildren would share stories of seeing the ghost of Rose standing at the top of the stairs in the late hours of the night, always around midnight. She would turn and look behind herself before disappearing.

'It was the same every time she appeared. She would do the same exact thing. Oh, and sometimes she'd scream and yell, and make things move around the house.'

'Oh my,' Christine said, 'she was pushed.'

Yukiko stared at her for a moment and said, 'I had the same thought. It was the first recorded death at Ravenstone House.'

'You mean murder,' Mary said.

'It may give us some idea as to why she is so angry,' Christine said.

'There could be another reason why she is so angry,' Yukiko said, once again finding her eyes drawn to the ceiling.

'Why, Yukiko?' Mary asked.

Yukiko finished the last of her drink. It wouldn't be her last vodka of the night, though.

'Because the records claim the person who pushed her was, how you would say, known to her.'

'Fuck,' Christine swore. 'Someone in her family sent her to her death?'

Yukiko nodded.

'Yes. Her firstborn. Her son.'

———

Finley waited as the two men came into the room. He closed the door. David and Quentin wondered why, but didn't question it.

The air in the room was as cold as a walk-in fridge: even colder than the main area of the basement.

Quentin instinctively slid his hands into his pockets and moved his limbs around in an attempt to warm up.

'I know you're going to ask me why I brought you in here,' Finley said.

David went to answer but simply nodded. Quentin did the same.

'This is where it happened,' Finley said solemnly.

David studied him for a moment. It took him a few seconds, with it being almost freezing, to think he may have an idea of what Finley meant.

'This is where they took your life.' As the words left his mouth, David could feel his throat tighten with sadness.

Finley stared at the floor for what seemed an eternity.

'They took all our lives in this room,' Finley said with a sad look on his face.

David and Quentin shook their heads.

Over 130 children, if the maths were right, had died in this tiny room.

'Can I ask you both a question?' Finley said.

'Yes,' the men answered at the very same time.

'Would you help us get to where we should have gone when our bodies were taken away from us?'

David shook his head in confusion. 'What do you mean?'

Finley Sproule had waited forty-five years for this very moment.

As he said the words that came next, he could feel the spirit of every single child who had been trapped at Ravenstone cry in hope.

'If those who killed us die, we will be set free,' he said.

Quentin and David now took their turn to stare long and hard at the young ghost.

As the words sunk in, David could still feel his body in ways he'd never felt before. The same went with Quentin. It was as if they weren't offended by what Finley had proposed.

Quentin stood there and without any thought, said, 'So what you're asking us to do, Finley, is take the lives of the people who took yours, and those of all the other children.'

Finley simply nodded.

'Wow. It's quite the task, young Finley Sproule. If we got caught, we'd spend the rest of our lives in prison. As much as I would like to speak to these terrible people, I'm not sure if killing them would be good for our own lives,' David said.

Finley once again studied a spot on the floor.

He seemed unperturbed by David's honest opinion of the request.

'If I was able to help you do this, and you'd never get caught, would you consider it?' he said.

Quentin took a deep breath and wondered how Mary would take this new development.

'Well, you'd have to explain how you'd do it. We would have to go away and think about it,' David said.

Finley had one more ace up his sleeve.

He believed this would get at least David over the line.

Maybe Quentin too.

He had come this far.

He'd waited all this time.

He was so close now, he knew he had to use it.

It might make the difference.

'I want to show you one more thing. It may shock you, but it may help you decide if you want to help us,' Finley said.

David wondered how bad it could be. He'd had a stint in the Royal Air Force; in his life, he'd seen all sorts of shocking things.

'Step closer. You need to see this.' Finley motioned for both men to come further into the room.

As they did, he pointed to the floorboards.

When David's torch found the spot, he immediately saw the large dark ring imprinted on the floor.

It was big enough for someone to stand in, but not much more.

As he started to wonder what it could have been, Finley said calmly, 'If you stand in the circle, I will show you.'

Quentin raised his eyebrows. He, too, was trying to figure out the significance of the ring on the floor.

Something deep inside David told him that not for all the tea in China should he stand in the ring. But his curiosity quickly won over.

He took one last look at Quentin, and turned to Finley.

'I'll do it. Tell me what to do,' he said.

Finley stepped directly next to the ring and said, 'Step into the ring. Then hold out both your hands.'

As David took a step closer, Finley added, 'This may be the most confronting thing you have ever seen in your life. I hope you can handle it.'

David could feel his taekwondo training kick in.

'Let's do this,' his mind shouted at him.

He stepped into the ring.

Finley moved closer and raised his arms into the air.

As David took a deep breath, Finley lowered his hands.

The burst of light that exploded in David's eyes was so bright, he wondered if he'd be permanently blinded.

CHAPTER TWENTY

'So, what happened?' Mary said.

Yukiko stared at the window in the dining area for a moment before turning back to Mary.

'Ravenstone House stayed in the family, but as the children grew older, they wanted to move. The ghost of their mother was too much, especially for the oldest son, who confessed to the murder on his own death bed decades later. In fact,' Yukiko shook her head, 'murder and crime seemed to flourish in the family starting with the murder of Rose Lloyd.

Christine let out a sigh. 'I sort of wish I'd spoken to you before we bought Flat Two,' she said.

Yukiko stared at Christine, 'I wish I'd spoken to me before we bought Flat Three.'

She took another sip of her vodka before she went on.

'The sons became hardened criminals. Together, the three of them ran an organised crime syndicate. Bad, bad people. They were known to bring prostitutes here to this very house. But what's more, these women were often never seen again.

'The syndicate eventually went international. They

started doing business in Eastern Europe. Drugs. Prostitution. Racketeering. Theft. Even human trafficking.'

Mary sat back in her chair, feeling sick. But Yukiko wasn't finished.

'I haven't even started on the orphanage period yet,' she said.

Yukiko took a breath and a sip of vodka.

'Anyway, the family were eventually, around the time of World War One, accused of sending money to connections in Eastern Europe, to fund the Triple Alliance.'

When Mary raised her eyebrows Yukiko said, 'this is who England fought in the First World War.'

'Oh shit,' Mary responded.

'When it came out, the three brothers and their families fled England. Apparently they ended up in Austria–Hungary. They never returned to England, at least on record, anyway.'

Yukiko knew she was dragging her heels and the story was taking too long.

'I'm sorry, I will try and speed this up,' she said.

She shifted in her seat and took a deep breath.

'Ravenstone House was sold to another wealthy European family. This new family were secretive and very rich.' She shook her head in amazement. 'Although people believed it was some other random family, many believed it was the Lloyds, who'd bought it back, but under a fictitious name.'

'What the hell?' Christine said.

'So this other "family",' Yukiko held both hands up and with two fingers emphasised the word 'family,' 'decided to turn Ravenstone House into an orphanage.'

A few months after the announcement, the place received its first children.

Mary could tell the story was weighing heavier on Yukiko as she continued to tell it.

'Ravenstone House was first lauded as a place of warmth and compassion. A place where all the "less privileged," orphans who had been abandoned, could find safety and protection.'

'But within the first three months of the orphanage opening, there were three deaths. Two five-year-old boys, twins actually, and an eight-year-old girl. Records show authorities investigated, but were convinced by the people running the place that the deaths were accidental.'

Yukiko shook her head. 'All three drowned in a bathtub, or so the report claimed.'

'Anyway,' Yukiko sat up straighter, 'I digress. For the next three or so decades, this place saw hundreds upon hundreds of orphans come and go. Records show the majority of these found homes where they were raised by the adopting parents.'

'But there seemed to always be a shadow hanging over the place. Staff who worked here were known to the locals to be rude and unsociable. The guy who ran the place was charming and forthcoming to the authorities, but some believed this was all a front. His son who worked here was a carbon copy of him. At some point, the father returned to Europe, and his son took over the running of the place.

'Some say the guy, and the son, too, had a thing for children, if you know what I mean. The place grew a reputation of being haunted by children who had died here. But still they came.'

Christine rose to her feet unsteadily and walked around the kitchen. Ravenstone House was starting to feel more evil as every hour passed. And her husband was currently downstairs in the basement.

'Rumours started to circulate more publicly after the end of the Second World War that Ravenstone House was run and staffed by what in later years would call paedophiles. And they were all in on it together, those who worked here. They'd cover for each other, especially the guy in charge.

'But it was the disappearance of,' Yukiko took a drink of her vodka, 'a young Scottish teenager in the early fifties, along with a sexual abuse case of a female worker by a male co-worker, which turned up the heat on the orphanage.

'The boy had been handed over to the orphanage because his father, an alcoholic, couldn't find work in London after moving here with his wife from Glasgow. He and his wife were never seen, nor heard from, ever again. The people who ran the orphanage stated he had been transferred to an orphanage back in Scotland.

'But this kid's uncle, who had worked and travelled abroad, had recently returned home to Scotland. With news of the disappearance of his brother and wife, he felt he owed it to his nephew to try and find him, in the hope of raising him.

'So when he went searching for his nephew, the orphanage in Glasgow where he was supposedly sent to had no record of him arriving there. The guy decided to check the other dozen or so orphanages in Glasgow too. The kid wasn't at any of these either. The head of Ravenstone House insisted the transfer had taken place. But the kid had vanished into thin air. Ravenstone House claimed he may have run away, and they eventually went with this version. But many in the community around here were convinced he'd never left Ravenstone.'

Christine read Mary's thoughts, or so it seemed. They realised the significance of this part of the story.

Both women met each other's eyes, both wide eyed.

Finley Sproule.

He'd never left Ravenstone.

David's first instinct was to panic.

The light was so bright he couldn't see a thing.

He knew he was in the basement of Ravenstone House, but felt as if he were a million miles away. He had the sudden taste of something sour, and his tongue felt as if it were glued to the top of his mouth.

Suddenly, light turned to black.

Now the panic began.

It started in the deepest pit of his stomach, and over the next few moments it would rise slowly but surely.

A flash of something flew past him. Monotone colours, all moving quickly, circling him as if he were standing in the eye of a hurricane.

He felt as if he were standing in the middle of a large cave. The smell was unbearable. Whatever it was, it was putrid and impossible to ignore.

As they began to slow, he realised what the blots of colour were.

Children.

They flew past him as if they had wings.

They were not unfriendly, but he could feel their tension, their sorrow.

Their pain.

Suddenly, one stopped dead in front of him.

Mother of God.

It was Heather.

David recognised her immediately.

But she was not the Heather he'd first met upstairs.

She came across as someone else, with dirty, matted hair, and a scowl on her face. Her eyes were bloodshot and distant; her teeth were yellow, and her breath was cold and foul. She had blood down one side of her face. It was dry and caked on.

She screamed at him, saying something at the same time.

He couldn't understand what she was saying.

She lifted up her dirty dress to reveal a body riddled with bruises on every limb, and across her torso.

David felt as if he wanted to scream himself.

And as he did, Heather screamed too, but sprang up and pushed against him, wrapping her arms around his neck.

She screamed in his face, and a moment later it was as if her consciousness was part of his.

David was trying everything he could to push it away, but nothing worked. He felt as if he were suffocating, and his own shouts of 'let me out' fell on deaf ears.

As the torment continued, suddenly his vision went black, but only for a split second.

Oh, my fucking Lord, he thought.

He found himself in the coat-rack room of the basement.

Hanging from the coat rack.

A candle burned in the corner of the room.

He kicked and screamed.

He realised he was now a child, in a filthy dress, hanging helplessly from the coat rack itself.

A second later, a large hand came out of nowhere and hit him in the face so hard, he wondered if he'd lost a couple of teeth. But whoever had hit him disappeared from view.

David, his face reeling from the pain, heard something next to him. When he turned, he saw three other children hanging on the coat rack alongside him, suspended there by belts around her waists.

The one right next to him was another girl.

She was either asleep, passed out, or—no she couldn't be —dead.

Her head sagged forward as if she were a rag doll. Her arms and legs were limp.

All of a sudden, three men entered the room. They stood on the far side and seemed to be a fine mood.

All had grins on their faces.

David wished he'd not stepped into the ring.

The big one on the far left said to the other two, 'What's your pick?'

David could feel the blood drain from his face. He started to feel dizzy.

He kicked and went to scream, but one of the other men stepped a few strides closer, now in arm's reach.

He grabbed the bottom of David's face and squeezed it so hard he felt like his jawbone was going to snap.

'Shut your trap, if you know what's good for ya,' he said, the smell of alcohol on him so strong David wanted to vomit.

Two of the men were so young, David thought they were barely eighteen years old. The third was much older, with a bald head and wisps of hair on the sides.

The guy stared at the girl next to him and snickered to the others, 'I think little Patsy may be off with the fairies.' But when he turned back, he said, 'So I guess this one here will do.' He turned back to David and smiled with a set of awful teeth.

He lifted David from the hook by wrapping his hand around his neck…

———

After several more minutes of torture and misery, David was back in the cave.

Heather's spirit was again standing in front of him.

But this time, it was the angelic Heather: the sweet little girl he'd seen for the first time upstairs.

When she evaporated into the open air, a moment later, another child stopped in front of him.

As the new child, this time a little boy, stepped closer to David, it dawned on him that he was going to see through this child's eyes just as he'd seen through Heather's.

David waved his hands in front of himself and said, 'No, not again, please! Enough, I can't do this!'

But the boy shook his head and screamed no, and in a split second came at David with the speed of a cheetah.

David felt the pain and anguish start all over again but this time shouted, 'Enough! Finley! I've seen en—'

David's vision suddenly exploded in dazzling white light.

But the sensation was as if he'd been thrown out of a plane without a parachute.

David opened his eyes.

He was back in the ring room.

He spun and saw Quentin standing there, looking at him.

David muttered something that Quentin couldn't understand.

David stepped out of the ring, lunged at Quentin—

And wrapped his arms around him.

David burst into tears.

'Heather,' he gasped, still sobbing. 'They raped her, and then they killed her. Right here in this room. I saw it—*felt* it—through her eyes.' He caught his breath and stepped back. 'Whatever you do, don't stand in the ring.'

Quentin, horrified into silence, could only nod. He could see David was clearly coming out of what appeared to be shock.

But as David began to compose himself, Quentin could see him turning back into the taekwondo instructor who could bust down walls with his bare hands.

'Did this happen to you all?' David asked Finley.

The boy stared at him, and twenty seconds later said, 'Yes.'

David glanced at Quentin with determination infused with anger on his face.

He turned back to Finley.

'Tell me how we can get them,' he said.

CHAPTER TWENTY-ONE

QUENTIN LED DAVID INTO HIS FLAT.

Christine and Mary rose to their feet.

'You just missed Yukiko,' Mary told the men.

Neither of them seemed to hear Mary's comment.

'You alright?' she said, giving Q a kiss.

As Christine did the same, she could tell David seemed to have been to Hell and back.

'What about you, my dear hubby? You holding up okay?'

David collapsed onto the bar stool, sitting heavily.

He glanced over to Quentin and said, 'Please tell me you have whisky somewhere in this fine flat of yours.'

Quentin went searching for his whisky.

David turned to Christine and smiled weakly, reaching for her hand.

'Ladies,' he met his wife's eyes before turning to Mary, 'you may need a shot of whisky on standby too, for what I'm about to tell you.'

———

David had two shots of whisky on the trot.

He had yet to speak.

When Quentin poured him a third, Christine said, 'You have classes tomorrow. Are you sure you want to have another one?'

David turned to his wife. 'They may be cancelled. I'll see how I go,' he said. Then he rose to his feet and rested both hands on the bench. 'We all need to move out of here,' he said, looking down to the floorboards.

Christine now stood to her feet and walked up to David, clearly taken aback by his surprising statement.

'Why, David? I thought we were going to try and sort things out and make it work,' she said, almost pleadingly.

David wiped his brow before quickly downing his third shot.

'Because I'm going to burn this place, basement and all, to the ground,' he said.

Christine could see hurt in his eyes, but it was quickly replaced with anger.

'We are going to help the spirits of all the children get to where they belong.'

Christine shook her head. 'What happened down there? You are not making any sense, my dear husband.'

———

David spent the next thirty minutes going over every detail of what happened.

Christine and Mary cried openly when he told the women about the experience of seeing Heather die.

They, in turn, told the men what Yukiko had said, leaving nothing out.

'The two guys I saw were barely adults. Many of these terrible people could still be walking the streets, especially those two. They are the most evil of human beings,' he said.

David stood before walking to the opposite side of the kitchen. There, he stood deep in thought.

Christine watched him intently, a look of concern firmly on her face.

'I'm no vigilante. I've never done or considered anything like this,' David said.

Christine shook her head. Mary and Quentin could tell the mere talk of this made her feel very uncomfortable.

'Can't we go to the police? Surely they can track these terrible people down and justice can be served,' she said.

'And the police interview the spirits of the dead children? This would go nowhere, quick,' David said.

Christine's face said it all. She was against the idea. Her face was turning more ashen by the minute.

'Finley swears black and blue it will work,' David said.

Christine met Mary's eyes, hoping for some support, but she found Mary strangely pensive. Mary appeared to be open to the idea.

'My heart cries out for those poor children, it does. But we're not going to jail for this,' Christine said.

She had a point.

Her husband, to her surprise, seemed to be on another page.

'They'll be trapped here forever,' David said.

Christine shook her head. 'We aren't the judge, jury, and executioners, David Banks.' She bit her bottom lip, knowing they rarely, if ever, had words.

Mary pictured little Heather.

She recalled the feeling of her spirit touching her and kissing her on the cheek.

To think she died in the way she did.

And the guy who murdered her could still be out there.

She thought about him for a moment.

Was he now a father? Maybe even a grandfather?

131

Was he known in his community as an upstanding person?

Or was he still as evil as he had been when he raped and murdered a tiny, defenceless little girl?

These people were the polar opposite of what she believed in, deep in her heart. Children, no matter who or where they came from, needed love, support, and above all, someone to care for them.

Someone to protect the kids from evil.

Like the evil of Ravenstone House.

Mary reached over and held out her hand to Quentin.

'We ask Finley if he can tell us anything about these people, names especially,' she said. 'We ask Yukiko if she can start searching for anything she can find on people who worked here.'

David's eyes lit up.

'And?' Quentin stared at his fiancée for an answer.

'We track one of these evil bastards down.' She stood straighter. 'We test Finley's plan. If it works, we'll go from there,' she said.

CHAPTER TWENTY-TWO

REGGIE BLOOD BLEW OUT THE CANDLE ON HIS PITIFUL little cupcake.

It was stale, and stolen.

So was the candle.

He'd squandered his last twenty quid on his favourite wine and cigarettes. But he'd also managed to buy six cans of spaghetti on special. He'd never know they were much cheaper than normal canned spaghetti for a reason. They were for infants.

But there was no money left for a birthday cake, so he stole the cupcake and the four pack of candles.

Reggie Blood's birthday was today.

Happy birthday, Reggie.

You piece of shit.

Seventy years on this bleak planet, he pondered.

He took in the scene around him and wondered if he'd be here another winter. If so, he thought, he'd be screwed. With no proper heating and no power, he knew that as he grew older, no amount of blankets would keep out the biting cold.

The beat-up caravan had been his home for the last

decade. But he'd been kicked out of the Holmpton Seaside Caravan park a year ago. Not paying the rent was the main reason. However, he also gave most people the creeps.

Holmpton was a little seaside village forty minutes from Hull, 155 miles from London on the east coast. Reggie's little rusting metal box now sat behind the Hook's Lane Fishing Pond, five minutes inland from the Holmpton Village. The dump on wheels sat behind a small mound of dirt and was surrounded by trees, virtually hidden from the outside world. He'd known the owner of the spot, a cranky old bastard of a man, who said he could put his caravan there if he tended to the pond every week or so. The owner had lost his sight thanks to a full-blown stroke a year ago. It was a miracle he was still alive. The old guy knew there was no way he could tend to his beloved little pond full of fish anymore.

Reggie hadn't tended to the pond for months.

The only time he bothered was when he'd steal a fish for dinner. And the way he was going, there'd soon be no damn fish left.

The thought of checking out of this miserable life was almost a holiday he was looking forward to.

Where the ghosts of the past could no longer haunt him.

But he was worried that when he died, maybe they'd be there waiting for him.

Reggie had known from an early age he had a problem.

But he'd stopped his evil ways by the time he'd reached his thirtieth birthday.

In his distorted mind, not having done anything bad for the last forty years meant he was off the hook.

For the last four decades, he'd not been evil.

So in the eyes of the Lord, he was redeemed.

Christine bumped into Yukiko two days later. A lunch invitation was a welcome distraction for Yukiko from her woes at home.

Over lunch, she'd confide in Christine things she'd told only a couple of people in her life.

Yukiko had been sexually abused by a couple of older boys at school when she was six years old. Although their actions saw the two punished, the emotional scars would take Yukiko years to recover from.

So when Christine asked if she would help to locate these people for Finley, if they were still alive, Yukiko agreed almost immediately.

But with conditions.

This would be her only involvement. Yukiko would track down the employment records of the orphanage staff and pass on the information to Christine. Nothing more. Nothing less.

Yukiko told Christine that finding people was one of the things she did best. No matter how old the case, over the years she'd found people co-workers never seemed to be able to.

She believed she had a gift for it, but more importantly, she simply never gave up, and exhausted avenues most people never considered.

She had the reputation, at work, for being able to find people no matter how hard they tried to fall off the edge of the earth.

There wasn't a patch of dirt on the planet where you could hide from Yukiko Parsons.

⸺

Yukiko welcomed Christine's dinner invitation with open arms. A week or so after having lunch with her neighbour,

Yukiko found herself flying solo. Andrew had been called back to the States on urgent business matters, so she was currently fending for herself. Yukiko was a good cook, but found it laborious after a long day at the office. So when she was on her own, she resorted to less Michelin-star dishes: toast, two-minute noodles, and cereal.

Christine rested the Beef Wellington in the middle of the table.

When Quentin and Mary arrived with wine and dessert, Yukiko was especially happy to have been invited over. She relished the social contact with these friendly and very down-to-earth people.

Andrew being away had given Yukiko the breathing space she felt she needed. He was being difficult about the need to leave Ravenstone House, and this was only putting strain on their marriage. He wasn't super-social, either, so Yukiko knew he'd have declined the dinner invitation if he was home.

Christine hadn't invited Yukiko to dinner to press her for what they nicknamed 'Oli': the orphanage list. The list of known employees who'd worked at the Ravenstone House for the Less Privileged.

So it came as a surprise, after dinner was served and enjoyably eaten, when Yukiko cleared her throat amid the banter.

'I have something I need to show you all.' Yukiko spoke quietly.

Quentin and David's conversation about the future of English Premier League football came to a grinding halt.

Mary and Christine, along with Yukiko, were in the middle of discussing the people who lived upstairs.

While their silence gave some background music the fore, Yukiko pulled a neatly folded piece of A4 paper from her handbag.

'I've made some inroads, ladies and gentlemen. This is

only the start. There are six names on the list so far, but I imagine it will grow as I go forward and dig deeper,' Yukiko said.

David scanned the list. He drew a deep breath as he viewed the names and last known addresses of the people on it so far.

Five men. One woman.

David met eyes with Quentin and Mary a few seconds later. He could see the anticipation in their faces.

'Quentin, we need to take this list to Finley. We need to ascertain, each time we get a name, if they were one of the good guys,' David took a sip of wine, 'or one of the bad guys.'

Everyone around the table agreed.

Mary leant forward and asked the question they'd all been thinking about ever since David and Quentin's last visit to the basement.

How would Finley help the four of them avenge all those children's lives without getting busted?

'How's this going to work?' Mary met eyes with Christine and Yukiko before peering over to David.

David read the names on the list once again before casting his gaze into the distance.

'Finley told me, when we are ready, he'll run through how it can be achieved,' David said.

Christine began to clear the plates as Mary rose to her feet to help.

After a moment, Christine glanced around their flat and wondered how long they would end up living there. It was the first time the thought had crossed her mind.

She stopped and waited for David to meet her eyes.

When he did, she stared at him for a few moments before saying resolutely, 'I guess you and Q will be visiting him tonight.'

CHAPTER TWENTY-THREE

DAVID REACHED THE OPEN DOORWAY TO THE RING room.

He and Quentin stood there wondering if they would call out for Finley, or if he'd know they were there and come of his own accord.

A moment later, David felt something touch his leg.

He jumped so high he thought he would hit the ceiling.

Heather.

She'd latched onto his leg, wrapping her arms around it before looking up to him.

'David, I'm so glad you've come down here to say hello,' Heather said.

David smiled. 'It is nice to see you, Heather. Is Finley around?'

Finley appeared as if on cue.

'I've been looking forward to seeing you both again,' he said.

After a few moments of silence, David took a deep breath and said, 'We're ready to start.'

Quentin stepped forward and said, 'But Finley, there's one more thing we need from you. We need to know—of all the people who worked here, were there any good people? Or was everyone who ever worked here evil?'

Finley stared at Quentin for what felt like an eternity. David was going to ask the same question. It was critical. It would be a dealbreaker if they couldn't distinguish the good employees, if any, from the bad.

'Yes. There were good people who worked here. But normally, not for long,' Finley said.

David turned to Quentin. Right, now they had this extra complication.

He turned back to Finley.

'We have someone tracking down the list of known people who worked here, Finley. We have six names to start with.' David pulled the piece of paper from his pocket and opened it.

He scanned the list of names:

1) John Heen
2) Archie Glaggin
3) Bradley Fletcher
4) Lynne Dalton
5) Reggie Blood
6) Josef Leitner

'How will we know who the good people were?' David said before meeting Finley's eyes. 'And how will we know who the bad guys were?'

Finley turned and ventured back into the small room.

When he came close to the notorious ring on the floor, David burst out, 'Please don't ask me to step back into the ring.' The tension was evident in his tone.

Finley shook his head.

'I know how this can be done,' he said.

Quentin and David nodded to him from the doorway.

'I will step into the ring. You will give me a name, which I will repeat. The children will tell me in the way we talk to each other.'

Quentin could feel his nerves firing.

'And you will tell us?' David asked.

Finley shook his head. 'The pain of their name will be too great for me to repeat. I have the ability to control things such as the light above you.' Finley pointed to the old globe hanging from the ceiling above the two men.

'If the light brightens, the name is of someone evil,' he said.

Quentin couldn't help but turn his head upwards and study the light. It hung about four feet above him. His senses made him stand away from being directly underneath, as if it were a wrecking ball that weighed a tonne.

Finley stepped into the ring as David watched on.

David held the list up while Quentin pulled out his torch to give his neighbour enough light to see the names.

'We are ready,' said Finley. 'Give me the first name.'

'John Heen,' David said slowly.

'John. Heen,' Finley repeated.

After close to two minutes, Quentin was the first to realise it was happening.

He had a sick feeling of being watched. The sensation crawled up his back like a centipede.

Out of nowhere, a rush of arctic wind came straight from the ring room.

He turned to David, who was staring at the globe.

'Did you feel that?' he said a second later.

The globe's intensity grew stronger, and when it peaked the two men had no doubt the guy was bad.

The light dimmed again. Quentin could feel the blood pulsing in the side of his neck.

After the next two names were read, the two men started to wonder if all six were bad guys.

But the next name was a female's name.

To their relief, after David called out the name, Lynne Dalton, the light remained unchanged. There was no gust of wind, nothing. They would note this on the list once they returned upstairs.

When David called out the next name, Reggie Blood, the time between the name being called and the light changing was much quicker.

David suddenly felt as if he was going to vomit.

A flashback hit him as if it were a train travelling through the Tube at a hundred miles an hour.

'Heather, no!' he heard Finley shout.

David felt her first before he'd had time to do anything.

Heather had reappeared and was holding onto his legs as if her life depended on it.

David wanted to scream as the vision of the man's face came to him.

The smell of his breath. The look in his eyes.

As Heather struggled to hold onto his legs, it dawned on him who Reggie Blood was.

He was the man who took Heather's life.

The light's intensity increased.

David shunned the brightness and at the same time realised Heather had disappeared.

The light dimmed.

David suddenly felt out of breath.

'You okay, mate?' Quentin put his hand on David's shoulder.

David felt as if he'd been punched in the chest.

'One more name on the list,' he said, 'and we are done.'

Quentin turned and met Finley's eyes.

The apparition nodded to him. David handed the list to Quentin and said, 'You can read out the last one.'

Quentin felt as nervous as hell.

David had read all the other names out, so Q only had to read one. It was no big deal, but he felt as if he were going to pass a kidney stone the size of a house brick.

'Josef. Leitner,' Quentin said.

This time, the reaction was instantaneous.

Not one second had passed before the light hanging above started to brighten.

But this time, the brightness seemed to continue.

Before they knew it, David and Quentin were shielding their eyes from the blinding light.

They could no longer see into the ring room.

David tried to hold his hand up above his eyes to see if Finley were still there.

'No, no! get away!' David thought he heard Finley shout, as the doors of the ring and coat rack rooms both slammed shut, and the light above pulsed blinding and white.

The doors opened quickly before slamming shut again.

The wire fence of the cages David was leaning against started to shake violently.

David and Quentin muttered their own profanities as they instinctively turned, feeling someone's presence.

All they could see was darkness, even though the light of the globe was now as bright as the sun.

Out of nowhere, someone appeared.

It was the old lady from the top of the stairs.

How they could smell her breath was another mystery they would mull over for aeons.

It was foul beyond belief: the stench of dead animals rotting in a ground of human faeces.

'THE BOSS.' The words she screamed would somehow come back to both Quentin and David in the days after this horrible encounter with her.

The two men fell backwards, landing on the floor.

The light above, now so bright it was impossible to keep their eyes open—exploded.

David and Quentin, luckily, had their eyelids already glued shut, but they rolled over quickly as the glass from the globe rained down.

After a few moments of pitch black, they flicked on their torches and came to their feet.

'She's starting to piss me right off.' David turned and tried to muster a smile at Quentin.

'She's one angry old bag. I wish she'd chill the fuck out,' Q said.

The two men stared at each other for a moment, and David eventually said, 'Well, I think we have what we need.'

As the men started to make their way towards the staircase, Heather said, 'Finley has something he wants to give you.'

———

Quentin and David walked to the entrance of the ring room.

Finley stood close to the wall on the far side.

In front of him, in the middle of the ring mark on the floor, sat a small glass bottle.

'Come in closer. Let me explain what this is,' he said.

The two men came back into the room.

'What I am about to tell you, you will find very hard to believe. But it's the truth,' Finley said.

He waved Heather over, whispering into her ear a

moment later. She smiled before disappearing through the open doorway.

'There is liquid in this bottle. If it comes into contact with one of the evil people who killed us, they will meet the same fate we did.'

David and Quentin stared at the bottle, thinking the same thing.

'Where did it come from?' David said.

Finley, with a shake of his head, said, 'You wouldn't believe me if I told you. So for now, I won't. But trust me. If it touches the monsters—they will die. It will help you do what is needed to be done. Without, how do you say, getting blood on your hands.'

CHAPTER TWENTY-FOUR

THE NEXT NIGHT, CHRISTINE AND DAVID SAT IN silence at their dining table.

In the middle was a small bottle of liquid. They'd all talked about it for some time before the others went home, and found believing what it could do hard to digest.

Now, David couldn't stop seeing the face of Reggie Blood.

He was the monster who raped and murdered Heather.

David could feel his anger building.

'What are you thinking?' Christine said.

She'd been watching her husband from the corner of her eye. She could tell the guy was buried deep in thought.

Eventually, without turning to her, he reached out his hand and found her lap. She took his big hand in hers and they sat for a few moments in silence.

David had described every detail of what he'd seen and felt when Finley had touched his hands.

Only when he cried in her arms, lying in bed afterwards, did she truly believe it had happened.

David had only cried twice in his life.

Besides, the guy never bullshitted. Except for the time he told her he'd enjoyed *Cats*.

When he turned to her, she could see the mist in his eyes. David had a heart of gold, and was the most decent man she'd ever met.

'We need to put this little bottle to the test,' he said.

Christine's apprehension swelled.

Things were now getting serious.

'What are you going to do?' she said, nervously.

David reached over and picked up the bottle.

As he held it, he turned to Christine, and with a look of determination, said.

'This weekend, we track down a monster. And we see if this bottle of potion works.'

Christine swallowed.

She wished they'd never found this flat.

'And does this monster have a name?' she said.

David stared off into the distance.

'Reggie. Blood,' he said, without turning to her.

<hr/>

One week later

'Nice ride,' Quentin said as he and David pulled out of the curb.

'My brother has a thing about Ford Escorts. He has four. Loves the cars more than his wife, I think. I'm surprised he lent me the cabriolet,' David said, adding, 'maybe with it being a nice day and all, he was feeling generous.'

The two men drove down the main road of Lacham, enjoying the fresh air and sunshine. Life's good in a convertible, they say.

David decided this was the day he'd pay Reggie Blood a visit, and Quentin said he'd gladly come.

The old bottle was in the boot of the car, along with seven one-litre bottles of water. Six of these were in a shrink-wrapped six-pack, with the seventh on its own.

They'd bought them at their local Tesco yesterday.

David had added a teaspoon of the potion to the seventh bottle.

He resealed the bottle tightly.

The address of Reggie Blood was a caravan park in the quaint seaside village of Holmpton.

Yukiko's dossier on Blood painted a grim picture. He hadn't worked, officially anyway, for at least twenty years. He'd been living off the taxes of the fifty-million-plus workers of the United Kingdom since.

Caravan parks seemed to be his thing. The current one had been his home for about eight years.

Theft, drink-driving, and assault were constant themes on the guy's police records, which covered three quarters of his life. The last time he'd been in jail was for indecent assault of a ten-year-old girl, about twenty-five years ago.

So he'd been lying to himself when he thought he'd been a good man for the past four decades.

⸻

'I'm a long-lost relative. My da's dying wish was for me to visit Reggie and make sure he's doing okay. My da was Reggie's father's brother and all. So here I am.'

David had laid on the Liverpool accent as thick as Marmite. His uncle actually had lived there his entire life, so all he had to do was pretend to be him. It seemed to work.

The woman gave David an ordinary look.

It wasn't him; it was who he was asking about.

Reggie Blood.

She seemed to want to say much, but kept it to, 'Reggie frigging Blood. We booted him out of the park last year. Creepy, creepy man. Sorry to speak badly of him, you being his relative and all.'

David felt as if he'd been punched in the crown jewels. He hadn't minded the drive up from London. The roads were quiet, the sun was shining, and it had given him a chance to get to know Quentin.

David was disappointed he'd not get the chance to see if Finley's potion worked.

And being honest, he wanted to lay eyes on the bastard.

As David nodded silently, muttering a sincere 'thanks anyway,' he turned and walked to the door.

The woman seemed to take pity on him, for as he had the door almost open, she said, 'If you want to see him, I can tell you where he lives now, if he's still there.'

David turned and smiled. 'Thanks. Da will be thankful!'

The Hook's Lane Fishing Pond was a five-minute drive from the Holmpton Seaside Village Caravan Park.

The place had seen much better days.

David pulled up and studied his surroundings. The lake in front of him was no bigger than a regulation Olympic-sized swimming pool, and the water was a murky grey. How fish still lived in it was anyone's guess.

Quentin was the first to spot a small shed on the other side of the lake. Behind this was a large mound of dirt, obviously from when someone had etched out the lake from the ground. Decent sized trees sat behind the mound, which made it look a little mini forest of sorts. The place oozed an eerie, desperate feel.

A pathway stretched from the car park along one side of the pond, where it met up with a shed on the opposite side.

'You want me to come?' Quentin asked.

David studied him for a moment. 'Why don't you wait here?' he said.

As he stepped out of the car, he noticed the concerned look on Quentin's face.

'Believe me. I want to break this guy's face. But I know I can't touch him. It's okay. I assure you I will stick to the plan.'

Quentin smiled. 'I believe you. Don't be too long, huh? The sooner we're out of here, the better.'

'Agree,' David said.

<hr />

No one ever visited Reggie Blood.

Old Morris McDonald, who owned the fish pond, was the only one who'd ever come beyond the mound to where his caravan was. And that was only to hassle the shit out of Reggie for not doing as he'd promised.

But he hadn't come for months.

So when he heard the tap-tap on the caravan door, his bowels tightened violently.

His first instinct was to ignore whoever the hell it was.

He was nursing a hangover as big as the fish pond, and getting out of bed seemed too big a task.

Sod it, he thought.

Tap.

Tap.

BANG.

Now his heart started to race.

Whoever it was had no intention of leaving. The tap on the door had now become even harder.

He decided to pull the dirty blanket over his head and try to pretend he wasn't there.

But the guy knocking had now moved to the front of the caravan and had spotted him through one of the front windows.

'Reggie? Reggie Blood?' the man said.

'What do you want?' Reggie's voice croaked.

'Reggie. My name is Steve. I'm from the Hull City Council. We are on the road checking in with pensioners and the like. People doing it tough. We're handing out rations of water during the warmer months. Thought you'd like some.'

Reggie stared at the guy through the broken window. The man had a smile on his face that was in no hurry to go away.

Reggie eventually sat up and, after catching his breath, watched the man walk back around to the door of the caravan.

One thing he never had a regular supply of was drinking water.

He for a moment wondered if this was a gift from the gods.

'I'm coming,' Reggie coughed before struggling to his feet.

When he opened the caravan door, the man who called himself Steve stood there holding a six-pack of water. Oh, and an extra one too.

'I had a spare one. Thought you could use it,' David said.

He stepped forward and put the bottles of water on the floor of the caravan, literally between Reggie's feet.

Reggie felt uneasy.

It was the way this guy who called himself Steve was staring at him.

His smile was still there, but his eyes had narrowed. The guy had hands the size of baseball mitts, and a part of old Reggie Blood could feel the blood draining from his face.

'Err, thanks.' Reggie had barely said the words before a coughing fit saw him hunched over for a good long while.

David watched the old man coughing and wondered what would be the harm in belting the living shit out of the evil son of a bitch. But a vision of Christine came into his mind, and he knew he couldn't do it. He'd promised her he wouldn't touch the guy.

'Why don't you take the water and get yourself sorted?' David stepped back and knew he needed to leave, or he might end up knocking the old bastard's lights out.

Reggie closed his door and fell back on his bed.

His head hurt and his vision spun for a few moments. His throat was dry. If he could stand up, he'd treat himself to a bottle of drinking water.

'Thanks, Hull City Council,' he muttered.

CHAPTER TWENTY-FIVE

IN THE TWO WEEKS AFTER DAVID AND QUENTIN DROVE out to Holmpton, Yukiko kept working on the list of people who'd worked at the orphanage.

Andrew was into his third week of his two-week trip to the States, and she was starting to feel a niggle in the back of her mind.

The last time they spoke on the phone, he was still pressing her to agree with his demand: move.

Like the others in the downstairs flats of Ravenstone House, she could feel something in her bones that told her to do the opposite: stay.

In the meantime, on another typical Friday in old London town, no one had heard anything further about the goings-on for one sad sack of shit. Reggie Blood.

Between the four of them, they'd watched the papers and listened to the news on the radio and the TV. Every day. They also began to believe the death of a decrepit old man, living in squalor in the countryside, would probably not make any sort of news anyway.

David had suggested he and Quentin drive back up there, pay a visit to the Hook's Lane Fishing Pond, and see how old Reggie was going. But Christine and Mary unanimously agreed that the next road trip of England's version of Starsky and Hutch was not going to happen. All jokes aside, it was too risky.

Being a Friday, David and Christine organised their favourite end-of-the-week spread: fish and chips. Lacham had one of London's oldest chippies, just a stone's throw from Ravenstone House.

David bumped into Mary on his way to fetch dinner, and asked if she and Quentin would like to come over.

'As long as I can bring some beer and wine to wash it all down,' she said excitedly. David had solved her biggest issue of the day: what to have for dinner that night.

When David had walked three feet, he spun around and shouted to Mary, 'You guys like some mushy peas on the side?'

Mary shook her head before smiling. 'If you aren't the best neighbour I've ever had, I don't know who is. Yes please!'

———

Flat One was fast becoming a halfway house of sorts. Quentin and Mary were spending at least one evening a week there, sometimes two. And in a moment, Yukiko would be there too. Christine and David admitted they were enjoying the others' company.

As was the custom in many households around dinner time, the television at Christine and David's flat stayed on, but with the volume down so the guys could chat.

As the four chinked their wines and bottles of beer, Quentin toasted, 'To the weekend.'

A moment later there came a knock on the door.

Yukiko had come for another reason, but the four refused

to take no for an answer when she tried to decline their offer of dinner.

After she'd finished eating, she said, 'I have a few additions to my list, and information.'

'Do tell,' Christine said.

Yukiko produced another list. With the revisions, it was now twenty names long.

When she showed David, he let out an exhausted 'Phew.'

Were they supposed to dispose of all twenty?

Was this the only way to free the spirits of Finley, Heather, and all the other poor souls trapped somewhere below?

'I thought there would have been more,' Yukiko said. 'The orphanage operated for thirty or so years.'

Christine nodded, 'Maybe there were many who weren't even on an employee list.'

Mary leant forward and agreed. 'Yukiko, do you think more names will appear through your searches? I guess at some point the names have to run out.'

Yukiko shook her head, 'I'm not sure, to be honest. My searches are in specific records from the City of Wandsworth archives. I don't know if I'll find other records or documents with more lists of names and so forth. Maybe. Maybe not.'

David sat forward, and after taking a long drink from his beer he said, 'You're doing a fine job, Yukiko. Whatever you can find is helpful.'

Yukiko sat back and took a drink of her wine.

'There's a few other things I've found out,' she announced to the four neighbours.

'Maybe you'll need another glass of wine if you're going to do some more talking,' Christine said.

Yukiko smiled as Christine leant over and gave her a big refill.

———

'So this name—Leitner. It seems to be repeated regularly. At least two times, as far as the employment records.'

David and Quentin shared a frightened look. Both men seemed to go a lighter shade of pale.

Mary was first to see the men react to the name.

'One was in charge of this place, right?' she asked Quentin before he nodded and took a big drink of his beer.

When he swallowed it all, he cleared his throat and said, 'Old happy-go-lucky bitchface—' He suddenly wondered if she'd come out of the ceiling and smack him around the ears.

He continued as David watched on intently. 'When she came down to the basement to say hello, she made a big deal of the name. Well, the one who was on the first list, Josef, I think? She said he was the boss. Screamed it, in fact.'

David continued where Quentin left off. 'My gut feel is he was most probably,' he found himself shaking his head at the horrific thought, 'the ringleader.'

After some silence, Yukiko said, 'I'm afraid to tell you, this is how it looks from what I've found so far. I'm going to continue digging,' Yukiko took another drink from her wine, 'but what we may have here was a group of people who actively abused, and murdered these children, and did it together. What's more, it may have been run by a family.'

As the other four mumbled various words to each other, more profanities and words of disgust, Yukiko put her hand up.

'There was one other thing, not important at this point in time, but interesting all the same,' she said.

Quentin, Mary, and Christine all had their eyes glued to Yukiko. David was now staring at the television.

A second later, without a word, he jumped to his feet and shuffled over to the TV, turning up the volume.

'This family vanished off the face of the earth in 1955. One year before Ravenstone House closed down for good. And when I mean vanished,' Yukiko leant forward to make her point, 'I mean evaporated. It was as if they'd never existed. And believe me,' she smiled, 'if I have lost their trail, it means they have must have moved to the moon, or maybe Mars.'

'Or maybe someone took care—' Quentin went to say, but was cut short by David shouting, 'Guys, guys! Check this out.'

'In other news tonight,' the anchor said, 'comes the mysterious death of seventy-year-old Reginald Arthur Blood, from Holmpton, Kingston upon Hull.'

David was literally holding his breath.

As footage of the Hook's Lane Fishing Pond was shown to the left side of the news anchor, the five stood watching a crane pulling a caravan out of the pond.

David gasped.

Reggie Blood's caravan was upside down, being pulled out by its axle.

'Locals say Reginald Blood was a drifter who's lived on the grounds of the fishing pond for about a year. But mystery surrounds how his caravan, with him in it, came to be upside down in the water. And what's more, it appears all the fish in the pond wound up dead too.'

The news anchor referred to his notes before meeting the camera again.

'Authorities claim there was no sign at all of the caravan being moved from its original position. They have so far found no tyre marks, no drag marks, or any evidence of heavy haulage entering the property to move it either. It was as if his caravan simply rose in the air of its own volition before taking seventy-year-old Reginald Blood to a watery death.'

David spent a while staring at Quentin. Neither man could get the vision of the old bottle sitting in the middle of the ring out of his head.

Finley's liquid had avenged its first death.

CHAPTER TWENTY-SIX

After Yukiko finished her wine, she told the others she had to go back to her flat to get ready for Andrew's call. From her demeanour, they could tell she would have preferred to stay and drink another bottle of wine on her own. Probably straight from the bottle too.

After she left, they talked quietly about what they all thought of Andrew. At that moment, he was not part of the inner sanctum of Operation Revenge. And from the sounds of what Yukiko had said about her husband, he would not be any time soon.

As the night began to drift towards bedtime, David surprised the other three by coming straight out and saying it.

'We need to find another, and now. It will prove to us all —one hundred per cent, if Finley's potion works.' He took a drink of his beer before concluding, 'This is the only way. What do you all think?'

'If these monsters are still alive, they don't deserve to be. No amount of jail time will cut it. If they're old, the authorities will give these people a slap on the wrist. Or better still for them, they'll end up in some low-security jail with a tennis court, VHS movies every Saturday night, and probably a foot rub once a month,' Mary said.

As Mary's words hung in the air, it was Christine's turn.

'They did unspeakable things to those poor, defenceless kids.'

As the tears formed in her eyes, she met David's look and said, 'You want to know why we're here? Why we bought this flat?' David went to say something, but Christine answered for him. 'Fate.'

They sat in silence with the word ringing in their ears.

'Christine,' Mary sat forward with resolve, 'maybe it's our turn to visit the basement,' she said.

Quentin shook his head, but Mary waved him off.

'I want to hear it straight from the children,' she said.

'Okay. If you guys want to go down there, that's fine. But before we call it a night, two more items on the agenda,' David said. 'Let's pick another name from the list, now. And tomorrow, we will meet for lunch to reconvene.'

'John Heen.' David had asked for the corner table at the cafe, which was well away from other people.

'Address?' Quentin said.

He'd already memorised it.

'Last known address was in West Worthing, down south,' David said.

As the cafe grew busier, they lowered their voices.

'Where's *Get Smart*'s cone of silence when you need it?' David laughed.

Christine gave him a slap on the arm for the lame joke.

'What do we know about this one?' Mary asked.

'Fifty-seven years old,' David said.

'Blimey. How old was he when he worked there?' Quentin asked.

'He started in 1950, at seventeen. He stayed there until its closure in '56. He married in 1965, had two boys, twins. His wife only lasted six years before she packed her bags and, with her two sons in tow, upped and left him,' David said.

'Do we know why?' Mary said.

'Let's just say, from Yukiko's dossier, the police reports from the time painted a fairly unsavoury picture of the man,' David said.

'Lunch will be here soon, my darling husband. Get on with it,' Christine said.

'The wife came home one day early from work, unexpected,' said David.

'When she walked in the door, she heard muffled noises upstairs. Upon investigating, her husband and the twins were not anywhere to be found, not in the boys' room or her bedroom.

'Well there was only one other place they could have been. Not thinking anything of it, she waltzed into the bathroom. She expected to see the twins to be in the bath and her husband sitting on the edge supervising.'

David shook his head.

'But when she walked in, he was not sitting on the edge of the bath.'

None of the other three spoke. So David came straight out and said it.

'I told you how old the boys were,' David said. 'Five years old. Well, their father was in the bath too. All three were naked.'

As they all took a deep breath, David held up his hand.

'The mother, as per the police report, said there was something else. And this was the reason she pulled the plug and left him for good. And also why the police laid charges on him.

'There was no water in the bath.'

———

Lunch took longer than usual.

No one complained. After David went through the rest of the dossier on Heen, they were in no hurry to eat.

John Heen remarried, but his second wife found out about his past. She thanked the Lord above she'd borne no children to him, packed her bags, and moved to Ireland—never to return.

By the time John Heen had turned the ripe old age of fifty, he'd been single longer than he'd been married. A cancer scare, due to his lifelong addiction to cigarettes, saw karma appearing to knock on his door.

But as he got the all-clear on the cancer, he made a cocky comment to a fellow patron at his local pub. 'I've done some bad things in my life, but I've been forgiven. I'll grow old and see my days out drinking beer here with you.'

Fate must have been listening. Or was it karma?

John Heen was diagnosed with early-onset Alzheimer's six months later.

Seven years later, the guy was still hanging on, but the incurable disease was taking its grip.

Mary would tell the others what she knew of the disease. It was a terrible and tragic affliction that rarely, if ever, had a happy ending. He could live for years to come, though not in the greatest of health.

And with him now in care at the Worthing Respite Centre, West Worthing, ideas flowed as to how to get to him.

As lunch ended and the bill was paid, one person

gingerly put her hand up and said, 'There's only one person sitting here with the credentials to get into the place.'

Nurse Mary.

But she wanted to do one thing first, before she paid Heen a visit.

Talk to the children he murdered.

CHAPTER TWENTY-SEVEN

'Are you sure you want to do this?' Quentin asked.

Mary stood at the basin in their bathroom and studied her fiancé in the mirror.

'Visit the basement, or visit a murderer?' she replied.

Quentin stood against the edge of the doorway and studied her.

'I feel a connection to the spirits of those poor children,' she said. 'When I came into contact with Heather the first time, it was as if she touched something in my soul. I know this all sounds a bit like I've been smoking some seriously good weed,' she smiled at him, 'but I feel we ended up here for a reason.'

'And the reason is, honey?' he said.

'To finish this,' she said.

<hr/>

Christine was still wearing a plaster cast, but her broken arm was coming along well, and she no longer needed a sling.

David and Quentin briefed the women on every detail of

the basement, leaving nothing out. David's suggestion they tag along was shot down.

Three times, he told them not to step into the ring.

The third time, they told him they believed they'd got the message.

The men would wait in David and Christine's apartment, counting down the minutes with a cup of tea and an unspecified amount of shortbread biscuits, with some Premier League on the telly.

Torches were checked and double checked. Suitable clothing, akin to what you might wear for a dog-sled race across the North Pole, was worn. The women were ready.

'Remember, if the old bag turns up, get the hell out of there. Or,' Quentin smirked, 'at least ask her to brush her teeth.'

Mary and Christine rolled their eyes in unison.

David's dad jokes were unfortunately rubbing off on Q.

'Shit,' Christine said when they arrived in the basement, 'this place is next-level creepy.'

Mary could feel the cold even with two layers of clothing on.

'Christ, and they say the North Pole is cold,' she said through chattering teeth.

With no working lights, they shone their torches around and could feel their senses going into overdrive.

Mary moved to the first room before standing in the open doorway.

'The ring room,' she said to Christine.

They spotted the closed door of the coat-rack room.

The men said Heather would appear first, then Finley.

When the women had been standing there nearly five minutes, they were about to turn around and go upstairs.

'Nurse Mary.'

Her voice was so distant, Christine and Mary locked eyes on each other to ensure it wasn't their imagination.

'Nurse Mary.'

They spun around and felt a sense of relief.

Heather stood in the middle of the room, smiling.

'Hello, Heather,' Mary said.

The girl walked towards her before lifting her arms into the air.

When Mary hugged her, something told her it couldn't be possible, to feel contact with a spirit of someone who was dead.

Christine leant down to hug Heather too, with one arm, and a moment later could feel the most unusual feeling coursing through her body.

'Would you like to speak to Finley?' Heather said. A rhetorical question.

'Yes, we would like to speak to Finley,' Mary smiled, 'if it's not too much trouble.'

Heather nodded before raising her hand to her mouth and failing to stifle a tiny giggle.

'Finley thinks you're pretty,' Heather said.

Mary could feel herself blush.

'It's okay, Nurse Mary. Finley knows you're going to marry Quentin one day. He likes him too.'

'What are you saying, you cheeky little thing?' Finley had appeared out of the shadows. Both women blinked. They'd not even see him appear.

'Finley, we'd like to ask you something, if it's okay with you.' Mary wasted no time getting on with it.

She could feel the cold slowly working its way into her bones.

Finley walked a couple of paces and stood next to Heather.

As was his custom, he reached over and put his hand on her shoulder.

'Go ahead, Mary,' Finley said. 'What is it you'd like to ask me?'

—

It took Mary a couple of minutes to articulate what she wanted to say. What she hoped for was to speak to the children who had come into contact with John Heen. She couldn't explain why, other than that she wanted to know the extent of his evil ways.

'I suggest we maybe step out of this room and go out there.' Finley indicated where the cages were.

'They don't like this room, do they?' Christine asked.

Finley stared at her for a long time before he finally said, 'That's not why I am suggesting out there.'

—

Mary had instinctively decided to kneel on the floor.

She didn't want to intimidate the children.

After a few minutes with Christine by her side, Finley walked out of the ring room and said, 'If you could turn off your torches for a moment.'

Mary gulped. Pitch black was not one of her favourite things in life. Especially down here. She could hear Christine hiss as if taking a sharp intake of air. She obviously felt the same.

But they did as Finley requested.

CHAPTER TWENTY-EIGHT

When Finley spoke, he sounded a thousand miles away.

'You may turn your torches on now,' he said.

Ending the torture of the darkness was a welcome relief.

Mary was able to get her torch on first, but dropped it a moment later.

She now realised why meeting the children had to happen out of the smaller rooms.

She couldn't believe the number of them standing there.

Heather stepped out of the shadows and faced the two women.

'You wanted to talk to the children who came into contact with John Heen,' she said.

Mary rose to her feet. There were at least three dozen children standing there looking at her.

Mary said, 'John Heen killed you all?"

Every child stared at her before turning their innocent little faces in Finley's direction.

They locked their eyes on him and did not waver.

Finley stepped forward and spoke.

'Mary and Christine are our friends. They're going to

help us get to where we belong. Can I ask, any of you, if the man called John Heen made you come to me, for our friends here, please put one of your hands up in the air.'

It took a few seconds. But when the last little arm went up into the air, Christine reached for Mary's hand.

At best guess, Mary surmised at least three quarters of the children put their hands up.

'Oh, sweet Lord,' Christine said.

It was the look on their faces.

The deepest sadness she'd ever seen.

It's not our fault.

We did nothing wrong.

Mary nudged Christine. 'Hold it together. We need to get through this,' she said.

Christine nodded before taking a deep breath.

'This man, John Heen—I will be visiting him soon, children. I am going to make sure he is taken from this earth, as he so wrongfully did to you all,' Mary said.

She turned to Finley and said, 'Would it be okay if a few of these children spoke to me individually? I would like to know what John Heen did.'

Finley studied Mary before eventually turning to the children.

'I know this may be difficult for you all. But Mary would like to talk to some of you, to find out more about the evil man, John Heen. Who would like to talk to our good friend, Nurse Mary?'

Bless those beautiful children, Christine thought.

They all put their hands back up.

Four days later

Christine drove another Ford Cortina down Lacham High Road, after picking up one of her brother-in-law's four beloved Cortinas from his place in Wandsworth.

Sitting next to her was Mary.

David and Quentin fiercely debated the decision to have the two women drive down to West Worthing to pay Mr John Heen, mass murderer of children, a visit at his respite hospital. But when Mary first proposed the cover plan, both men couldn't disagree that it was a good idea.

The men's worry was more about the women's safety than anything else. But as Mary said, a man bedridden with Alzheimer's is probably a low risk.

Still, when David reminded the two how many times he'd killed, they did see his point.

Mary's original idea of waltzing through the doorway as Nurse Mary was replaced with a much better idea.

Christine would pose as Heen's second wife.

Mary would be the miracle child Heen had fathered but his wife had never told him about.

They practised Irish accents ad nauseam, and once the two women believed they could pass themselves off as residents of the land of Guinness and green pastures, they felt good to go.

So their story went, they were visiting Heen to tell him they'd forgiven him for being a creep and to introduce his long-estranged daughter to him, now he was on his way to the next life.

Mary said this was the one of the times she hoped there were such a place as Hell. Men like Heen belonged nowhere else.

The potion, this time, went into a small bottle of drinking water.

It found its way into Christine's well-proportioned handbag.

The traffic en route to West Worthing was light for a Wednesday, which suited Christine fine. With the sun out, the greenness of the land was nice.

'It's beautiful down here, isn't it,' Mary said while looking out the window.

Christine glanced at Mary quickly, prompting her to look over.

'You left out many of the stories the children told us, when you were telling Quentin and David,' she said. It was more of a statement, but had a hint of question to it.

Mary stared at Christine for a time before turning her gaze back to the view passing her by.

'If the boys heard what we heard, I think they would have come down to West Worthing and made a right mess of this guy's face.'

Christine watched the road in front as the continued down the A24. Although she could see the road in front of her, the faces of all those children were there too.

'Finley said he was one of the worst,' she said.

Mary did something out of character a second later.

She punched the passenger's-side door seal, startling Christine.

'What chance did these kids ever have?' she turned, and Christine could see the anger in her eyes, 'especially when two men teamed up?'

They drove on for another few miles before Mary shook her head.

'The sick bastard had something about baths, right?' She didn't wait for Christine to say anything and continued. 'He'd take a bath with the kids.' She gritted her teeth. 'They wouldn't have known any different. They wouldn't have questioned it.'

Christine reached over and placed her hand on Mary's shoulder. Mary was probably recalling what the three of the spirits of the children had told her.

'But there were five of them in the bath. He told them to be still so they wouldn't spill the bathwater,' Mary went on, her voice full of cold rage, as though she'd have liked to stop but fury pushed her forward. 'But how could you? One of them flinched from him and spilled the water, so he—' She started crying. 'He drowned him. And then, because they screamed, he drowned the others, one by one, with their friends looking on, as another man stopped them getting away.'

The white of Christine's knuckles showed through the skin as she gripped the wheel.

CHAPTER TWENTY-NINE

The West Worthing Respite Centre had seen better days. Built in the early 70s, it obviously hadn't been made over since.

The smell of iodoform, the most commonly used disinfectant in hospitals, was particularly strong here. Where she worked, it wasn't this pungent. It filled her nostrils and only heightened the undercurrent of anxiety coursing through her veins.

Christine had told Mary, when they'd pulled into the carpark, to let her do all the talking. She told Mary to come across as the subordinate daughter. Don't make eye contact with anyone, come across as a bit shy, and so on. Christine would take the lead until they got into Heen's room.

The two nurses at the reception desk smiled when Christine introduced herself, though Mary could see the disdain in their eyes at the mere mention of the name John Heen.

They checked notes, and Christine for a moment wondered if they would let her and Mary see him.

When she turned to look over to Mary, Mary herself saw the two nurses whisper to each other. When one shrugged her shoulders a moment later, the body language said it all.

They wondered why a long-lost divorcée would bother visiting an ex-husband after all these years, regardless of the whole long-lost daughter thing, but decided—what do they care?

'Room 19. Turn left at the end of this hall. Last room, right side, at the end of Wing A. We'd thought Mr Heen could use some peace and quiet. There's no other patient currently in Wing A.'

Christine wondered why the nurse had told her all this.

Maybe she wanted the guy's ex-wife to know they didn't like him, and had put him as far away from the staff and other patients as they could.

When Christine turned to see if Mary had heard what the nurse had said to her, the look on Mary's face confirmed it. Both women knew what the other was thinking at that very moment.

—

Wing A of the West Worthing Respite Centre was as eerie as the basement of Ravenstone House. The hallway lights were either out of action or deliberately turned off. Most of the rooms leading off the wing had their doors shut.

The smell too—it was a mixture of iodoform and something else that Mary couldn't put her finger on. Whatever it was, it was uncomfortable to her senses.

Their footsteps were quiet, but if you were the only person in the wing, you would have heard the sound.

As they walked closer to Room 19, they heard what sounded like a squawk. 'It's about bloody time. You nurses are supposed to tend to me more than once a day.' The voice came from somewhere distant.

Mary and Christine met each other's eyes and took a

deep breath. They wished they hadn't, with the smell, but it was too late.

———

The eyes of the patient in Room 19 were fixed on the open doorway.

When Christine reached it, she could see the surprise in his eyes at the sight of a complete stranger.

At fifty-seven years old, the guy had clearly seen better days, Christine thought.

His skin was a sickly ashen pallor, shiny from his large forehead down to the thick brow above his eyes, which reminded her of a ferret's—small, dark, and beady.

He was as skinny as a rake, his cheekbones pronounced and with dirty stubble covering a large chin and the bottom half of his face. When he opened his mouth, his teeth revealed a lifelong romance with cigarettes. Yellow and crooked.

Thin, ghostly-white, and unkempt hair straddled the sides of his skull, and a wisp of the stuff seemed to be ready to float away on the top, adrift on a sea of baldness.

Christine was not a supermodel, by any means. But this guy must have worked at the cookie factory where they pressed his face into the dough to make ugly biscuits, she thought.

'Who the fuck are you?' he barked, though his voice was meagre.

'Darling,' Christine walked into the room proper.

Oh, kill me now, she suddenly thought.

The smell.

Either the guy had pissed himself about a week ago and they hadn't changed the sheets, or he hadn't had a shower in months.

He reeked.

Christine, focused on the mission, pushed on.

'It's Patty,' she bellowed in an Irish twang, 'come to wish you all the best in the afterlife, and to bring someone you may want to meet before you go.'

Mary, now at the doorway, was quietly impressed. Christine should be an actress on the BBC, she thought. She had it nailed.

When Christine moved to the end of the bed, it took him a full minute to realise there was someone else now standing in the doorway.

'Patty?' Heen was clearly confused. He stared at Mary for a long time, and when he eventually spoke, spittle came out of his mouth along with his words. Charming.

'Who the hell are—'

What broke his sentence off was a distant memory. He was having a moment of coherence, but it wouldn't last long.

'Patty?' He lifted himself into a more upright sitting position.

When Heen saw Mary move from the corner of his eye, he glanced at her for a moment before turning back to Christine.

'Patty, you walked out on me twenty years ago. What the hell are you doing here now?'

The venom in his voice was weak, but it was still there.

Christine stood silently for a few moments. For a second, she was about to drop the act, but realised she'd have to keep it up for a moment, especially in case one of the nurses decided to come and check on the only patient in Ward A.

They wouldn't.

'I'm glad to see you too,' she rested both hands on the railing of the bed. 'I see you haven't lost your tongue.'

Heen sat staring at her with those sneaky little beady eyes.

Christine took a short breath. The smell of him was strong, and if she'd taken a deeper one, she might have brought up her breakfast.

'I came today so your daughter,' she turned and smiled at Mary, 'our daughter, could come and meet you. And say goodbye.'

Heen's eyes didn't stray from Christine. He kept staring at her. What Christine didn't know, was what was going on behind those beady little eyes of his. The pilot light of coherence was slowly being blown out.

'A daughter? I have a fucking daughter? You told me you couldn't get pregnant. Now you're here all these years later with some kid and you say it's mine?'

Mary decided to jump into the theatrical fray.

'Daddy, you shouldn't speak to mammy mean. It's not nice.'

Heen cast his little ferret eyes at Mary.

A small but noticeable grin slipped across his face.

'If you're my daughter, come a little closer and don't be shy,' he said.

Mary could feel the hairs on her neck prickling. The guy was the creepiest human being she'd ever been in the presence of.

She caught a glimpse of Christine, who was watching her with apprehension.

Mary took a couple of steps forward. The smell now was overbearing. No one in her hospital had ever given off such an odour. No wonder they put this guy in his own ward.

While Mary had Heen's attention, Christine scoped the scene in front of her. What she'd had hoped for was something close to him, a cup or glass on his bedside table with water in it. She would figure out a way to get some of her water in his. He would drink it, and if Finley's potion did what it was promised to do, the creep would die.

181

His bedside table was sparse. A box of tissues, empty. Packets of one-serve biscuits, empty. A women's magazine, years old.

When she spotted it, her heart skipped a beat.

A cup with a straw.

But there was a slight problem.

It was lying on its side, empty.

She turned her attention back to Mary, who'd inched a couple of feet closer. Her body language spoke volumes. She was feeling very uncomfortable being this close to him.

Heen patted the side of his bed closest to Mary and smirked. 'Why don't you come and sit, pretty daughter, so your old man can see you better.'

Mary turned and glared at Christine.

She didn't want to get any closer to him than she was.

'I won't bite, you know.' Heen's tone said otherwise.

Mary shook her head. 'If it's okay with you,' she now stood right next to his bed, 'I may just stand here instead.'

Heen nodded.

As a sickening grin appeared and dribble crept out of his mouth, he suddenly lunged forward.

His hand sprang out and landed directly between Mary's legs. A second later, John Heen was groping Mary's crotch.

It happened so quickly, it took Mary a good two seconds to realise what the decrepit old man was doing.

She jumped two feet into the air before swinging her arm and hitting Heen's forearm at full tilt.

'You filthy old man!' Mary screamed.

She grabbed his chest with both hands. His hospital gown was soaked in sweat.

As she began to shake him, Christine sprang into action.

She dropped her handbag on the floor, and it fell open to reveal its contents.

Spotting the drink bottle, she knew this could be her

opportunity to break up the stoush, offer him some water, and slap the son of a bitch in the face before walking out.

But as her hand reached the bottle, she gasped.

The bottle was empty.

⸺

'You've gotta be kidding me,' Christine said to herself.

As Mary continued to hurl abuse at Heen, Christine's head spun at a thousand miles an hour.

All the theatrics had been a complete waste of time.

She cursed herself for not checking the lid of the bottle before slipping it into her handbag.

She decided it was time to get out of there.

She jumped to Mary's side of Heen's bed.

Mary had the guy by the scruff of his pyjamas and was verbally abusing him. She knew Mary's anger was coming more from her knowledge of his actions at the orphanage than from him groping her.

'Enough!' Christine pulled Mary back.

As Mary let go of Heen, she said, 'You will burn in hell for what you've done. Trust me, bathtub boy.'

Christine led Mary to the entrance of his room and said, 'We're done. Wait here.'

Christine turned and realised her handbag was still sitting on the floor at the end of Heen's bed.

Christine took the four or so steps there, and as she did, took one last look at Heen.

The guy was staring at her as if he was wondering what the big deal was.

They locked eyes on each other.

For a second, Christine felt as if he knew she wasn't Patty.

The grin was back, and it made her want to step over and smack him in the teeth.

When she turned her attention to her handbag, she saw something else.

Then, glancing back up to Heen, she saw the guy was sweating—bad.

Christine was about to put on the best performance of her life.

She pulled her handbag up and stole a glance over to the entrance of the room. Mary was standing out in the hallway, her back turned.

Christine stepped over to the side of Heen's bed.

'You're being a little naughty, Mr Heen,' Christine said.

He sat back and made (as she hoped) the fatal mistake of thinking she was playing down his disgusting actions of a moment ago. With, of all people, his very own 'daughter'.

As she smiled at him, Heen replicated the expression on his own ugly face.

She watched his right hand twitch, knowing at any moment he could do the same thing to her as he'd done to Mary. But she stepped right next to him and put her right hand firmly on his. He would not be groping her today.

'Now, now, John.' Christine dropped her left hand into her handbag and pushed aside the few items in there to get to what she wanted.

A packet of tissues.

Now drenched in the water from the bottle.

When she'd spotted them a few moments ago, the idea was hatched.

'You're sweating—here.' She pulled out the tissues, which were practically dripping wet.

She hurriedly ran the soaking tissues all over his face.

When she got to his mouth, he started to gag.

His face was turning red. All she could do now was hope and pray.

Christine let go and took a step back. The tissues were still stuck to the man's face.

'What the fuck are you trying to do, Patty, drown me?' Heen barked. As he pulled the wet tissues away, Christine was sure her plan had worked.

'I think I left my keys in the car,' Christine said, and started to walk out of the room.

'You always were a fucking bitch,' Heen bellowed, before he lost sight of Christine.

He closed his eyes and wondered what the Christ had just happened. He took a deep breath and thought, at least I got a grope of the young one, and it felt good—

A presence in the room startled him, and his eyelids flew open.

His daughter.

It was Mary.

She hit him so hard in the nose, she broke it in two places.

CHAPTER THIRTY

UNLIKE HIS PALS REGGIE BLOOD AND JOHN HEEN, seventy-five-year-old Archie Glaggin had somehow etched out what appeared to be a normal existence.

Married for forty-plus years, with three adult children, five grandchildren, and a career as long as his marriage, driving trains, nothing on the outside of Archie's life betrayed his time at Ravenstone House for the Less Privileged.

He blamed the Leitner family for his sins.

But that was rolled-gold bullshit.

He'd fantasised about what he eventually did at Ravenstone way before he'd set foot through its front doors.

He quit the orphanage in 1955, one year before it closed.

He hoped that when its doors shut forever, it would hold in all the deep, dark, and horrible sins that had taken place within its four walls, some of which involved him.

He'd found God within five years of leaving Ravenstone. And having confessed his sins to the almighty being above, he believed he'd atoned for them.

Glaggin moved to Glasgow not long after quitting his job at the orphanage. There, he laid bricks as he had in one of his many jobs before the orphanage, but returned to the borough of Wandsworth in the year the world lost the U.S. president John F. Kennedy. 1963.

And for the last twenty-seven years, he had lived in Tooting, which, ironically, is two miles from Ravenstone House.

Funnily enough, Glaggin had made it a habit never to venture into Lacham, especially Lacham High Road. It was as if by laying eyes on Ravenstone House, it would be able to spot him, and would scream out what it knew.

But from time to time, especially with his wife working part time as a volunteer in Lacham, just around the corner from Ravenstone, it couldn't be avoided.

So when he'd noticed some time ago that the place was draped in scaffolding, and surrounded by men in hard hats in the midst of feverish activity, his heart sank to the depths of the tunnels his trains would travel through when he worked for the Tube.

His intuition served him well.

Ravenstone was coming after him.

━━

David and Quentin donned their detective hats.

Glaggin's address was a street in Tooting, only a couple of miles away.

It looked like many others of the ubiquitous row houses in the suburb, where some streets were near identical to others. But Glaggin's house was at the very end of his street, affording him the rare opportunity for a double garage, which fronted onto the side street next to his home.

When David and Quentin strolled past one sunny Saturday morning, they spotted Glaggin working on an old rust bucket of a bygone era, in his messy and very disorganised garage. Both doors were open, and Glaggin had pulled a trolley and other items out onto the sidewalk.

Tools, a couple of tyres, and a rusting old forty-four-gallon drum: the crap practically blocked the pavement for anyone trying to walk past.

If David and Quentin hadn't checked the guy out, David would have been tempted to tell him to clear all the shit off the pavement. It was a hazard for God's sake, Glaggin.

As if Glaggin had read David's thought on the matter as he walked past, he pulled his head out of the bonnet of the old car and offered an apology of sorts.

'Sorry for the mess, gents. I've got too much stuff in me old garage to get around the old beast.' He smiled as David waved off his apology.

'It's no big deal. We can walk around it,' David said, and a second later disappeared from view.

And with those words, Glaggin returned to the engine bay of his old rust bucket. David and Quentin walked on, and David started to formulate a plan for Mr Archie Glaggin.

In the end, it didn't matter. The plan would not go ahead.

⬜

Bradley Fletcher was the last remaining name on the original list. Quentin, Mary, and Christine pondered the news about where he lived after David had checked the origins of his address in his copy of the *AA Road Atlas*.

Fletcher lived on a farmlet not far out of Bangor, Wales. To drive from Lacham to Bangor was a smidgen over five hours.

David felt as if he couldn't ask his brother for another lend of one of his Cortinas. But the only other option was to hire a car, and that was voted down. It would be a trail that could be followed if a local saw the hire car at Fletcher's farmlet.

So with a boxful of his brother's favourite beer delivered to his door, and assurances the petrol tank would be full to the brim when the car was returned, David borrowed Cortina number three. The brown one.

The next issue was one of human resources.

Who would take the leisurely five-hour drive up to Wales?

They quickly binned the idea of drawing straws, and with no clear way to decide who would go and who would stay, the final decision was made.

Road-trip time, people.

With an overnight bag packed and now in the boot of the baby-shit-brown Cortina, which came with an equally appalling dark-brown leather-look top, the foursome met at 7am sharp on yet another Saturday in their hometown of Lacham.

The plan was straightforward, as far as logistics went. If they achieved their goal and made some sort of contact with Fletcher, they agreed they would drive back home as soon as the deed was done. If they didn't catch him, they'd stay overnight somewhere and hope he was home the next morning.

As they had previously, when two of the four had set off on a similar mission, they recorded the dossier—in this case for Fletcher—to memory and then disposed of it. This included the address. David seemed to have a photographic memory when it came to addresses, so remembering it was his thing.

With five long hours of road to navigate and only a handful of cassette tapes in the glovebox of Cortina number three, they had plenty of time to talk about everything and anything.

———

As they left the outskirts of London, David knew it was time.

He abruptly pushed the eject button on the tape player, to everyone else's groans.

'You cannot stop Phil Collins,' Mary barked from the rear. '*But Seriously* is one of his best albums ever!'

Christine shot him a dirty look as she spotted David taking an unlabelled cassette from the center console.

'It better not be Iron Maiden,' Christine said, a mock look of anger on her face, 'or you will meet another Iron Maiden in about three seconds flat, my dear.'

David shook his head enthusiastically, the smile on his face threatening to split his cheeks in two. 'This is a special treat for you all, now we're going on a road trip together for the first time.' He grinned.

As the cassette player gobbled up tape and they heard the ding-dong sound at the start, the other three sat glued to the speakers.

A second later, Christine wished it actually had been Iron Maiden.

When the accordion started to pump out of the speakers, Mary and Quentin met each other's eyes and wondered, 'What the—?'

But their puzzlement faded as a lady started to sing a merry folk song: 'Didn't we have a lovely time—'

Christine leant over and cuffed David in the back of the head.

'Our neighbours are too young to be put through the torture of Fiddler's Dram!' Christine laughed as David sang along at the top of his voice.

He checked out the scene in the rear-view mirror, and

when he saw Quentin and Mary staring at him as if he'd lost his marbles, he laughed harder than they'd seen him do thus far.

'Well,' he turned the song down, 'we are on our way to Bangor, and it is a lovely day. Not sure about the lunch for under a pound, though.'

Mercifully, he pulled the tape out a second later and put Phil Collins back on.

<hr>

After Phil Collins weaved his musical genius on sides A and B, David left the music off for a while.

Christine sat sideways so she could better see Q and Mary sitting in the back seat.

'Bradley Fletcher. Another candidate for employee of the year at the Ravenstone House for the Less Privileged,' she said.

Mary and Quentin nodded. They'd heard snippets about the man, but not the full story.

'On the first look, another one who walked away and got on with his life as if Ravenstone House, and its depraved secrets, never existed.'

'How old is he now?' Mary asked.

Christine met David's eyes for a second, but he said nothing.

'He's due to turn seventy in a couple of weeks, the dossier told us.'

'Family?' Quentin inquired.

'You'd start to think there is a bit of repetition going on here,' Christine said.

David nodded. He knew what she meant.

'Another divorcée. I'm starting to think all these wives

may have found out about their husband's past? It seems to be a pattern.'

'Glaggin's still married,' David said.

'Well, he's the rarity,' Christine responded quickly.

She adjusted her seat belt so she could get more comfortable.

'Wife left him twenty years ago. Yukiko's file said she got on the next ship heading for Australia and never returned. The woman now lives in Perth, along with their two children. By all accounts, they haven't set foot in England since. They have no contact with him.'

Christine took in the view through the rear window of the Cortina, behind Quentin and Mary. For a moment, she was thousands of miles away, in Australia. She'd travelled there twice. It was a beautiful place.

'You've gotta ask yourself once again,' Christine met Quentin and Mary's eyes, 'the guy's kids disowned him. And his wife did the same?'

Mary nodded. 'What gets me is these guys are not in jail where they belong. So all their families and partners seem to maybe have realised they are all creeps, but still they walk free.'

As the car fell into silence, David chimed in. 'Apart from what the dossier tells us,' he took a long and careful deep breath, 'I'll admit to you all now I found out more about this one, Fletcher, from Finley.'

David spent the next few moments talking about Fletcher. He did his best to convey what Finley had told him without giving all the details. He didn't think they would take it well.

Fletcher had a thing about lollipops.

He'd been known in the orphanage as the lollipop man. He seemed to always have a perpetual supply in his bag.

This was how he got the kids into a room alone. But then

he would use the lollipops in a way you weren't supposed to. And when he wanted to try and get one of the kids downstairs into the basement, he would offer five in one go.

What was most heartbreaking was a few of kids agreed to the bribe—so they could eventually share the lollipops with their roommates. They never got the chance.

Quentin surprised the other three with his fury.

'When we stop off at the next service station for petrol,' he hissed, 'I'm going to find the biggest lollipop they sell. And when I get to meet this one Fletcher, I'm going to take the fucking lollipop and shove it up his—'

Mary put her hand firmly on his leg. Cutting in, she said, 'Hold it together, Q. It's okay.' She leant over and kissed him on the cheek. 'We'll make sure Fletcher pays for his sins. Hopefully today.'

CHAPTER THIRTY-ONE

THE FARMLET WAS WELL HIDDEN, NESTLED ON THE other side of the forest they'd driven through. If you drove five miles faster, you'd miss it for sure. The entrance of the property was actually in the forest itself. The small road snaked its way out and into some limited open land.

Either Fletcher had gone to pains to hide his little place from the outside world, or he'd become extremely complacent in the upkeep of the trees, vines, and anything else that grew on his property.

The guys debated a raft of ideas to get the potion and Fletcher doing the tango, and decided to roll with things as they unfolded when they got there. Christine and Mary would be in charge of the potion, held in two drink bottles.

David pulled the Cortina through the impossibly narrow entrance, the gates open but long overgrown with vegetation. He thanked himself for not being in something wider like a Jag. It wouldn't have fit.

The Cortina crawled its way around a small bend with the forest hanging ominously overhead, and the small house finally came into view.

David and Christine both let out a small gasp when they left the forest and entered the clearing.

The house was a shit-fight, to be blunt. Bradley Fletcher was either a straight-out hoarder in his advancing years, or he didn't care about the garbage and crap that almost suffocated the front of his house in all directions.

A well-worn two-door Mini, looking close to death, sat in a tiny clearing that led to the front door of the cottage. The car was more rust than metal.

Whatever would happen to lollipop man, when he left this life someone would probably throw a match to the place. Clearing the land of all the garbage, overgrowth, and junk would take an army of people weeks to do.

David was able to pull the Cortina up in a small clearing among all the crap and vegetation. He knew there was no way in hell he'd be able to turn the car around.

Christine took off her seatbelt and said to David, 'Come on, let's get this done, shall we.'

David took his seat belt off and opened the car door. When he walked to the front of the car, he waited until Quentin and Mary hopped out before starting to wend his way through the chaos of the front garden to the door.

This would be the Christine and David show to start with today.

Quentin and Mary stood together at the front of the car and found each other's hand. Mary took a deep breath and met Q's eyes. She wondered how the next few minutes would go.

Christine and David reached the front door of the cottage. It appeared as if it would fall open at the slightest touch.

They took one last look at each other before Christine reached out and knocked on the door.

It only took a few moments before they heard the low and subtle sound of movement inside. Christine stole a glance down to Quentin and Mary, and as she turned to see if David wanted her to knock again, they heard a voice approaching the front door.

'Who in God's name is disturbing my drinking time?' The voice sounded almost comically annoyed.

Christine was about to tell David what she thought, but a moment later they heard a thud on the other side of the door.

A small piece of the door, three quarters up, suddenly disappeared before a bloodshot eye appeared in its place.

'Who ar-re you-u, whad do-oo you-oo wa-and?'

Christine smiled at the single eye and wondered how'd he react if she stuck her finger in the hole.

'Hello there,' she beamed from ear to ear, 'I was hoping you could help us? We seem to be lost.'

Fletcher's eye stayed there for a moment. But after a long pause, he blinked. He mumbled something to himself, sounding excited.

Fletcher stepped back from the front door and pulled it open. He almost pulled it off its hinges, which had David in stitches. But the drunk kept his game face on.

Fletcher stood shakily on his feet. Christine could immediately smell his breath. The guy was three sheets to the wind, drunk as a proverbial skunk.

'Sorry to disturb you, sir,' Christine let her rehearsed words flow, 'as I said, we are lost and—'

Fletcher glanced at her as if in a daze, but his expression changed.

'Hold on a second.' The guy's voice suddenly seemed clearer.

He swallowed before taking a long stare at her.

'I know who you are,' he said.

CHAPTER THIRTY-TWO

Christine's reaction was to freeze. The guy was old but his eyes shone sharply.

Christine went to say something, but once again the man at his front door jumped in over her. Her heart stopped as she thought how badly this had gone already.

How did Fletcher know her? Had someone tipped him off?

She was about to make a hasty exit but the guy said, 'You're Cathy Lesurf!'

Fletcher stared at her before a smile broke out on his face, minus about six teeth.

He licked his lips and said to David, 'And you must be in the band too, right?'

Christine had no idea what was going on.

But not a second later, Fletcher brought the curtain down on the mystery.

'You're the lead singer of Fiddler's Dram!'

David couldn't believe what he was hearing.

As he was about to turn and share a confused but amused glance down to Quentin and Mary, Fletcher began to sing. 'Didn't me have a loooveely tyme the dayy wee went to

Banged Door, bootiful dayy wee have supper the way and not more than wee poond or more.' And as he sang, his right arm swung from side to side.

Christine peered over to David as if to say, 'What do we do now?' but David had other ideas.

'It's been a while since anyone has recognised us. We're glad to see we still have fans out here,' he said.

Fletcher could see Quentin and Mary standing there, but from his distance, and given he was blind drunk, all he saw were two people. Quentin and Mary were far too young to be members of Fiddler's Dram.

'Well, whatever it is you need,' Fletcher said, falling over himself with enthusiasm, 'come on in and let me help you.'

But as Christine and David stood wondering if this was actually happening, Fletcher added, 'But I wouldn't mind if you could sing me your biggest hit.'

David turned to Quentin and Mary, waving.

This was going to be an interesting few minutes.

———

The inside of the cottage was no better than the outside. The guy had let the place go. And he was a hoarder, for sure.

When he stumbled into the lounge room, there was nowhere to sit but one other spot on a filthy old couch next to Fletcher.

'So, I'll help you get to wherever you need to go, but first,' he held up an empty bottle of whisky, 'any of you care for a little drink?'

'Thanks for the offer, but we may pass if it's alright with you,' David said.

Fletcher nodded. 'Fine,' he said, taking a swig. 'More for me,' he slurred through the top of the bottle.

Three of his guests seemed to have eyes that told him nothing.

But one was different.

That one's eyes were telling him something.

Fletcher couldn't put a finger on it, but it was as if raindrops of clarity were falling into his drunkenness.

He scanned over to the two women and the other man. They remained pensive.

When he met the other guy's eyes, his adrenal gland gave him a shot of fear.

Fletcher sat back in his chair and closed his eyes. After a few moments, he opened them and said, 'So, are you guys going to sing my favourite song before I help you?'

Christine turned to David, trying to shake her head in a way that Fletcher wouldn't notice.

She took a deep breath. 'Alright, you lot,' she said, making eye contact with the others, 'from the top.'

As she and David started to recite the words, and David thanked the stars above he'd happened to play it in the car, all but one of their band joined in.

By the time the second verse had kicked in, it was basically Christine and David singing, and Mary humming along as best she could.

Fletcher had his eyes closed the whole time, swinging his arms from side to side as if he were at Glastonbury having the night of his life.

When the song eventually finished and the room went silent, Fletcher slowly opened his eyes, with a big smile still on his face.

'Thank you, I really enjoy—'

His sentence was cut short.

When he met eyes with the one who'd made him feel uneasy a few minutes ago, the man was giving him the death stare.

But that wasn't why he began to panic.

The guy had something in his mouth.

A lollipop.

Fletcher seemed to clam up. The joy of hearing one of his favourite songs being sung felt a million miles away. He pulled himself to the edge of the couch and wished he'd never let these people in.

As he stood, he mumbled, 'One minute. I need to visit the little boys' room.'

As Fletcher stepped between his guests and his adrenal gland started pumping the 'fight or flight' solution into his bloodstream, even his foggy and paranoid mind knew there was only one option.

Flight.

As he shuffled off around the corner and a moment later they heard a door shut, Mary was the first among them to spot it.

'What the hell are you doing?' She watched Quentin stick the Chupa Chup back in his mouth. 'Are you out of your freaking mind?'

David and Christine realised what Mary was going on about, and it was the first time they legitimately got angry with Quentin.

Christine shook her head. 'Are you trying to fuck up this one, Quentin? What's got into you?'

'So I've got a Chupa Chup in my mouth? So what?' he snapped.

David heard what sounded like a door closing.

He muttered a profanity under his breath before something caught his attention through the lounge room window.

'What the hell?' he said.

Fletcher was on foot, running away from his cottage at speed.

———

David watched Fletcher for a moment before turning back to the others. 'He's got a bit of speed for an old drunk,' he said, and gave Quentin a dirty look. 'We'd better go after him.'

They found the back door a few moments later. There was so much crap in the house, they wondered how Fletcher had made it to the back door.

David and Quentin broke into a run with Christine and Mary tailing a few strides behind.

On reaching a mass of overgrown ivy, the four ran round it and found themselves in open land. The rolling hills seemed to stretch as far as the eye could see.

David was the first to spot Fletcher.

'There,' he said.

Fletcher was either a marathon runner when he wasn't drinking his way to the grave or, more likely, he felt like he was running for his life.

'We have to stop him going wherever the hell he is going,' David said before breaking into a sprint.

The other three followed suit.

Fletcher glanced over his shoulder. He could see the people coming after him, and sped up. It was pointless.

In his dazed and panicked state, he'd failed to realise he was running into a dead end.

In front of him was a small dam that stretched wide enough to have him trapped if he continued to head where his feet were taking him.

'Leave me alone,' he shouted, turning his head back. 'Get off my property and go away!'

By the time he'd turned back to see where he was, it was too late.

He was cornered.

———

When David approached Fletcher, he could see the panic in his eyes.

'Why did you run away from us?' David said.

Fletcher studied David's face before his eyes darted to Christine and Mary's. As Fletcher shuffled backwards, feeling the soft earth around the dam turning to mud, he caught Quentin's eye.

Quentin had lost the lollipop, but none of his anger.

With his chest still heaving, Fletcher bent over to try and catch his breath.

When he met Quentin's eyes, he spoke as if the run had made him sober. 'I knew one day you would come for me.'

Quentin stepped forward a couple of feet and shook his head. 'What in God's name are you talking about? I have no idea who you are,' he said.

Fletcher shook his head and kept staring at Quentin.

'You know,' he said.

Mary and Christine had literally stopped breathing. If there was any oxygen in Wales, it certainly wasn't around the hills of Crymlyn.

Quentin stepped another foot closer, and by now Fletcher had gone into some sort of self-induced trance.

He took another step backwards and could feel his shoes in the mud. Another two feet and he'd be stepping in the shallows.

A cloud had passed overhead, casting the land in a

monotone grey light. The wind had picked up and the women shivered in the burst of cold that had come from nowhere.

Fletcher was delirious. He cast his eyes back to Quentin as if he knew he was about to die.

'You know I'm the lollipop man,' Fletcher laughed.

Quentin shook his head. 'I don't know what the fuck you are talking about, you drunk,' he said.

David was about to interject but Fletcher shook his head and grinned.

'I saw the look in your eye in the house. I've not seen that look for close to forty years. It's part of the reason I moved up here.'

Quentin was secretly yearning to step two feet closer and knock the smart-ass grin off Fletcher's face.

It was like the guy was getting off on being so arrogant.

'Chupa Chups.' Fletcher grinned. 'It's a pity they weren't around when I was.'

Quentin turned around to ensure David, Christine, and Mary were all hearing this.

Each one met his eyes, and when he turned back to face Fletcher, the guy was now staring straight at Mary.

He was looking her over.

Like she was a lollipop.

He smacked his lips before straightening his back, and with a set jaw he said, 'I sure would have loved to use a Chupa Chup on you. A bit older than usual, but tasty all the same.'

His eyes remained on Mary as the words sank in.

'What did you just say?' she demanded.

Fletcher cocked his head before lifting his left hand to his face and licking his index finger as if it were a lollipop.

'I said,' his face now was dark and suddenly evil, 'I wish I could get you alone with a giant-sized Chupa Chup.'

Mary wondered later where her explosion of anger had come from.

Without even thinking about what she was doing, she lunged forward and a second later was in his face. As if another force was driving her, she thrust her hand into her handbag. How she got the bottle cap off would be a mystery she'd never be able to figure out.

'You disgusting old man,' she shouted, and splashed his face with a dose of water. 'You can wash your mouth out, you filthy bastard.'

David and Christine looked at each other and wondered how the hell the sequence of events had ended up here.

Fletcher, his face now dripping with water, licked his lips and kept his eyes trained on Mary.

But he turned to Christine and said, 'Cathy Lesurf, I always had a thing for you.' He put one hand on his crotch and smiled. 'I'd stick a lollipop up your behind whilst I was fuc—'

His filthy words were suddenly cut off.

David had pounced, pushing Quentin and Mary out of the way in the process.

Without a second's notice, he slammed his open-palmed hand straight into Fletcher's upper chest.

The old guy's feet literally lifted off the ground for a second before he landed backwards in the mud, his head and upper body splashing in the water of the dam.

David turned to the others and said, with a tone of authority, 'We are done here. Now.'

As they all started back to the car, only David, being the last person to walk away from Fletcher, heard the man's evil and deranged laughter as he lay on his back in the mud.

He wasn't dead.

Yet.

CHAPTER THIRTY-THREE

One week later

YUKIKO INFORMED THE CREW THAT ANDREW WAS returning to London that weekend. No one asked her how she felt about it. Her face said it all.

She went on to say that she'd reached a dead end with the orphanage list.

She'd exhausted all available avenues for finding anyone who had ever worked at Ravenstone House for the Less Privileged, and believed her work was done.

The two couples told her that without her input, they'd be nowhere. They'd all grown fond of Yukiko.

So now the list had topped out at twenty-three people.

But this excluded the Leitners. In the time the orphanage was in operation, at least three family members had worked there. At one point, the father had been in charge, but eventually he handed responsibility for the orphanage to his son. Their whereabouts remained unknown: they'd all disappeared into thin air when the place closed in 1956.

Finley and Heather confirmed that of the twenty-three people on the list, thirteen were child murderers.

Of that thirteen, one was female. Eight were still alive. (Make that seven, now that Reggie Blood was swimming with the flatheads in the Hook's Lane Fishing Pond.)

This left ten of those who had worked there that were good people.

A handful of these uncovered the abuse first-hand, witnessing it with their very own eyes, often by accident.

Some had tried to intervene, but to no avail. They found themselves suddenly unemployed, with only vague and unfounded reasons given for their sacking, followed by threats they knew should be taken at face value. Sadly, most never spoke another word of their time at Ravenstone House.

At least two defied the death threats and still went to the authorities.

But it was a futile gesture.

The accusations were denied, and envelopes thick with money made those accusations disappear.

———

Being a Friday night, the fish and chips were reigning supreme.

'So, Yukiko,' Christine took a couple of chips, 'do you think Andrew is going to want to go back to New York?'

Yukiko took a long drink from her white wine. 'It's the feeling I'm getting from him.' She shook her head. 'I don't like the Big Apple. Nothing against fruit,' she laughed at her own joke, 'but it's not London, if you know what I mean.'

Mary smiled, 'I've only been once. It's quite the city. Certainly a different vibe to London.'

Quentin felt like talking shop, so he waited for a pause in the conversation and said, 'So, Yukiko. I'm curious about the Leitners. The owners.'

'In all my years as a forensic investigator,' she shook her

head, 'I could count on one hand the amount of people I couldn't track down.' She turned to Quentin. 'If you'd afford me some speculation…'

Quentin nodded immediately.

'My guess is they fled back to Austria,' Yukiko continued. 'This is where they seem to have roots. They were well connected. I actually am starting to wonder if this whole orphanage,' she seemed to hesitate as if uncomfortable about what she was about to say, 'was some sort of set-up from the start.'

She could see the looks on their faces and knew they hadn't understood what she was referring to.

'Something struck me. It was more about this family than anything else. Although they seemed to disappear from the face of this earth,' she took a sip of her wine, 'to have people disappearing, even entire families, and then re-emerging with another identity altogether, is something to consider.

'The amount of children who died here, it's mind-blowing,' she said.

The four nodded together as if by subconscious agreement.

'You think the people who worked here did all this…' She shook her head instinctively as the thoughts ran through her brain. 'What I am trying to say is… I think there was a chance this mysterious family…'

The hypothesis was disturbing to even think, let alone say. '…had set all this up. And people paid to abuse the children.'

Christine dropped her wine glass on the table. She wasn't angry with Yukiko. It was the realisation of what she'd just said that made her indignant.

'Oh my Lord.' Christine reached out her hand for David. 'You think they bought this place to take advantage of the orphans? But worse—they let people come here and do it for a price?' Christine said.

David let go of Christine's hands and rested both his elbows on the dining table. He met eyes with his wife before turning his gaze upwards, as if he wanted old Rose to come. When he stared at the middle of the dining table, he said to no one in particular, 'We need to end this. Now.'

He uncrossed his arms and made an effort to smile, looking over to the others around his table.

'We work the list until we run out of names. We must free the spirits of these children,' he said.

David placed his hands on the table.

Without looking up, he said, 'And they, the monsters who are still alive,' he gritted his teeth, 'need to meet their maker. They need to answer for their evil sins.'

⊏⊐

Two days later

England's largest open-air freshwater pool was a place David and Christine had loved as long as they'd lived in the borough of Wandsworth.

The Tooting Bec Lido was busy that day, with the mercury hovering around 27 degrees and the sky devoid of clouds. It was always like this when the weather on a Sunday was so good.

Christine had packed the usual picnic lunch for herself and her man, the sort of gourmet feast we'd all like to get stuck into after unrolling the picnic blanket.

As Christine placed the basket down in the middle of the blanket, David stood up and began to undress. Obviously he was planning on taking a dip before having some lunch.

When Christine turned her attention from the picnic basket to her husband, she gasped in horror.

'David Banks—' As she cursed her husband's name, she realised by the grin on his face that he was trying to wind her up.

He stood there in nothing but a pair of fluoro G-string bathers.

As a wolf whistle came across the lawn, Christine burst into a fit of laughter.

David would do this from time to time. Do something silly.

It always had the same effect on her.

'Get your shorts back on,' she tried to compose herself through the hiccups that a fit of intense laughter would always bring on, 'before the young 'uns get here!'

David pulled his pants up, and just in time. Christine spotted Quentin and Mary a second later, walking from the entrance towards the grassed area.

They arrived as David was almost finished tying his bathing shorts up.

'You're not swimming today?' Mary mused to David.

David gave her a surprised look. He was still wearing his swimming shorts. 'Er, not sure what you mean.' He pointed to his bathers with a confused look.

Mary smiled at Christine before turning back to David.

'Well, we thought you were about to go for a swim in your *real* bathers.' She nodded to his shorts and grinned.

David blushed before Christine started to laugh so hard she immediately got the hiccups again.

'I've got to get myself a pair of those,' Quentin said, shaking his head as he and Mary laughed.

As the younger couple settled onto the blanket with their own lunch, David spotted something in the corner of his eye, not thirty feet away.

'Well, I'll be damned,' he said underneath his breath.

'What is it, darling?' Christine said.

David took one final, careful look over Quentin's shoulder before sitting back and checking out the contents of the picnic basket.

'Whatever you do,' he said in a conspiratorial tone, 'don't look over behind Quentin.'

No one budged, so David said, 'Archie Glaggin, one of the guys on the list. He's sitting right over there.'

Quentin remembered the name.

'The guy who was in his garage when we walked past his house.' He looked David in the eye. 'Who's he with?'

David afforded Glaggin another careful look. The guy wasn't even looking in his direction. 'A woman. Not sure who, but it could be his wife. Most probably. She's as old as he is.'

David was about to say something, else, but another thought fell out of the sky and landed with a thud in his lap. 'Jesus Christ,' he gasped, before looking around at the other three people sitting on the blanket with him.

'You girls wouldn't have by chance brought any of Finley's potion with you, would you?'

Christine and Mary raised their eyebrows at the same time.

Mary spoke first, 'It's my RDO for hunting bad guys. Christine?'

Christine shook her head and patted David lightly on the arm. 'Sorry, darling, I didn't know we were on call today.'

David nodded and took no offense at the girl's humour. But the look on his face remained serious.

Christine leant forward and said, 'You're not thinking what I think you're thinking?'

David's eyes narrowed.

'We need it.' He glanced in the direction of the huge

Tooting Bec Lido pool. 'In the bloody pool, when the man over there goes for a swim.'

Christine understood what he meant in an instant.

She went to get up and make her way back to their flat. The round trip, if she hurried, would be forty minutes at least.

Mary shook her head and grabbed Christine gently by the arm.

'No, Christine.' Mary literally pulled her back down to the blanket. 'I'll go.'

As she rose to her feet, she indicated to Quentin that he should give her the keys to their flat.

'With your arm still recovering,' Mary stood up and was ready for the mission at hand, 'I can go. I'll run there, and run back.'

She pecked Quentin on the forehead and said, 'You wait here and make sure David doesn't get tempted to go for a swim in those fluoro G-string bathers while I'm gone.'

David smiled.

Mary had spunk.

And was also the fastest runner.

———

'Shit,' David said between mouthfuls of his chicken and avocado sandwich, not two minutes after Mary had left.

He took one more careful glance behind Quentin and screwed his face up in frustration.

'The fucker is going for a swim now,' he cursed.

———

It was the longest forty minutes of their lives.

Forty-six, to be exact.

While David and Christine took turns watching Archie Glaggin and his companion lazing about in the pool, the two had time to tell Quentin something.

They were going to tell Mary as well, but with her fetching the potion, Christine decided Quentin could pass on the message.

'Quentin,' Christine waited until she had his full attention, 'Bradley Fletcher, the creep who was obsessed with baths, is dead.'

Quentin dropped his bottle of soft drink in his lap mid-swig.

'How'd you find this out?' Quentin said. 'We've been watching the news and listening to the radio around the clock.'

Christine shared a subtle smile with her husband before she turned her attention back to Q.

'I called the respite centre this morning,' she said.

'When we went there, it was glaringly obvious they all hated Heen. They never came out and said it. It was their expressions. The way they spoke about him. The way they reacted when I arrived and introduced myself as his ex-wife.' Christine shook her head and smiled faintly at the memory. 'I got the impression they even hated me for ever being married to him. The person I spoke to at the reception desk must have been the president of the John Heen fan club.'

Before Quentin had a chance to ask her what she meant, she continued. 'She seemed to have no problem telling me precisely what happened to him. Details you'd think you wouldn't tell even an ex-wife.'

Quentin stared at her with curiosity.

'They found him in the bathroom,' she said.

Quentin's eyebrows shot up. 'Don't tell me—he was in the bathtub.'

Christine shook her head. 'No. There was no bathtub in

his bathroom, as you would expect. But it was, in fact, you could say, another source of water.'

Quentin shrugged his shoulders.

'His head was wedged—inside the bowl of the toilet,' she said.

'Bullshit. No way,' Quentin said.

'She told me his head was wedged so firmly in the bowl, they had to smash the toilet with a sledgehammer to get him out,' Christine said.

Before Quentin could say another word, Christine patted him on the arm, 'She also told me this. His body was—how do I say this—suspended upside down, in mid-air.'

'You've got to be kidding me,' Quentin said.

'No, no, no,' David hissed as he watched Archie Glaggin and his swimming partner slowly making their way towards the edge of the pool.

'Damn it. We've missed a golden opportunity,' he said.

CHAPTER THIRTY-FOUR

Quentin was the first to spot her.

Mary.

She was running at full tilt inside the pool grounds.

She had some ground to cover.

Fortunately for her, one of the lifeguards was on lunch, and the other was doing his best to chat up a young lass in a bikini. His attention was fixed on the young girl's blue eyes and smile.

Glaggin and the unidentified woman were now halfway back to the edge of the pool.

Mary had taken a moment before she left the Tooting Bec Lido to make a mental note of what Glaggin and the woman looked like. She spotted the two as she drew closer.

David was about to rise to his feet but Christine suddenly pulled him down. 'Wait,' she said.

Mary realised there was no way she or anyone else was going to make it into the pool with the potion while Glaggin was still swimming.

He was almost at the edge of the pool now.

In a swift, almost mesmerising move, Mary ran for her

life along the edge of the pool while pulling the lid off her water bottle.

Whatever she had in mind, she had literally seconds to get there.

At that moment—a miracle occurred.

Glaggin had reached the edge of the pool and was about to get out. But the woman he was with said something, and he turned back to her.

As she swam the last couple of feet towards him, Mary was about the same distance away on foot.

When the woman made it to Glaggin, she sheepishly put both hands on his shoulders and attempted to push him under for a bit of fun. Glaggin decided he'd do the same, and as they were both trying to push each other under the surface, Mary arrived.

She turned the bottle of water upside down and squeezed with all her might. The water spurted out and showered Glaggin and the woman.

Mary leapt into the air, diving over the man and woman in the pool before her.

Only a handful of people paid any attention to a woman diving into the pool—clothed.

But three kept their eyes glued to her every move.

They watched on as they lost sight of Mary, who had yet to come up for air.

———

Mary could easily swim underwater for twenty-five yards or more on one breath. She was fit and she knew it.

She made the other side of the pool, thirty-three yards away, with ease. But as she turned back to see what was going on with Glaggin and his friend, she froze.

They were looking directly at her, and the look on their faces was alarming.

'You!' Glaggin shouted as his female friend made a groan-like sound.

Quentin, Christine, and David now rose to their feet to get a better view of what was going on. Meanwhile, Mary wondered what the hell she was going to do.

Glaggin & Co. were now making their way back across the pool towards Mary.

The sounds they were making were really starting to freak her out. Low, guttural moans, as if they were in pain but at the same time very, very angry.

As they reached the middle of the pool, Mary could have sworn she heard Glaggin say, 'You think those children can get to—'

Mary felt a mild shockwave in the water, as though a tiny bomb had detonated in there somewhere. Glaggin and the woman stopped dead in their tracks. They were now right in the middle of the pool.

Mary would tell the others later that it was at this point the crazy shit started to happen.

The temperature of the pool began to rise.

She watched other swimmers in the pool reacting.

People started to ask each other what was going on.

Others started swimming for the edge.

And yet the water got warmer and warmer.

Mary tried to move, but somehow was unable.

She felt as if something was holding her in the pool.

Steam started to rise from the surface.

Swimmers screamed in fear.

Mary started to feel dizzy from the heat.

Glaggin & Co. threw their arms into the air.

Their eyes were fixed on Mary.

Mary found herself putting her hands in the air too, to try and cool her body down.

A second later, she felt hands grabbing hers.

Quentin and David.

As they pulled her from the water, they could see the steam rising from all over the huge pool.

Thankfully, there was no one left in the water but Glaggin and the woman.

The hundreds of people who'd gone to the Tooting Bec Lido that day to cool off were now watching Glaggin and his friend standing in the middle of the pool, making the most disturbing noises while their arms remained steadfastly up in the air.

But a second later, they both dived into the pool with their arms forward, and for a second were completely underwater.

Glaggin and the woman's legs shot out of the pool a few moments later, as if they were both doing a handstand.

What.

The.

Hell.

As Mary's feet landed on the ground, something else happened.

It would be one of the borough of Wandsworth's most talked-about events for years to come.

As if an earthquake were about to split England's largest pool in half, the water in the pool exploded into the air.

Those standing around the pool ran in all directions, more from instinct than fright.

As David, Mary, Quentin, and Christine ran towards the closest tree for cover, they gasped in amazement.

The water had shot up at least a hundred feet into the air.

Quentin shouted, 'My God, look,' pointing to the

middle of the pool, where sat a perfectly shaped gigantic block of ice in the shape of a cylinder.

Sticking out of the top were two sets of ankles.

As Quentin heard David ask, 'What is it?' dozens of other people pointed at the bizarre object.

And a moment later, well over a million gallons of steaming water came raining down across the entire pool and surrounding grounds.

Today would mark two things.

One, it would be the turning point.

And two, people from the yard up north would now enter the fray.

Scotland Yard.

CHAPTER THIRTY-FIVE

DAVID AND CHRISTINE AND QUENTIN AND MARY all sat in silence nursing a stiff drink.

It had been a few hours since the cataclysmic event at the Tooting Bec Lido.

The conversation was minimal. All were speechless from what they'd witnessed.

After fleeing the pool, they'd agreed to watch the nightly news together, to see how the story would be covered.

When the clock chimed six, Mary turned on the television and returned to the couch. Her heart beat faster as the seconds ticked by.

What happened had been her doing, she'd been telling herself all afternoon.

After a thirty-second intro, the BBC evening news began.

'Good evening. Bob Freeman, along with Frances Brown, with the news this Sunday the 24th of June 1990.'

The major news stories being covered that night were read out first in summary.

Mary wondered if what happened at Tooting Bec Lido had actually made it on, when they'd got to the sixth news story but nothing of it had been mentioned.

It was the last major news story.

'And lastly, we'll cover off the accident at Tooting Bec Lido today,' said Frances Brown, 'which has resulted in the deaths of two people.'

All four shared curious looks.

They'd have to wait about fifteen minutes to be put out of their misery.

But the news story right after the Tooting Bec Lido 'accident' would have the four falling off their couches.

⸺

'Thanks for staying with us,' Bob Freeman said as the news came back from the commercial break.

'England's largest outdoor pool, Tooting Bec Lido, found in the Tooting Commons between Tooting and Streatham, is under lockdown today after the drowning deaths of two people.'

Frances Brown, his co-anchor, continued as a file-footage photo of the pool appeared on the green screen behind them.

'Witnesses claim a sudden change in the pool's temperature saw the water become so warm, steam was seen rising from the water's edge.

'We cross now to Kim Mackay, who is at the Tooting Bec Lido live. Kim, are you there?'

The reporter nodded as she came into view, standing out the front of the pool.

'Thanks, Frances,' Kim said as she straightened her shoulders and got down to business.

'Witnesses we have spoken to this afternoon claim the temperature of the pool suddenly increased. They spoke of people clearing out of the pool quickly, but the two elderly victims, for some reason, were not able to get out quickly enough.'

At this point, David, Christine, Mary, and Quentin could feel there was something unusual about the news report. Something wrong.

'Will the pool remain closed?' Frances at the news desk asked the reporter.

Kim nodded. 'Yes, Frances. While investigations continue, the Tooting Bec Lido will remain closed until further notice. Back to you, Frances.'

'What in God's name?' David shook his head.

'They covered it up, lock, stock, and barrel. They omitted everything else. The explosion of water. The block of ice. Glaggin & Co. upside down. You've got to ask yourself why,' he said.

Mary remained glued to the television screen.

She was beyond surprised by what had happened—more in shock.

'Let's face it,' Christine said, getting everyone's attention, 'how would anyone have explained what happened today? You'd bet the authorities decided it was simply beyond explanation. I'm not surprised, to be honest.'

But as soon as she'd taken a sip of her whisky, she added, 'What I want to know is this. Why did the woman who was with Glaggin die too?'

David was about to enter the debate when Mary squealed and her arm shot out to grab Quentin's leg.

They turned to her as she said, 'Look, look.'

Bob Freeman was talking, but in the background they saw something that silenced them.

'Police in Bangor, Wales, came across a very unusual and quite macabre event of their own when they arrived at their station this morning for another day of work.'

'You've got to be bloody kidding me,' David said.

The vision was of two policemen covering a Mini-Minor with a tarpaulin. The car itself sat on the pavement right at the bottom of the steps leading up the front door of the police station.

He'd remembered the car because he once owned one. And recently, he'd seen the same one on the telly, in someone's front yard.

'The deceased driver of the Mini-Minor is yet to be identified. But what has puzzled the police in Bangor, is how he came to be sitting in the car directly outside the Bangor Police Station.'

As the cameraman zoomed in on the Mini for a few seconds before it was covered by the tarpaulin, David and Christine grabbed each other's hand.

The inside of the car was full to the roof with water.

But it was what was floating in the water that caught their attention.

Dozens upon dozens—of lollipops.

Bradley Fletcher, aka the lollipop man, was dead.

How his body had come to be sitting in the driver's seat was anyone's guess.

After draining the car, the local police would find something they would not share with the press.

Wedged in every orifice of Fletcher's body—a lollipop.

CHAPTER THIRTY-SIX

ANDREW PARSONS' FLIGHT FROM NEW YORK WAS delayed. Pilots with wives who are due to give birth should not be taxiing a British Airways 747 jumbo onto the main runway at JFK, especially when the flight was on schedule. They should be at the hospital. It's only fair, right? To the paying passengers, I mean. Let another pilot with less pressing issues fly the darn plane, please.

After a gruelling ten hours more crammed into his economy cabin seat, Andrew was ready to rip someone's head off if they even breathed at him the wrong way.

The guy needed to take a chill pill—and if he couldn't buy those anywhere, maybe try meditation.

Heathrow International Airport greeted Andrew with the sort of homecoming anyone flying across the Atlantic would wish for.

Long queues. Delays at every point. Hundreds of people devoid of any manners or decorum, tired and pissed off. All trying to get to the one place they so desperately wanted to be. Home.

And as Andrew fought his way through the crowds

towards the taxi rank, his stress about what he was planning to do increased.

He would be telling Yukiko tonight.

It's either me, in New York, or I'm no longer your husband.

Actually, there's something we know that Yukiko doesn't. Not yet.

He was hoping she'd decide to stay in London.

Parsons lacked the kind of bollocks most men possess.

He didn't have the balls to walk in the door and tell Yukiko the truth: he wanted out.

Andrew hoped that instead, he could use Ravenstone House as the excuse for him to end the marriage. Because Andrew was confident Yukiko was in love with London.

Just like he was in love with a co-worker.

In New York.

But Ravenstone House would not approve of his dishonest tactics.

It would take action.

⸻

'Nurse Mary.'

Mary was sleeping lightly, and felt Heather standing there before she was roused from her sleep.

'Hello darling,' Mary said, her smile foggy, but enough to melt Heather's spirit.

The smile, combined with the word 'darling,' always had the same effect on bonny Heather.

She stepped forward and gave Mary a loving kiss on the cheek.

Mary had already fallen in love with the little girl long ago. She prayed that one day she would bring her own Heather into the world.

Mary and Christine knew they were out of what they privately coined 'holy water,' more commonly known to the four as simply 'Finley's potion.'

So Mary had left Heather's ring on her bedside table.

She didn't want to go downstairs and ask for Finley.

The basement still made her skin crawl.

'Heather,' Mary reached out for her hand, 'we are out of the special potion Finley has been giving us.'

Heather smiled at her.

'I'll ask Finley to give you some more. If you'd like to come down to the basement, I'll see to it for you.'

Before Mary could say, 'I'll send Quentin down, if that's okay,' Heather was gone.

Mary found Quentin's shoulder and gripped it lightly, 'Honey, it's your turn to fetch the potion.'

Ten seconds later, Quentin roused from his sleep.

'And I'd just hit 186 miles at Silverstone,' he said. Mary wondered if he'd been a racing car driver in his previous life.

'Okay, I'll go,' he mumbled.

—

Quentin checked the time on the microwave oven, though he was still half asleep.

It was 11.59pm.

If he'd been more awake, he'd have had second thoughts about leaving his flat at that time of night.

With slippers on his feet, long-legged pyjama bottoms, and a Pink Floyd T-shirt indicating he'd attended the *A Momentary Lapse of Reason* tour a couple of years ago, he fumbled his way out of the front door of his flat.

It was at this point he froze.

Andrew Parsons was standing at the bottom of the staircase to the upstairs flats.

229

'Andrew?' Quentin took a couple of steps forward.

His eyes were fixed on something at the top of the stairs.

A thought came to Q's mind, and he cursed himself for forgetting.

The stroke of midnight—it was the Rose Lloyd moment.

The old lady of Ravenstone House was probably the meanest ghost in London, maybe even all of Great Britain.

Quentin was keen to get downstairs, get the bottle of potion, and get the hell back into his flat.

But something felt five-ways weird right now.

Andrew's eyes were locked onto something at the top of the stairs, and it was starting to freak Quentin out.

He went to take another step forward, but Andrew then turned and locked his cold eyes directly onto Quentin.

Without a second's warning, he slowly opened his mouth and shouted, 'Fuck off, asshole. And mind your own business.'

And with those friendly words, Andrew turned his eyes back towards the top of the stairs.

Quentin made a wise decision.

Get the potion, and get home.

———

'You mustn't be out there in the hall at midnight,' Heather sheepishly said to Quentin, who was still clearly shaken by what had just happened.

He'd fumbled his way down to the basement as quietly as he could. He was so freaked out by whatever had been going on with Andrew in the hallway, he'd had no time to feel uncomfortable about being down in the spooky basement.

Finley materialised from the shadows and pointed to the ring on the floor, where another bottle sat.

When Quentin picked the bottle up and was about to get

his shivering bum back upstairs, Finley said, 'You guys are doing an amazing job. I can't explain to you, Quentin.'

Quentin stopped and decided he'd give the young ghost at least a moment or two of his time.

'Can't explain what, Finley?' Quentin said.

Finley smiled over to Heather and said, 'The children. Actually, me too. We can feel the doorway to where we are meant to be—slowly opening. It's the most incredible feeling. It's given us more hope than we've ever had before.'

Quentin glanced down to Heather. He felt moved by a terrible pity for her.

'None of you deserved what happened to you,' Quentin said.

'We, I mean myself, Mary, David, and Christine…' He realised he'd forgotten someone. 'And Yukiko: we're happy to have had the chance to make things right for you all.'

Heather ran to him and wrapped her arms around his legs.

'Thank you for helping us,' she said.

Finley leant over and tapped Heather on the shoulder, 'Now, now, bonny Heather. You'll make Quentin blush.'

Quentin shook his head from side to side, 'Mary and I think Heather is one special little girl.'

He grinned, 'Promise me you don't tell Mary I told you this,' he didn't wait for a response, 'but we both love you back, Heather.'

Finley smiled from ear to ear. Finally, after forty plus years of being there for Heather, he felt as if she was finally experiencing what he'd wished he could have given her by the truck load.

Parental love.

As Quentin made his way back upstairs, Finley said, 'One other thing.'

Quentin turned to him.

'With half of the monsters dead, it's made something else happen,' he said.

'What?'

'Whatever force was keeping us trapped here, we've never been able to leave the boundaries of Ravenstone House. Never. But now,' he said with a look of satisfaction, 'something, today, broke us free. The rules have changed.'

Quentin stared at Finley for a moment as the penny dropped.

Archie Glaggin had died today.

And the woman he was with, too. Quentin would later find out why.

As Quentin was about to tell Finley about Glaggin, and the day's extraordinary events, he heard the mother of all thumps on the floorboards above him. It was so loud he almost dropped the bottle of potion.

He immediately thought of two people: one living and one dead.

Andrew Parsons.

Rose Lloyd.

This can't be good.

CHAPTER THIRTY-SEVEN

DAVID AND CHRISTINE WERE ALREADY IN THE HALLWAY when Quentin arrived from the basement, having been awakened by all the commotion. Quentin quickly stashed the bottle of potion inside their open front door, and by the time he stood back up, Mary was already at their own front door looking over to him.

Her face said it all.

What in God's name?

Quentin could hear voices coming from upstairs. There were people screaming and muttering words he couldn't decipher.

At least one or two people were coming down the stairs now.

At the bottom, in a crumpled heap, was Andrew.

David and Christine were standing over him.

Christine turned and saw Mary standing in her doorway.

'Mary, get on the phone. We need an ambulance as soon as it can get here.'

When Quentin got a bit closer, he could see Andrew was motionless, parts of his body at such grotesque angles it made him want to be sick.

Most of his body was lying up on the stairs. His head was the only thing touching the actual bottom floor.

'My God!' one of the women coming down the stairs screamed, 'we heard all this ruckus in the hallway,' she said.

By the time the woman made it down to the last few steps before having to squeeze past Andrew, she was clearly out of breath.

Another woman was coming down behind her. When the second woman made it to the bottom floor the first said, 'We live upstairs. We heard some strange noises, and an old woman's voice we couldn't understand.'

The other woman chimed in.

'We've seen the old lady a few times. That's one scary-looking ghost.'

David checked Andrew's pulse again, as he had done a moment ago.

It was weak, but it was still there. In the distance, he could hear the squawk of an ambulance's siren. He hoped it was the one heading here.

The woman whose name was Helena spoke, putting her hand to her chest as if the words would cause her pain.

'The ghost of the old lady was just standing there. She was looking down the staircase. This is the fifth time we've seen her there. It's the spot she always goes to.'

Helena stared at Andrew and could feel her emotions getting the better of her.

'This guy. All of a sudden, he appeared. He'd walked up to the top of the stairs as if he was going to confront her.'

The ambulance was now heading down the street. David could feel a sense of relief, at least, knowing it was only a few moments away.

Christine patted the woman from upstairs on the back as she continued. 'The ghost of the old woman went ballistic. This guy was almost face to face with her. He was one step down from her. He said nothing. As if he was trying to intimidate her.'

'Or the ghost of the old lady had put him under some sort of spell or something,' the other woman said.

As the ambulance arrived, Helena said, 'A second later she shot forward, making this godawful sound, and either she somehow was able to push him, or he lost his balance and fell backwards.'

'What the hell?' Yukiko had appeared, and when she saw it was Andrew lying there, she screamed.

David shot forward and cut her off as she ran to her husband.

'Yukiko, wait.' He pulled her into his arms. 'He's got a pulse, but he's in a bad way. He might have broken his neck. Let the paramedics tend to him.'

Christine stepped over to David and took the shocked Yukiko from him.

'He was supposed to be home hours ago,' Yukiko said between laboured breaths. 'What happened to him?'

'We've yet to figure it out,' Christine said, as Quentin let the two paramedics in the front door of Ravenstone House.

———

Andrew was admitted to the Royal London Hospital.

As of Monday morning, Andrew was in an induced coma, with his condition listed as serious but stable. Miraculously, Andrew had only suffered two broken legs, a fractured left hip, and a broken right arm. Plus, he'd sprained his left wrist and had a severe concussion. But even after tumbling down the long flight of stairs at Ravenstone House, he hadn't broken his neck as David had suspected. That was the miracle.

Yukiko had stayed by his side since he arrived at the

hospital. She would have reconsidered doing this if she knew what her husband had been up to in New York.

Setting himself up for a new life that didn't include her.

And then there was what he'd planned to tell her after he arrived home.

Andrew didn't need to be conscious for his life to begin unravelling.

———

Quentin arrived at work feeling like his eyes were hanging out of his head. The last night's events involving Andrew, along with what had happened at Tooting Bec Lido during the day, had put sleep out of reach.

'Well, well, well,' his colleague Tim said when Q walked into the office.

'It looks like someone's partying ways are still going full throttle, even with a big ol' ring on the little lady's finger,' Tim teased.

Quentin ignored the jibe and took a long and clumsy gulp of his coffee.

'Oh, man,' said Tim, speaking softer now, 'you look like a well-dressed turd. Did your fine woman keep you up all weekend?'

This roused a smirk from Quentin before he reached for his coffee again. After another gulp, he ushered Tim to grab a chair and bring it to his desk.

When he'd finally done so, Quentin scanned the office to ensure no one was too close.

'Ravenstone,' he shook his head, 'it's a fucking loony bin. One of our neighbours had words with the old granny ghost last night and is now in a coma.'

Tim shook his head. 'I'm starting to wonder if you and Mary buying a flat there was a good idea, yeah?'

Quentin leant forward and rested his head on the desk.

'Man, you need to take some time out,' said Tim. 'Let me handle the workload today. Why don't you finish early?'

'Mate, I appreciate the offer,' Quentin said, 'but there's one little catch.'

Tim shrugged his shoulders, not sure what he meant.

'What?' he said.

Quentin took a deep breath as the thought of what he and Mary had to do that night. His father's house was closer to Q's work than home, so it was no use going home early.

'Dinner,' he said helplessly to his best friend, 'with the lord mayor.'

———

Quentin somehow managed to get through the whole day without falling in a heap. He seemed to get his second wind after speaking to Mary during his lunch break. Five strong cups of coffee may also have helped.

Mary had called Christine before Quentin and found out the latest on Yukiko's husband. His condition was serious but stable, and the good news was that the broken bones, fractures, and sprains would eventually heal.

The neighbours were all worried about Yukiko, and knowing the guy would recover was good news for her. So Q felt slightly more upbeat. But he still had dinner with his father to get through.

'You ready for tonight?' Mary said, seconds before she rang off from the call with Quentin.

'I'd rather run down Oxford Street in a pink tutu,' he said. 'I'll go whisky for whisky with him. That'll help.'

———

Wendy Moss had been Quentin's father's maid for as long as Quentin could remember. She was a tall, big-boned woman with a head of auburn hair that she wore in a tight ponytail 364 days of the year. Quentin had always loved the smile on her friendly face, which went with green eyes and big, frequently red cheeks.

When Quentin's mother passed away, Wendy seemed to take her sudden death very hard. The two women had an exceptionally good relationship over the years, though at the time Wendy had always only ever been a part-time employee in the Brookes household. Six months after the death of Janet Brookes, her widowed husband decided it might be better if Wendy worked for him full-time. And since her own husband had passed a few years earlier from a rare form of cancer, Wendy decided the extra money wouldn't go astray.

Especially after Janet's untimely death, Wendy had figured out she could trust the Q-man. She had watched him grow into a smart, bright, and solid young adult.

She would often confide in him when she could, and what she'd told him recently didn't surprise Q in the slightest.

The demands of the lord mayor's office were relentless, and Bernie had become what most people would describe as 'a bit of a prick.' His mood toggled between cantankerous and surly, and Wendy would be lucky to get a smile from him maybe once a week.

Mary had finished work an hour earlier than usual, so when she arrived at Quentin's office and saw the state of her future husband, she knew she had to get him out of there.

He had a mountain-sized bear to deal with in the evening.

Bernie Brookes.

So they headed for Quentin's father's house earlier than scheduled, thinking what was the harm? Q was still the lord mayor's son, after all. They were family.

Quentin wondered if a pre-Bernie drink would help his mood.

His old man had a thing for whisky and liqueurs, and his bar rivalled some of the best in the city. It was kind of old-age cool, and full to the brim with bottles of alcohol Quentin often wondered where on God's earth they'd come from.

He knew there would be something there to take the edge off his day and, more importantly, what was to come.

'Look at you,' Wendy said excitedly as she opened the door for Quentin. 'And your future wife looks as good as you do. Come on through,' she said.

When Quentin and Mary arrived in the kitchen, they were confronted with the irresistible aroma of the sort of roast beef you'd happily pay four times the restaurant price for.

Quentin eyed Mary and grinned. 'Ever thought about leaving this place,' he asked Wendy, 'and coming and taking care of us two at home?'

As Wendy pulled a tray from the oven of the best-looking roast potatoes Mary had ever seen, she turned to Quentin and smiled faintly.

'I hear things about Ravenstone,' she returned the potatoes to the oven, 'which makes me want to refuse the generous offer, Quentin. But thanks anyway.'

After a few seconds of awkward silence, Quentin attempted a smile before saying, 'maybe I'll get us a pre-dinner drink.'

He left Wendy and Mary in the kitchen, and headed to his father's bar.

As Quentin poured himself two fingers of Cardhu eighteen-year-old single- malt Scotch whisky, his mind whirled in a sea of thoughts. Most centred around Ravenstone.

He'd already poured Mary her favoured pre-dinner drink, Malibu rum, but after pouring his drink next, he seemed stuck in a daydream.

Not for long.

'Quentin Brookes, what are you up to?'

The voice was soft, but it still scared the shit out of him.

Wendy.

'Are you okay, young man?' she said.

Quentin fumbled with his whisky and managed a sip, which made him feel better. 'I am now,' he said, and pulled off a smile.

Wendy turned and glanced into the hall.

When she turned back, her face was serious.

'Your father,' she hurriedly checked her watch, 'is due home any moment. I'd better make this quick,' she said.

Quentin put his drink down and leant in closer. 'What's going on?'

Wendy seemed to gather her thoughts, and was about to say something but hesitated.

'Wendy, if Dad is almost home, you'd better get on with it,' he said.

'Your father's starting to worry me,' she said.

Quentin shook his head. 'The old man's not been the same for years. Let's be honest: he's been a different man since Mum died.'

Wendy nodded.

'He's drinking more these days. When he gets home, he seems to only ever do the same thing: drink and fall asleep in his chair by the fire.'

'I get the feeling he's losing the plot. The press are saying he needs to call it a day,' Quentin said.

Wendy took a deep breath.

'Last week, I worked later than I usually do. Your father had guests, and it dragged on a little,' she said.

She made one last check of her watch and took a quick look out the window. The weight of what she was about to say felt like it was pinning her down like a block of concrete.

'When I came to say goodnight, he was sitting in his chair, I thought he was asleep. He was muttering to himself. I couldn't understand it. But there was one word I could hear as clear as day.'

Quentin thought he heard a noise in the house somewhere, but ignored it for the moment.

Big mistake.

He was too focused on what Wendy was trying to tell him.

'But not only this,' Wendy seemed to pinch her lips shut as if she were about to say something unspeakable, 'he's been burning documents, and letters, in the fire.'

'Bugger me,' Quentin said, 'what were they?'

Wendy shook her head, 'No idea, but I could see documents going up in flames.'

Bernie Brookes entered his home a moment later. But he used the back door, as he did just a little more often than never.

After grunting at Mary, he ventured to find Quentin, unaware that Wendy was with him.

'But the next day, when I was cleaning out the fireplace,' Wendy had seconds before Bernie arrived at the door to the bar, 'I found a partially burnt letter underneath the fireplace grate.'

Wendy thought she heard something in the hallway, so she quickly turned and started to close the curtains.

Quentin ignored the world around him.

'Who was it from? And what was the word you heard him say?'

'Janet,' she whispered.

'What are you two doing?' Quentin's father tried to make it sound humorous, but failed miserably.

'Talking about you,' Quentin returned the comment with his own attempt at irony.

But when father and son made eye contact, there was no humour in their eyes.

CHAPTER THIRTY-EIGHT

WENDY'S ROAST WAS MICHELIN-STAR QUALITY. IT HAD to be, given Bernie's expectations.

Q had opted out of his usual accompaniment for a beef roast, a good Australian merlot or cabernet sauvignon.

After the look his old man had given him when he arrived home, Quentin decided to stick with his original plan for dinner. Whisky for whisky with the lord mayor.

He knew at some point he would opt out, but for now, the whisky was helping to keep his nerves under control.

The conversation, or lack thereof, was much like it was last time. Every time.

Devoid of any quality or substance. Vanilla.

How are you? Fine.

How is work? Good.

What have you guys been up to? Not much.

After Bernie downed his second whisky before even finishing his dinner, Mary and Quentin shared their usual look.

Here we go again.

'So, how's things at the office, Bernie?' Mary decided to try and break the awkwardness.

He glanced in her direction before picking up a piece of meat and shoving it in his mouth.

He chewed on it forever, at no time taking his eyes off his plate. He was doing it on purpose.

Quentin was about to let him have it. He thought his father was being a contemptuous son of a bitch.

After a sip of his whisky, he cleared his throat to moan about his constituents. 'They are getting sick of me, I can feel it. And to be honest,' he threw a cold stare in Quentin's direction, 'I'm getting damn sick of the people too.'

Well, Quentin thought, this is going well.

'Maybe it's time to tend to the garden a little more.' It was Quentin's usual line every time Bernie hinted at quitting or being ousted from office. But his father never warmed to it. As a matter of fact, it insulted him.

And on some level, Quentin knew it.

Mary kicked him underneath the table.

Bernie seemed to ignore the comment, and went about demolishing his dinner.

Without looking up, he said, 'They tell me the old house of yours is starting to fall apart, and strange shit is happening. I told you buying a flat there was a stupid idea.' He emphasised the word *stupid*, which only angered Quentin more.

Mary dropped her knife. That it hit the side of her plate was an accident, but it had the desired effect.

'Would it be possible to have a nice dinner for once, you two?' she said quietly. She was sick and tired of father and son swapping insults over the dinner table. It was bloody immature, to be honest.

Bernie almost spat the roast potato he had in his mouth back onto his plate.

'Two things, young lady,' he barked.

Mary instantly regretted her words. Oh, my Lord, what have I done? she thought.

Bernie's toupee moved awkwardly as his jaw set in an angry expression. 'One, Ravenstone House is a bad, bad place,' he said. 'They should have demolished it decades ago. You two are imbeciles for buying a flat there. Idiots. And two,' he levelled his fork at her pointedly, 'don't you ever, ever, speak to me like that again. You hear me?'

Quentin burst out of his seat, almost upending both his chair and his dinner. He wished he could take it with him: he was only halfway through.

But enough was enough.

'Sit down,' Bernie shouted in a deep, guttural tone.

'Go to hell.' Quentin tapped Mary on the shoulder to indicate they were leaving. 'Mary was just trying to diffuse the usual crap between us.'

As he moved away from the table, Quentin shook his head and pulled his hair with both hands to show how frustrated he was.

'Quit the damn job, Dad. It's turned you into one hell of an arsehole. I can't deal with you like this anymore.' To his credit, Quentin said it with more sincerity than anger.

Bernie remained steadfast in his seat. He glared at Mary and for a second, she thought she saw regret in his eyes. She was wrong. When he turned his gaze to Quentin, it was colder than ever.

Then he picked up his knife and fork, and turned his attention back to his meal.

Quentin and Mary stared at each other, wondering if what they were seeing was actually happening. It was surreal.

Quentin took Mary's hand and led her gently out of the room.

As they passed his father at the table, Bernie lashed out by pointing his knife at Quentin.

'I was always an arsehole,' he sneered. 'You just don't know me well enough, boy.'

The way he said *boy* made Quentin's blood run cold. Or was it the dark expression on his puffy, red face? Either/or. Maybe his father was right.

When Quentin and Mary entered the hallway, Wendy appeared from nowhere with Mary's handbag. The look on her face said it all: she was worried, and by all accounts scared.

'Are you going to be alright?' Quentin said.

Wendy ushered the two down the hall towards the front door.

'Yes, I will stay in my room for a little while. Once he heads off to the lounge room, I'll clear the table and finish the kitchen. I'll be fine,' Wendy said before she hugged Quentin and Mary goodbye. As she opened the front door, she nodded to Mary's handbag, waiting for Quentin to see what she was getting at.

When he glanced back to her, she could see the surprise in his eyes.

After Quentin and Mary made it to the pavement, Quentin waited until they were two houses down the street before he stopped Mary and reached for her handbag.

She wondered what he was doing, but Mary saw what hadn't been there when they arrived at Bernie's house for dinner.

Quentin pulled it out.

A faded standard-sized envelope.

Slightly burnt on the edges.

'Bernie' was written on the outside.

In his mother's handwriting.

When Quentin and Mary arrived home, a note underneath their front door diverted their attention from the disastrous dinner at the lord mayor's house.

'Come see us. D + C.'

———

'Tea? Coffee?'

'Johnny?'

Mary diverted her gaze straight to Quentin.

'Quentin Brookes,' she gave him a questioning look, 'haven't you had enough whisky tonight?'

Quentin shook his head.

Dinner with his father had rattled him.

David had waited for Quentin to confirm he wanted a whisky over a tea or coffee.

'Two fingers, rocks.' Quentin winked at Mary, who rolled her eyes. 'Or no rocks,' he said.

'I guess dinner didn't go well,' Christine said.

'He's getting worse.' Mary stared off into the distance. 'We don't know how much more of his moods we can handle.'

Christine passed Mary her cup of tea.

David gave Quentin his whisky and purposefully let the room fall into silence. He was keen to change the subject.

'So,' he slowly descended into his own bar stool before reaching for his cup of coffee, 'we've been summoned, people.'

Quentin and Mary shared a confused look before turning back to the third-dan taekwondo master.

'God, the cops have been here?' Quentin said.

Christine smiled as she met David's grin.

'No doubt they'll be here sooner rather than later,' Christine sipped her tea, 'thanks to what happened to Andrew last night, but no.'

'Oh,' Mary felt something in her stomach flutter, 'let me guess,' she said.

Christine and David nodded silently.

<hr />

As David went down the stairs to the basement, Christine, directly behind him, said, 'This is the first time we've all been down here at once. The four of us, right?'

Quentin, behind her, grunted in the affirmative.

Minutes before they'd finished their drinks, Christine told Quentin and Mary of Finley's surprise visit only an hour or so earlier. He'd appeared out of nowhere and scared the living wits out of the couple, who were in the middle of eating dinner. He'd spoken briefly before disappearing into the shadows.

The basement was as cold as ever.

A butcher could keep meat down there.

Quentin felt strangely at ease, which would have been ironic, after what had happened at his dad's house. Only, David would admit later that he'd poured Quentin four fingers earlier, not two.

This had certainly helped him calm down. Now being slightly tipsy, he had a dose of Dutch courage.

When they arrived at the ring room, they stood wondering what to do next.

But they all knew the only thing to do—was wait.

There was no doorbell for Finley.

A minute of silence later, Heather appeared from the dark room, animated and enthusiastic as ever.

'Nurse Mary. Christine. David. Oh, and Quentin too,'

she said all their names in perfect English, followed by the most beautiful and sincere smiles.

'Hi, Heather. It's so nice to see you, darling,' Mary said.

Heather wanted to hug her, but Finley came out of the shadows and said, 'Now, bonny Heather, what have I told you about getting too excited?'

Heather gave him an unhappy look, but it only lasted a second.

Finley walked closer and smiled.

'Heather thinks once this is all over, she can stay with you,' he patted her head affectionately, 'but I've told her when we're set free, we go to another place.'

Heather glanced up to Finley, and for the first time since meeting her, Mary thought she saw a frown on the little girl's face.

'But, Nurse Mary,' Heather's bottom lip quivered, 'I told Finley I want to stay with you.' She stole a glance at Quentin. 'And Quentin too.'

When the silence in the basement was broken by a far-off sound, Heather added, 'I want to be your daughter.'

Christine stifled a sob.

'Now, now, bonny Heather,' Finley crouched down to her, 'let's talk about this later. We need to discuss other things tonight.'

Mary wiped tears from her eyes. Quentin could feel his heart cry out for her. He took a deep breath and regained his composure.

Finley said, 'We are close to the end.' He motioned for the four to step out into the larger area of the basement. When they did, he stood at the doorway to the ring room. 'David, would it be okay if we ran through the list one more time?'

David nodded before venturing into the boiler room, which was the third small room in the basement.

He found his well-hidden piece of paper which contained the list of all the employees Yukiko had been able to track down.

He asked Christine to hold the torch so he could view the list.

There were only four names left, along with a reference to a 'Leitner,' presumably the Leitner son who'd taken over from his father and run the orphanage until its closure:

Richard Bailey
William West
Fitzroy Brown
Annabelle Pendalson
Leitner? Josef?

After David had called all the names out, Finley said, 'Annabelle Pendalson is no longer on the list.'

The four met each other's gazes for a moment, not sure what Finley's comment meant.

'She died recently?' David asked Finley.

'Yes,' Finley nodded.

'How?' Christine said.

Finley stared at her for a long time before slowly shaking his head.

'I can't explain to you how we know she's dead. We just know. The children who she killed told me. It's a feeling. But we don't know how she died. So I can't help you there.'

David, Christine, Mary, and Quentin all stood wondering what a glorious coincidence it was. She would be one less person to go after.

'But some of the kids reminded me of something last night. Annabelle was in cahoots with one of the other workers here. They were as thick as thieves.'

'Who was she thick with?' Quentin said the words, but

realised how drunk they sounded.

Finley met eyes with Heather as a rare frown came over both their faces at the same time.

'Archie Glaggin,' Finley eventually said.

It took Mary only a few seconds to realise.

'Oh my Lord. The penny just dropped for me.'

Heather suddenly took a step back, as if Mary's words scared her.

Finley saw the reaction and glared at Mary.

'How did you know we called her that?'

Mary shook her head, confused. 'What do you mean?'

Finley stared off into the distance. At the same time, spirits of some of the orphans materialised in front of him.

He knew it would have been the children whose fate had seen them cross paths with Annabelle Pendalson.

He turned and with sad eyes said, 'Annabelle Pendalson. "Penny" was what we all called her.'

'Makes sense,' David said. 'Pendalson. Penny.'

Finley shook his head before closing his eyes, struggling with the pain the children in the cages were channelling into him.

'No David,' Finley said, 'they called her penny because she would offer kids a penny.'

Christine could feel her stomach twist.

'To do what?' she asked, not wanting to know the answer.

Finley put his hand on Heather's shoulder before bending over and whispering into her ear.

She disappeared without a second's notice.

'You've been through much pain, children. Go off now, I don't want you to hear these words I'm about to speak.'

Quentin and Mary, from where they were standing, turned their heads and saw all the children standing there. Mary could see the sadness in their eyes.

When they were gone, Finley said, 'Those children don't need to hear what I'm about to tell you.'

He stood in silence for a moment.

'She would give the children a penny. To put their hands on her, where a woman goes to the toilet. Boys and girls.'

Christine felt as if she was going to be sick. David, hell, he was ready to dig this bitch out of the ground and smack her in the face.

It was Mary who solved the mystery. She'd had the thought a while ago, but now it all fitted in place.

'Archie married her.'

Quentin let out a gasp.

'Fuck. She was the woman in the pool with Glaggin. It's why she died alongside him,' he said.

———

A few moments later, the conversation returned to the job at hand. They rejoiced at the two-for-one deal—with the passing of Archie & Co. at the Tooting Bec Lido, they could now turn their focus to the last names on the list.

David read them out. The last name, Josef Leitner, was ruled out for now. The guy was a ghost, pardon the pun. He'd disappeared with the closure of Ravenstone House back in 1956. David wondered if he was buried here somewhere too.

But Finley said the children all felt as if he was still very much alive. Somewhere on God's earth.

For now, the other three names would be on their radar:

Richard Bailey
William West
Fitzroy Brown

Finley produced another bottle of his potion before they left him for the night. When all this was over, he would ask Finley what the liquid was.

As they were about to leave, Christine said, 'One last thing, Finley. Yukiko's husband. His name is Andrew.'

Finley nodded. 'Yes. The one who ran into Rose Lloyd.'

'What happened?' Christine said.

Finley shook his head, 'She's an angry, bitter woman. This is not the first time it's happened. When I was alive, I killed one of the workers here at the orphanage. She did the same thing she did to Yukiko's husband.'

Mary said, 'What does she do? How can she hurt people?'

Finley shrugged his shoulders.

'Rose has the ability to change herself into an apparition of her younger self. She was once a beautiful lady.'

'A power many would like to have,' David said.

'She did the same thing when I was alive, to a man who worked here. He was a cruel man. He would punch and slap us. Sometimes, he would even bite children. But one night, two children snuck out of their beds. They were heading for the kitchen. When they came down the hallway, the guy was standing at the base of the stairs. He was staring up at some-one. One of the kids watched him walk up, and a few seconds later, heard his muffled groans before he came crashing back down. He landed at the bottom with his head pointing in the wrong direction. They saw Rose. But she was young and very pretty. A second later, right in front of their very eyes, she changed back to how we'd normally see her: a scary, old mean lady.'

'Why would she have done this to Andrew?' asked Mary.

'You'll have to figure it out. She would only change into her younger apparition for a reason,' Finley said before he disappeared into the darkness.

CHAPTER THIRTY-NINE

DAVID AND CHRISTINE CRAWLED INTO BED. THE evening had been eventful, revealing further layers of mystery wedged into the walls of Ravenstone House.

Both of them were avid readers. David loved nothing more than the current Stephen King novel to send him off to sleep. Christine would read the latest women's magazines.

But that night, they both felt in no mood to read.

The more stories they heard of the people who worked at Ravenstone House, the more drained they would often feel.

When David drifted off into silence, Christine said, 'Penny for your thoughts? Oh—' She put her hand over her mouth and cursed. 'I will never say those words again,' she added.

David continued to stare at the ceiling before he turned to her.

'I don't blame you for not wanting to.'

'But to answer your question,' he rolled over to his side to face her, 'here's what I was thinking.'

Christine rolled onto her side and faced her husband.

'Richard Bailey. His current address is in Clapham

Common. The next on the list was a guy by the name of William West. He's in Brixton Hill.'

David let the comment hang in the air between them. His wife eventually let out a solitary 'And?'

'They live quite close to each other,' David said.

'Sorry, honey,' Christine smiled genuinely, 'I love you, but it's been a long day. What is your point?'

David grinned at his wife's directness. It was part of her DNA. He'd always admired it.

'I wonder if they still know each other. I wonder if they're friends.'

Christine knew her husband had a point, even if it had taken a moment to get there.

She nodded in agreement, and before she could articulate the same thought in words, David added, 'And let's face it. Clapham Common and Brixton Hill aren't too far away from Furzedown, either. You wonder if maybe a few of these sick bastards kept in touch from the old days.'

Christine shook her head. 'I wouldn't discount any of those theories, my love. You never know. Maybe they had. And you wonder what they'll be thinking if they know of the mysterious deaths of Archie Glaggin and Annabelle Pendalson.'

As David went to reach for the switch of his bedside lamp, he said, 'Fitzroy Brown. Something is gnawing at me about that name.'

Christine pecked him on the cheek and said, 'Why?'

'It rings a bell. I can't tell you from where, but it does,' David said.

'Well, you can ding the bell all you want in the morning, darling.' Christine smiled before she snuggled up to him for the night.

━━

The Mount Pond Arms Hotel was found within the expansive eighty-nine hectares of the Clapham Common. Nestled less than fifty feet from its namesake, the Mount Pond, it was a dump. If you call a run-down hotel a dive, the Mount Pond Arms Hotel would get a gold medal for the sport in the next Olympics, hands down.

It was half a pint away from being condemned. In less than a couple of Premier League seasons, the ramshackle building would be brought back to the dirt it had been hastily erected on 137 years earlier.

Being a seedy dive, it attracted a clientele to match.

Only the bottom end of Clapham and the surrounding borough's demographic hobbled through the doors. Everyone else avoided the place like the plague, which they feared they'd actually catch if they set foot inside.

The main bar of the Pond was busier than normal for a Wednesday afternoon, filled to capacity with a tightly packed twelve people. The barman stood behind his keep and wondered how he would cope.

Although only half of the drinkers were smoking, the air was a thick as the London Fog of '52. It added to the seedy feel of the place. As in many old pubs in Britain, natural light was almost unabashedly frowned upon. At the Pond, there were virtually no windows.

It looked like it was ten o'clock at night, but in fact it was only three in the afternoon.

The air was thick as pea soup with smoke, and also reeked of stale piss, a century of spilt beer, and the various fruity odours of patrons who'd rather buy a pint of beer than a can of deodorant.

Two men stood in one corner, either side of a flimsy bar

table, though there were plenty of places to sit. Frequent drinkers at the Pond, they knew it was safer to stand. Stories of men peeing their pants while sitting on the chairs were not rumours.

The small table was full of empty pint glasses.

'Are you going to farkeen get 'ver here, barman, and clean our farkeen glasses away, or what?'

The taller one, with the fluid tongue of a true English gentleman, held the barman's gaze before bursting into an explosion of laughter. As the barman came over with a tray, the man clipped him over the back of the head.

'If you weren't my little shit of a brutha,' he put a couple of the glasses on the tray for him, 'I'd stick one of these pint glasses in your neck for being so sheet at your job.'

Richard Bailey, ladies and gentlemen.

Richard 'the Old' Bailey, as many of his drinking buddies had called him over the years, was one mean prick.

Standing at six foot five, no one had messed with him in his early days, when he was in much better physical shape. He was 'top boy' in his local gang, in his hometown of Bootle, near Liverpool.

He had a large, narrow face, with dark-brown eyes. Teeth that would never make it into a toothpaste commercial were framed by thin, smug lips, below a big misshapen nose that had been punched too many times. His black hair, now thinning, had for half his life been tied into a greasy ponytail.

The Old Bailey had become his nickname because he'd spent seventy percent of his time on earth going in and out of the place.

Petty crime, drugs, assault, theft, and a murder charge, he'd somehow gotten out of.

His police record was a lifetime's resume of misery, both suffered and bestowed on others.

And he was one of only a handful of the workers of the Ravenstone House for the Less Privileged to have been charged with a crime he committed there, which gave him his first long-term stint in prison.

'Go easy on your brother,' his drinking buddy smirked, before savouring the cold of his seventh pint touching his lips.

William West.

The colour of paper could have originated from the tone of William 'Wild' West's skin. Pallid, pasty, take your pick. His face, neck, and head were permanently coated in a thin veneer of sweat. Although he wasn't an albino, he was surely trying to imitate one. His hair had long receded into the abyss behind his small, beaver-like face, while his gut had extended as if he were pregnant with the thousand pints he'd drunk over the years. Suffice to say, the guy wouldn't be making the front cover of any magazines soon, if ever.

They called him 'Wild' West because he was anything but.

He gripped his pint as if he had hold of his baby-carrot-sized appendage. With hands as sweaty as the rest of him, he didn't want the beer to slip out of them.

'And what are you gonna doo about 'at,' Bailey snarled, before eventually curling his lips at the edges.

The fact was, West was no match for Bailey.

He was a clear foot shorter on a good day, and West was twenty kilos heavier at least. Think of the two as a creepier version of Laurel and Hardy.

The two men had remained friends, on and off, for a long time. Ever since they'd met at work about forty years ago.

Bailey was heading towards the bottom of his ninth pint. West was lagging behind as normal. He couldn't ever keep up with the taller man, but Bailey didn't care in the slightest. West was paying for the beers, as he did most of the time. He owed Bailey, and they both knew it.

They hadn't seen each other for close to a year. The last time, West had hoped it would be the last. Bailey was still, after all these years, a son of a bitch. And Christ, did the man smell.

But when Bailey contacted West suggesting they get together for a pint, West had resigned himself. It had been a year since the last time he'd seen him.

Bailey was, West thought, three sheets to the wind, proper. Bailey's giveaway for being blind drunk was how loud he got. It was truly concerning how lubricated his lips became.

Bailey lit another cigarette, sucking on the thing as if his life depended on it.

He turned to West, before his focus drifted away into the distance.

'Did you farkeen hear?' Bailey said.

West put his beer down and felt like a new layer of cold sweat rolled over his entire body. He wanted to tell Bailey to keep his voice down, but he knew that might not end well.

'You talkin' about those at the Lido?' West said.

'Farkeen way to meet our maker,' Bailey snorted.

He dropped his now empty pint before waving at the bartender for another round. His brother reluctantly nodded.

'Farkeen creeps,' Bailey said to West before blowing smoke in his face, 'but Penny sure did give good head.'

West shook his own head in disgust, but didn't want to offend the Old Bailey, so he said, 'Well, they're now gone, and their creepy ways and secrets.'

After Bailey's brother brought over another two pints, West added, 'You hear 'bout the lollipop man, right?'

Bailey butted out his cigarette before turning to West, 'Do I look like the farkeen BCC?'

West knew Bailey had meant to say the 'BBC,' as in the British Broadcasting Corporation, but could not be bothered correcting him.

West leant forward and shook his head. 'Fletcher. You know, the one known at the place as the lollipop man. He's dead too. Died the other day.'

Bailey stared at West for an eternity. Now on his tenth pint, the guy was struggling to figure out what the hell West was talking about. He eventually, somehow, figured it out.

'Well, there you go. Fletcher, Archie, and his mole of a wife, all dead. Big farkeen deal,' he said, loud enough for just about the whole bar to hear.

West cringed. He started to wonder if going to the toilet and not coming back would be a good idea. The only problem with the Pond Hotel was that the side door had stopped working years ago. Stuck shut. There was only one way in and out. If he did a runner, Bailey might see him. Damn it.

West put his beer down and scanned the room. Save for a couple of guys standing at the bar with their backs turned to him and Bailey, there were only two other men there. And they were sitting in a huddle right over in the opposite corner.

'Richard,' West said. He waited for Bailey to make eye contact, which took him forever.

When he eventually looked at him, West said, 'You may have forgotten. It's been a while since we've seen each other.'

Bailey glared at his friend's sweaty head. 'Forgotten what, mate?'

West wiped the sweat off his considerably large forehead before wiping his hand on his trousers.

'I stayed friends with one of the other guys from the orphanage,' he said.

Bailey shook his head and reached for his packet of cigarettes. As he stuck another smoke in his mouth, he said, 'Not sure where the farck this is going, chubby, but you can get on with it if you bloody well like.'

West bit his lower lip before wishing he was on another continent, thousands of miles away from this shit of a man.

'John Heen. He worked there too. Died two weeks ago. Don't you find it a little coincidental, Bailey?'

Bailey lit his cigarette and shrugged his shoulders.

The guy had never been intelligent. And now he was completely pissed, his mind was working on single-digit output.

'Sounds like Ravenstone fucking house is catching up with us all,' Bailey snickered, reaching over and grabbing West on the shoulder.

'Sounds like you'd better savour the beer in front of you, chubby,' he laughed.

West didn't share Bailey's flippant attitude.

'Come get us, little children of Ravenstone!' Bailey shouted.

This resulted in his brother the barman shaking his head, and brought stares from the two men huddled in the corner.

The two men standing at the bar with their backs turned to Bailey and West simply met each other's eyes without moving their heads at all.

They were both thinking the same thing.

The sooner this one was swimming with the fish, the better. And his fat little mate as well.

The stockier one of the two reached down and felt the object in the front pocket of his army pants.

He wondered how soon he would get to use it. There had been no opportunity at the pub.

David would get his chance.

Just not here.

Somewhere close. Underground.

CHAPTER FORTY

David and Quentin left the Mount Pond Arms Hotel.

The smell of the place would remain in their nostrils for hours.

Bailey had announced to West that they would head into the city and undertake an impromptu two-man pub crawl. He said it like he was announcing it to the entire pub. West felt ill with the thought. He'd hoped Bailey had enough beer for one day. Nope. The man was on a mission. The only guy happy with the idea was Bailey's brother.

It would be the last time he saw his older brother in the flesh.

David weighed his options. His gut told him the two men would go into town on the Tube. Guys like these two never caught cabs. They'd rather keep the fare for more beers. So when he and Quentin left the pub, he headed towards Clapham South Station.

There they were. Bailey's height made him easy to find. He was a walking beanpole with a black ponytail sticking out the top.

'What's the plan, my man?' Quentin asked him as they kept a safe distance, tailing the two men.

David walked on for a few steps before he turned and smiled at Quentin.

'No bloody idea,' he grinned, 'but let's just see if something presents itself.'

David had identified both men the previous weekend, thanks to the dossiers on them from Yukiko. Both had police records, which meant photos on file. Although the photos were old, he recognised the two after staking out the addresses in their files.

He and Quentin had actually been following Bailey that particular day, hoping for any chance to get some of the potion in contact with him. They couldn't believe their luck when he ended up at the Mount Pond Arms Hotel to meet up with West, another name on the list.

As they stood at the bar listening to the drivel coming from both men, they wondered if another two-for-one deal would eventuate. But with the bartender keeping a watchful eye on his older brother, it would prove impossible to orchestrate—at least at the Mount Pond Arms Hotel.

'We should become private investigators,' Quentin quipped. He'd just crossed Nightingale Lane with David, and they were now walking down the pavement towards Clapham South Station.

Bailey and West were a good fifty feet in front. David was fairly confident they'd successfully tailed the men without Bailey or West noticing they'd been followed.

Wishful thinking, Mr Banks.

As the two men walked into the entrance of the station, David realised something.

'Shit,' he said, 'quick!'

He broke into a sudden sprint.

Quentin put two and two together.

If a train came in a moment, Bailey and West might make it onto a carriage while he and David missed it.

Quentin ran after him.

As David reached the station, he caught his breath and ran towards the escalators with Quentin in tow.

Quentin heard David's words ahead of him: 'Shit, shit, shit.'

The rush of wind and the sounds were unmistakable.

A train was right that moment pulling in or out of the station.

David kept going. Quentin was having trouble keeping up.

As they reached the bottom of the long escalator, the first thing David noticed was that the station was empty.

They must have all made the train.

David headed towards the platform for the city-bound train.

When he came through to the platform, he cursed himself.

'Fuck it,' he said to himself through laboured breaths.

The platform was empty.

A second later, he saw movement halfway down the platform.

'You've gotta be kidding me,' David said, and a moment later Quentin made it to his side of the platform. Q was looking down to the other end of the platform with an intent look that disturbed him. Following his eyes, David saw Bailey and West had just come out of another access tunnel not forty feet away.

But what unnerved David the most was that Bailey was looking at them.

David stood and stared at Bailey, and for a second he thought the mission was blown.

He quickly ushered Quentin to head towards the other end of the station. The platform ran out about twenty feet away from them; after that, there was only the pitch-black tunnel, through which the next train would soon come hurtling.

When they were within about ten feet of the end, David stopped and turned his attention to the wall on the other side of the platform. 'Don't look at them,' he told Quentin. 'Look straight ahead.'

And it was all Quentin wanted to do, to turn and see what their quarry was doing. His senses were going into overdrive.

Out of the corner of his eye, he was sure he could see Bailey walking in their direction, with West trailing behind him.

Doing his best to be inconspicuous, David turned to see what was behind him. On a bench seat, someone had left the remains of their lunch: a half-eaten roll in a paper wrapper, and an empty plastic cup.

He thought it could be a good idea to back towards the chair and sit down. If Quentin followed, they might just look like two everyday people waiting for the next train.

'Oh, shit,' Quentin said a second later.

Bailey was ten feet away.

'What the fark are you lookin' at?' he barked.

Quentin froze, but instinctively turned his head to Bailey. 'Who, me?' he said.

'I says, are you farkeen lookin' me?' Bailey shouted. His teeth showed, his lips in a snarl.

David grabbed Quentin by the arm, pulling him away from the edge of the platform just in case.

'Hey you, fucker,' Bailey was now almost within six feet

of David, 'hold on. West?' Bailey turned to his drinking buddy. 'Weren't these farckers at the farking Pond?'

West nodded. 'They were standing at the bar. What the fuck, Bailey? Are they following us?'

Bailey turned back to David and Quentin.

His eyes went wide.

'Farking pigs or somethin'. West, you know what I do to farking pigs?'

Quentin wondered if he was going to get a hiding.

But he remembered who he was with.

David.

Taekwondo master. Third dan, you motherfuckers.

'Oh shit!' Quentin cried out.

The underground station had suddenly plunged into pitch darkness.

It all happened so fast.

The second the lights went out, David felt someone right next to him. But it wasn't Quentin.

'David.'

Shit, he knew the voice.

Finley.

'Pour as much of the potion as you can into the cup on the bench behind you, right now,' the boy said.

David pulled the bottle of potion from his pocket and fumbled for the bench.

Somehow, in the darkness, he found the cup.

He quickly poured the liquid until he felt it overflow.

As soon as he dropped the bottle on the bench, the lights came back on.

Bailey and West had stumbled backwards somewhat, with Bailey only centimetres from the edge.

'What the fark is going on?' he shouted.

'I have no fucking idea,' West groaned.

The lights throughout the station flickered off and on again, as if there were an electrical fault.

But when they steadied, Quentin felt every hair on his body pulsate in fright.

On the train line, from one end of the platform to the other: children.

It's not our fault.

We did nothing wrong.

Finley was at the very end of the platform, pointing at Bailey and West.

The two drunks were staring at all the children, and had gone completely silent. West was trembling.

A sick, sly grin appeared on Bailey's face.

He pointed to Finley and waggled his finger.

'So you farking kids have come for us too, huh?'

Finley stood motionless.

David wondered what would happen next.

It was the first time he'd seen any of the children outside the walls of Ravenstone House.

Bailey took his arrogance to the next level.

He glared down at the children.

They, in turn, stared back.

None of them looked angry, just pensive.

Bailey reached down and unzipped his pants.

'You've gotta be kidding me,' David said under his breath, 'he's not going to—'

As Bailey pulled his appendage out of his pants, he stood closer to the edge of the platform, ready to piss out onto the train line.

'Go to the bench and hold on for dear life,' David and Quentin heard Finley say. As if driven on autopilot by his words, they did as exactly as they were told.

'Put the cup of water on the platform. Quickly, David,' Finley added.

Just as David did this and made it back to the seat, they heard the almighty rumble.

A train was coming.

With his appendage in his hand, Bailey laughed, 'Farking train is coming, kids, best be on your way or else—'

A second later, West screamed.

A train was about to explode out of the tunnel.

But this one had something surrounding it.

A wall of water.

<hr>

'Hold your breath!'

David managed to shout the three words before he and Quentin were engulfed by the tidal wave of water exploding with the train out of the tunnel. It was an incredible thing to witness.

It hit the platform with the might of a sledgehammer, throwing Bailey into the air with West a few feet behind him.

As the train came through the tunnel, it seemed to drive the avalanche of water ahead of it.

As the train screeched to a halt, David and Quentin watched the wall of water disappear into the other end of the Tube tunnel.

They were soaking wet, but alive.

David realised the cup of potion was long gone.

People were stepping out of the train, some screaming, others looking at each other in bewilderment.

The platform was drenched in water. It rolled back onto the tracks in slow motion. It dripped from everything, high and low.

And old lady who'd been on the train stepped out and

pulled from her bag a compact umbrella, which opened with a 'poof'. She shuffled her way carefully across the wet platform, as if this were a daily occurrence.

David and Quentin both rose to their feet and started to walk down the platform towards the front of the train.

People were still coming out. Eventually, the train driver came out of his compartment, shaking his head.

'I've been driving trains for twenty-five years,' David heard him telling a passenger, 'and I've never seen this before.'

Quentin followed David to the other end of the platform in silence.

No one seemed to be hurt or injured.

But two people were nowhere to be seen.

Bailey and West.

They would be found somewhere in the underground complex of Clapham South Station.

CHAPTER FORTY-ONE

BUILT IN THE EARLY 1940S, THE DEEP-LEVEL AIR-RAID shelter had been designed to protect up to 8,000 Londoners from the frightening German air raids of World War II. It was one of eight the British government built adjacent to Tube stations in London.

Sitting directly beneath the Morden train line, the Clapham South Station air-raid shelter was extensive. Two main tunnels stretched a whopping 350-plus metres over two levels, accompanied by connecting tunnels and other facilities such as kitchens, washrooms, and lavatories.

Only one access tunnel directly connected Clapham South Station to the war-era shelter. And this, as you would expect, was secured from curious eyes by an ominous gate of wrought-iron bars, and a padlock just as menacing.

Next to the Anson shelter, one of eight designated wings in the facility, was one of four lavatory blocks. This was where police would eventually find the body of sixty-three-year-old Richard Bailey, of Clapham Common, and with him sixty-seven-year old William West, also deceased, of Brixton Hill.

How the two men made it all the way from the station

above, and through a series of tunnels, to the lavatory block close to 150 feet away, would be the first question Scotland Yard detectives pondered. How the wrought-iron gate was blown open and off its hinges was another mystery.

It was no coincidence that these detectives were also investigating the bizarre deaths of Archie and Anna Glaggin at the Tooting Bec Lido. For there was a direct connection between the two sets of untimely deaths.

It took forensic investigators close to two hours to get to the bodies of Bailey and West, which were suspended upside down in a chunk of solid ice at least twenty feet thick.

But the mysteries didn't end there.

Bailey was much taller than the low-hanging ceiling of the shelter. When the police eventually got to the two, Bailey was suspended upside down, alright. But his neck was clearly broken, with his head turned perpendicular to his body. It was the only way, whoever—or whatever—had done this could have managed to hang him upside down in the lavatory block.

As with the Glaggins, only the feet of the victims were left protruding, at the very top of the huge block of ice.

***

David and Quentin slipped into the dazed crowd of train passengers after finding no trace of Bailey and West.

Strangers continued to mutter profanities to each other about what they'd just witnessed. But they all moved with purpose, keen to get to ground level.

With CCTV cameras still a year or two away from becoming part of the decor at Clapham South Station, Quentin and David were fairly safe from detection, though someone looking carefully might have wondered why among all the others hurrying from the station, two were wet as drowned rats. Rather than calling attention to themselves by soaking the seats in the back of a cab, the men decided to get some exercise and walk home.

———

'What in God's name happened to you?' Christine's eyes widened as David walked into their kitchen in a dishevelled state.

'I had a shower, clothed,' David quipped, and gave his wife a light peck on the forehead before shuffling off to the bathroom.

Ten minutes later he reappeared, showered and squeaky clean.

'How did you and Quentin go with, er, what was his name?' Christine asked while putting the finishing touches on a lasagne that was soon to reappear as dinner.

'Bailey,' David said, reaching into the fridge for a beer.

He waited until he'd had at least two welcome swigs of ale before speaking further. He needed it.

'You wouldn't believe it if I told you, honey,' he said, clearly exhausted, and still more shaken, by the day's events.

'Well, before you tell me all about it,' Christine put the lasagne in the oven and closed the door before turning back to him, 'I'll tell you this first, before I forget. The guys upstairs want to meet up with you and me and Quentin and Mary tomorrow, for brunch. Yukiko, too, if she's able. They want to talk about what's going on here at Ravenstone.'

David took another long pull from his beer and nodded.

'Good,' Christine said. 'I'd said we would be there. Mary said yes too. I'm sure if Mary's there, Q will only be one step behind. I suggested we meet at Moose's Cafe. Okay with you?'

David nodded again.

'Now,' she stepped up the island bench that separated her from her husband, 'tell me all, Mr Banks.'

David smiled. 'Grab a chair.' He flicked his head towards a bar stool next to him. 'You're going to want to take a seat for this one, Mrs Banks.'

Moose's Cafe was a leisurely ten-minute walk from Ravenstone House. Named after the owner, Sharon Molloy, her secondary-school nickname had become one of the top destinations in all of Wandsworth for a decent breakfast, brunch, or lunch—take your pick.

Christine had chosen it for their get-together with the upstairs residents for three reasons: good coffee, amazing food, and a nice shack out the back for private functions.

David, Christine, Quentin, and Mary arrived early to briefly run through what they would and would not openly discuss with the neighbours.

It was a forgone conclusion that they would keep their mission for the children a secret. There was no need for those upstairs to know. With their work drawing to a close—or so they hoped—they saw no reason for anything to change.

'Ah, here they come.' Quentin's seat at the big table in the shack afforded him a direct view into the courtyard, where he could see about half a dozen people approaching.

Christine nodded. 'I remember the two women up front. They saw old Rose Lloyd at the top of the stairs with Yukiko's husband.'

David, being the very type of an extrovert, and closest to

the door, sprang to his feet to open the door for the group to enter.

'Hello! Welcome!' David said.

Quick and hasty introductions were made with outstretched hands, in the shack dominated by a well-weathered but solid wooden table.

'Hello, I'm Helena, Helena George,' the woman said. 'And this is my friend Frances McKendrick.' She looked at Christine and Mary. 'I believe we've already met.'

'Yes,' Christine said, 'on the terrible night with Andrew from Flat Three.'

'How is he doing?' Frances inquired.

Christine could feel her chest hurt for Yukiko. 'He's still in a stable condition, as far as I know.'

David stepped closer to two men who had arrived with the group.

'David Banks, Flat Two, and over there is my wife of forty glorious years,' he said, grinning towards Christine.

The taller of the two echoed David's smile. 'Hello. Ross DeBel is my name, and this sorry excuse for a flatmate is my best friend, Neil Olney.'

Neil shook David's hand firmly and shook his head. 'One thing you learn once you get to know Ross here,' he flicked his head in the other's direction, 'is the guy has patented a way of talking pure bollocks.'

They all laughed before shuffling to a seat and preparing to sit down.

The last couple attending the catch-up stood awkwardly at the door. Christine could tell they were either shy, or as nervous as hell. Maybe both.

'Hello,' Christine said, leaning over the table and stretching her hand in the direction of the woman.

'Christine Banks, Flat Two,' she smiled, 'and this gaggle

of people over here is David, my husband, and Quentin and Mary from Flat One.'

'Hi there,' the young woman smiled weakly, 'I'm Martine Nicholls, and this here is my husband, John.'

John Nicholls' eyes darted from one side of the big table to the other. He went to reach for Quentin's hand, but doubted he could make it, so he pulled back and gave an awkward wave to everyone else at the table instead.

With everyone seated, the discussion could get underway.

—

Brunch orders came and went, and the conversation stayed light as candyfloss while people ate their food and drank their coffees, teas, and orange juices. All manner of conversations fluttered around the shack until the last of the meals were finished.

David and Christine met each other's eyes and knew what the other was thinking: time to get this show on the road.

David cleared his throat and humorously tapped his knife on his mug of tea. 'Okay, everyone, shall we get down to why we're all here?'

The shack fell into silence.

'Alright,' David said quietly, 'who wants to start this?'

Ross DeBel put his hand up.

'Ross,' David said, 'it's all yours.'

Ross met the eyes of his friend, Neil, who seemed to say something without speaking.

'It goes without saying that Ravenstone is one seriously haunted house, right?' Ross said. The group agreed with nods and murmurs. 'They say the old lady, who most of us have seen, was thrown from the top of the stairs to her death. She's one seriously pissed-off old bag.'

Neil cut in. 'I heard round the traps that there's over a hundred orphans buried under the house itself. Murdered.'

Helena had her turn, seemingly unperturbed by Neil's report that they were living over a pile of dead bodies. 'Back to the old lady: they say her name is Rose Lloyd. Her husband was the original owner of Ravenstone back in the early 1800s. The guy apparently liked to share his love around. Quite the philanderer, they say. I don't know if what I've heard is true. But the theory is he ordered one of his sons to do the deed. To kill his wife. Sneak up and push her down the stairs. That's is why she is so angry.'

Everyone seemed to take a deeper breath all at once. Frances, Helena's flatmate, leant forward. 'Whatever happened to the man from Flat Three, Andrew,' Helena nodded next to her, confirming Frances had his name correct, 'has the two of us completely freaked out.'

She put her hand to her mouth, her emotions slowly coming to the boil, 'and now there's these stories of the orphans who were killed here. And are still here.'

Helena draped her arm over Frances' shoulder, comforting her. 'Not sure about the rest of you, but we don't think we can continue living there,' she said.

John and Martine Nicholls seemed to shift in their seats at the same time, before John shook his head and said quietly, 'We hear noises at night. We've both heard children's voices. And Rose Lloyd, fuck me: if I had a pound for every time we've woken up to her standing in the doorway of our bedroom giving us dirty looks…'

Martine closed her eyes and stifled a sob, her head drooping towards her lap, but she kept silent.

'…I'd have enough money to buy the place outright,' John concluded.

Neil sat forward and spoke to the four inhabitants of the downstairs flats. 'You guys. Have you heard anything, seen anything?'

Quentin's eyes remained fixed on Neil, and he was the first to speak. 'Hell yes,' Quentin said. 'We've heard noises in the night which seem out of place. And...' he wondered how far he should go, but knew it was best to say something. If he, Mary, Christine, and David all said nothing, it might raise alarm bells.

'...we've all had a visit from the old lady too.'

Mary watched the reaction of the people from upstairs, and wondered where this meeting was going.

'And you're all going to stay on?' this from Martine, who had a voice as quiet as her husband's. Crikey, Mary thought, don't ever go to the basement and stand inside the ring on the floor.

David, Christine, Mary, and Quentin weren't sure what to say.

'We're not sure, to be honest,' David lied, and Quentin and Mary concurred.

<hr>

When David heard Helena's conversation with Neil and Ross, he almost patted Christine on the leg to get her to stop talking to John and Martine.

'What did you just say?' he said to Helena.

She shifted her gaze to David as the conversations around her quickly dissipated.

'My father knew a few people who worked at Ravenstone House when it was the orphanage,' she said.

David could feel a ball-bearing the size of a tennis ball slide into his throat.

Sensing his unease, Christine placed her hand on David's

right knee, underneath the table, to try and get him settle and to take a breath.

'He worked in a grocery shop across the road from the orphanage, straight after the war,' she said. 'He's old as the hills now, but sharp as a tack.'

'The couple who died in the Tooting Bec Lido the other day—he remembered these people. Don't tell me how he knew their names—Archie Glaggin and Annabelle Pendalson —but he did. They eventually married.'

She took a sip of her tea before she continued.

'He worked in the area for many years after Ravenstone closed. Maybe he used to see some of these people still around the place.'

'Where does he live now?' David said.

Helena waved in the direction of the window, 'Dad is one stubborn old bastard,' she said light-heartedly. 'He's still in his own flat in Clapham Common.'

Helena was not done there.

'I've begged him to stop shuffling across the grounds of the Common to drink his one pint a week at the Mount Pond Arms Hotel. But Dad says he has to try and help it stay open. He's been doing it for years. The place is a cesspool.'

Just the mere mention of the place had David and Quentin shift in their seats. Shit, they'd been there only yesterday, for God's sake. This six degrees of separation was getting too close.

David and Quentin knew it wasn't out of the question for him to have come into contact with Bailey and West, especially if he remembered the two from Ravenstone and they drank there as often as the old man did. But they had to swallow the sense of dread they were both starting to feel.

'Tell the guys what he once told you about the other guy who worked there,' this from Frances, Helena's flatmate.

Helena shook her head as if she didn't want to bring it

up. But with four people at the table seemingly hanging on her every word (David, Christine, Quentin and Mary) Helena couldn't help herself. It had been a while since she had this much attention.

'Dad brought this story up when I told him I'd purchased the flat at Ravenstone House. There was this dark-skinned guy,' she quickly scanned the people at the table, 'Sorry, I'm not racist, I'm just telling you what he said.'

No one reacted, so she continued, 'Okay, so he was Jamaican, or maybe from the West Indies; anyway, Dad said he'd come over and buy groceries from him every week. One day, Dad asked what his name was. The guy told Dad to just simply call him "Fitz".'

Helena looked at Frances, who gave her a 'get on with it' look.

'So Dad, being the nosy sod he was, couldn't leave it there. He's always, as long as I can remember, always had a thing for names. He can remember my primary-school teacher's full name after all these years. Anyway,' she shook her head, 'I digress.'

'For God's sake, get on with it,' David thought.

'Someone else from the orphanage came in one day, another nice chap, and Dad, being Dad, mentioned the other guy to this man. "You know Fitz? Oh, I've forgotten his full name," he said to this other guy, who was trying to get the right money for his groceries from his pocket, or so Dad's long-winded story went.

'Anyway, the guy finally put Dad and his silly head out of their misery. The guy's name was Fitzroy Brown. He'd come over here on the ship, the *Windrush*, remember?' Helena scanned the room, but pretty much only David nodded. He remembered the story.

The *Windrush* was a ship that brought Jamaican workers over to England in 1948, and they—'

David recalled where the refugees had been housed for the short term, once they'd arrived here. It was a coincidence he could park for now. He let himself come back to the room.

He picked up Helena's story, and wondered if she would be done by dinner time.

'Anyway, sorry to do this, but I thought it were interesting.' She shot a worried look at Frances, who she could tell was starting to urge her to get to the end.

'Okay, so the crux of this story is this. This guy Fitz, one day, simply vanished, stopped coming into Dad's shop. When Dad asked one of the other workers where Fitz was, the guy told him he'd not turned up for work last week, and hadn't been seen since. This wasn't long before the orphanage closed its doors forever. But Dad also has a thing for conspiracy theories and such. Don't ever have a cup of tea with Dad,' she smiled to herself, 'the guy will bore you to death with all his hoo-ha about every conspiracy known to man. Especially the homegrown stories.'

She had David's full attention. This little get-together may have been potentially useful after all.

Just get to the point, Helena, Christine thought.

'Dad told me about ten years ago. I just dismissed it as another one of his stupid theories. There were so many, I used to just tune out most of the time. But for anyone who cares...'

'...Dad swears Fitzroy Brown disappeared for a while but came back to London under a new identity. He says he remembers the guy's eyes. His mannerisms. He swore on his life he thinks it's true. Fitzroy Brown is now Jacob Brown. You all know him, right?'

David and Christine met each other's eyes.

Jacob Brown was an elected member of Parliament.

A British MP.

CHAPTER FORTY-TWO

The brunch meeting at Moose's Cafe ended shortly after Helena's story ended. They all agreed to stay in touch. But it would be the last time they were all together.

David and Christine opted for a walk home after they said their goodbyes to their fellow residents, while Quentin succumbed to Mary's pleas for a leisurely stroll down Lacham High Road to check out some clothes stores. The pain in his eyes was such that you'd think Mary had kicked him in his crown jewels.

'Talk to me, Mr Banks,' Christine said to David once they were well out of earshot of everyone else.

'You think Helena's old man is on the money?' he said as he reached out to hold his wife's hand as they strolled together.

Christine walked for a few moments before answering him.

'Right now,' she turned and met his eyes, 'everything is on the table.'

Christine meant you couldn't completely rule out what Helena's old man had said. If the guy was still sharp, who knew? His wild theory just might be true.

That would take this thing to the next level. Most of the other people on the hit list had belonged to the fringes of society. Bums, derelicts, and so on.

But if Helena's dad was right, and this Jacob Brown, MP, had once been Fitzroy Brown, he would be all but untouchable.

If he was brought to answer for his sins, it could blow everything wide open, and that may have repercussions.

The couple continued to walk while they discussed and debated the day's meeting. Deeply engrossed in their conversation, they didn't realise they'd walked all the way back to Ravenstone House until they were almost at the doorstep.

As they approached the front door, they heard someone speak behind them.

'Do you two live here?' the calm and confident voice asked.

David and Christine glanced at each other before turning around.

David stepped back down to the pavement before making eye contact with the stranger.

'Yes. We do,' he said.

The guy smiled. Without taking his eyes off David, he slipped his hand into the inside of his suit.

He pulled out his wallet and said, 'Alright,' then flipped it open to reveal a police badge.

'Detective Inspector Megevand, CID. Would you mind if I came in to ask you a few questions?'

———

David led the inspector into the hallway of Ravenstone House.

Christine followed at the rear, busy arranging her thoughts.

'They did a fine job with the renovations,' the policeman said, his eyes venturing from the floor to the ceiling.

'Come, our flat is this way,' David said.

Once inside their flat, Ian did the same thing as in the hallway, looking around the flat with what seemed to be a keen interest. 'What a lovely place you guys have,' he said.

But truth be told, the feeling coursing through Ian was anything but welcoming. Something was gnawing at him deep inside: a sense of darkness, sorrow, death.

The feeling would remain until he left.

While he checked out their home, Christine took the opportunity to check him out.

The inspector wore a smart, dark-blue suit. It appeared to have either been tailor-made, or the guy had the body of one of those well-built mannequins you saw in department-store windows.

He would be six foot at least, she surmised, with strong, broad shoulders. His shoes were spotlessly clean and polished to a high shine. She smiled as David watched her checking him out.

'Put the kettle on, darling,' Christine said, winking at her husband.

She wondered how long ago he'd lost his hair. She pitched his age at somewhere around the mid-forties. If she could check his license, she'd see she was about right: he was forty-four.

Inspector Megevand made bald look good.

His fair complexion made her believe his roots were somewhere in Britain.

His gaze was serious, but with blue eyes and a nondescript nose, he was anything but intimidating. Only his square, set jaw gave the hint that he could be if he wanted to.

And it was only when David offered him a tea that his

lips parted to reveal a good set of white teeth. Before that, she hadn't seen him smile.

⸺

'Nice and easy,' David thought as he reached over and placed the cup of tea in front of the inspector.

Christine could tell David was nervous, but she doubted the inspector would notice. It didn't matter. Most people the world over would feel the same way if an inspector asked to come in for a chat, Christine thought. Right?

Ian took a sip of the tea and said, 'English Breakfast. A good drop. So,' he wiped his lips lightly with a thumb, 'you don't mind if I ask you a few questions?'

Christine slowly ventured to the side of the island bench where her husband stood.

'No problem,' David straightened his shoulders and took a deep breath. 'Please go ahead. What can we do for you?'

'I'm investigating the bizarre deaths of one Archie Glaggin, and his wife Anna, at the Tooting Bec Lido a couple of weeks ago,' Inspector Megevand said.

'I saw something on telly about it. Very odd indeed,' Christine said.

Megevand took another sip of his black tea before resting it on the saucer. He nodded before pulling out his notepad and flipping it open to a page, then turned his gaze back to the couple.

'Well, it doesn't end there. Yesterday, two men died at Clapham South Station. There's a similarity in the circumstances of both their deaths and those of Mr and Mrs Glaggin.'

David raised his eyebrows.

'Awful news, inspector, but I,' David turned and patted

Christine on the back, 'we don't know anything about these events.'

Inspector Megevand nodded, but his face remained pensive. The look in his eyes unnerved Christine. She did her best to try and remain calm.

'Alright,' the inspector slowly rose from the stool before taking one last drink from his tea. 'Thank you for the tea, and your time.'

As Christine and David led him out of their flat and to the front door, the inspector shook both their hands and said his goodbyes.

When he reached the pavement, he turned and said to David, 'By the way, have you been to the Mount Pond Arms Hotel recently?'

David panicked. His response probably came too quickly.

'Where?'

Megevand held his gaze for a few seconds before making eye contact with Christine. He smiled before turning and walking away.

<hr>

Quentin felt as if he were in his own version of Hell. But millions of men the world over had to endure the same pain.

Clothes shopping.

With your woman.

For her.

Bloody.

Hell.

They were currently at store number four.

Quentin loved Mary, which allowed her to stretch his patience far further than anyone else.

But like a giant rubber band, sooner or later, it would spring back with an almighty force. Snap.

'What do you think, darling?' he'd been asked the question so many times, he'd been starting to zone out.

'Looks absolutely fabulous,' said the young shop assistant standing behind the counter.

If Mary had been trying on a hessian potato sack with holes cut for her arms, legs, and head, the girl would probably have said the same thing, Quentin surmised.

Only when the silence lengthened did he realise it was his cue to answer.

Honestly, the dress was pretty, but it did not suit her. He was torn between telling the truth and risking being dragged to another five stores, and telling her it was nice.

'Um, er...' Damn it! Quentin chastised himself. He couldn't lie to her, so even in his hesitation she knew the answer.

'Right,' Mary huffed before spinning on her heels and heading back to the change room.

The shop assistant wisely added no further comment.

Quentin shook his head and wished he had a magazine to read.

The coffee he'd had with brunch a little while ago was giving his breath a fragrance the rear ends of camels were famous for. He reached over and pulled his fiancée's generously sized handbag towards him to look for her mints.

He might have been be bored shitless, but at least his breath wouldn't threaten to blow back on him and knock him out.

When he put the packet of mints back in the handbag, something right at the bottom caught his attention.

For the rest of the day, he'd be asking himself how he'd managed to completely forget about it.

It was the letter Wendy, his father's housekeeper, had given to him.

Just as he was about to grab it, he heard movement from the change room.

Mary was coming out in another new dress.

Actually, Quentin immediately thought this one appeared perfect on her.

It made him feel good to tell her the truth.

'Spot on,' he said, giving her a perfunctory wave as if to say, 'Get it off, you're buying it.'

When she closed the change-room door, Quentin reached in and pulled the envelope out. He could taste the bile, a dead giveaway that he was nervous, even with a mint in his mouth.

He took a deep breath and pulled the piece of paper free of the envelope.

His mother's handwriting made it look like she'd written the short letter under duress. Her normally neat, cursive script was haphazard, even panicked. It unnerved him.

It took him a couple of moments to re-read the words, checking his eyes had it right:

Bernie.
Our marriage was built on lies.
The sort of lies one cannot forgive.
I want it all.
This is the only way, Bernie, your lies can remain
locked away from the outside world.
Your soon to be ex-wife.

CHAPTER FORTY-THREE

QUENTIN WAS DISTRACTED FOR MOST OF THE WALK BACK to Ravenstone House.

When they arrived home, he sat in the kitchen as Mary went about her business.

'Want anything—' Mary abruptly stopped her question mid-sentence when she saw the look on Q's face.

Her eyes spotted the piece of paper sitting in front of him on the bench.

'Read this.' He passed it over to her.

The couple had found their way to the couch.

Both were working overtime to try and understand what Quentin's mother's letter meant.

'Can I ask you a question without offending you, my love?' Mary said carefully.

Quentin shook his head. 'What a silly thing to say,' he said.

He watched Mary stare into the distance. Like many couples, they could often tell each other's thoughts, and it didn't take long for him to figure it out. 'Did Dad, have something to do with the "accident",' he paused until she met his eyes, 'which took my mother's life?'

The knock on their door made the two jump.

Because when the third-dan taekwondo instructor tapped on anything, it was always with the force of a hammer.

Quentin was on his feet and at his front door in a few strides.

'It's been a while.' Quentin smiled.

'You and Mary, come quick, hurry,' David said.

Mary was already halfway to the front door when Quentin turned and nodded in the direction of Flat One.

———

They found David and Christine in the middle of their lounge room with their eyes fixed on the television. They barely turned their heads when Quentin and Mary arrived.

'What are we—'

David cut Quentin's question short. 'Wait, wait,' he interjected as the ad on-screen ended and the evening news came back on.

'And now to the mysterious goings-on at the Clapham South Station yesterday, where passengers aboard a city-bound train experienced what you could say was their own version of a house-of-horrors water slide. We cross to Kim Mackay, who is on the scene live at Clapham South Station. Kim, what can you tell us?'

The reporter stood at the entrance to the station, which was entirely cordoned off with police tape.

'Thanks, Bob.' The reporter adjusted her earpiece to sit more comfortably. 'As you have said, passengers on a 3.20pm city-bound train had one hell of a scary experience here yesterday. Passengers who have given statements thus far spoke of a sudden explosion of water not far from when the train arrived at the platform. It came from nowhere, as if the train had hit a wall of water. But all this water seemed to travel along with the train before it exploded out into the station.'

The reporter paused to catch her breath before continuing.

'Miraculously, no one on the train was injured, including the driver, who, rightly so, has taken leave until investigations of the mystery have been completed. Transit authorities are citing a water leak even though no further water seemed to appear after the train came to a halt at the station. But,' Kim's expression grew serious, 'police have informed us of the deaths of two men who were waiting for the train on the platform. Their bodies were found in the train tunnel about twenty metres further down. Police have said initial indications are that the two men, known to police, appear to have drowned. Back to you, Bob.'

David went to say something, but Christine slapped him as she realised the news anchor had more to say. 'This, in addition to the mysterious goings-on at the Tooting Bec Lido, which also resulted in the deaths of two people, have the residents of the borough of Wandsworth wondering if something is amiss in their neighbourhood.'

The news anchor checked his notes before his eyes met the red dot on the camera in front of him.

'Sources within the police, who wish to remain anonymous, claim there are rumours that the people in both events were connected in some way.'

His next words would forever change the lives of those four residents watching the news together.

'The four people killed not only knew each other, but once all worked in an orphanage located in Lacham, which closed under a cloud of controversy thirty-four years ago, in

1956.' Frustratingly, Bob checked his notes again. 'We believe it was called Ravenstone House for the Less Privileged,' he finally said. 'Although the building has largely lain derelict since its closure, it was recently converted into modern flats, where some residents are now living in fear thanks to paranormal activity taking place there of late.'

If David, Christine, Mary, and Quentin thought that was the end of it, they were mistaken. The camera angle changed and now the other anchor, Frances Brown, took her turn.

'Reporters covering another news story in Central London today decided it was time to ask the lord mayor, Bernie Brookes, for his take on the strange goings-on around Lacham and Wandsworth.'

When Quentin's father appeared on the screen, he could feel a cold shiver pass over him.

'My lord mayor, my lord mayor,' a couple of the reporters said as they pointed large microphones towards Bernie Brookes' face.

'My lord mayor, what are your thoughts on what's been happening around Lacham. People dying, drowning, all connected, allegedly, to the Ravenstone House orphanage, which itself has a long and dark history.'

Brookes seemed to digest the reporters' words.

'Bad, bad place, the orphanage.' He glared at the reporter. 'Should have been torn down decades ago,' he said coldly.

But when he said the next words, he stared into the camera, and Quentin felt as if he were speaking to him directly.

He may as well have been.

'But those damn developers, who care for nothing but profit, they renovated the place, much to my disgust. What's worse,' here it comes, Q, 'my only son ignored my pleas and stupidly bought one of the flats there.'

The words punched Quentin in the stomach with the force of a nuclear warhead, and he momentarily felt woozy. Then his father said one more thing. 'As far as these dead people, you're asking the wrong guy. I haven't heard of these events. But if you believe the rumours of the orphanage and how children were treated there, they probably deserved it.'

Shit, Bernie, don't hold back, Mary thought.

Christine turned the TV off.

All four stood in stunned silence for a few moments. Eventually, like zombies, they shuffled to the island bench and found bar stools to collapse onto.

'What the fuck,' Quentin said.

David turned to Christine. 'Johnny. Glasses. Stat,' he said.

———

They talked for a while.

David and Christine discussed their impromptu chat with a member of the police force earlier in the day.

As he took his first sip of whisky, Quentin decided he wouldn't tell them about the contents of his mother's letter just yet. He'd park it for now; its implications were too heavy to deal with.

The four knew that thanks to the lord mayor of London, the spotlight on Ravenstone House would grow brighter now. Especially due to the deaths of the Glaggins, Bailey, and West. It was probably only a matter of time before investigative journalists uncovered the recent deaths of the other workers connected to the orphanage.

The last thing David said to the others before Quentin and Mary retired for the night was that he wanted to know how Finley and the children had been able to appear from nowhere at Clapham South Station the day before. It had to mean something. And he knew there was only one way to find out.

Ask Finley.

He asked Mary if it would be okay with her to put Heather's ring out on her bedside table when she went to bed that night.

And he asked Quentin if he would come and get him for a visit to the basement, if Heather came.

Q looked tired, but there was a glint of resolve in his eyes.

He wanted this all to end.

CHAPTER FORTY-FOUR

'Nurse Mary.'

Those two words filled her heart with an overabundance of love.

Mary would never be able to explain it to anyone, not even Quentin, even though he, at least, would probably have believed her if she tried. She didn't even think there'd be a shrink in the world who would understand it.

So she just let it happen.

'Hello, my darling,' Mary knew reaching out for her may have seemed forward, but she no longer cared. A gut feeling told her this whole thing at Ravenstone House could, and probably would end at any moment.

And that would very likely mean that she'd be left dearly missing bonny Heather.

She reminded herself for the thousandth time: you are not supposed to be able to physically feel the spirit of a dead child.

'Nurse Mary.'

'Yes, Heather.'

'I love you. And Quentin too.'

Mary held back a cascade of tears.

'You will always be in our hearts, bonny Heather.' She'd taken up Finley's affectionate way of speaking to the girl.

'I don't want to be in your hearts, Mary. I want to live here with you.'

'When this is all over, my darling, we will try and work something out,' Mary couldn't think of anything else to say.

'Nurse Mary.'

Mary smiled openly. The spirit of the gorgeous little girl was endlessly endearing.

'Yes, honey?'

'Did you want to just say hello to me tonight, or … ?'

Mary shook her head and basked in the rays of the little girl's sunshine of pure innocence.

'Bonny Heather, would you like to go and ask Finley if David and Quentin can come and speak to him tonight?'

'Nurse Mary.'

'Yes, Heather.'

'Anything for you.'

David had decided to crash on the couch.

His hope was at some point in the evening, there would be a tap on the door. So instead of taking the risk of waking his darling wife from the cute little snoring thing she'd been doing for years, he'd stay in the lounge room.

Tap tap.

Mission accomplished.

'Alright?' David asked Quentin when they arrived at the door to the basement.

As Quentin opened the door and found the handle still cold as ice, he turned to his neighbour.

'I'm chuffed to bits,' he said, but David saw through his sarcasm.

'It's your old man, isn't it?' David spoke tactfully, but it stopped Quentin mid-step.

'Next time we've got a few pints in front of us,' Quentin said, shaking his mood into shape, 'we can talk about Bernie Brookes.'

'Deal,' David said, venturing into the basement before closing the door.

———

The basement was frightfully cold. Somehow, it seemed to be getting colder.

The cages were still empty, but the men could see ice forming on them. Someone had put three or four boxes down in one of the cages a while ago, but they were gone now, and the cages would stay empty.

As the lone light globe swayed from side to side, Quentin blew air into his cupped hands. Even with a coat on, he could still feel the chill biting into him. He might consider wearing a balaclava next time, even if it ended up scaring the shit out of Finley and the kids.

He was about to turn to Quentin and ask him if it was getting colder still, when Heather appeared from the shadows.

'David, Quentin,' she said, and as usual, she ran for Quentin as if he were her long-lost father.

'Hello, Heather.' Quentin patted her lightly on the top of the head, and she stood back and smiled up at him.

'Bonny Heather,' Finley said, stepping out of the ring room, 'I'm going to give up telling you not to do that.' He stopped and smiled to David and Quentin.

'Finley,' David nodded, 'it's good to see you again.'

'Thank you for seeing us tonight,' Quentin added. Finley

knew he owed the four an eternity of gratitude, not the other way around.

'You guys made it out of the station safely?' Finley asked.

David met eyes with Quentin before turning to the boy.

'How was it possible? How were you able to be there? I thought you were trapped within the boundaries of Raven-stone House?'

Finley leant down to Heather and whispered in her ear. She slipped into the shadows and out of sight. Then he addressed the men.

'I told you. Up until the deaths of Glaggin and Pendal-son, we were never able to move beyond the walls of Raven-stone House.'

'But now you can?' said David.

Finley turned to him slowly. 'Yes. If any of you come into contact with one of the monsters of Ravenstone, we are somehow able to come to you.'

The two men met each other's eyes with curiosity.

Finley's next words surprised the two men.

'I won't lie to you; some of the children think it's the most exciting thing ever,' Finley said. The two men could see he did not share their excitement at all.

'I don't know what to say, Finley,' said David. But a thought did come to mind. 'You saved the day, yesterday, at the station.'

Unlike with the living, compliments did not register with Finley. They didn't bring a warmth to his chest, or make him feel good.

But he could tell by the look on David's face that what-ever David was saying meant he'd done a good thing.

'Can I ask you one other question?' David said.

'Yes,' Finley said.

'The water at the station. Where did it come from?'

What Finley said made no sense at all.

He turned and pointed into the ring room.

It was yet another piece of information that David and Quentin would spend years attempting to remove from their memories.

And nightmares.

The two men walked up to the entrance of the room before Finley spoke.

His words were painfully slow.

But probably nowhere as painful as his death.

'Many of us were drowned.

'Inside this room.

'Upside down.'

CHAPTER FORTY-FIVE

Jacob Brown, MP, was a twenty-year veteran of the Conservative Party. As the member for the constituency of Streatham, he had risen through the ranks of the Lambeth City Council after arriving in Brixton from the island of Jamaica in 1959.

As with many MPs, he had moved on from council chambers to the House of Commons.

Charismatic and charming, but sometimes arrogant, with an apparent 'short fuse' not normally seen in public, Brown was well known in Brixton for his dedication to supporting the people of his multicultural borough.

Although his distaste for the Conservative Party's current leader, once dubbed 'the Iron lady,' by a Soviet journalist, was known to a few insiders, he'd remained in good stead with her and most of his fellow MPs.

Brown stood at around five foot nine inches. Given his Jamaican ancestry, his hair was soot black with tight, firm curls. His face was long, with a mouth often compared to a horse by his less politically correct opponents in Parliament. He would say they were only jealous of his big smile and good looks. But with a visibly receding hairline, there was no disguising his move towards old age as he hit his sixties.

And Brown was not without his controversies.

Shady deals in his days as a member of the Lambeth council had dogged him for many years.

Rumours of infidelity had also followed him into the House of Commons, but since other MPs were in the same boat from time to time, nobody put much effort into substantiating them.

His first wife could have done so easily.

So could his second, since she'd been having an affair with Brown when he was married to his first.

But today, Brown's mind was nowhere near the thought of his infidelity as a badge of honour, which was how he usually represented it to himself.

He'd barely touched his breakfast, and his coffee, normally the first thing to disappear from the table, had gone cold in the still-full mug.

His head was buried deep in pages three and four of the *Sun*, which were all about Ravenstone House—its dark history, rumours of it being haunted, and the like. The stories connected to the recent deaths of the Glaggin couple, and of Richard Bailey and William West.

His wife had opted, that morning, to catch up with a couple of girlfriends for brunch, leaving Brown home alone for the time being.

It was much to his relief, because it meant he could sit and read the reports for the third time without having to hide the grave expression on his face from her.

It seemed an eternity since he'd even remotely thought of that period of his life.

The place.

Those people.

What he'd done.

What they all had.

It wouldn't be the first time Brown wished he could have his time over again.

Just then, he had only one regret.

Coming back.

———

Quentin, to his credit, remained stoic and dignified after his father had publicly ridiculed him on national television.

Wendy Moss had contacted him the day after Bernie's appearance on the news, and told him how sorry she was to see his father speak of him in such a way. She told Quentin his father had continued his downward spiral, and these days was an angry, unapproachable old goat. Most nights, he wouldn't venture home before 10pm, and she would often find his dinner uneaten in the bin, or still in the fridge the next day.

She told Quentin she felt it may be was time to resign from employment as his father's housekeeper.

Quentin couldn't stop thinking about the letter, which was now safely hidden in his bedroom. Mary hadn't mentioned it again, which suited him fine. He was reconciled to having to approach his father, confront him with the letter, and demand answers.

Over at Flat One, Christine received a welcome visit from Yukiko the Tuesday after the big weekend of events ending with the 'incident' at Clapham South Station.

Yukiko informed Christine that Andrew was on the mend. But with two broken legs and a shattered hip, he'd be in hospital a while yet.

Yukiko said a co-worker from Andrew's New York office

had called the hospital on a number of occasions, checking on his condition, and now he was out of the coma, was speaking with him often. Yukiko thought it was nice to see Andrew had been popular enough at work that anyone would care to call from the other side of the Atlantic.

Christine declined to tell Yukiko what her personal thoughts were on this co-worker from New York.

Though he could now sit up and talk, Andrew could provide no insight into what happened the night he returned from the Big Apple. He recalled nothing of speaking to an angry old ghost named Rose Lloyd before falling backwards and almost killing himself.

With reporters now frequently annoying the residents of Ravenstone House, by mid-week David made the executive decision to install a lock on the basement door.

No one argued, because it was too cold for anyone to go down there anyway.

David did not want a sneaky, pesky reporter slipping into Ravenstone House and poking around down there.

It would forever remain the creepiest place he'd ever set foot in.

But a part of him felt as if it was his duty to protect what was there.

The spirits of the children.

David had seen Finley while he was installing the new lock on the basement door. When he'd appeared, David came close to putting the drill through the palm of his hand. The kid sure knew how to scare the wits out of him, even now.

He'd told David there was another bottle of potion waiting for him in the ring room.

David made no secret to Finley of his concerns about the police now investigating the deaths of at least four people on the employee list, which had put Ravenstone House on national television and sent reporters to pester residents.

Worse, the last guy on the list was a member of Parliament. David said the risk of getting close to him was too great.

To David's slight frustration, Finley seemed to take all the concerns as water off a duck's back.

He told David they were so close now that he could see the light at the end of the tunnel. Only at the very end would David realise there was more to this from Finley than mere cliché.

As David was leaving the basement with his refill of special potion, Finley told him one more thing.

Just get in the same room as Brown and have the potion and some sort of cup in your possession.

He, along with the children, would take care of the rest.

David wouldn't realise until the following weekend just how big a room it would be.

It would only take another three days for the next piece of the puzzle to fall into place.

And fall, David and Christine said to each other, was apt. The opportunity that presented itself, felt as if it had literally fallen from the heavens above.

The odds were about 6.4 million to one, even when you thought of it with six degrees of separation in mind. When Frigyes Karinthy came up with the theory in 1929, he must have had this sort of scenario as his prime example.

One of the news stories on the BBC six-o'clock news that Wednesday evening edition had featured the upcoming concert of the newly formed 'Three Tenors' due to take place on Saturday night.

Fresh from their debut at the 1990 FIFA World Cup concert in Rome, Plácido Domingo, José Carreras, and

Luciano Pavarotti accepted an offer from Her Majesty Queen Elizabeth II to perform at the Royal Opera House in Covent Garden.

Although the concert itself had been announced previously, David and Christine noticed something in the story that got the two of them thinking of old Karinthy and his theory.

The list of dignitaries who would be attending the gala event was the usual who's who of British high society.

But the story was mainly concerned with how Prime Minister Thatcher would not be attending due to escalating tensions in the Middle East. In less than a week, Saddam Hussein's army would invade neighbouring Kuwait.

As the news story began to draw to a close, the reporter said that in the prime minister's absence, a handful of MPs would attend the event.

As the reporter ran through the names of those attending, stock photos of each appeared as she read out the names. The last one captivated David and Christine's attention: Jacob Brown, member for Streatham.

David and Christine shared the same thought. David's sister worked at the Royal Opera House. Getting tickets for Saturday night's concert would be easy.

As a thirty-year veteran of the establishment, Abbey had a permanent family pass that meant she and any member of her family (yes, in-laws included) could attend any event held there.

Although they'd not made plans to attend Saturday night's concert, David was on the phone to his brother as the six-o'clock news went to the ad break after the story. And by the time the break ended, David and Christine had realised they'd better dust off their black-tie attire.

They had a concert to attend on Saturday night.

'It's going to be one eventful evening,' Abbey gushed to David on the phone during the commercial break.

Little did she know how true this would be.

CHAPTER FORTY-SIX

'Well, well, well.' Quentin shook his head before meeting Mary's eyes.

She whacked him in the arm a second later.

'Quentin Brookes, future husband and father of my unborn children, where are your manners?' she blushed.

David and Christine stood in the middle of Quentin and Mary's lounge room.

It was Saturday, the night of the gala event, and the first time the couple had seen their neighbours dressed to kill.

Black tie.

'Move over, Mr Bond,' Quentin smirked.

Christine smiled.

'David will not mind me telling you, if he'd dusted off his old tuxedo, you would have thought he was the Penguin from the Batman movie!'

David gave his best penguin impersonation—a series of low-pitched squabbles.

This put Mary in a fit of laughter, with Quentin one step behind.

'And may I say,' Quentin said after the laughter dissipated, 'Mrs Banks looks mighty fine tonight.'

Christine wore a long-sleeved black sequinned dress, which hugged her figure nicely, Mary thought.

Her high heels were jet black and impossibly shiny.

Seeing her with her hair up in a perfectly formed bun, and wearing just the right amount of make-up, Mary said, 'David, you'd better keep an eye on this one tonight: she may attract plenty of attention.'

'As Quentin would attest,' David reached over and took Christine's hand in his, 'when your partner is a beautiful woman, it comes with the territory.'

God, would someone send a bucket to Ravenstone House, Lacham, London, stat. Compliment overload in Flat Two.

'Alright,' David ushered Christine towards the door, 'I think our taxi is here, my darling.'

'You all set, Mr Bond?' Quentin asked.

David patted his right chest, checking that the flask normally reserved for something a little sharper than holy water was sitting comfortably in his suit pocket. 'I am,' he said. A small cardboard cup sat collapsed in his pants pocket. This worried him more than the hip flask. How he would explain it if checked when they entered the Opera House, he wasn't sure.

But evidently, it was just a paper cup. If it was confiscated, so be it. He would have to figure something else out.

'Have a wonderful evening, you guys,' Mary said as the Bankses slipped into the cab.

David smiled before waving through the window, but as the cab pulled out from the curb, someone walking towards the entrance of Ravenstone House made him do a double take.

His heart dropped like a stone, but there wasn't a thing he could do.

It was Quentin and Mary's turn.

Inspector Megevand gave David a friendly little wave.

'Quentin Brookes?' he said as he arrived at the bottom of the stairs to Ravenstone House.

Quentin and Mary shared a glance.

Christine had described the inspector in detail to Mary.

He was a looker alright. Mary kept the thought all to herself.

'Yes?' Quentin's answer was anything but rhetorical; he knew who the guy was.

'Detective Inspector Ian Megevand, CID. Do you guys mind if we chat for a moment or two?'

———

The Royal Opera House was resplendent.

The crowds in and around its entrance were all dressed to impress. Black tie as far as the eye could see.

The buzz was infectious, Christine thought as they crossed Bow Street to be swallowed up by the hundreds of people already congregating at the entrance.

Camera crews, reporters, and press photographers were out the front behind a cordoned-off area, feverishly flashing their cameras and making the scene all the more electric.

But David was feeling anything but buzzy.

His nerves were getting the better of him.

Part of it was his feeling of duty to the children, and the other half was, simply put…

…the guy was shitting bricks.

This was next-level.

He wasn't dumping the potion into a cup on an empty train station platform with the lights flickering on and off.

The capacity of the Royal Opera House, he knew, because his sister-in-law Abbey had told him years ago, was well over two thousand people.

And he would be there with his bottle of potion and a paper cup, and no idea what was going to happen.

Finley had been typically vague. But David knew all he could do was go along with what he'd been told to do, and hope Finley would take care of the rest.

As he and Christine entered the line feeding into the entrance of the main hall, he suddenly felt very much alone, as if all of this hinged on him.

Don't worry, Mr Banks; here's one thing you will realise very soon.

You are *not* alone.

A hundred and thirty-five orphans will be there with you.

In spirit.

<hr />

'Mind if I call you Quentin?'

Quentin nodded. 'Mr Brookes kind of feels a bit formal, if you ask me.'

He went to say something to Mary, but she quickly waved it off. 'Mary is absolutely fine with me, thanks, Inspector.'

The couple had invited Megevand into their home.

Christine had said he'd come across as relaxed and friendly when they'd first met him. Mary thought making him stand outside might come across as a bit cold, and signal that they had something to hide.

Quentin and Mary sat together on one sofa, and the inspector sat on the other. Quentin had switched on the radio for some background music to fend off the possibility of an awkward silence.

'I'm not sure if your neighbours across the way mentioned my visit the other day. Do you know your neighbours?'

Mary nodded. There was no law against knowing your neighbours. 'Yes, we know David and Christine. You could say we're friends. They did mention your visit,' she said.

She's confident, Megevand thought. She'd have to be. He knew she was a head nurse at one of Britain's busiest children's hospitals.

'Okay.' The inspector unbuttoned his suit jacket at the front and relaxed just a little. This would save him a couple of minutes of explaining. 'So they would have told you I'm investigating the strange deaths of workers at the orphanage which once operated in this building, many years ago.'

Quentin felt anxious.

'Quentin, I imagine you have heard of these deaths?' Megevand said.

His face must have given something away.

Quentin sat forward. 'Yes. We are all aware of the deaths of these people. Can I ask you a question, Inspector Megevand?' he said.

The inspector nodded. Phew, Quentin thought, the guy's blood must have been the same temperature as the basement below. The guy oozed calm, or maybe it came in an aftershave.

'Is this a murder investigation? I was under the impression these deaths appeared to be strange accidents in both cases?'

Mary shuddered, but she didn't show it.

She may have asked this question later in the conversation, maybe after they'd sussed the inspector out somewhat. But she thought it was too significant a question to ask this early in the piece.

Megevand switched on his training. He sat for a moment, drawing out his answer to see if delaying it would make the couple give anything away.

It might be a nervous tic, a touch of the nose (a dead giveaway) or a part of the face somewhere close.

Either they weren't nervous, or they were holding up well.

But Megevand knew. And the couple didn't know what he knew.

Time to roll.

'Quentin, your father is Bernie Brookes, the lord mayor of London, right?'

Q stared at the inspector for a moment before muttering, 'Yes.'

'Okay, we'll park this for now,' Megevand said before taking a deep breath and throwing his first punch, so to speak.

'Quentin, have you ever been to Hull, up north? There's a quaint little place just outside there. Holmpton. Know it?'

Bang.

He could see the telltale signs on Quentin. Subtle, but there all the same.

Recognition.

'Once, in a trip to Moors National Park.' Quentin answered the question, but his mind was in a total free fall.

Reggie Blood.

'How the fu—' Quentin went to ask himself.

But now it was Mary's turn.

'Mary, a random question for you, if I may.' Megevand smiled, casting his probing gaze at the nurse.

Mary had barely nodded before the inspector said, 'Ever been to West Worthing in your travels? You know, down south?'

Mary could hold her own, but this was serious shit.

John Heen.

The fucking creep who groped me.

Lying to a member of the police force would potentially have consequences, so she thought of Quentin's response.

Do it quickly, Mary.

'Yes, a weekend drive once.' She smiled her million-watt smile, 'Nice part of the world, I might add.'

The inspector carefully sized up the couple.

Son of the lord mayor, he thought.

Balls of steel? Maybe.

Head nurse. She'd spend her life around children.

Either she put it on, or genuinely loved kids. Most nurses do.

He'd read the files, buried deep within the archives at Whitehall Place under an inch of dust, on Ravenstone House for the Less Privileged.

They made his skin crawl.

The place was a cesspool of the sickest people. And there had been only a handful of convictions, if any.

But back to the couple sitting in front of him.

Megevand, without taking his gaze off the couple, reached into his suit pocket and fished out his notepad.

Only after flicking the first few pages did he take his eyes off the two.

'Reggie Blood. John Heen. Bradley,' he glanced up from his notes and completed the man's full name while staring at the couple, 'Fletcher. To add to this list, Archie and Anna Glaggin, Richard Bailey, and William,' he had to look back to his notes, 'West. Do any of these names mean anything to you?'

Quentin recalled the first time he'd heard these names.

And now, they were all dead.

Quentin shook his head. 'Other than what we've heard on the BBC,' he lied, 'can't say I have.'

Megevand stared at Quentin for a time.

Quentin had regained his composure.

And he thought—the fuck with this. Those people did the most unspeakable things to all those children before conspiring to murder them in cold blood.

They'd drowned Finley.

Heather.

His heart hurt for her.

That gorgeous little girl.

And someone had snuffed the innocent life out of her.

By drowning.

At six years old.

It was enough to make Quentin feel sick.

'They all worked here, right?' Mary said evenly.

Megevand nodded.

'They murdered scores of children, orphans who, by the worst hand of fate, were sent here,' she said.

Megevand liked this one.

Her confidence and poise were impressive.

She'd make a good cop, he thought.

'That's the rumour,' he replied.

Mary acknowledged his comment.

She hastily grabbed her fiancé's hand before rising to her feet, and would have pulled Quentin up with her even if he hadn't wanted to.

'We have a dinner engagement tonight, Inspector, so if you don't have any other questions, may we?'

The inspector slowly rose to his feet.

He stepped over and outstretched his right hand to shake Quentin's, and then Mary's.

'Can't say I can distinguish your accent, Inspector Megevand.' It had bugged Quentin since the guy had introduced himself. He couldn't put his finger on it.

There was something unique about it.

'I'm from up north, originally.' It was all he said before he walked to Quentin and Mary's front door. 'We'll talk again soon.' He smiled, before leaving Quentin and Mary at their front door.

When he reached the foyer, Megevand stole a glance upwards at the staircase stretching up to the second floor. 'If only you could talk,' he said, before exiting into the night.

CHAPTER FORTY-SEVEN

DAVID'S PASSIONS IN LIFE—DID NOT INCLUDE architecture.

If you asked him, he'd tell you he recalled not being able to spell the word for a grade five spelling test.

You wouldn't find him staring up at buildings or structures oohing and aahing.

David was not that type of guy.

But every time he entered the Royal Opera House, he thought it was one of the most spectacular rooms he'd ever seen.

The ceiling alone made him want to stare upwards all night instead of at the stage. It was spectacular up close: the plush red everywhere, mixed with yellow and gold, and dozens upon dozens of ornate and beautiful lights dotted throughout the theatre. You couldn't escape the glow of the lamps, or the feeling of standing in a place that was essential to the very fabric of London's being.

It may have burnt down twice, but people had been entertained within those very walls for over a quarter of a millennium.

Christine smiled as David stared up at the ceiling.

They'd just been taken to their seats, and David couldn't help himself.

'Stunning,' he said to his wife, without making eye contact with her.

'You look pretty good tonight, too, my love.' Her response made him grin from ear to ear.

But he kept staring at the ceiling.

'Alright, you,' she patted him on his leg, 'you'll pull a muscle if you don't stop looking up, honey,' Christine said.

David admitted to himself that his neck was starting to strain, and turned back to her, still grinning.

'What is it about this place?' he asked her.

Christine smiled at her husband. It amused her that he was always transfixed by this theatre despite otherwise having zero interest in buildings.

Their seats were on the first of the four main levels above the main seating on the floor, and directly to one side, if looking forward from the rear of the room. It afforded the couple one of the best views they'd ever had at the Royal Opera House. They'd never been this close to the action before.

A cancellation only an hour earlier had given Abbey and her two guests the opportunity of a lifetime. A party of three hadn't been able to make it—something about a private jet and a pilot with food poisoning.

It also let the couple take in their surroundings without the need for high-powered binoculars.

David, with his line of sight only three feet above those seated on the main floor of the theatre, realised that in front of his very eyes were television and movie stars, soccer players, cricketers, golfers—my God, David thought–socialites, business leaders. He recognised many politicians, and thought he may even have spotted Jacob Brown halfway across to the other side, but wasn't sure. David had seen him out the front when they first arrived, so he knew he was here.

And that was all before he spotted the people taking their seats on the second level on the other side of the theatre.

His head started to spin.

Queen Elizabeth II and various members of the royal family were being shown to their seats.

His chest tightened. If anything happened here, it would be on him.

What *was* going to happen? David wondered.

What did Finley and the other children have in store for the two thousand people there, including Brown?

David chatted to Christine before the performance, but his mind was focused on one thing only. Well, maybe two: the potion and Jacob Brown, MP for Streatham.

He took another careful glance towards the man sitting thirty feet away. He wore a tux, too, and chatted to people around him as casually as you would have it.

Christine had made a salient point only a moment ago. If somewhere along the line, they had this wrong, and Jacob Brown was not Fitzroy Brown, whatever little event they imagined might happen, would not happen.

For only if he were one of the monsters from the Ravenstone House for the Less Privileged would the potion do its thing. Whatever that was going to be.

If this was some long-winded case of mistaken identity, the guy would walk out of the Royal Opera House none the wiser. Maybe just with a story to tell.

Or maybe not.

CHAPTER FORTY-EIGHT

DAVID CHECKED HIS WATCH.

It was the sixth time he'd done so in the last five minutes.

Christine had noticed, but knew it was better not to say anything.

She decided the best thing to do was keep Abbey distracted. With so many famous people there, that was easy: there was much to talk about.

David could feel his nerves heading towards a red line.

It would be only a few moments before the show started.

He had no damned idea what to do or when to do it.

All he'd been told was that when the time was right, he should put as much of the potion in the paper cup as he could, and leave it—somewhere.

What the hell? As his apprehension began to overcome him, it messed with his logical mind.

This is ridiculous, he was thinking, but that train of thought was abruptly cut off as the orchestra made its last, subtle sound checks, the hubbub of the two thousand people in the theatre faded to quiet hums and whispers, and it began.

A handful of the decorative lights across the multiple levels, started to flicker ever so subtly.

Within five seconds, the number of lights flickering on and off doubled.

Some of the bigger lights focused on the stage started doing the very same thing.

People's whispers fell to silence.

David and Christine met each other's eyes, and their thoughts were as one.

They're coming.

And they weren't thinking about the three tenors.

The stage lights flickered more powerfully, and a moment later, to the gasps of hundreds of people, every single light in the theatre began to flicker haphazardly. It was like no light show the audience had seen before.

The strobing was now so frenetic that people were starting to get visibly worried. They hid their eyes.

But after about ten seconds, the lights started to die down. David could hear people's sighs and mutters of relief.

David turned to the stage. The curtain, parted in the middle, began to close.

The audience thought it was part of the show. They held their breaths in anticipation, waiting for the three tenors to appear.

But the second the curtains closed—all the lights went off. Even the lighting on the floor to show people to their seats.

David felt Christine's hand find his and grip tight. He slipped the other into the inside of his tuxedo pocket, and pulled out his hip flask.

Once the flask was out and wedged between his legs, he extracted the flattened paper cup from his pants pocket.

People were starting to murmur, but most still believed the darkness was part of the show.

A single light on stage flickered before coming on.

All the others along the edge of the stage did the same.

'Mother of God,' Christine said.

Christine and her husband would be the only two people in the Royal Opera House who knew who all the people on stage were.

They weren't grown-ups.

Finley stood at the front of the stage.

Holding his hand was sweet little bonny Heather.

She stared out into the auditorium with fascination.

Behind the two stood the spirits of the rest of the 133 children from Ravenstone House.

Hundreds of people still actually believed this was part of the show they'd come to see.

Wow.

Finley and Heather started singing.

It made David and Christine's heart ache.

By the time they got to the end of the first line, the rest of the children joined in.

'Twinkle, twinkle, little star,
How I wonder what you are.
Up above the world so high,
Like a diamond in the sky.

When the blazing sun is gone,
When he nothing shines upon,
Then you show your little light,
Twinkle, twinkle, all the night.'

For the next verse, people throughout the audience started to hum along.

David could not believe what he was seeing and hearing.

'In the dark blue sky you keep,
And often thro' my curtains peep,
For you never shut your eye,
Till the sun is in the sky.

'Tis your bright and tiny spark,
Lights the traveller in the dark,
Tho' I know not what you are,
Twinkle, twinkle, litt—'

The stage manager appeared at stage left.

He did not look happy.

He stumbled on something as he walked into the stage proper, and as he lost his footing, he fell towards the children —and directly through at least half a dozen of them.

'What the hell is going on here?' he said as he regained his footing.

The children moved out of the way before giving the stage manager the dirtiest of looks.

Finley watched the man stumbling around, then turned and faced the audience. 'We are the murdered children of Ravenstone House for the Less Privileged,' he said.

As the words echoed throughout the theatre, David could hear gasps all around him.

The stage manager, still not believing what he was seeing, lunged for Finley—and went straight through him.

'There is one here tonight,' Finley addressed the audience as if public speaking was second nature to him, 'who killed many of us orphans.'

David cast his eyes to Jacob Brown.

The MP darted his gaze around the audience. Most of the crowd were doing the same, as if the person Finley spoke of would stand up and make himself known.

'This song is for him,' Finley said.

He turned and nodded to the children.

They started to hum, and as they did, they swayed as if they were the happiest 135 children ever seen.

Christine felt tears begin to stream from her eyes as they started to sing.

'Rain, rain, go away.
Come again another day.
Little Arthur wants to play.
Little Arthur—wants to play.'

David watched on as one of the orphans stepped forward: a little boy about ten children down from Finley on the right side of the stage.

They'd find out later that his name was Arthur.

'Rain, rain, go away.
Come again another day.'

Then all the kids screamed as loud as they could.

'IT'S NOT OUR FAULT!
WE DID NOTHING WRONG!
RAIN RAIN, WASH HIM—AWAY.'

* * *

The entire theatre plunged into darkness again.

A second later, the fire-system sprinklers malfunctioned.

There was no fire, but they exploded into life.

As the rain came down inside the Royal Opera House, David realised this was how they were going to get to Brown.

He quickly opened his flask, haphazardly popped open the paper cup, and poured in the entire contents of the flask.

He leant forward and put the cup on the railing.

People around him were trying to get away from the water raining down. But there was nowhere to go.

Someone shouted, 'The doors out are locked! What the hell is going on?'

David reached out and found his wife's hand. He could just make out her shape in the darkness.

'You okay, Mrs Banks?' he said.

'I'm good if you're good,' she replied.

A voice hastily came over the PA. 'Please, everyone, remain seated. We're trying to turn off the sprinklers and get the lights on.'

The person at the doors shouted again. 'Why don't you just get these bleeding doors open, you lot?'

David kept calm.

Like most of the people trapped inside the theatre, he was getting drenched.

The only people who were able to escape the deluge were the royal family.

But not before Her Majesty had seen the orphans with her own eyes.

The sprinklers stopped, and emergency lighting flicked on throughout the immense theatre.

Miraculously, a man with a sprained ankle and a heavily pregnant woman whose waters had broken were so far the only casualties of the commotion.

Christine was the first to hear it: a low hum that she could feel passing through her.

She spun around and met her husband's eyes.

'Me too,' he said. 'What in God's name was th—'

A second later, people seated on the ground floor started muttering profanities.

'I'm stuck!' a woman squealed.

'What is happening?' came another woman's voice from the ground floor. 'I can't move my legs! My feet are stuck in something.'

The decorative lights started to flicker again, as frenetically as they had before Finley and the other children appeared.

The low hum David, Christine, and Abbey had heard grew stronger.

As David watched on in fascination, scores of the celebrities who had been slowly milling out of the theatre were now literally stopped in their tracks.

'It's the water!' someone shouted.

'It's starting to turn to ice!' another bellowed.

'What the fuck!' This was a well-known business leader. 'I can't move my feet. Help, someone!'

The lights throughout the theatre were now pulsing in such a way that even David was starting to feel a bit nervous.

Christine was now huddled up against him. They were both wet to the core, and David could feel Christine shiver.

'The ice! It's rising. Please, help!' This supermodel was famous for her outbursts, but now sounded like a helpless little girl.

The water was at least a foot deep, and David could see it turning to ice.

'Oh my Lord,' David said, 'this is going down, honey.'

She knew it could only mean one thing.

Fitzroy Brown was here.

By now the panic was as contagious as the common cold.

Most of the people who had been on the ground floor for the show were experiencing their own version of total bewilderment.

The lighting was pulsing on and off, accompanied by the low hum of a deep vibration that could barely be felt, let alone heard.

As David watched the scene unfold, he suddenly grabbed his wife's arm.

'Christine, there,' he said.

She turned and followed her husband's gaze to Jacob—aka Fitzroy—Brown.

The ice around him and about a dozen people nearby was at waist height.

The men shouted and the women screamed.

At this point, the hum mysteriously stopped.

David and Christine met each other's eyes.

Suddenly, every light shone so bright, the couple had to shield their eyes.

A second later, all 467 lights exploded into thousands of tiny shards of glass.

The auditorium fell into darkness once more, and David and Christine could hear people screaming from every corner of the theatre.

The glass from the lights had fallen on hundreds of people.

'This is intense,' David said. 'When is this going to en—'

As the emergency lights flickered on, Christine grabbed David by the arm.

'Oh my fucking Lord,' Christine swore.

CHAPTER FORTY-NINE

It was an ice sculpture like no one had ever seen.

In the area where they knew Jacob Brown had been sitting, and then standing a few moments ago, was a gigantic block of ice at least sixty feet high, and about twenty feet thick at the base.

It tapered off towards the top, like a Christmas tree.

At the very pinnacle of the massive block of ice were two shoes, sticking out of the top.

Whoever the shoes and feet belonged to was upside down.

The screams and cries heard throughout the theatre were now so loud, Christine blocked her ears.

Because other people were stuck in the massive block of ice too.

Some had just their heads sticking out. An arm here, a leg there.

David felt as if someone had punched him in the stomach.

This wasn't meant to happen. Other people weren't meant to die.

He would only find out later that the people stuck inside the ice sculpture were still alive.

A large pocket of air surrounded each person.

Eventually, they would be freed and live to tell the tale.

There would be only one death.

But as the emergency services arrived on the scene of the chaos, it was Abbey who had Christine do a double take.

'Look at the shape of the ice,' Abbey said.

As more torches were shone onto it, what Christine saw made her inhale sharply and wish for a very strong glass of alcohol.

The huge ice structure was in the shape of hundreds of children standing side by side. Each level was like a tier, and as it got higher, the tiers grew smaller.

Their arms reached outwards as if to say, 'Help us.'

Christine started to weep.

The faces of the ice children all had their mouths wide open, as though screaming in pain.

Christine turned to David

'I want to go home,' he said.

'I do too,' she said, 'let's get out of—'

But unlike the other two times ice had trapped the monsters of Ravenstone, something different happened.

Right before the eyes of hundreds of amazed and horrified onlookers still in the theatre, the entire sculpture exploded.

Ice shattered in a thousand directions.

People screamed as shards of ice rained down.

But David and Christine noticed something.

A big block of ice remained.

It was about six feet tall and three feet thick.

It was perfectly round.

Sticking out of the top of it were two shoes.

David and Christine arrived home, a littler earlier than they'd expected.

They'd dropped Abbey off at her home in Wandsworth a few minutes earlier.

David and Christine knew Quentin and Mary would still be up, and they were keen to tell the two what they'd just witnessed.

'Lord, what happened to you two?' Mary said after answering the knock on the front door.

'We were just checking you were home,' said David, whose wet hair had dried in the shape of a skunk.

Christine was one step behind him. 'We'll go get changed,' she said, 'and be back in a jiffy, okay?'

Mary could see a now-familiar look in her neighbours' eyes.

Some serious shit had happened.

━━

'Oh, I had put the kettle on,' Mary said when the couple walked into her kitchen.

David was holding a full bottle of Johnny Walker.

'The kettle may not cut it tonight, folks,' he said.

Quentin let out a mild wolf whistle.

'Bleedin' 'ell,' he said in his best cockney accent, 'A bottle o' Johnny Walker Blue Label you've just plonked on our kitchen bench, my friend.'

'Refer to my last comment.' David smiled, but Mary and Quentin could see anything but happiness in his eyes.

━━

David was right. Tea wouldn't cut it.

Four shot glasses made their way to the kitchen bench within two minutes of the Bankses' arriving at Flat One.

Thirty explicitly detailed minutes later, with close to half of the bottle of Blue Label gone, it was done.

David welcomed the numbing of his nerves after his fifth shot.

He rarely, if ever, got drunk. Now he didn't care.

They all knew who the guy would be, feet up and frozen in his ice coffin.

And regardless of who he may have been back in the old days, he had until recently been an 'honourable' member of Parliament.

Hence, the occasion for David's rare and very old bottle of Johnny Walker Blue Label.

They all knew nothing would be the same after tonight.

'We should check in with Finley,' David said, looking to the others for their thoughts.

'I guess I'll leave the calling card out,' Mary said.

'Nurse Mary.'

'Nurse Mary.'

'Nurse. Mary?'

Mary had crashed.

She'd done the unthinkable.

She'd had three shots of whisky.

She wished she hadn't.

Mary felt a little queasy.

'Hello, honey,' she said when she eventually roused herself from her whisky-induced coma.

Bonny Heather.

The smile on her face was enormous.

Mary stared at her for a moment and thought, wow, she must have enjoyed her night out.

'My bonny Heather, you look like you had a wonderful evening.'

Heather stared at her long enough for Mary to wonder if she'd said something wrong.

'Can I tell you a secret?' the little girl whispered.

Mary wondered where this was going, but had grown so fond of Heather, she had enough patience for her to last a lifetime.

Heather stepped so close, Mary could almost feel her little lips on her face.

'Do you promise if I tell you,' Heather said, 'it remains a secret to you and me?'

Mary thought nothing of it, knowing it was another sweetness about Heather she was going to dearly miss.

'I promise, my darling,' Mary said.

'Okay,' Heather said.

With Mary experiencing a bit of a hot flush from the alcohol, she had her duvet pulled back.

She'd pulled her Duran Duran tank top up somewhat, trying to get some cold air onto her burning stomach.

Heather raised her hand and placed it on Mary's belly.

Mary felt a buzz pass through her entire body.

'There's your own little baby in there,' Heather said, smiling so brightly Mary was taken aback.

'How do you know?' Mary could not hide her shock.

'I can feel her in there.' Heather smiled.

Mary could feel the tears in her eyes as she struggled to hold back her emotions.

'You are going to make the finest mother in the world,' Heather said.

It took Mary a moment to recover from the shock. The

spirit of a gorgeous little girl had just told her she was pregnant.

Mary asked Heather if David and Quentin could see Finley tonight.

'Of course,' Heather said before disappearing into the darkness a moment later.

———

The change in Finley was clear even to two men well on their way to varying degrees of a hangover.

'Alright?' David said after Finley appeared from the ring room.

Finley stepped up the closest he had ever been to the taekwondo master.

'You're a good man, David Banks. You did good tonight. All the children want to thank you,' Finley said.

'All in a day's work, my boy.' David nodded.

'I hear it was quite the show,' Quentin said, feeling slightly left out.

Finley turned to him and with a shake of the head said, 'I'd never been to the Opera House when I breathed, Quentin.

'It was the most amazing sight. If it weren't for David, and the monster Fitzroy Brown being in the same room, we'd not have been able to go there.'

Quentin patted David on the back with gusto. 'Look at you go. You're the hero, David,' he said.

David, his head still hurting from the expensive but very smooth whisky, waved his hand in Quentin's direction.

'The inspector will be back before we know it,' David said, meeting Quentin's eyes.

Finley stood back and glanced over to the cages.

'There's something I need to tell you before you leave me tonight.'

His happy demeanour had darkened.

'Finley,' David stepped forward, 'what is it?'

Finley took a step back.

'I, I can't explain it,' he said.

Quentin felt a shiver pass over him.

On instinct, he turned around, and froze.

The cages were full of children.

But this time they were all crying.

'We felt him there tonight.' Now it was Finley who cried.

'Who? Brown? But he's—' David went to say.

Finley held up his hand, cutting David off.

'No, him!' he shouted. 'He—was there tonight.'

He'd realised who Finley was referring to.

'The boss. Are you sure?' David said.

Finley nodded. He slipped into the ring room and out of sight.

'Excuse me?'

David and Quentin met each other's eyes before finding the source of the little voice.

A little boy, stared up to the men through the cage and said,

'It not our fault.
We did noffing wong.'

CHAPTER FIFTY

CHRISTINE COULD NOT BRING HERSELF TO TELL YUKIKO what her gut was telling her.

Andrew, Yukiko's husband, was cheating on her. Christine couldn't prove it, yet. But everything she'd been told thus far had her thinking. And we know she was on the money.

When Christine had seen Yukiko in the hallway that morning, she'd seemed a shadow of her former self. She was already tiny and sparrowlike, but now she seemed even more so.

The stress of what had happened to Andrew, and his feelings of wanting to get the hell out of Ravenstone House, were getting too much for Yukiko.

Christine felt so sorry for her. She invited her in for a cup of tea and a natter. And some shortbreads.

'He refuses to come back here, Christine,' Yukiko whimpered.

Part of her could understand it. He'd almost died in this house.

'What does Andrew expect to do, if he can't come back here?' Christine asked.

Yukiko took a bite of the shortbread biscuit.

Christine watched her patiently. She knew she was finding all this tough at the moment.

'This friend of his in New York has a friend who lives here,' Yukiko said eventually.

Here we go, Christine thought.

'He can stay there if he wants, apparently. The guy who owns the flat is away on a work assignment in Australia for another three months.'

I'm waiting for it, Christine thought. If I hear what I think is coming, comes, my suspicions will go from ninety-nine percent to one hundred.

Yukiko took another sip of tea, and another peck at the shortbread.

'His friend offered to come over and stay with him,' Yukiko said.

The statement hung in the air as if it were a chandelier made of lies and manipulation.

This is bullshit, Christine thought. Yukiko was being taken for a ride.

'Honey.' Christine stepped over closer to Yukiko and spoke very, very softly.

'Were you part of this plan to stay at this other flat? Did Andrew or this friend of his include you in the idea?'

Yukiko stared at Christine for a moment.

'No. I don't know why,' Yukiko said.

Christine could not help but shake her head.

What sort of fucker is this guy? she thought. Seriously.

'Yukiko, don't you think it's a little unusual?' Christine hesitated in making the statement, but it just came out.

She could see the cogs in Yukiko's head turning, if very slowly.

'Maybe,' Yukiko said, but added, 'if you are talking about unusual, can I tell you what happened this morning in my flat?'

Christine reached for her tea and nodded. 'I have a new take on unusual after the last few weeks, but please, tell me,' she said.

'Don't repeat this to anyone,' Yukiko said. 'They'll think I've gone stark raving mad.'

Christine, with a shake of her head, smiled. 'Honey, if you've gone mad, so have all of us.'

Yukiko managed a feeble smile. It was the first Christine had seen from her that day.

'Alright,' Yukiko said, mustering her courage.

'This morning, I had my daily shower. I like it hot, and it steams up the bathroom to no end, like a sauna.' Yukiko tried to reach for another smile but it eluded her. She could see Christine waiting on her every word, so she went on. 'So when I came out of the shower, and after I dried myself, I went to the bathroom vanity.' She instinctively put her hand to her mouth as she recalled the vision. 'And when I reached it, someone had written words in the fog on the mirror.'

'Shit,' Christine thought. Now she could feel a cold breeze pass over the back of her neck.

'My God, Yukiko,' Christine said awkwardly, 'what did it say?'

Yukiko closed her eyes and put her hand to her mouth again.

'Scribbled words. As if it were written by someone with skinny, scrawny fingers,' she said.

'And?' Christine said.

'Adulterer HE IS. why I pushed him.'

⬜

David, in the meantime, had gone for a Sunday-morning walk. Christine had opted to stay home, which suited him fine. Walking alone was therapeutic, especially after what had

345

happened the night before. He took his time walking the streets of Lacham and eventually ended up at the Tooting Bec Commons.

He couldn't escape the thought of what Finley had said at the end.

He'd hardly slept last night thinking about it.

The boss of Ravenstone orphanage had been in the audience at the Royal Opera House last night.

But what frustrated him more than anything, was that all Finley had to go on was 'a feeling.'

Nothing else.

Who the hell is he, this guy? David wondered.

Quentin had figured out one part of the mystery by the time they'd reached the top of the basement stairs last night.

David hadn't understood why the other guy wasn't suspended upside down in a block of ice like Fitzroy Brown had been.

'He buggered off before the rain came,' Quentin had guessed.

And he was right.

In the week to come, millions of Brits would find out the back story of one Jacob, or rather Fitzroy, Brown. He'd slipped out of the UK in the summer of '55, only to return under another name and new identity in 1959 or 1960.

'And now we have another,' David told the ducks swimming around the commons pond. They ignored him, mostly. 'A man who did the most despicable things possible, before buggering off somewhere and then coming back.' The ducks still had no idea what he was going on about. 'And I'll bet all the whisky in Scotland he returned, like Brown, under a new name.'

He let the words fall into the pond as the breeze blew up and sent a pattern across the lake. The ducks saw no food coming from the man, so they waddled off.

'Well, well, what a small world. Fancy bumping into you here.'

David turned, and with the sun blinding him, had to put his hand up to shield his eyes.

His face instinctively tightened when he saw who it was.

Inspector Megevand.

'Mind if I join you?' Megevand said.

'Be my guest, Inspector.' David quickly put his thoughts into some sort of order as Megevand sat down next to him on the bench seat.

'Nice day for it.' Megevand smiled, though his eyes stayed focused on the water in front of him.

'You live around here?' David said quietly, as he looked at the ducks on the other side of the pond, 'or are you following me?'

Megevand smiled.

'Romford,' he said. 'I was over at the Tooting Bec Lido, and decided to take a break. It's nice around here, so I thought a walk would be good.'

The inspector turned to David. 'I saw you from a distance. You were walking as if you had much on your mind.'

David took a long, deep breath through his nostrils. It always calmed him. He needed it right now.

'No more than the average middle-aged man living in this busy metropolis we call home,' he said.

Megevand shifted to sit sideways on the bench seat, facing David.

'You know why I became a policeman?'

David kept his eyes fixed on the ducks on the far side of the pond.

'I'm sure you're about to tell me. Why did you?'

Megevand stared at David for a moment before his lips finally moved.

'I wanted to catch the bad guys,' he said.

'You're a good man, Inspector,' David said, and he meant it. 'The world needs more men like you in it.'

The inspector accepted the compliment with a nod, but his face remained expressionless.

'So, tell me, David Banks, do you think you're one of the good guys, or one of the bad guys?' he said.

David smiled, but his eyes fell away from the inspector's stare. When he eventually looked back, he nodded. 'What does your gut tell you? Am I a good guy or a bad guy?'

The inspector stared at David for a time before turning away. He rose to his feet and stepped over to the edge of the pond.

David watched him intently, hoping he would leave so he could return to his own thoughts.

When Megevand eventually turned around, his expression gave nothing away.

'My intuition tells me you are on the side of good,' he said.

He stepped a foot closer so he was looking down at David.

'But it also tells me you know more than you are letting on, Mr Banks. That, or you're trying to protect someone.'

One person came straight to David's vision.

If there was one person he was trying to protect, it was him.

And he wasn't even alive.

Finley Sproule.

Megevand could see David was lost in thought, so he leant down, and for the first time his tone was anything but friendly.

'The heat on this thing, Banks,' Megevand became serious, 'it's now up full blast. Especially after last night. It's funny, you know,' Megevand stepped back a fraction but had lost none of his bite.

'Your brother's married to an employee of the Royal Opera House. I'll refrain from asking you where you were last night,' David realised the inspector was looking down at him hard now, 'so you don't have to lie to me.'

David went to say something, but Megevand held up his hand. 'Save it.'

The inspector slipped his hands into his pockets and kicked at a small mound of dirt in front of him.

'My boss, and his boss, and the one above him. They're all going to want answers on this now, with Brown's death. This is going to go all the way to the top.'

Megevand saw something in the corner of his eye. It was another detective in the distance, waving at him to come back to the Lido.

Just before he walked off, Megevand stepped closer to David, sending a cold chill down the other man's spine.

'So you'd better figure out when you're going to start telling me what you know. My tolerance for liars is wafer-thin at the best of times.'

CHAPTER FIFTY-ONE

THE CONSERVATIVE GOVERNMENT WAS IN MELTDOWN.

Prime Minister Thatcher deflected the 'Brown Affair' to her deputy, Sir Geoffrey Howe, while focusing on other 'more relevant issues,' in her own words. The constituents of Streatham, Brown's electorate, did not take kindly to this.

Her pal George W. Bush, aka the president of the United States, had sent his troops into Kuwait, and the Gulf War was on. Shortly, Thatcher would send Britain's own armed forces into the fray.

On the domestic front, her recently introduced 'Community Charge,' better known in the press as the poll tax, was still biting her on the behind, to put it mildly.

The latter would be cited as one of the key components of Thatcher's ousting from the leadership of the Conservative Party later in the year.

Meanwhile, the press were having a field day with the 'strange happenings' at the Royal Opera House the previous Saturday night. The BBC nightly news ran various stories about the evening for a full week afterwards.

The death of a prominent member of Parliament under

such mysterious and bizarre circumstances, witnessed by so many people, was unprecedented.

———

One week later

'Oh my God!' Christine shrieked.

'What amazing news!' David said as the couple hugged Mary and then Quentin.

'Yes…' As Mary spoke, all she could see was bonny Heather's pretty little face when she first told her.

'…I'm up the duff!' She put her hand to her stomach and patted it gently.

The head nurse had snuck in a visit to her own GP during the week, and her doctor had confirmed it 100 per cent.

'Well, well.' David put his arm around Quentin. 'Are you ready to become a father, my boy?'

'You bet,' Q said, but the butterflies prancing around his stomach said otherwise.

After the commotion died down, the two couples sat around Quentin and Mary's island bench, sipping on their teas and coffees. Of course, the shortbreads were there too.

'Are you going to tell your father?' Christine said carefully.

Mary met Quentin's eyes before they both emitted something akin to an 'um.'

'I don't know if he'll care. Wendy finished up last week. We're not keen to go around to Dad's without her there, to be honest,' Quentin said.

'Well, if you guys want, we can come with you. If you need the moral support. He's still your father, Quentin. Maybe the news will make a difference to him.'

'Are you sure?' Quentin asked.

The Bankses nodded.

'How bad can he be?' David said, smiling.

'Ever poked a polar bear in the eye with a knitting needle?' said Mary, with a shake of her head.

———

The mid-afternoon train trip to Bernie Brookes' home gave the four time to read the weekend tabloids.

Most, if not all, of the Saturday papers had extensive coverage of 'the Brown Affair,' but tied in with 'the Ravenstone House Mystery.'

At one time or the other, mutters of 'Jesus' or some other profanity could be heard behind a newspaper being held up by one of the four as the train hurtled through the tunnel.

Mary sat next to Quentin, both of them reading their own copy of *The Sun*.

Pages four, five, six, and seven were dedicated entirely to the 'Brown Affair' and the 'Ravenstone House Mystery.'

'Christ. They've listed all the names of those now dead who worked at the orphanage,' Quentin said.

'The story about Heen, the one Christine and I visited— they've interviewed the workers at the respite centre. The article goes on to say Heen's ex-wife hasn't set foot in the UK for ten years.'

Quentin could sense Mary's apprehension building.

'It's going to be okay, babe,' he said. 'Even if they find out you two visited him, his death had nothing to do with you. They can't pin it on you, okay?'

Mary heard Quentin's words but felt only marginally better.

David dropped his paper. 'Jacob Brown,' he said. 'This article states they believe he and a few other workers of the orphanage slipped out of Britain in the middle of the night. They knew the authorities were starting to get suspicious, so they took off.'

He went back to his paper and read on. 'It was shortly after they'd jailed an orphanage worker. His name was Richard Bailey—oh shit, I remember him. He was the guy from the Pond Arms Hotel. We followed him to the station.' David nodded over to Quentin. 'They say Bailey went to jail for raping one of the female staff members at the orphanage. But the article goes on to say William West was involved in the rape as well.'

A few moments later, David took a breath and continued, 'I'll let you all guess what I mean. Anyway, the press found this lady. She's still here in London. She said Bailey had taken the rap for West, even though she insisted to the police that he was involved. In the end, they were happy with just one scapegoat. Oh, bloody hell,' David met Christine's eyes, 'this lady remembers "the boss" too. She said he was like a chameleon. He had ability to come across as a saint. But behind certain closed doors, she said, he was literally the devil incarnate.'

Christine dropped her own paper and joined in, 'Here it says they believe they slipped out on a ferry to Belgium under assumed identities.'

'What would possess Brown to come back to England?' Mary asked.

'If this article is correct, they say he went back to Jamaica. Maybe he found London a more attractive prospect than life in Kingston?' Christine said.

'*The Sun*,' David said, glancing at the paper on his lap before he turned back to his wife and Quentin and Mary, 'they had a whole page dedicated to this Leitner family. The article alleges the family were involved in child-trafficking as far back as World War I. It's alleged they were involved in trafficking imprisoned Jewish kids out of Nazi-occupied Poland and Austria, to all four corners of the globe. They had links to the Nazis, who thought nothing of what they were doing. Two of the brothers ran the operation out of Austria, but the other brother stayed in London. They say it was this one who, under a cloak of complete deception to the outside world, ran the orphanage as if he was an honest member of British society.'

David took a breath before he went on.

'But when certain ex-employees started to talk about what they believed was going on, the pressure started to mount on him. He offered his resignation and handed over the reins to his son. He moved into a mountain retreat overlooking Lake Wolfgang, Austria, where his other two brothers still lived.

'The article paints the worst of pictures here. They alleged that the people who ran the orphanage allowed people to enter the building with the sole purpose to molest children—for a price.'

Christine chimed in, showing her copy of the *Daily Mirror*. 'This says the son knew things were catching up with him, too, after being at the helm for a number of years. The Bailey case appeared to be the last straw. They think he fled the country with Brown in 1955. And his whereabouts are still unknown to this day.

'But now, with the idea Brown had re-entered Britain five years after fleeing, they're starting to wonder if "the son," did the same. The theory being, they had a person in the UK to continue their co-ordinated efforts at human trafficking across Europe and the rest of the world.'

David and Quentin looked at each other for a long time, as the train jostled along at twenty miles an hour through the tight tunnel.

'He's here, alright, and still alive,' Quentin said.

355

A second later, the train started to slow.

They were coming into Bank Station.

CHAPTER FIFTY-TWO

THE WALK FROM BANK STATION TO QUENTIN'S FATHER'S home usually took about one minute.

For Quentin, it felt more like he'd just walked from Lacham to Mansion House. Mary could see it. David and Christine had shared their usual glances, and from the way he trudged onward, they had more than a sneaking suspicion of Quentin's mood. But they walked at his pace.

Mary knew that even though Q had backup of sorts, she could tell he was still unsure if it was a good idea to come and see his old man.

As they rounded Bernie Brookes' street corner, Mary stopped.

'May be a good idea if we lose these, you think?' she said, holding up her newspaper.

She turned to Quentin for confirmation.

It took him a second to realise why.

'Even at the best of times, he's never had a good relationship with Fleet Street,' he told Christine and David, and nodded to Mary.

For the head nurse, it was more about Bernie thinking they'd been reading up on the 'Ravenstone House mystery' after he'd made it very clear, both publicly and privately, that he thought buying the flat there was a bad idea.

With the papers binned, they walked on.

When they arrived at the entrance to Bernie Brookes' home, Quentin was barely breathing.

Mary, God love her, had a look of resolve on her face. She was obviously channelling Linda Carter, the American actress who'd played Wonder Woman on TV.

Maybe it was her impending motherhood.

Or maybe she felt it was time to tell Bernie Brookes what she really thought of him.

———

Tap. Tap.

Quentin stood back.

'Breathe,' Mary whispered to her fiancé.

'Shut up smarty pan—'

His response was cut short when the front door opened slowly.

'May I help you?'

No bloody way, Quentin thought, Dad has replaced Wendy. He hadn't been aware.

'May I help you?'

Mary was about to nudge Quentin forcefully. 'Answer her, you nimwit,' was the sentence which entered her mind.

'H-e-l-l-o, my name is—Quentin. And this here is my fiancée, Mary. These two people with us are our friends David and Christine.'

David thought the look on the new maid's face was priceless.

Either English was her second language or she had no goddamn idea who Quentin was. Actually, he was right on both counts. She must have been seriously new to Mansion House.

'Oh. I'm—sorry.' The housekeeper stared at Quentin as if he were an alien, but managed a weak smile.

'You're Bernie's son?' Her question, in an accent as thick as a glass of tar, was not even remotely rhetorical.

Quentin stared at her a moment, astonished. It wasn't her fault, he knew. But the new housekeeper being like this made Mansion House feel so foreign to him now.

He felt like a complete stranger.

The new housekeeper wouldn't have been over five foot tall, Quentin figured. Of Eastern European lineage, she had mousy-blond hair pulled tightly into a bun, and was diminutive, almost frail. But she had a friendly face, even if at present it was pretty much blank.

'Yes. I am Bernie's son, Quentin. And who may you be?' Q asked as pleasantly as he could.

'Oh. My name is Isabella. I am the housekeeper,' her words were rehearsed, Christine thought, maybe the only ones she spoke most of the time.

Quentin felt sorry for her. She wasn't suited to working for the tyrant his father had turned into. But just then, he had other issues to deal with.

'Is my father home at present, Isabella?' Quentin said.

'Yes, he is,' the housekeeper said.

Quentin stepped forward.

Mary went to say something when at the same time Isabella held up her hand. 'Should I not check Master Brookes will want—see you?'

'Master Brookes?' Quentin thought. Bloody hell, the old man was getting too big for his own boots.

Quentin turned to Mary and saw the alarm in her eyes. When looked to David and Christine, he sensed they were thinking the same thing.

'Yes, you're right,' Quentin said as he stepped back. 'Please, tell Dad I am here to see him,' he added with a shake of his head.

———

The last ice age was supposedly 1.8 million years ago, give or take a few.

But today, Quentin thought, you'd think it was still going.

Or maybe the ice age of 1990 was confined within the walls of Mansion House.

'I've not had a day off in three months. So you'd better tell me why you have come here, unannounced, and without any warning. And why you've thought it fitting to bring complete strangers into the home of the lord mayor of London!'

Quentin's reaction, in the face of such an onslaught of unnecessary aggression, was priceless.

'Is this how you greet your only son, his future wife, and their friends, Father?'

'You could have made an appointment!' Bernie barked.

'Bleeding hell.' Now it was David's turn to speak his mind. He'd expected Q's dad to be a bit of a grump, but shit, Mary was right. 'Polar bear and knitting needle is right,' he muttered privately to Christine, 'but maybe the needle ended up being poked up his a—'

'My friends here, David and Christine, thought it would be an honour to meet you today, so they thought they'd come along with Mary and I for the impromptu trip over here.' Quentin grinned.

'And where do you both come from?' Bernie glared at David and Christine as if they were peasants.

'Lacham,' David said, rather quickly and tersely.

Bernie's lips turned into a snarl.

'Oh, don't tell me,' the lord mayor said, sitting back on the armrest of a sofa just behind him, 'you guys live in Ravenstone House too?'

Christine could feel the tension in the air suddenly rise.

'Correct,' David said. 'We are Quentin and Mary's neighbours across the hall.' Christine realised David knew where this was going. The only thing they underestimated was how ugly it was about to get.

'Well, you'd be as stupid as my son and future daughter-in-law?' Bernie hissed.

With a smile that did nothing to flatter his ageing and increasingly bitter face, he slipped onto the sofa proper, and that was when Mary noticed the glass of whisky sitting on the side table.

Shit, it was barely the afternoon and he was already on it.

David met Christine's worried eyes. As a married couple of forty years, they were able to communicate their thoughts to each other in a look.

David: I am going break this pasty old piece of shit's nose in about thirteen different places.

Christine: you will not break this pasty old piece of shit's nose in about thirteen different places.

A smirk wavered in the corner of David's mouth.

In an alternate universe, at this point David would have jumped the six steps between himself and Quentin's father, to give him a nose job free of the rigours of plastic surgery.

But he took a deep breath.

'Sir,' he said, 'you are well within your rights to have your own opinion. A man of your stature and success commands nothing less.'

Well done, David.

'Alright,' Bernie took a gulp from his whisky, 'now we have established the intelligence level of the four people standing in front of me, tell me why the hell you are all here.'

———

The four found a place to sit.

'Dad.' Quentin found himself almost stuttering, but took a moment to breathe.

'Mary and I have some news to tell you. We thought it would be better to tell you in person. I'm hoping it will—'

'Oh for Christ's sake, boy-' Bernie turned and shouted 'Is-a-bell-a, another whisssky, now.'

Aha, so the old git was three sheets, Christine thought.

'—how long is this going to take?' the lord mayor bellowed.

David met Christine's eyes again. This fucker was next-level.

Mary found herself staring down to the carpet.

She wished they'd never come today. Quentin should have just sent him a letter, she thought.

'Cat got your tongue, boy, or are you waiting for the boss to take over for you?'

Fuck you, Mary fumed to herself. He'd made some stupid reference about this once before. It was nothing more than an insult to Quentin, Bernie implying Mary was the boss in their relationship. She thought it was an awful thing for a father to say to a son. It was as insulting as it got.

'Quentin,' Mary said, and waited for him to meet her eyes. When he did, she added, 'Just tell him. I think we need to leave, now.'

Isabella appeared from the hallway with another whisky.

After she disappeared into the hallway, Quentin stared at Bernie for a moment.

'Mary's pregnant, Dad. You're going to be a grandfather. Okay?'

Quentin rose to his feet and Mary followed suit.

David and Christine were already on their feet. They couldn't wait to get as far away as they could from this horrible excuse for a father, and a human being.

Quentin turned to David and Christine and said, 'Meet us out the front, won't you?'

David and Christine nodded in unison, and as they turned to say goodbye to Bernie, the lord mayor gave a stupid, condescending little wave, while his eyes remained fixed on Mary and Quentin.

'Right.' David grabbed Christine's hand and they slipped into the hallway, a moment later they were, much to their relief, on the pavement outside Mansion House.

'You got anything to say?' Quentin asked his father, his anger building.

Bernie stared at him for a time, and said nothing.

He turned and found his fresh whisky, and after taking a long drink, he shouted, 'Isabella?'

When she appeared from the kitchen a moment later, he said, 'Please see my guests out, won't you?'

Mary exchanged a disgusted look with Quentin, and without even looking at her future father-in-law, stormed out and headed for the front door.

Quentin turned back to his father and through gritted teeth said, 'What in God's name is wrong with you?'

When Quentin stepped into the hallway, he could see Mary waiting for him at the front door.

He nodded and made his way towards her.

When Quentin had made it halfway down the hall, his father said, 'At least your child will have plenty of kid ghosts to play with at Ravenstone House, so the papers say.'

Mary hadn't heard what Bernie said.

But Quentin had.

A fuse inside his head flipped.

He stopped dead in his tracks.

He spun around and in a fit of rage ran back into the lounge room at a pace.

By the time he'd made it to his old man, Mary was almost screaming in panic.

When she made it to the entrance of the lounge room, she saw Quentin with his hands around his father's neck.

'Quentin, no!' she shouted.

Quentin let go of his old man and stood back.

'I know about Mum, you fucking evil piece of shit. She was going to leave you. She found out something about you, right?

'A woman who spent half her life catching trains in the Tube slips off the edge in front of an oncoming train?'

Mary was already dragging him out of the lounge room by the time Bernie had regained his composure. Another thirty seconds and she wondered if Quentin would have strangled him to death.

When they were halfway down the hallway, they heard the lord mayor laughing.

Quentin stopped. Mary grabbed him by the arm and kept moving towards the front door, but not before Bernie thought of the perfect comeback to Quentin's tirade.

They would never be sure if they'd heard him right, but they swore it sounded like this:

'I did nothing wrong.

'It's not my fault.'

CHAPTER FIFTY-THREE

THE TRAIN TRIP HOME WAS COMPLETELY DEVOID OF conversation.

The disastrous visit to Bernie Brookes' home was on everyone's mind.

Especially Quentin's.

He knew the relationship with his father was all but fucked. Excuse the French, ladies and gentlemen, but that's exactly what he was thinking.

He wondered if it could get any worse after today.

It could.

As they walked out of the Lacham Tube Station, David mumbled something about beer, and fish and chips for dinner.

The other three mumbled their own version of it being a good idea.

They walked on in virtual silence until they rounded the corner of their street.

'You've got to be fucking kidding me,' said Quentin, while Mary simultaneously exclaimed, 'What in God's name?'

David and Christine simply stared at each other and said, 'Oh no,' at the same time.

There were at least four marked police cars parked outside Ravenstone House.

Quentin lost count of the number of policemen standing out the front. They were directing people walking past onto the other side of the road from both directions.

As they walked closer, David could see more cops walking in and out of the front door. What he assumed were plain-clothed officers stood out the front as well, in suits.

A small group of onlookers stood directly across the street, watching the goings-on. Quentin, Mary, David and Christine walked up to the group.

'What's happening?' David inquired to one, before sidling up to the group like a curious passer-by.

'They've been here for about half an hour or so,' the guy told David. 'They arrived out of nowhere,' the man next to him added. 'I thought a robbery was taking place inside, or so it seemed.'

A lady close by said, 'My money's on the Jacob Brown thing. There's rumours around here he was one of the orphanage workers. I'm telling you,' she announced to anyone in the group who cared to listen, 'it's a bad place over there. It's full of ghosts of the children, and supposedly a cranky old lady who was killed because she'd found out her husband was shagging all the servants behind her back. They say her husband, after finding out she knew, made his son do it. Pushed her off the top of the stairs, they say.'

David turned and met his wife's eyes. She'd heard everything the lady said. Mary had too.

Quentin watched in some sort of paralysed fascination as the upstairs neighbours were escorted out of the front door, much to their dissatisfaction.

'You have no right to do this!' Quentin heard Ross, a guy

from upstairs, tell one of the policemen who was ushering him out onto the pavement.

'Easy, easy,' the policeman said, 'the sooner we conduct this operation, the sooner you get to go back to your flat.'

Quentin looked on, feeling no need to go across the road and ask what in God's name all the police were doing inside Ravenstone House.

A thought entered his mind.

'I wonder if this was Dad's do—'

His words were cut off by the appearance in the main doorway of Inspector Megevand, who instantly spotted Quentin, Mary, David, and Christine standing across the road.

He took two steps down to another policeman and muttered something in his ear.

A second later, Megevand and the policeman walked across the street.

'Good afternoon, residents of flats one and two,' Megevand said firmly, would you all mind following me please?'

━━

Megevand took the four into the hallway of Ravenstone House. Police were everywhere. Cops had entered their two flats, as well as Yukiko and Andrew's. The front doors all wide open, as if there was some sort of big party going on.

Megevand told the four to follow him again, and a second later they all stood at the door to the basement.

'Who put this padlock on this door?' he asked.

David's gut had told him the whole situation had arrived at a critical juncture. Time was just about up.

'I did,' David said.

'Can you tell me why?' Megevand asked.

367

David nodded, 'With all the press going on about this place, I didn't want any journalists going down there and poking around.'

Megevand stared at him for a time before he leant in closer and with dead eyes, said, 'Go get the key. Now.'

David stepped back, and after making eye contact with the others, shuffled off to the entrance to his flat.

About forty-five seconds later, he appeared back in the hallway, holding a key up in his hand.

Megevand waited for him to return before shouting to two cops at the entrance of the main door. 'Reilly, Kennedy, could I borrow you both for a few minutes please?'

As the two cops made their way down the hallway, he turned to David and said, 'Unlock it, if you wouldn't mind.'

As David took the padlock off the door, Megevand told the two uniformed policemen, 'These four are coming with me downstairs. I don't want anyone, and I mean *anyone*, to either enter or leave this doorway until I say so, right?'

The two cops nodded. 'Yes, Inspector,' they said together.

'David, you lead the way,' the inspector said.

Christine and Mary felt the cold of the basement hit them like a hammer as the door opened.

———

As the five arrived at the bottom of the stairs, Megevand said nothing for a few moments.

Somewhere upstairs, as they'd made their way to the basement door, he'd acquired a torch, which he now turned on and panned around the basement area.

'This place is creepy,' he said to no one in particular.

Mary and Christine huddled together while David and Quentin stood and kept a close eye on what Megevand was looking at.

The inspector started by walking to the third room, the one with the boiler and other appliances in it for the flats upstairs.

He poked the torch in, and a moment later, without saying anything, stepped back, before going to the next doorway.

The coat room.

He stood at the entrance and shone his torch inside.

'Bad stuff happened in here,' he said without turning to the four, 'I can feel it in my bones.'

David went to say something, but instinctively, Christine grabbed his arm and with a shake of the head indicated—don't say a word.

Megevand turned and focused on the open doorway to the ring room.

As he stepped over to the last room, the four took a breath. Megevand stood in the doorway, and for the first time they saw him clearly shiver. From the cold maybe, or something else?

Oh, Christ.

Unlike the other two rooms, for whatever reason the inspector stepped into the ring room.

'I—' David went to say, 'I'd be careful in there,' but found only the first word could leave his mouth.

Megevand studied the room, noting the terrible state of the wood-panelled walls, and the wall on the far side of the entrance.

As he stepped closer to the ring on the floor, David and Quentin wondered if he knew it was there.

'Fuck,' Quentin said, looking over to Mary as they watched in silent horror as the inspector took another step closer to the ring.

As the floorboards creaked, suddenly a gust of ice-cold wind blew in from the main area of the basement and straight into the ring room.

The inspector instinctively turned to see where the hell the gust of wind had come from.

But as he did this, he stepped backwards.

Both his feet were now directly inside the ring.

'Argghhh!' he shrieked as his body suddenly went completely stiff, as if he had just been electrocuted standing up.

The inspector's torch went off.

The lone light bulb out the front of the room grew brighter until it blinded David, Christine, Quentin, and Mary.

A second later it exploded, again.

The basement was in complete darkness.

Yukiko checked in at the nurse's station as she had done many times before when visiting her husband.

As she walked down the hallway towards his room, she could feel a huge range of emotions swirling within her.

But the one enabling her to put one foot in front of the other—was confidence.

When she arrived at the open doorway to his room, she could hear the low hum of her husband talking to someone.

When she took the five or so steps into his room, she already knew who it was.

Her.

She could already smell her perfume.

Under other circumstances, she would think it smelled pretty good.

But not today.

'Hello, Andrew,' Yukiko said.

If he could, her husband would have jumped ten feet in the air.

'Hi, Yukiko.' He shifted uncomfortably in his bed. 'I wasn't expecting you until later in the day.'

The woman sitting on his bed rose to her feet.

'Hi. I'm Jane,' she said.

Yukiko smiled.

I know who you are, she said to herself.

'Well, I thought I would drop in earlier today,' Yukiko said. She turned to the woman. 'So you would be the one having sex with my husband?' she said.

'How dare you?' The woman scowled. 'I don't know what you're talking about!'

Andrew snarled, 'Jane is a co-worker from New York, Yukiko. Why would you say such a ridiculous thing?'

Yukiko, with a shake of the head, stepped to the edge of her husband's bed.

'You remember the night you fell down the stairs?' Yukiko said.

'How could I forget?' he said.

'Do you know why you walked to the top of the stairs in the first place?'

Andrew wasted no time in responding. 'As a matter of fact, I do. There was a woman standing there, staring at me.'

Yukiko glanced at Jane before turning back to Andrew.

'She was a ghost, Andrew. The ghost of old Rose Lloyd. She died on those very stairs.'

Jane and Andrew both laughed as if Yukiko was stark raving mad.

'She was a young woman. I thought she was one of our neighbours from upstairs,' Andrew responded arrogantly.

Yukiko shook her head.

'She'd found out her husband was cheating on her. And

371

when he found out she knew this, he had their son push Rose off the top of the stairs—to her death.'

'You're obviously one of those people who believes in silly ghost stories,' Jane scoffed. 'Personally, I don't.'

Yukiko ignored the woman and turned back to Andrew.

'She made you come up the stairs so she could push you from the top, because you are like her husband, a cheater.'

As Andrew started to shake his head, doing his best to deny Yukiko's claims, Jane rose and said, 'Think whatever you want to think.' She looked at Andrew. 'I can see why you'd want to spend more time in New York. Your wife is a paranoid storyteller.'

Yukiko waved her hand in the air and said, 'It doesn't matter. Andrew, I want a divorce. Oh,' Yukiko smiled, 'and this is what is going to happen. I'll have the flat.'

As Andrew and his co-worker broke into laughter, Yukiko laughed too, making the two feel suddenly uncomfortable.

'You see, one of my bosses,' she caught Jane's eye, 'happens to be good friends with your husband's very own brother. So, if you think for a second he won't tell your brother-in-law what's going on between the two of you,' Yukiko grinned, 'try me.'

As she stepped back towards the doorway, she waved to her soon to be ex-husband and said, 'You have two weeks to send me your new mailing address and to sign the flat over to me once you receive my paperwork. Or else a trans-Atlantic phone call will be made.'

CHAPTER FIFTY-FOUR

THE SOUNDS OF THE AMBULANCE ROARING TOWARDS Ravenstone House sent a wave of relief over the four.

Constables Reilly and Kennedy were racing down the stairs moments after Quentin had shouted out, 'We need help down here!'

Megevand had let out a godawful shriek, seconds before they all heard what sounded like an explosion.

Bits of brick and plaster had flown out of the ring room, but David and Quentin had already dived out of the way.

When everything went still, David realised there was no sound coming from the ring room at all.

He crawled on his hands and knees into the room in the pitch black, where he found the inspector under a pile of debris.

His torch was just out of his arm's reach, but David had found it and fumbled with the switch.

Thankfully, the torch came back to life.

Being a taekwondo master, David had learned first aid years ago. He'd saved three people so far from certain death.

Today, hopefully, the number would rise.

Megevand had no pulse.

Like a man possessed, David grappled with the bricks and mortar lying over the inspector.

Mary and Christine helped clear the debris as David frantically began CPR.

'Come on!' he shouted to the man lying on the floor, pulling at his chin before pushing air from his own mouth into his.

David continued to push on Megevand's chest, but to his heartache, there was no response.

'You are not dying down here!' David shouted, looking over to Christine, who could see his determination turning into sorrow.

'No, he will not.' The words cut through the air with such clarity, it almost hurt David's ears.

Finley.

He'd appeared from nowhere, and was now crouching down directly on the other side of the inspector, staring calmly into David's eyes.

'One more time, David,' he said quietly.

As David started beating on the inspector's chest and giving him one more mouthful of air, he watched Finley place both his hands on the inspector's forehead.

'He cannot die,' David heard him whisper.

About ten seconds later, David felt it.

Megevand's chest heaved.

As he breathed his first breath, he coughed a mouthful of dust straight into David's eyes. David didn't care. He turned to Finley.

He was gone.

The two uniformed police arrived.

'We need to get the inspector upstairs,' David said.

'What happened?' a cop asked Mary and Christine.

Both peered into the ring room.

'There was some sort of explosion in there,' Mary said.

When one of the cops pointed his torch into the room, Christine and Mary saw it.

They both gasped, their hands flying to their mouths.

A large hole had blown out in the far wall, opposite the entrance of the ring room. In what appeared to be the original wall, made of wood panels directly behind the bricks, was another hole halfway between the floor and the ceiling.

Christine could feel a familiar chill pass over her as she met Mary's eyes.

The chute was big enough for a person to enter.

CHAPTER FIFTY-FIVE

Ravenstone House was now a crime scene.

All residents were put up in a hotel about a quarter of a mile away.

The events in the basement had not been made public—yet.

David, Christine, Mary, and Quentin were told not to speak a word of what had happened down there.

Inspector Megevand was taken to the Royal London Hospital, and was currently in a stable condition.

He looked like he'd been hit by a bus, with cuts and bruises over much of his face, but was conscious and in good spirits.

The same could not be said of his superiors.

They were under enormous pressure to put a lid on the investigation of the death of Jacob Brown and all the other strange events leading back to Ravenstone House.

The British press were having a field day on the story: painting in lurid strokes the death of an elected MP with a murky, evil past, and unravelling his connection to the orphanage, whose other employees had also been dying recently.

The Thatcher government, already struggling to justify their involvement in the Gulf War and the ongoing revolt against the poll tax, wanted the story to go away. Immediately.

At midnight, the decision was made in a government office that a news conference would be held out the front of Ravenstone House. The government would put an end to the story, denouncing Jacob Brown's involvement in the saga of the orphanage, but would announce that the deaths of the other ex-employees were simply coincidental. They would also cite that without any evidence of the actual deaths of children at the orphanage many decades ago, this was just another ghost story made up by bored people who'd heard strange sounds in Ravenstone House.

Talk about denial.

All they needed to figure out was who would be the best person to front the news conference: someone, ideally, who shared their desire, to bury it.

It was the deputy prime minister who hit on the perfect person for the job. He'd shared more than his fair share of whisky with him. And with the guy having come to owe the deputy PM more than one favour over the years, he knew he could make him do it whether he wanted to or not. He could not, and would not, refuse.

The lord mayor of London.

———

The news conference was set for four in the afternoon.

By lunchtime, everyone in Lacham knew about it, including all those staying at the Lacham Travelodge.

When Quentin found out his own father was going to front the conference, he couldn't believe it.

'Of all the people they could have thought of,' he said to Mary, 'they had to choose my fucking father.'

Mary could not find even the weakest of smiles for her fiancé.

'Well, at least we'll all be there to watch him lay on the bullshit,' she said.

'I have a sneaking suspicion there'll be a decent crowd there today,' David said across the table from Quentin and Mary.

'Bernie Brookes is not the most popular of people around here,' Christine said, making eye contact with Quentin.

He nodded. 'I wonder why.'

———

There were so many onlookers, the police had blocked both ends of the street.

Locals stood alongside reporters and cameramen, all jostling to get a good vantage point for the news conference.

Microphones were set up so the lord mayor would stand on the landing of the entrance to Ravenstone House, at the top of the steps.

With five minutes to go, David, Christine, Mary, and Quentin found a patch of familiar people when they arrived.

The other residents of Ravenstone House.

'Well, well,' David said, coming face to face with Helena and Frances from one of the flats upstairs, 'fancy seeing you guys here, huh?'

'There's not much else going on,' Helena said to David with a smirk, 'Hey, meet my dad. Dad?' Helena turned to a friendly looking old guy standing close.

He stepped forward and put his hand out, 'Albert George,' he said to David.

'Nice to meet you, Albert,' David said, shaking his hand

and thinking, wow, this guy's hand is like a vice.

'I used to work at the grocery shop across the street, when this was an orphanage,' Albert told him, with surprising sharpness for a man of his vintage.

David let go of his hand and said, 'Right. Helena told us you have a photographic memory for faces.'

The old guy smiled proudly, 'Can't explain it, young fella.' He looked at Helena before shrugging his shoulders. 'I can remember a face from fifty years ago.'

David could see the crowd getting excited. It was time for the news conference to begin.

'You remembered Jacob Brown when he worked at the orphanage, right?' David said.

Albert George nodded vigorously.

'And the others too. When I saw their faces in the news-paper, the other workers who all died recently, it was like only yesterday. All of them came into my store at one time or the other,' he said.

When the thought struck David, a part of him cursed himself for not thinking of it sooner. He wished he'd thought more of involving Helena and Albert in the investigation, but he'd been too worried about letting others in on the secret that he shared with Christine, Quentin, Mary, and Yukiko, of their mission of revenge on behalf of the children of Ravenstone.

As he heard the reporters starting to say, 'Here he comes,' knowing they were talking about the lord mayor, he leant in close to Albert and said, 'Do you remember the people who ran the orphanage? The father and son?'

Albert stared into David's eyes with an uncomfortable clarity. His thin, ageing lips turned into a grin a second later.

'Yes. Especially the son.'

'Why the son?' David said.

'Because he molested one of my workers at the store one

day.'

David took a breath. 'I'm sorry.'

'It was on the day he, Brown, and the other fuckers left town, never to return,' Albert said. 'She was never the same. She took her own life five years later. I blame myself for it. I've thought of that evil bastard's face every day since.'

'Ladies and gentlemen,' a government official announced from the steps of Ravenstone House, ' This news conference is about to begin. Please remain quiet. Here is the lord mayor of London, to speak today.'

Bernie Brookes stepped up and adjusted some of the microphones.

Dressed in a dark-blue suit, he looked like he'd have paid a million pounds to be anywhere else.

He hated talking to the press at the best of times, let alone with an audience of what in private he called, 'civilians'.

Charming.

Okay, the sooner I do this, the sooner I can go home and get pissed, he thought.

'I am the lord mayor of London. My name is Bernie Brookes.'

No shit, Sherlock, was the simultaneous thought of many standing there.

'I am here at the request of the government, to put an end to the rumours, ghost stories, and shenanigans surrounding Ravenstone House.'

Many in the audience, especially the residents of Ravenstone House, considered calling what had happened there 'rumours' and 'ghost stories' an outright lie. But before anyone could scoff, the lord mayor barrelled on.

'I know lots of people love a good ghost story. Hell, my mother used to tell me spooky stories when I was a boy. But enough is enough. The government, as I do, has more important things to worry about. If anyone thinks the recent deaths of said individuals dotted all over the United Kingdom, including the MP Jacob Brown, are connected to this very building behind me, their minds have taken a leave of absence.'

As the crowd mumbled and murmured, Brookes waved his hand in the air with authority.

'This building should have been torn down decades ago. It may have once been an orphanage, but soon became a place where drunks and drug addicts partied and caused trouble.'

At this point, Quentin felt his guts churn.

'I told the developer, a man I knew, that renovating this decrepit, run-down building was a bad idea. I told him nothing good would come of it. Now, as we can see by recent events, all it has done is drum up all these fanciful tales of ghosts, and people who supposedly worked here more than four decades ago suddenly being found dead.'

A reporter at the front of the crowd held up his hand.

'Eight people, my lord mayor. All of whom worked here. All dead within a few weeks of each other. Are you telling us this is nothing more than a coincidence?'

'Did I give you permission to speak?' Brookes roared.

'Fuck me,' Quentin said to Mary, 'someone got out of the wrong side of bed this morning.'

As the crowd began to grow impatient with Bernie Brookes' lack of decorum, he tried to continue his rehearsed speech.

'The government is discussing the future of this building with the Wandsworth council. There is a view from some that the building should be vacated and torn down.'

If the lord mayor thought he was already unpopular with the constituents of Lacham, he'd just put a noose around his neck.

Ravenstone House residents Ross DeBel and his mate Neil Olney decided enough was enough.

Without a word, they both began to move from their vantage point with the other residents, and towards the lord mayor.

'Oh, shit, what's happening here,' David said to Christine, as the residents watched their two neighbours push their way through the crowd.

Suddenly, Helena and Frances, who lived next to Ross and Neil, decided to follow. They obviously had a problem with what the lord mayor had just said too.

When Helena started to move, her father, Albert, must have decided to go, too, perhaps for moral support.

The crowd as a whole erupted in noise as these people started to push their way forward.

'And what about the people who live here now, lord mayor!' shouted Ross.

'Who the fuck do you think you are standing up there and telling us what we've witnessed with our very own eyes is made up?' Neil added.

The lord mayor was ready to rip heads off.

He planned to personally call the deputy PM when he got home and tell him he was a bastard for making him do this.

'I'm the lord mayor of London, you dimwit. All of you,' he pointed at Neil and those standing nearby, 'are morons if you think for a second ghosts even exist. Especially some old bag and a group of sad-sack feral orphans!'

Oh shit.

It was on.

Ross lunged forward, breaking through the reporters.

Before the one or two policemen standing too far away to do anything could react, Ross reached the bottom of the stairs.

But in his rage, Ross stumbled and fell, pretty much making a fool of himself in the process.

This gave the cops time to make the distance and grab him.

But as they did so, he reached out for the lord mayor.

'You arrogant fuck!' he shouted.

Bernie Brookes stepped backwards to ensure the guy didn't get too close to him.

As the cops wrestled with Ross, Neil decided he'd jump in and defend his flatmate.

He, too, lunged for Bernie, but one of the cops wrestling with Ross grabbed at him.

The lord mayor thought it was quite funny, but didn't want any of these idiots to get their dirty hands on him. So he took another step back.

With the front door to Ravenstone House wide open, Bernie stepped back into the doorway without realising he had, enough for his body to be just over the threshold.

A gust of wind exploded from the inside of the building, blowing hats off heads among the audience.

A moment later, everyone heard the screams of an old woman. If Bernie Brookes had turned towards the staircase, he would have seen her standing there up the top.

The ghost of Rose Lloyd.

As the cameras kept rolling, the apparition came flying down the stairs at breakneck speed.

She appeared behind the lord mayor a second later, and with more ungodly shrieks, she was somehow able to push him.

Bernie fell forward, back through the front door, flew off the top landing and into the two policemen still wrestling with the two residents of Ravenstone House, collecting the microphones on the way.

The ghost of the old lady, catching herself in front of everyone standing there watching, changed into her younger self.

The gasps of the large crowd fell into silence as she stepped to the open doorway.

'Your father murdered me, Josef!' she said, pointing to Bernie Brookes as he struggled to get back on his feet.

'This is all fake!' the lord mayor shouted. 'Someone is staging this. You are not real, and neither are the ghosts of all these orphans who never died here. And my name is Bernie Brookes!'

Someone standing close to David, Christine, Quentin, and Mary was the first to see them. Others in the crowd spotted them a moment later, and began to scream even before Mary began pointing to one of the upstairs windows.

A moment later, other people in the crowd did the same.

In every window, upstairs and on the ground floor, were the faces of dozens of the ghosts of the orphan children of Ravenstone House.

'Mother of God,' one of the reporters shouted before he turned to his cameraman, 'You getting all this, Chip?' he said.

The guy nodded without taking his eye from the viewfinder.

The ghost of Rose Lloyd turned back into her scarier version and pointed down to the lord mayor.

While this was happening, Ross, who was still scuffling almost on top of Bernie Brookes, found his left arm suddenly free. He grappled with Bernie and in his good fortune, found something to grab hold of.

The lord mayor's toupee.

As he pulled, Bernie groaned and wildly flung his fist in

the guy's face, but missed and hit one of the policemen with such force, he broke the guy's nose right in front of the press and their cameras.

When he eventually got to his feet, he snarled and threw the microphone stands out of the way, and crawled, angrier than he'd been in years, back to the top of the landing.

He stood there and tried to regain some sort of composure, knowing his toupee was still in the fist of a guy a few feet away. Without the rug, he looked completely different.

'This news conference is over!' he shouted.

As the policeman with the broken nose glanced up to Bernie, Ross and Neil stopped scuffling and went to the officer's aid. Later, it would help their cause in court, but that's not why they did it.

Helena and Frances were there, too, rendering what assistance they could—moral support, mostly.

But Helena stopped dead when she noticed her father, who had come to join her, staring at Bernie Brookes as if he'd seen the devil himself.

'Mother of God,' Helena's father said.

'Dad, are you alright? What is it?' Helena said.

'It's him.' As he pointed at the lord mayor, Helena could see tears rolling down her father's cheeks.

Bernie Brookes met Albert George's gaze.

The two hadn't seen each other for forty years, and each saw the recognition in the other's eyes.

'Nothing ever happened here,' Bernie shouted into the crowd. 'The stories of dead orphans,' he took one last look at Albert before straightening his tie and looking over the top of the audience, 'are just a silly old wives' tale, made up by locals who had nothing better to—'

The lord mayor would not finish his sentence.

The street rumbled as if it was going to collapse beneath them.

Suddenly, the long-dead garden beds on both sides of the entrance pushed upwards. Dirt erupted ten feet into the air and a moment later two massive explosions of water rained down on anyone standing within twenty feet of Ravenstone House.

People ran in all directions.

As David, Christine, Quentin, and Mary watched on in awe, they could still see the ghosts of the children in the windows, standing there as if there was nowhere else they'd rather be.

Bernie Brookes jumped for the pavement, but was reluctant to run into the crowd for fear of having the shit kicked out of him. As water began to gush from the gigantic holes on both sides of the entrance, the lord mayor stood back up on the top step, and waved both hands in the air in a futile attempt to restore calm.

'Go home! There is nothing to see here!' he bellowed.

His words were swallowed by the nightmarish scene unfolding in front of the large crowd of shocked onlookers.

Children's bones, dozens upon dozens, flowed out of the basement and onto the pavement in a torrent of water.

People started to scream as they realised what all the stuff in the water was, but a moment later it got worse.

Tiny skulls poured from the garden beds in the gushes of water, and onto the pavement like shells on a beach.

But as the carnage unfolded, two men found each other's eyes.

One's thoughts were murderous.

I want to put my hands around your fat neck and strangle you, you fucking monster, thought Albert George.

The other was on another page entirely.

I wish I'd never come back, thought Josef Leitner.

CHAPTER FIFTY-SIX

THE WHOLE AREA AROUND RAVENSTONE HOUSE BECAME a crime scene. Both ends of the street were blocked off to stop the press and curious onlookers getting nosy.

In the mid-1930s, the designers of the ever-expanding London Underground train network had decided to link to the District Line what in later years became the Northern Line.

A cut-and-cover tunnel began construction in Lacham, extended through Earlsfield and connected to Wimbledon Park Station. But at some point, the contractors realised they would have to tunnel underneath large sections of both Lacham and Wandsworth, and decided to dig directly under dwellings without the consent of the owners.

But as the impending war with Germany grew on the horizon, all infrastructure works in England were halted.

At some point, engineers also questioned if the link between the two lines was necessary. The project was abandoned and the tunnel mostly filled in. But when war broke out in 1939, even that work was hastily mothballed.

Police investigators soon discovered the origin of the children's remains: a section of the abandoned Tube tunnel.

With Josef Leitner refusing to provide any answers, the police would be forced to conclude someone had, at some point, discovered the abandoned section of the Tube tunnel directly underneath Ravenstone House.

It was in fact Josef's father Franz, who had overheard two men talking about it at a local pub one evening. Coincidentally, the place was none other than the Mount Pond Arms Hotel.

But it was Josef who had come up with the idea to dig an access tunnel down to the void. He wasn't sure what he would do if they were able to reach the abandoned tunnel, but knew it may one day serve a purpose.

The abandoned section of the tunnel they discovered was at least twenty feet high, about thirty feet wide, and fifty feet long.

Access to the secret tunnel to the void below was hidden successfully by a small door built on the far wall of the ring room. When closed, it looked like a closet.

The police concluded that when the decision was made to close the orphanage, Josef Leitner had ordered a brick wall built to hide the access tunnel. Though a couple of his workers had told him they'd filled in 'the chute'—to the void below—he'd never checked to see if they were telling the truth. In fact, they'd decided it wasn't necessary and had lied to him.

It took five days to drain the water from the basement of Ravenstone House and the section of the abandoned pre-war Tube tunnel found below its foundations.

The police would, in the end, estimate they had found the skeletal remains of between 130 and 150 children down there, along with the bodies of at least ten unidentified adults.

David and Christine visited Inspector Ian Megevand in hospital five days after the extraordinary events in Lacham.

They could both see genuine happiness in the policeman's eyes when they ventured into his private room.

'How are you feeling, Inspector?' David said.

The inspector held out his hand for David to take.

'Feeling good. I'm actually being discharged this afternoon. Back on the clock tomorrow,' he said.

'I hear I owe you one hell of a thank you,' the inspector said.

'Not at all, Inspector,' David said with a shake of the head. 'You always treated us with respect. And I wasn't going to let you take your last breath in such a terrible place.'

Megevand nodded. 'Close the door and find somewhere to sit,' he said.

Once the door was closed and his two guests were sitting down, Megevand said, 'Josef Leitner, huh? How's Quentin holding up?'

'He's in a lot of pain, Inspector,' Christine said.

'Okay, from this point on, I insist you both call me by my first name. Ian,' he said.

They both nodded, but he could see they were deep in thought.

'Quentin's struggling to come to terms with it all,' Christine said. 'I think it's all the more difficult because of his mother's death. But the press, to our amazement, have gone pretty light on him.'

'I've heard,' said Megevand. 'I'm amazed how that came about. She's never done anything like this before.'

The queen.

Having seen the spirits of the children with her own eyes at the opera before she and the rest of the royal family were whisked away, she made an extraordinary public plea for the press and the public to leave Quentin alone, and to give him some space and respect.

Megevand stared into the distance before meeting David and Christine's eyes.

'He's still refusing to talk to anyone,' the inspector said, knowing they knew who he was referring to.

Bernie Brookes was currently in custody, in an undisclosed location somewhere in London.

'What I would give for five minutes with him,' David said to Megevand.

The inspector smiled.

'Well, I will be getting it tomorrow. And it will be more than five minutes, I can assure you.'

David and Christine both gasped. 'You can pass on our regards to him, if you will,' David said.

'Oh, trust me, I will. But in the meantime, I think it's time the three of us had a little chat.'

▭

'What happened to you when you stepped into the ring?' David said.

'Before I passed out, I saw things I hope I never see again,' Megevand said quietly.

Christine reached over and patted him on the arm. 'If you don't want to talk about it, you don't have to.'

Megevand placed his hand on hers. 'No. I need you both to know,' he said. The inspector opened his eyes. 'Do you know what the ring mark on the floor was? Did you ever figure it out?'

'I have my suspicions,' David said. 'But still never—'

Megevand closed his eyes and said, 'It was from a forty-four-gallon drum.'

When he opened his eyes, Christine could see tears.

'They had it there in the room for a reason. And there's also a reason why it was so close to the hole in the wall.'

Megevand, with a shake of the head, said, 'They drowned the children in the drum. Do you know why all those people who died were found upside down, and sometimes in blocks of ice?'

David realised the awful truth.

'They held the kids upside down, those fucking animals. The water was cold as ice,' the inspector said.

Christine wept, holding out her hand to the inspector, who shook his head as his own tears came.

'I saw this. When I stepped into the ring, I suddenly was in the room, watching the men kill the children this way. When I saw it—the visions—they were killing two kids at once. One of the men doing it was Bernie Brookes, clear as day. When the poor kids stopped flailing around, the men pulled the kids out and shoved the lifeless bodies into the chute. It was the saddest thing I've ever seen,' he said.

After a few moments, the inspector regained his composure.

'I also saw a couple of the children. Their spirits. They said to me—you two, and Quentin and Mary, were saints. They told me they were giving you a special potion. And when this came into contact with those who had killed the children, they would be taken from this world. They told me the only way for the kids to go to the afterlife was for all the monsters to be taken from the earth.'

David and Christine shifted awkwardly. David went to say something, but the inspector waved him off.

'There's more, but before I tell you—I need you to both know your secret will remain as such. You saved my life. I saw for myself what you were trying to avenge.'

David felt relief pass over him.

After a few deep breaths, he said, 'Can you please put me

393

out of my misery, Ian, and tell me, if you know…' Megevand stared at him for a moment, so David came straight out with it. 'What was in the potion?'

Megevand smiled, as he shook his head in surprise.

'If I was told this six months ago, I would have not believed it. But now I do. It was their tears,' he said.

Christine turned to David as she started to cry again.

'It's okay,' the inspector said, 'it's over.'

'It's why the place leaked when we first moved in. There was always drops of water leaking from the ceiling. Oh my God,' Christine said.

Megevand turned back to David and grinned.

'Is there any chance you had any of the special potion left?' he said.

Christine smiled to the inspector and reached for her oversized handbag.

CHAPTER FIFTY-SEVEN

In the early hours of the next morning, Inspector Megevand called into his office at Scotland Yard. Always an early riser, he wanted to get into the office before most of his co-workers started. He wanted to gather his files and his thoughts. It would be easier to do both without other people around.

The inspector made his way to the top-secret location where Bernie Brookes was detained in the heart of London, and picked up something important on the way.

Megevand had only been there once before: it was a location mostly used by MI6. A place off the grid, so to speak.

As he drove into the city, he wondered how this meeting would turn out. He couldn't wait to get there and get on with it.

⸻

'My name is Inspector Ian Megevand.'

Silence.

'I understand you are reluctant to speak at all,' he said a moment later.

More silence.

The inspector shifted in his chair to get a little more comfortable.

He took in the room for the second time. There was nothing else to do as he waited in vain for the man sitting across the table to say something.

The room was medium-sized, with the walls and floor of polished concrete except for one wall with a gigantic mirror built into it. Two people stood in the room on the other side of the mirror, with cameras filming the interview.

A single downlight sat directly above the table. It did nothing flattering for the man sitting across from him.

'Your name is Bernie Brookes. But you were once known as Josef Leitner. Is this correct?'

The man stared at something in the distance, to the left of the inspector's expressionless face.

Still in his business shirt and pants, now crumpled and dirty, he looked like the proverbial fish out of water.

Thanks to Ross—or was it Neil?—of Ravenstone House, Brookes looked almost naked without his toupee.

But his eyes still conveyed something else.

Unadulterated arrogance.

Megevand spent another five minutes telling him what he knew. He asked Brookes questions every few moments, trying to get him to say something. One question was how he'd enjoyed the show at the Royal Opera House only a couple of weeks ago, which he'd hastily left before things got crazy. He'd been filmed entering the building with other dignitaries, so there was no use denying it.

At one point, as the clock on the wall on the other side of the mirror said he'd been at it almost ten minutes, Bernie Brookes stopped staring off into the distance and cast his dead eyes directly at the inspector.

The tiniest grin passed over his mouth, as he prepared for what he evidently thought would be the ultimate insult.

He closed his eyes and crossed his arms like he was going to have a nap.

And after about thirty seconds, Megevand knew this was the perfect moment.

Bernie Brookes pulled his little stunt for about five minutes. Truth be told, he did feel as if he'd fallen asleep for most of it.

So he decided to slowly open his eyes and see how the inspector was going with it.

But Megevand had a trick of his own to play.

It was the thing he'd picked up on the way to this secret location.

And when Bernie opened his eyes, there it was.

Quentin.

'Hello, Dad,' Quentin said.

Bernie Brookes, if he could, would have fallen back on his chair, reeling in surprise.

But with the chair bolted to the floor, all he could do was show the initial shock on his face, as if someone had just bitch-slapped him with a fucking big fish.

Maybe a trout.

'I am only here to ask you one question.' Quentin leant forward and stared long and hard into his father's eyes.

'Yes,' Bernie Brookes said without a moment's notice.

Quentin hadn't even asked, but his father had already pre-empted the question and answered in in the affirmative.

Did I have anything to do with your mother's death?

Yes.

The two men stared at each other for a time.

'Why?' Quentin eventually said.

Josef Leitner slowly shook his head.

'You said only one question, boy. Now fuck off and stop wasting my time.'

Quentin calculated how long it would take him to jump the table and break the fucker's neck.

Brookes senior would soon wish his son had done him this favour.

But the monster of Ravenstone wasn't finished.

As Quentin stared at him, knowing he had no real comeback now, the arsehole decided enough was enough.

It was time to try his last trick, this time on Quentin.

He closed his eyes once again.

But that was his gravest mistake.

When he'd opened his eyes a couple of minutes ago to see Quentin sitting there, he didn't see what Quentin had brought into the room with him.

Something he'd borrowed from Inspector Megevand.

Something Inspector Megevand had borrowed from Christine Banks.

Now it was in a nondescript paper cup.

The children's tears.

It's not our fault.

We did nothing wrong.

Many had been killed at the hands of the very man sitting opposite Quentin.

Quentin rose to his feet without making a sound.

He turned and cast a glare at the mirror to his right.

He knew Inspector Megevand would be standing there.

If he could have seen through the one-way mirror, Quentin would have seen the inspector silently nodding to him.

Do it.

Quentin leant down and picked up the cup.

'Open your eyes so I can at least say goodbye to you, Father,' Quentin said.

It worked.

Bernie Brookes opened his eyes.

'It was all your fault.

'And those poor children, so help you God, did nothing wrong.'

Quentin threw the contents of the paper cup straight into the face of a monster.

EPILOGUE—PART ONE

Bernie Brookes was taken back to his cell within the secret MI6 facility, pitying Quentin for thinking that throwing a cup of water at him would upset him.

It hadn't.

His cell was a long way from Mansion House, barely ten feet wide and deep, with no windows. A stark, bright light had been fixed into the ceiling twenty feet above, and a brutal-looking metal toilet in one corner. No toilet paper in sight, though. There was a single mattress on the floor. No blankets, no pillow.

Bernie didn't bother to complain. There was no point.

He tried to sleep, but couldn't.

Time stood still for him.

So when the decision was made to transport him to another location in London, he didn't realise he'd been in his cell for close to twenty hours.

But what was more—nothing had happened to him.

What had been in the cup of water? Just water?

Was it missing the special ingredient?

Or was this the ultimate case of mistaken identity?

The trip to Bernie Brookes' next destination would see him cross the River Thames en route. He knew, simply by looking out through the window of the car, that they were heading towards Tower Bridge.

Two unmarked police cars escorted the car he was in, one at the front and one at the rear.

It was a smidgen after five in the morning.

He had a good idea why they were transporting him from one place to another at this hour. The death threats the lord mayor's office had fielded in the week since the events surrounding his ill-fated news conference in Lacham were next-level. Mansion House had closed by the middle of the week due to concerns of the staff's own safety, even though the target was no one but Bernie Brookes himself.

Mansion House had also been vandalised.

The words 'monster' and 'murderer' had been graffitied on the walls, windows, and doors. Police had since sealed off the building for fear of further reprisals.

Isabella was nowhere to be found.

As the motorcade turned into Tower Bridge Road, Brookes spotted the lights of the HMS *Belfast*, which had sat moored in its current position on the River Thames since the early '70s.

He'd always despised it. He'd always had a secret hatred for anything British, but only Fitzroy Brown, and his associates over in continental Europe, ever knew this.

It all happened at breakneck speed.

The lead car had just crossed over the centre of the bridge.

As the car Brookes was in reached the middle, it slammed to a stop.

'What the fuck?' the driver said to the policeman in the front passenger seat.

'What are you doing?' the guy said.

'I didn't!—It wasn't me!' the driver shouted back.

The car's engine had died. The electrical system was the same.

The driver jumped out of the car and realised the other police car behind him was at least 200 metres further back down the road.

'What the fuck are you doing?' the driver of the rear car shouted to him.

'Our car cut out. What the hell are you doing?' he shouted back.

'My car went dead too,' the cop responded.

The lead car was now at least two hundred metres ahead, and the driver of Bernie's car was running back towards the centre of Tower Bridge.

The two policemen stuck in the middle of the historic bridge were the first to hear the sound.

'You've got to be fucking kidding me,' one said to the other.

The bridge was moving.

Designed to pull up like a classic drawbridge, from each side, the two spans moved up towards the heavens usually around a thousand times a year.

In a matter of seconds, both men realised the horrible truth of the situation.

The car transporting Bernie Brookes was sitting right across the line where the two spans joined.

Suddenly, the two men felt sick. Their desire to be as far away from water as possible was so profound, both instantly began to dry retch. The driver vomited a moment later. What came up: icy water.

Without another word, they both ran, the feeling of dread growing stronger by the second.

As the spans began to lift, Bernie Brookes sat stunned in the back seat of the sedan.

He opened his door, but immediately closed it again to stop himself from falling forty feet into the murky waters below.

At this point, the spans stopped moving.

By now, the cops were running to both ends of Tower Bridge to try and find whoever was responsible for this fuck-up.

From a distance, you might think the spans had barely moved, but they had done so just enough to suspend the car holding Bernie Brookes between them, with all wheels now hanging in the wind.

It was a surreal sight.

'Oh my Lord,' one cop shouted to the other as he saw something from the corner of his eye.

Hundreds of metres down the River Thames, something was hurtling straight at the Tower Bridge.

The policeman would find it hard to describe when interviewed the next day.

When the other members of the force standing at the other end of the bridge saw what was coming towards it, they had to blink to make sure they were seeing straight.

Two identical walls of water, the height of Tower Bridge itself and edged with jagged teeth of ice, reflected the lights on both sides of the river as they moved with terrifying speed, one from the east and one from the west.

Ahead of them came a disturbing sound: the screams of children, so loud the policemen witnessing the event held their hands over their ears.

A moment later, they arrived.

Thousands of black crows, out of nowhere and flying in from all directions.

Their destination—the air directly above Tower Bridge.

The two walls of freezing water and jagged ice collided in and all around Tower Bridge.

The crows circled directly above.

The sound of their cawing was bad enough, but alongside it the horrifying screams of children grew louder.

The policemen knew Bernie Brookes was in there somewhere.

But a moment later, the sound ceased. The crows flew off in all directions.

The two policemen who were in the car with Bernie Brookes shook their heads in bewilderment.

Then the massive formation surrounding the Tower Bridge made a shuddering sound before exploding.

What was left took the policemen's breath away.

It was like the formation that appeared in the Royal Opera House. But this one was five times the size.

A gigantic tower of ice, tiered like a wedding cake.

And each tier was formed of children with outstretched arms.

The men had all heard about the event at the opera, but this was much, much bigger.

One of the cops shouted to the others, 'Don't go any closer! Remember what happened at the Opera Hou—'

But his words came too late.

The giant ice formation erupted into a shower of exploding ice, and knocked them flat.

When the two cops got up from the road, they were both wondering if drinking at that time of the morning was permitted.

There was an object perched perfectly on top of the roof

of Bernie's car, which was still suspended between the two spans of the bridge.

They weren't sure what it was, so they walked closer.

When they were about fifty feet away, they could see it more clearly.

The ice was frozen in the shape of a forty-four-gallon drum.

Sticking out of the top were two feet.

By the time the sun came up over the Tower Bridge, the forty-four-gallon drum made of ice had all but melted.

Behind hastily erected tarpaulins, the officers on the scene wondered if they would ever report what they saw to the public.

All that was left of Bernie Brookes were the two feet seen sticking out of the drum.

The rest of him had exploded into tiny pieces.

EPILOGUE—PART TWO

Although the residents were allowed to return to Ravenstone House, all stayed elsewhere.

David, Christine, Quentin, and Mary grappled with whether to keep living there or move on. So did Yukiko.

No decision had been made about the fate of the huge cavern deep below the foundations, where the remains of all the children were uncovered.

And even though they'd met the spirits of many of those children, the five neighbours still had an uncomfortable feeling about the tunnel, especially knowing the remains of at least ten unidentified adults were also down there.

But for now, they would stay in their flats, and on the night after Bernie Brookes' demise on Tower Bridge, they would meet for what they knew may be their last dinner together at Ravenstone House.

The five sat around the dinner table and reflected on the last few months.

When Mary and Yukiko spoke of what future lay ahead for Yukiko, now she was single, Christine joined in.

'Yukiko, I think I may have the perfect man for you.'

Mary frowned, 'He'd better be made of the right stuff. This girl needs a man of dignity and respect!' she announced.

'Well, there's something I found out about a certain person we've all had recent dealings with,' Christine said, grinning.

'No. He's single?' Mary said, maybe a bit too enthusiastically for Quentin, whose face went limp.

'Yes, darling. Inspector Megevand is recently divorced; he mentioned it in passing at the hospital when we visited him.'

Mary gave Yukiko a nudge.

Yukiko blushed before whispering, 'Maybe.'

The wine and conversation flowed well into the night.

David was on a roll. Quentin could not get enough of the gags.

They thought all the weird stuff was over.

No it wasn't.

Halfway through another dad joke, the power in David and Christine's flat went out.

A second later, so did the three candles burning in the middle of the dining table.

When David relit the first candle, they all jumped.

They were surrounded by orphans.

David hastily lit the other two candles.

'Hello, children,' Mary said, struggling to contain the fright in her voice.

The children exchanged looks at each other before one smiled. Soon, there was an unnerving smile on every child's face.

'Children, children,' Finley said, appearing from the shadows, 'what have I told you about surprising our friends?'

He made his way through the mosh pit of kids and made it to the end of the table.

'Hello, Finley,' Christine said to him.

Finley smiled.

'Christine, David, Quentin, Mary, and Yuk-koko,' they decided not to correct him, 'we have come here tonight to do something, thanks to you all, that we never thought possible.'

Yukiko seemed frozen in fear, but kept her composure well.

'Finley, we are happy to see you and all the children tonight,' David said. 'But you have us wondering exactly—what is it you are here to do?'

Finley stared across the lounge room and into the dining area. The sea of children stared back at him.

'To say goodbye,' he said.

It took a moment to sink in.

'They're all gone?' Quentin said.

Here's the thing.

No one had spoken with Finley about who Josef Leitner was in 1990: Bernie Brookes, Quentin's father.

They'd wondered how to broach it with him. Quentin, Mary, David, and Christine knew the stone-cold truth. Quentin's father had hidden his true identity from his only son his entire life. And that's why they had decided to park it.

But now, the monsters of Ravenstone were all dead.

The children could now go where they'd waited an eternity to enter.

'The last one—is dead? The boss of the orphanage?' David asked.

'We all can feel it,' Finley said. 'He is no longer in this world.'

Quentin felt for Mary's hand under the table, and when

he found it, she held his tightly. For a moment, he could feel sadness rising in him, but then a vision of someone came immediately to mind.

His mother, Janet Brookes.

Whatever emotion he felt from knowing his father was dead had disappeared.

David leant over and placed his hand on his wife's shoulder.

'We're going to miss you, Finley,' David said. He glanced down to the sea of smiling faces and added, 'You are all the most beautiful children we have ever met. We wish we could have been your parents.'

The children stared at David while Christine fought back tears. The orphans smiled, but none understood what he meant.

Except Finley.

'You are the type of man I wished my father to be,' he said.

Christ. Now Mary and Yukiko were fighting a losing battle with tears.

'Do you mind if I ask you all to do one more thing?' Finley said.

'Of course,' Christine said, wiping her eyes.

'Can you go and sit on the couch? The children want to say goodbye to you.'

Yukiko decided to stay at the dining table, but watched on in fascination.

David, Christine, Quentin, and Mary squeezed onto the one sofa.

Over the next five minutes, all the children filtered past. Some smiled, others waved.

They lost track of who was who, there seemed to be so many.

Eventually, Finley asked the children to let him have his turn.

He stood in front of the two couples.

Then something occurred to Mary. 'Finley, I just realised. Where's Heather? I haven't seen her among the children.'

'I'm sorry, Mary. Heather's gone,' Finley said.

Mary could not hide her distress.

'I don't understand! Where has she gone? I thought she would be wherever you were,' she gasped. Then her tears came.

Finley shook his head.

'Heather loved you, Mary. When we realised we could go on to where we belong, she told me she could not come,' he said.

'Why?' Mary sobbed.

'Because she said she could not leave you,' he said.

Quentin put his arm around Mary to comfort her.

'I cannot feel her presence here. I don't know if she decided to go ahead of us because she could not bear the thought of saying goodbye. I won't know until we get there,' Finley said.

Mary cried. She could not control her sorrow.

'I'm sorry, Mary, but there's something else,' Finley said.

Oh Christ, Mary thought, there's more?

'Someone else has gone from Ravenstone House too,' Finley said.

Christine leant forward, 'Who?' she said.

As Finley found himself looking upwards, Mary's heart sank. She put two and two together.

'Rose? Rose Lloyd?' she said.

'Yes. She seemed to have disappeared the same time as Heather did.'

It took some time before Mary regained her composure.

Finley and the children stood there as if they had all the time in the world.

She reached her hand out and said, 'It's time, my dear Finley. You've waited so long, and now…' Mary scanned the room to see all the children, 'now you can go where the sun will always shine for you all.'

Finley smiled.

'We will never forget you. All of you. One day, we hope you come to where we are. Thank you for saving our souls,' he said.

He stood and stared at the four for the last time.

'It may be a good idea if you all close your eyes,' he said. 'The light may hurt,' he said.

They all did.

In a matter of moments, a mysterious light source in the room grew brighter. At the same time, there was a piercing, high-pitched squeal. Both grew to such intensity that the five squeezed their eyes hard and clapped their hands over their ears.

When the sound suddenly stopped about ten seconds later, so did the incredibly bright light.

They opened their eyes.

A moment later, the power to the flat returned.

It was over.

It's not our fault.

We did nothing wrong.

Finally, the spirits of the children were free.

EPILOGUE—PART THREE

Nine months later

Extensive Met investigations, which at certain times involved MI6 and Interpol, uncovered the elaborately woven web of deceptions that made up the life of Josef Leitner, who later became known as Bernie Brookes.

The orphanage, investigators concluded, was set up as a front by the three Leitner brothers, who would sell the orphans into the sick world of child slavery. But Josef's father, who the investigators believed was a closet paedophile, realised he had access to the children no one wanted, which allowed him to abuse the kids at will, without consequence. At this point, he came up with another money-making idea: offer the sickest people of society access to the children for a fee, and let them do whatever they wanted.

At some point, with the discovery of the huge underground cavern directly below the orphanage, the elder Leitner realised they could completely hide their wicked ways.

Fitzroy Brown entered England as a refugee from Jamaica

in 1948, on the SS *Windrush*. He was housed, of all places, in the air-raid shelter at the Clapham South Tube station. There, he met Richard Bailey, who would often sneak into the shelter to escape the cold London winters.

Bailey soon introduced Fitzroy to a young Josef Leitner, his boss at the orphanage, where Bailey and his friend West worked.

When West was arrested for the violent rape and abuse of one of the female co-workers a few years later, Fitzroy Brown was already ensconced in the 'Leitner family business.' He also abused children in his own right.

But Bailey, who was still spending stints in prison, decided to do West a favour, and took the rap for the rape.

Due to that latest case, rumours about the dark side of the orphanage grew much stronger.

People started asking questions about the recent disappearance of a fourteen-year-old orphan. Other accusations of child abuse were getting all-too regular. Brown and Josef Leitner decided the risk was getting too great. So in late 1955, they made the decision to shut shop. The wall in the ring room was covered up, and both Brown and Leitner, along with some others, fled England in the middle of the night.

After some time in Austria, Brown decided to return to Jamaica. But after only five or so years, life there bored him.

He contacted Josef Leitner, and his ex-boss from the orphanage came up with a plan. Although it cost Brown a considerable sum of money, the Leitner crime family successfully altered Brown's appearance enough, so they believed, that he could re-enter Britain under a new identity.

This gave the brothers the idea that maybe they should send one of their own to England. Having someone there would help co-ordinate their international drug-trafficking, money-laundering, and child-slavery businesses, on British soil.

Josef, tired of trying to run the family business his way under constant pressure from his father and two uncles, put his hand up to return to England.

He, too, had his appearance altered, but he often wondered if he had gone far enough. Bald by his twenty-fifth birthday, the toupee was the main element of his new look.

Fresh with a brand-new backstory, a crisp new British passport, and all other necessary papers, Leitner became Bernie Brookes, and began his new life in Manchester in the winter of 1960.

The decision was made before he left for England that this would be a long-term assignment.

When he met Janet Ashton six months after settling in Manchester, he did genuinely fall in love with her. He buried his sordid, murderous past deep inside his consciousness, and began a new life as a real-estate salesman, and later a council member, in his local borough.

Although having children was something he'd never wanted to do, the family back in Austria advised him to roll with it. If Janet wanted children, it would only help his cover.

After the first two babies miscarried, he thought he was off the hook. But Janet became pregnant a third time, and Quentin was born ten months later. Janet, fearing another miscarriage, decided one child was enough.

———

No one knew the backstory to the relationship between the lord mayor and the member for Streatham.

It was nothing for the lord mayor of London to rub

shoulders with many, if not all British politicians, so their relationship seemed normal.

But one night at the Brookes house, only a few years ago, Janet Brookes overheard a conversation that would eventually cost her life.

Retiring to bed that particular night, she could not sleep. Overhearing voices in the study, Janet made the fatal mistake of eavesdropping on the conversation.

What she heard broke her heart.

The two men were discussing the Leitner family business, which the two men were still connected to.

But when Brown mentioned the trafficked children and invited her husband to go with him to spend some 'quality time,' with a few kids, she felt like she'd died.

After four weeks of indecision, she decided to leave. But she wanted the house and half of his money. It was only fair, she thought.

The letter was the biggest mistake she made.

Although a conversation never took place between husband and wife, Bernie Brookes knew that whatever she may have known, it was too risky to allow it to come out.

When Brown told him he could take care of it, Brookes only asked once. How could he help him?

When the MP said he still had irregular contact with someone from the past, the lord mayor never asked him who.

He didn't want to know.

Through their extensive investigations, the police eventually spoke to a bartender who had recently been busted for dealing drugs in the hotel he worked at: the Mount Pond Arms.

As part of a plea deal, the guy told the police something his brother had once told him. When asked why he hadn't told the police at the time, he said he feared for his life. His brother was one seriously fucked up son of a bitch.

Richard Bailey.

He told the investigators that his brother had bragged one night, while off his face on speed and about fourteen pints, that he'd helped a lady in the Tube onto a train. Oops, his brother joked, the train came a fraction too early.

———

Ravenstone House was condemned, and the building eventually demolished.

Council building inspectors believed it was only a matter of time before the foundations of the building were compromised beyond repair, thanks to the cavern underneath.

Pro-bono lawyers, in a class action on behalf of all the residents of Ravenstone House, successfully sued the developer and the Wandsworth council for compensation. Although it took close to two years, all residents and tenants received their money back, and compensation for hardship.

Coincidentally, as the building came down, an ex-developer who had moved to Spain some time ago, and who had gone blind after his last visit to Ravenstone House, miraculously regained his vision.

Quentin and Mary, and David and Christine, could not believe their luck—Mary found two flats next door to each other for sale not long after they had to move out of Ravenstone House.

She found them, of all places, on a street called—Ravenstone Street.

What are the odds?

The Brookes' family home was sold and the proceeds frozen.

The government said that due to Bernie's background and shadowy past, the money could not go to Quentin, as it was from the proceeds of crime.

Quentin stoically accepted it.

But a secret deal was made that saw him receive a substantial payout under the auspices of his mother's will. They agreed that she, like Quentin, had never known of Brookes' secret past and life of organised crime.

———

'Easy, easy,' Mary said as Quentin yanked her out of the back seat.

To say she was heavily pregnant would be an understatement. Her belly stuck out so far, she struggled to even waddle.

But Christine smiled: she thought Mary shone with a motherly glow.

Quentin let go of her hands as she stood upright on the pavement.

'Crikey, when are you due my dear?' David grinned.

'What time is it?' Mary smiled.

She was due that very day.

The two couples turned and gazed over the small patch of land.

'Wow. Incredible,' Mary said.

'They've done an amazing job.' Quentin smiled.

After the council demolished Ravenstone House, in its place it had erected a park dedicated to the memory of the children.

On the far wall, 135 small plaques were placed looking out into the memorial park. Sadly, many of them, for orphans who had yet to be formally identified, remained blank.

In the garden beds, 135 peony shrubs were planted, one for each of the children who had lost their lives below.

Mary reached the wall with the plaques and found the two she was looking for.

She ran her finger over them.

Finley Sproule.

Heather MacLeod.

'Oh, I miss you, bonny Heather, and Finley too,' Mary said.

'Sorry for our tardiness.' The voice from behind her sounded genuinely apologetic.

Yukiko smiled, and there was a hint of a blush on her cheeks.

Holding her hand, Ian Megevand nodded. 'Our train was delayed, but we made it,' he said.

'Well, look at you two.' Christine smiled, looking at Yukiko. She was so happy for her.

Andrew, her soon to be ex-husband, had recovered enough to return to New York six months ago.

Two months later, his affair with his co-worker went public. The woman's husband, surprisingly, forgave her, but Andrew was unceremoniously fired from the company.

Christine was the one who'd played matchmaker. She contacted the inspector and insisted he ask Yukiko out on a date. It took him about two months to drum up the courage, but he did, and they'd been dating since.

Something in the middle of the memorial garden caught Christine's attention. She walked up to a council gardener tending to some of the plants nearby, and asked, 'Now, does this one seem a bit out of place?'

The gardener nodded, and as David reached her side, said, 'Do you guys believe in the weird stuff that happened here?'

The couple met each other's eyes and smiled. 'You could say that,' David said. 'Why do you ask?'

The gardener shook his head. 'Because I had to check if I could tell you.'

'Go on, then,' Christine said.

The gardener walked over to the bush Christine had pointed out. 'This wasn't here a week ago, when I was here last. But as you can see, here it is, and healthy as all the rest, like it was here the whole time. Now that's weird, right?'

The three of them stood there and studied it.

It was one hell of a healthy, vibrant thing, with big, happy red flowers almost smiling at them.

A Rose bush.

———

The crew had morning tea back at Moose's Cafe.

Ian turned to Yukiko. 'You think it's time?'

'We have a little story to tell you all,' Yukiko said, reaching over and holding Ian's hand.

The inspector cleared his throat.

'I wasn't sure if I was right about this,' he said, 'but after I started dating one of London's best forensic investigators, she decided to help me look into it.'

David, Christine, Quentin, and Mary all shut the hell up.

This sounded important.

'David,' Megevand turned to the taekwondo teacher, 'remember when I told you why I became a policeman?'

David nodded, 'To get the bad guys off the streets, or words to that effect.'

Megevand nodded.

After a pause, he took a sip of water and turned to Yukiko. 'Maybe you should tell the next bit,' he said.

Yukiko took a deep breath.

'Ian's adopted. His adoptive parents are as wonderful as he is. Kind-hearted, decent people.' She smiled at him.

'You see, Ian's Scottish. And I'll tell you all,' she giggled to herself, 'I like what's under his kilt!'

They laughed. Hearing Yukiko say something so cheeky was a breath of fresh air.

'Anyway, I spent some time tracing Ian's life back to Glasgow, where he was born. His parents gave him up for adoption: they were dirt poor, and his father was an alcoholic. The saddest thing was, Ian had a brother and a sister, and for whatever reason, his biological parents gave him and his sister up, but for reasons we cannot figure out, decided to keep the youngest one.'

The inspector continued the story. 'My parents, they moved here to London. Yukiko traced the family to Clapham South, of all places. But within a few months, they moved to,' he took a deep breath, 'Lacham.'

After a pause to take a sip of tea and a bite of his muffin, Megevand pressed on.

'My biological father, apparently, had no luck finding a job. It's a bit hard when you're drunk all the time. But I digress. In the end, they'd already given up my sister and I, so they went the trifecta and gave up their third, my little brother.

Quentin nearly coughed his coffee up and all over Mary.

'Finley.' He gasped as Mary patted him on the back.

Megevand met eyes with the four of them, but said nothing.

'He came to me after I'd stepped into that ring mark on the floor. At first I'd thought I was dreaming it all.'

As everyone around the table digested the news, Ian turned to David again.

'When I said I wanted to be a cop, yes, it was to get the bad guys. But the other reason was—to find my little brother. I had a feeling a long time ago he was dead. I reconnected with my biological father's own brother about fifteen years ago. He told me he'd searched for Finley around the time he disappeared from Ravenstone. They told him he was sent back to Scotland, but he didn't believe it.'

'You've blown us away, Inspector,' David said. 'Our heart goes out to you for your loss. Obviously, we all got to know him, in a sense. He was very much like you. Made of the right stuff.'

Megevand nodded, leant over, and patted David on the shoulder.

'I got to speak to him. Wherever we were, it didn't matter. It put a lot of feelings to rest. After I arrived at the hospital, it all came back to me. I wasn't sure if it had actually happened, so I decided to keep it to myself.'

The inspector turned to Yukiko.

'After I told Yukiko about it, she decided to see if we could find out if the connection was true, between Finley and myself. Well, as you all now know, it was. Finley was my little brother. And I don't think I could be more proud of him,' he said.

'What a story,' Mary started to cry, 'sorry, I am struggling with my—'

'Shit!' she said a second later, 'my water just broke!'

───

For the last nine months, Mary had hoped she wouldn't be in labour for more than six hours.

Nine hours later, at midnight, Christine and David told Quentin they'd need to go home: their bed was calling. They told him to call when anything exciting happened.

'How you holding up, darling?' Quentin said, knowing full well the answer.

'Better when this baby is born.' Mary winced.

At 2am, the nurses were coming every half an hour, and were starting to wonder if and when they would induce her. They decided, much to her annoyance, they would give her another two to three hours to see if little baby came of its own accord.

At 3am, Quentin was dozing off in the chair directly next to Mary's bed. When she heard his light snores, she wanted to throw something at him, not for the noise, but because she wished she could do the same.

She could feel herself dozing in and out of sleep.

At 3.17am, she thought she felt a presence in the room.

She gasped before throwing her hand to her mouth.

'Nurse Mary.'

Bonny Heather.

But there was someone standing next to her.

A tall, beautiful young woman.

'We came to let you know we've been keeping an eye on you.'

The woman smiled, patting Heather on the head.

'You will be a fine mother,' she said to Mary.

It took her another second before the penny dropped.

Rose Lloyd.

'Oh my God,' she said. 'Where have you been?'

Rose met Heather's eyes, and they shared a smile.

'Rose has been taking care of me,' Heather said.

Mary closed her eyes. Her eyelids felt like concrete.

When she opened them a moment later, Heather and Rose were gone.

She turned to Quentin, whose snores continued.

Pain exploded from her stomach.

As she groaned, Quentin practically fell out of his chair.

'Quentin!' she screamed. 'Something is wrong!'

Twenty seconds later, the room was full of midwives and one very panicked doctor. This was only his second delivery.

'We need to get this baby out right now,' the doctor said.

Mary was taken to the other room.

Her body was telling her something was seriously amiss.

Quentin was asked to wait outside.

———

As Mary struggled to retain her composure, surrounded by people, she felt as if she was going to die. The pain was so intense, she had passed out a couple of times already.

In her dazed state, as the midwives and doctor tried to deliver her baby, she stared into the corner of the room. Rose and Heather were standing there, watching. She found it comforting.

After another five minutes of agony, suddenly the midwives and doctor were silent.

This was the most disturbing part for Mary.

As she tried to figure out what was wrong, one of the midwives came into view.

Her face was solemn.

Mary's heart felt as if it would stop beating.

'I'm sorry Mary.'

Mary burst into tears, and as she shook her head, knowing her baby had died at birth, she found herself looking over to the corner of the room.

But when she did, she realised there was only one person standing there.

Rose Lloyd.

The doctor said something Mary could not understand.

The midwife who'd just spoken to Mary jumped up and went to the doctor's side.

Ten seconds later, Mary heard the sweetest sound.

A baby's cry.

——

Six years later

Mary was dog-tired. It had been a big day in the Brookes household on Ravenstone St.

Her six-year-old daughter, Heather, and her three-year-old son, Finley, had run her into the ground. They were so full of life, some days, they were like two Energizer bunnies on full tilt.

When Mary hopped into bed, a memory came to mind, of how she once would put a little ring on her bedside table, and bonny Heather would appear not long after.

To recall it warmed her heart.

She fished for the ring in the drawer of her bedside table, and found it eventually. She held the tiny object in her fingers and thought, for old times' sake, she'd leave it out.

Well after Quentin had come to bed and the house had been in darkness for hours, Mary sensed something by her bedside.

She half opened her eyes, as she heard the words that used to melt her heart.

'Nurse Mary.'

Bonny Heather.

Her heart filled with joy.

But when she turned on her bedside light, it was her daughter standing next to the bed.

Mary was confused. She tried to shake herself awake.

When her daughter saw the ring, she smiled before picking it up and studying it.

Then she slipped it onto one of her fingers before placing her hand on her mother's chest.

The second her little hand touched Mary, she felt the same feeling she did when bonny Heather McLeod used to touch her.

Mary saw a twinkle in her daughter's eye before she leant in and whispered to her.

'Nurse Mary. I knew I would find a way back to you.'

THE END

REVIEW THIS BOOK

You would be helping me greatly as an independent author by taking a few moments to review *The Luxury Orphanage* at the place you bought it.

I cannot thank you enough for taking the time to do this.

Grant Finnegan, 2020

Grant Finnegan's next novel is coming in late 2021.
It will pose this one question to you.

What is your karma?

KEEP IN TOUCH

Feel free to drop me a line at my website, grantfinnegan.com, or on Facebook at facebook.com/grantfinneganauthorAUS.

DISCLAIMER

All characters in this book are fictitious. Although the names used for some of these characters are of actual people (fans of my novels) there is no other connection whatsoever between the characters and these people. The story in this novel is based purely on imagination.

The Ravenstone House for the Less Privileged is also a fictitious place, as is the town of Lacham in South London. The Mount Pond Arms Hotel also never existed.

Some readers will find certain scenes in this novel disturbing. These scenes were created to show the depths of evil in some of the story's most unsavoury characters, so that readers can understand the heroes' response.

There are, and have been, many orphanages in England and abroad, that properly nurture and care for the children who need their care. This fictional story should not in any way reflect on these real orphanages and the incredible work they do.

ACKNOWLEDGEMENTS

I would like to thank the following people for their contribution to this novel.

My editor, Ben Hourigan, of Hourigan & Co. This is the fourth book I've enlisted Ben's services for, and it just gets easier each time. Thanks, Ben, for the good work you do.

Thank you to all those who have read my novels and sent me words of support. I now have regular contact with some of my readers, which is something that I enjoy immensely as an author.

Some of the characters in this novel are named after a few of these people: Kim Mackay, Helena George, Lynne Dalton, Ross DeBel, Doug Lozel, Wendy Moss, Frances Mckendrick, Frances Brown, Bob Freeman, Neil Olney, and Ian Megevand.

Andrew and Yukiko Parsons—with special thanks to Andrew for being there to debate storylines, plots, and everything in between.

David and Christine Windebank—naming two of the main characters after you was an honour and is my way of saying thank you for the incredible support you give me. Although David in real life is not a taekwondo instructor, apparently he does like to swan about the house in a kimono on the weekends. That's what Christine tells me. Okay, so I'm just kidding here.

For those who love their eighties movies, the character of bonnie Heather was named after Heather, Connor MacLeod's first love interest from one of my all-time favourite movies, *Highlander*. In the end, there can be only one. What a movie.

Quentin is another prominent name in this novel, and the character was named after my grandson. Q was the first person in the world to hear passages of *Flight 19, Part 2* as I wrote them, nursing him as a newborn in one arm and typing with the other. Perhaps I should have taken the hint when he fell asleep as soon as I began to read to him. My late mother's brother, who passed before I was born, also shared the name Quentin. His last name was Sproule, and it is no coincidence that the character Finley in this novel has the same surname.

Finally, as I have done in the last two novels, I save the last thanks to someone who helps make this possible. You endure early manuscripts at their most basic, and often most annoying, but still push on and help me. You never stop believing in my writing even when I find it hard myself. My beautiful wife, Sharon—thank you, honey. I love you.

ABOUT THE AUTHOR

Grant Finnegan is an avid reader of many genres, from action thriller to supernatural mysteries and many others.

Some of his favorite authors and strongest writing influences are familiar names: Stephen King, the late Clive Cussler (RIP), Janet Evanovich, Lee Child, and Douglas Kennedy, to name a few.

Grant lives in the bayside suburbs of Melbourne, Australia. Most days, he can be found walking along the beach with his wife, discussing the world we live in. If he's not there, he's in the kitchen cooking up a storm, at his desk writing, or otherwise staying active.

Grant's other favorite pastimes include snowboarding, windsurfing, and travelling the world. He has a soft spot for London and the United Kingdom, Queenstown, the South Island of New Zealand, and the island of Bali in Indonesia.

facebook.com/grantfinneganauthorAUS

amazon.com/author/grantfinnegan

Printed in Great Britain
by Amazon